Also by Mary Stanley

Retreat
Missing
Revenge
Searching for Home

The Lost Garden

Mary Stanley

headline
review

First published in Great Britain in 2006 by HEADLINE REVIEW
An imprint of HEADLINE BOOK PUBLISHING

First published in paperback in Great Britain in 2006 by HEADLINE REVIEW
An imprint of HEADLINE BOOK PUBLISHING

2

ISBN 0 7553 2516 8

Typeset by Palimpsest Book Production Limited, Polmont, Stirlingshire

Printed and bound in Great Britain by Clays Ltd, St Ives plc

Headline's policy is to use papers that are natural, renewable and recyclable
products and made from wood grown in sustainable forests. The logging and
manufacturing processes are expected to conform to the environmental
regulations of the country of origin.

HEADLINE BOOK PUBLISHING
A division of Hodder Headline
338 Euston Road
London NW1 3BH

www.reviewbooks.co.uk
www.hodderheadline.com

For
Justin Corfield
with love

Acknowledgements

I thank –

Norbert van Woerkom for the Dutch input and for the shared philosophy of I.T.N.,

Tacchi, turophile extraordinaire, for the French details and the laughter,

Flora Rees, for being a great editor and a special friend,

Michaela Grabinger, unmet friend and translator,

Carole Blake, my agent and supporter

My children Steffen and Sophie Higel,

All my friends at Headline Review and Hodder Headline Ireland

for their great work and support,

and

Dr Justin Corfield, for his constant help and friendship,

and for being one in a million.

To see a World in a Grain of Sand
And a Heaven in a Wild Flower,
Hold Infinity in the palm of your hand
And Eternity in an hour.

William Blake

PROLOGUE

There was a room.
 The daylight came through the side of the closed curtains and through a triangle at the top where they were not quite fitting.
 Through the side, a tiny section of the windowpane was visible, and through that the trees.

The wind blew the leaves on the trees.
 The trees were swaying.
 The leaves were falling.
 It would soon be winter.
 Tick –
 Tick –
 Tick –
 It sounded like a clock.
 But it seemed that it was getting slower.
 Tick –

Tick –

Tick . . .

After daylight there was nightdark.
   And then there was daylight.
   And then there was night . . .

Tick . . .

In the room there was a spider. He walked so carefully on a crack that spread across the ceiling. The crack elongated over time. Every movement of the spider took on a deliberateness of its own.

Tick . . .

The tick was a heartbeat.

And in that room, there was nothing, only a heart beating, a crack elongating and a spider spinning.

CHAPTER ONE

There was a woman. Esme Waters was her chosen name. She appeared serene and gentle, with eyes like clear-cut green glass. When she smiled, they smiled too. Tiny lines had appeared at their edges that matched the smile lines around her mouth. There was a slight tentativeness about her, a cautiousness that she tried to hide by carrying her head high and portraying an air of confidence. She stood in the tiny hallway of her rented Parisian apartment and checked herself in the gilt-edged mirror. She carefully applied lipstick to her mouth, stretching her lips so that it went on evenly. She brushed her hair out with the silver hairbrush her father had given her twenty-seven years earlier, for her fourteenth birthday. Reaching back, she coiled her hair into a chignon and pinned it with a clip, chosen from the selection on the tiny shelf beneath the mirror. Then, picking up her keys and handbag, she let herself out of the door on to the tiled corridor.

She was trying on her new life as she would a pair of new shoes. Wearing it for a little more each day, searching for a routine that would suit, looking for it to feel right. Like the previous morning, she used the stairs, coming down one flight to the ground floor, where she nodded politely to the concierge, and then she went out of the heavy glass doors on to the street. In an echo of the day before, she walked to the corner, before deciding what to do. She crossed the road to the café with its tables outside – the same café as the morning before. She liked routine. There was safety in familiarity, in creating a structure that she would recognise and in customising habits. She gave the impression of composure.

Jacob Althaus was sitting outside his local café, less than fifty metres from the building that housed his rooms where he saw his patients. The café was his regular early morning haunt, where strong black coffee and a croissant prepared him for the first hour of listening and probing. The June sun shone down on his head and shoulders, and he knew that it would be but a few days more before wearing a jacket in the heat would be unbearable.

He had a newspaper, *Le Monde*, beside him on the metal table, but he had not looked at it beyond reading the headlines. Sometimes he wondered why he bought the paper at all. What grief and sadness was not in it he would hear about from his patients during the course of the day.

His legs were crossed, and he glanced down at his well-polished shoes before flicking a minute speck of dust from his perfectly creased trouser leg.

Jacob Althaus was six foot tall, and had virtually no hair left. It had receded early and he had taken to shaving his skull in a successful effort to avoid being aware of any more hair loss. He was a heavily built man with sharp intelligent eyes, and the ability to tune in very closely to what was being said. He could read between the words to find the hidden meaning, and was adept at picking off the layers with which his patients veneered their lives, to come to the hidden depths that made up their soul, or their *essence*, as he liked to call it.

He glanced at his watch. He had a mere five minutes before he must leave. He lit a Gauloise.

And then he saw her.

Despite the noise from the traffic and the bustle of pedestrians on the footpaths, he heard the clickety-click of her heels on the pavement just behind him before she actually came into view.

She appeared perfectly poised, self-contained, almost like ice, her face immobile as she sat at the next table. A slender hand reached up and pushed back an imagined wisp into the chignon at the back of her head.

She turned slightly to signal to the waiter, and Jacob saw the jewelled clip holding her hair, and how the green in its stones matched the green of her eyes. He had his back to the sun, while she was facing it, and she reached into her bag and took out a pair of sunglasses. She turned again to try to catch the waiter's attention, as he stood with his back to the café door, his hands resting on the knot at the back of his white apron.

She raised her hand and he, with that studied rudeness of many a French waiter, gazed at the traffic.

'*Garçon*,' Jacob called, immediately catching his attention. '*Madame . . .*' he said, gesturing towards the woman with the glass-green eyes and the immobile face. He got to his feet. It was time to go and face the first patient of the day.

'*Merci*,' the woman said to him, a gentle smile on her lips as he passed the table.

He nodded in return as the waiter approached her, and he heard her ordering coffee as he headed down the street.

She had been there the previous morning, the same impassive mask on her face when she arrived. Then, she had entered the café. She had been served inside and had carried her coffee out into the sunshine. And then, having sat at the next table to his, and placing her cup so carefully on it without spilling its contents, she had suddenly moved forwards as though peering at something. Jacob watched as she looked at a small spider on the tabletop. She had leaned in towards it and then placed her hands on either side of it so that it was trapped. Leaving her bag on the ground as though totally unaware that it was singularly unsafe to do such a thing in Paris, she scooped up the spider and carried it over to the small potted bushes that surrounded the side of the café, where she deposited it with gentle care.

Coming back to her table she had taken a book from her bag, completely oblivious to the fact that he was observing her. Her face, which had lit up when she first saw the spider, had returned to its original calm state, but as he watched while she was reading, the mask had slipped again. And he was sure he had seen something else when in repose. A sadness, maybe, as she tilted her head towards her book, the inscrutable poise disappearing as she concentrated on her reading material, a pen in one hand, which she still held as she sipped her coffee.

He pushed thoughts of her aside as he entered the air-conditioned building where he worked, took the elevator up and faced the first patient of the day.

Esme Waters, having thanked the man who had attracted the waiter's attention for her, ordered coffee and a *pain au chocolat*. Having arrived in Paris a few days earlier, and settled herself into the apartment she had rented through an estate agent online, she was now trying to find a routine that would suit her to see her through the days and evenings. She assumed that most nights she would be with her lover – François Artois, a French gynaecologist she had met a little over eight months earlier and with whom she had been having a commuting relationship ever since. He had been out of town since her arrival, but there was nothing unusual in that. His work took him to hospitals in the suburbs of Paris and the hours he worked were sometimes very long.

After she had arrived and unpacked, she discovered she had left her copy of the play *Macbeth* on her desk in London and she had emailed her second daughter, Rose, asking her to forward it in the post. However, later that same day, while walking in a market, she had come across a stall with second-hand books, and quite coincidentally had found a copy of *Macbeth*, in English, in very good condition. She bought it, and emailed Rose again, cancelling the request.

It was this copy of *Macbeth* that she was now reading, pen in hand, marking certain passages as she had done in her original copy in London.

Esme's home and work were in London, but her daughters were now at an age where she could take a reasonable amount of time off. She had applied and been accepted for a sabbatical year from the Philosophy Department in the London university where she was a part-time lecturer. She also wrote for several academic journals, but this work would continue during her sabbatical. She had only re-entered the world of academia in the previous eight years, but became acknowledged, within a very short time, in her field as a scholar of modern moral thinking. She lectured in virtue ethics to first-year students, but her main interest was in normative and meta-ethics. She was occasionally invited to give lectures abroad in a variety of different universities and city halls. And those lectures she gave, initially not with any relish, but with a sense that she had something to offer, and that it was her duty to deliver.

And deliver she did. That sense of duty evolved into a feeling of satisfaction. She was good at what she did and it gave her pleasure.

She turned the page of her book but the warmth of the sun made it difficult to concentrate and the umbrella over the table was giving her little shade. The tables around were filling up and there was nowhere to move to. A baby in a buggy started to cry. Esme felt her concentration slipping. She glanced around to see if someone was attending to the baby. A woman was drinking coffee at a nearby table, and the baby wailed. Esme looked at its face and she shivered as she saw its too broad forehead and its crooked mouth. The woman pushed the teat of a bottle between its lips, but the bottle slipped and the baby howled again. Esme abruptly closed her book, reached for her bag, and went inside to pay.

There were times, she knew, when she must just walk away.

That evening, Esme, dressed in a tight-fitting cream suit, the jacket pinched at her waist, an ivory lace-topped vest just showing at the V-opening at her neck, in high heels, entered the restaurant where she was meeting François Artois for dinner. Just as she came in, François appeared behind her, slipping an arm around her shoulders and kissing her on both cheeks.

Before she could speak they were interrupted.

''*Allo.*' It was the man from the morning café, looming over them both. '*François,*' he said. His voice, though smooth, was rich in resonance.

If François was disconcerted he hid it well.

'*Jacob,*' he said. '*Jacob Althaus. Bonsoir.*' He hesitated as though momentarily unsure how to handle the situation. Then, 'Allow me to introduce my friend Esme Waters.'

He pronounced the name 'Yakob'. Esme would remember the coolness of Jacob's hand afterwards and the strength of his handshake. It was the perfect handshake – she thought that immediately. It was neither too weak nor too strong, neither too short nor too long. There was reassurance in it. Their eyes met, and she paused in her polite smile, knowing that he was looking into her, and that in some way they were connecting.

'Well,' François said into the momentary silence, 'we should find our table.'

'*Bon appétit*,' Jacob replied. 'Do enjoy yourselves.' He glanced around. 'I am meeting my wife. You remember Naomi?'

'Of course I do, and how is she? Do give her my regards,' François said as he took Esme's elbow and guided her away with what appeared to her to be unnecessary haste.

'It has been a pleasure meeting you,' Jacob said to Esme. 'I'm sure I'll see you again.'

Esme smiled at him over her shoulder as François almost pulled her away.

For a moment she thought she could now sense that there was something wrong, as if François did not want her to remain close to Jacob, that he did not want her talking to him. Then she brushed aside the thought. After all, François and she had not seen each other in several weeks. Of course he wanted her to himself.

'Do you realise that is the first friend of yours I've met,' she said. It pleased her to meet someone who knew him.

'Jacob?' he said. 'We went to school together, and university. I don't see much of him now, though. But tell me about you. The apartment – is it to your liking? And Paris . . . ?'

Esme felt he was behaving differently now from before, but she couldn't put her finger on it.

'The apartment is fine,' she replied. 'It looks much like the photos I'd seen – slightly smaller than I'd expected, but really it's more than adequate . . . yes, I like it.'

'A good place to work then?'

It was small talk. She was puzzled. Did François usually do small talk? Why did she not remember this?

'Yes,' she said, looking at the menu.

She was pleased to be sitting there with him. The last few days had been strangely disconcerting as she sorted her things in the apartment, thought about work, ventured forth on to the streets of Paris and, in some sense, started a new life.

On her visits to Paris over the last months, François was often too busy to stay a whole night in her hotel, and on occasion he had been suddenly called out of town. It had surprised her how much time a gynaecologist had to spend away, but in some ways this had attracted her. It meant that she would have space while living in Paris, and yet be guaranteed company. He was ordering the wine now, his finger scrolling down the wine list, suggesting types and vintages in a way he did not usually do, as though endeavouring to hold her attention or to distract her from something.

She glanced across the restaurant to where Jacob was now sitting with his wife against the far wall, a single candle lighting their table and a gentle glow reflecting on his face as he looked at the woman opposite him. She had dark hair, and Esme could see the gold on her fingers in the light from the candle, and the heavy bracelets hanging on her wrists.

Esme touched her own blonde-streaked hair and looked back at her companion. During the months she had been commuting between London and Paris, she had spent several short weekends in Paris, and a few longer ones in the Loire Valley or in Provence, where François invariably joined her. She tried concentrating on the menu, but she had a sinking feeling that there was something wrong. Of course she could be imagining it, she thought, as the waiter arrived at their table.

She asked about the fish. Her French was good but still not good enough to know which fish was which.

'*La daurade?*' she asked.

'The – how you say? – bream,' the waiter translated.

'Sea bream,' François said.

'Well, and how is the apartment?' he asked her, when they had selected from the menu.

She looked at him in puzzlement. He had already asked her that. He was always so loving and attentive on their stolen weekend meetings but she got the feeling now that he was not quite focused on her. And after all, this was their first full evening together since her arrival.

'Are you all right?' she asked him at one point.

'Of course I am. Just tired – looking forward to being alone with you.'

He seemed to hurry her through the meal and she got the impression that he wanted them finished and out of the restaurant, and she could not help wondering if he was concerned that either Jacob or his wife might come over.

Across the restaurant, Jacob Althaus was trying to concentrate on his wife. Naomi was talking about clothes or style or something, and his mind was wandering. He wished she had something else to interest her other than people and clothing.

He and Naomi had no children. It had been a deliberate choice on his part, and Naomi, for whatever reason at the time, had gone along with him, but now he felt she regretted it. She had godchildren in whom she invested a certain amount of time, energy and money. There had been a discussion once, long ago, which he remembered with a great deal of clarity.

'It is mere chance that I am still alive,' he had said to her, a young man, with black hair and dark intense eyes, holding her hand. 'I should have died like the others . . .'

He was referring to his family, to the total and utter annihilation of all related to him, bar his cousin Daniel, who now lived in Tel Aviv, and who, with him, had emerged from the Holocaust as the sole bearers of that strain of the Althaus stock.

'But maybe you survived for a purpose,' Naomi had said to him long ago. 'Maybe you survived because there was a reason, and maybe that reason was so that your name would not die out.'

'I cannot do it,' he said to Naomi.

It was in the early days of their love affair, and he was being honest, as honest as a young man can be with someone he loves. He wanted it clear from the beginning, so that she would know all the facts before progressing further.

And she seemed to understand. She appeared to have bought into his world-view, and had married him, knowing that children were not an option, knowing that he could not bear the idea of bringing children into a world where the crimes of the twentieth century resonated too closely, too clearly, too frighteningly.

But now, he thought, now, maybe that was a mistake.

Not a mistake from his point of view, because he had not changed his stance, but watching her across the table, with a little too much gold hanging around her neck, and adorning her wrists and fingers, he felt that his beliefs were not ultimately hers. He worried that he had coerced her into his way of thinking, and in so doing, she had given up what she really wanted, and that her needs had been overrun while he continued his work. His fulfilment came from listening to people's problems, learning what motivated them, and, where possible, helping them.

Esme Waters intrigued him. He was pleased to have heard her name. From that moment when he shook her hand and their eyes had locked he had not been able to rid her from his consciousness. She was there right through dinner somewhere on the edge of his mind with her glass-green eyes and that gentle aloof smile. He had been disappointed that his old college friend François Artois was having a relationship with her. He would have liked someone better for her. He saw François as a rather sick bastard who had freely admitted on graduation day that he had gone into gynaecology in order to spend half his life between women's legs.

'Doesn't that rather kill the mystery of women?' Jacob had asked him.

'No more than penetrating their minds must kill the mystery,' François had said.

Jacob laughed. 'You've got that wrong,' he said. 'Mental penetration enhances the mystery.'

'Well, so does gynaecology,' François replied.

'Each to their own,' Jacob said, amused. 'Although if I were, let's say, a butcher, I cannot imagine getting particularly excited about a cut of steak when I got home.'

François had chortled and said that Jacob knew nothing.

They were about to order coffee when Jacob said to Naomi, 'Shall we ask François and his companion to join us?'

'François?' She appeared surprised. 'François who?'

'François Artois. He's sitting across the room.'

Naomi looked across and he followed her gaze. The table was empty, a waiter removing the glasses from it, and dusting away whatever crumbs were on it. He was surprised, having been totally unaware that they had moved and left.

'I don't see them,' Naomi said.

'They must be gone. My mistake. I thought it would be nice . . .'

On their way out of the restaurant, Esme turned to François.

'You are coming back to my apartment, aren't you?' she asked.

'Well . . . I may not be able to spend the whole night.'

'Why ever not?' she said. 'The whole point of my taking the apartment here for the year surely is so we can spend a little more time together? Apart from my work, of course . . .'

'I really can only come back for a little,' he said, glancing at his watch. 'I've an early start in the morning.'

'We could go by your place and collect whatever clean clothes you need for the morning,' she suggested.

'Hmm.' He seemed doubtful.

That twinge of unease that she had felt in the restaurant prickled in her mind again. She had been looking forward to their first evening together and had assumed that he was too. She had wanted to show him the apartment she had rented, share the view, have a drink, enjoy an evening and a night without the constraints of time and travel.

He directed the taxi to her apartment, and she did not bother reiterating her suggestion that they should go to his home – a home she had never seen, because she had really never been long enough in Paris, and always too busy to visit. That she had never been there she had somehow assumed was because there were so many other things to do and they were both always in a rush as she flew into Paris, knowing she would be gone within forty-eight hours. And it had suited her.

The element of distance and restraint were characteristics that she thought were right for this relationship.

'François, I'm tired,' she said suddenly. 'Why don't we leave it for tonight? And tomorrow you can bring some things so that when you want to stay over it will be easy and you'll have what you need for the following day.'

'But I can come in for an hour or so now,' he objected.

'No,' she replied. 'I want our first night here to be a proper one, and as I said, I'm tired. I don't want to be getting up to let you out in an hour or so.'

He agreed then, and he kissed her on the street before getting back into the taxi. She let herself into the building and, deep in thought, went to her apartment.

Despite the perfection in her dress and her need for books, Esme travelled light. Of personal items, her apartment only contained the contents of a large suitcase and a large shoulder bag. Her laptop was open on her desk by the window, and a couple of books lay beside it. Her theory was that everything was replaceable, and if she needed something she would simply go and buy it. She was fond of her clothes – in fact she was quite attached to them – but she had taken with her just what she needed for her first season abroad, knowing that she could easily purchase for the next when the weather changed.

Food and wine had been delivered to the apartment the previous day, and she went now to the small kitchen and opened the bottle of brandy that she had bought for herself and François. The apartment was stylish and the kitchen utensils and accoutrements were of excellent quality. She took a crystal glass from the cupboard and poured herself a cognac, and then went and sat on a chair in front of the window looking out across the river where the lights reflected like coiling snakes in the water, while beyond, the rooftops of Paris were etched in the skyline.

She had left her apartment in London in what, she hoped, were the careful hands of her middle daughter Rose. Lily, the eldest daughter, was in Canada tracking geese, and Jasmine, the youngest, was in South Carolina with her father.

Esme had rented this furnished apartment in Paris on a six-month renewable lease. It was her intention to base herself there for most of the forthcoming year. The apartment was elegantly furnished, a combination of Scandinavian minimalism and French furnishings. There were no pictures on the walls; instead there were just large mirrors with somewhat ornate frames, but the size of these mirrors had the effect of magnifying the small surroundings. The bedroom housed fitted cupboards and a king-size bed with a rather lavish bedstead in a dark rich wood. The living room had comfortable leather chairs at the window, a glass-topped dining table with four rather rigid matching chairs, and a desk.

Sitting there in the window, cognac in hand, she contemplated François and the strange feelings of unease that had unnerved her both in the restaurant and in the taxi. She did not actually love François, but she had taken the apartment in Paris because of him. She enjoyed him, liked his company, needed his affection. But she knew that wasn't love. She knew that if she explained this to anyone, she would be found to be callous, but she felt she was doing no harm, and she needed someone loving with whom to spend her nights. François fulfilled this need when they were together. She knew he did not love her either, although he said he did. She felt that he had seen someone similar to himself in her, and that their relationship, such as it was, suited them both. She did not want to get involved with anyone – not deeply, anyway. Deep involvement brought pain and hurt to one party or the other, so Esme kept herself aloof from that.

Her maxim was to live life to its fullest, but to try never to hurt anyone else. It was what she had said to her daughters when they were old enough to understand. 'Seize the day. This is not a rehearsal. This is it. Do what you can to fulfil yourselves, but do not hurt others. *Carpe diem.*'

She had asked François early on in their relationship if he was married, and he had snorted in derision, saying something like, 'Marriage – bah, it ees not for me.' And she had laughed.

But it had never occurred to her to ask if theirs was an exclusive relationship. She had just assumed it was. Now she wondered if there was someone else in his life. She felt distinctly uneasy. Their affair had been going on for eight months. Shouldn't she have suspected something before now?

The pieces of the puzzle were falling into place. She wondered at her naïvety, at her not having thought about this before. But she had taken him at face value. She was surprised at herself. Surprised it had not occurred to her. If she was right and there was someone else, she did not know what she was going to do.

She knew that she had to make a choice and she wanted to be sure that she saw it clearly in her mind before tackling the situation. Were she to ask François if he was involved with someone else and he in fact was not, where was that going to leave her? And if he admitted that he was involved, then what was she going to do? Apart from this, she was now also puzzled by her own determination to have come to Paris.

It had been a good idea to take a year off work, and she was glad the Department had given her the time she needed because she was under a certain amount of pressure.

As a sideline and a distraction from the intensity of her work, Esme wrote crime thrillers. She wrote under the pseudonym H. Hastings. Her plan had been to complete the next of these during this year out, as well as submit her usual monthly articles to various magazines, and to have some time to herself. Because of her relationship with François, she had assumed that Paris was the most obvious place to be. Otherwise she would be travelling weekends again, or whenever suited François, and that would eat into her work and productive time.

She got up from the leather easy chair and went to her

computer to check her email. There were two work-related ones.

One was from her agent, giving her figures on her last book, which for some reason totally unclear to her had become a bestseller in Japan. Her novels explored the brutality of man to man, of one human being to another for his or her own ends. Her books were clever, guised as simple whodunits but exposing the knock-on effects of mindless selfish crime that left others either dead or damaged beyond repair. Her first two thrillers were based on the murders and violence of the Baader-Meinhof gang in Germany. Her most recent, inspired by a trip she had made some eighteen months earlier when she had been invited to give a lecture in Tokyo, had been translated into Japanese.

Her agent wanted to know if she was willing to go to Japan in September, as the Japanese publishers were keen to have her on some game show as well as the usual publicity that would take place. A further email was from her editor asking if she had an outline ready for her present novel and if she was going to be able to stick to the deadlines that had been imposed. Her editor was understanding, as always, and knew that her work and her lectures abroad somewhat limited the time she could give to her novel writing. But this was Esme's sabbatical year and she was expected to keep to the target.

Japan . . . she thought. There was no reason why not. She sat back in the chair with her cognac. If it was early September she could fly straight there from France and then back to Frankfurt where she was to give a lecture on moral relativism in the middle of the month. And after that? She was unclear. She had no plans other than being based in Paris. She was living on a daily basis, her diary for the year ahead marked with appointments in different countries. She filled them in and booked flights accordingly, only occasionally checking where she would next be. She tried not to turn down any invitations.

While Esme liked routine – in fact needed it to give her a sense of security within which she could work – she also liked being in different places as long as she could bring that routine with her.

Her mind was both puzzled and tired now. She needed to reassess what she was doing with François and why. She did not love him. She reiterated that to herself. It was quite clear in her mind. But she liked having a man in her life, albeit at the periphery. She realised now that by moving to Paris for the year she was bringing things to a head with him, and she did not know why she had done that. The way things were had been more than adequate, and now she was going to be forced either to confront him or to pretend that there was nothing wrong.

She stayed at the window for another two hours, just thinking – her thoughts going from her relationship with him, to her plans for the next novel. She was putting off going to bed, dreading the sleeplessness ahead, or, if she did sleep, fearing the dreams that troubled her nights. She thought briefly of Macbeth – a man who could no longer sleep, but it was he who had brought that about.

> Methought I heard a voice cry 'Sleep no more!
> Macbeth does murder sleep' – the innocent sleep,
> Sleep that knits up the ravell'd sleeve of care,
> The death of each day's life, sore labour's bath,
> Balm of hurt minds, great nature's second course,
> Chief nourisher in life's feast.

She poured another cognac and gazed alternately at the river and at the skyline, her mind wandering back and forth between her daughters and her present situation. She knew that her life was undergoing a change, she knew that the main reason for her taking this year off was because the girls no longer needed her – they were either growing or grown up. She was aware that her role as parent was altering. This unnerved her. She feared the meaninglessness of her existence although she refused to put it into such stark terms. She feared other things too.

The silence in the apartment was becoming oppressive.

Down below on the road, a car pulled up. She watched in horrid fascination as it stayed beside the pavement. Fears started growing in her mind, and having moved forward on her chair to stare down through the night at the stationary car, she suddenly found she could not move. She felt this overwhelming sense of loneliness and isolation, and with it came the fear. She stared at the car, hardly able to breathe. And then, of a sudden, a woman got out and blew a kiss back in to the driver and the car pulled away.

'It is nothing,' she told herself over and over when her breathing returned to normal. 'I am safe here,' she reassured herself.

CHAPTER TWO

For some reason Jacob was not surprised to find Esme already at the café when he arrived the following morning. He had briefly thought of postponing his first patient in the hope of having coffee with her, but then decided he ought not to, because if she and he were destined to meet again they would.

And there she was.

She was inside, at the bar, with a coffee in front of her. He did not know what had made him look inside that morning, as he usually sat down at one of the tables and waited there to be served.

She must have seen his reflection in the mirror behind the bar, because she half turned and he smiled at her.

'*Bonjour*,' he said. 'We meet again.' Even as he spoke, he felt it was a cliché.

She smiled back at him.

'Will you join me outside?' he asked. 'It is so pleasantly warm.'

She agreed tacitly by slipping down from the barstool.

He ordered for himself and carried her coffee out, placing two chairs at a table so their backs were to the sun, as he did not want her to put on her sunglasses – he wanted to look into those startlingly green eyes.

She seated herself by his side. The poise he had noticed before was there. Neither spoke for a moment as he waited for his coffee and croissant to be brought to the table.

'It is part of your routine to come here in the mornings?' he asked. 'I've seen you, you know. Not just yesterday, but the previous day as well.'

'Yes,' she said simply. 'I only arrived in Paris a few days ago. I'm here on sabbatical, a working sabbatical, and I'm still trying to find my way – how to combine work and play, I suppose.'

'Did you enjoy your dinner last night?' he asked.

She nodded. 'Yes. I hadn't seen François for some weeks. We've been together a while, but he was away when I arrived.'

Now Jacob nodded.

'You and he are friends?' she asked.

'We were in school and in university together,' he said briefly. 'Tell me about your work. What it is you are doing here, I mean.'

They spoke lightly that first morning, steering clear of the subject of François Artois. She told him about her work, her sabbatical, the novel she was about to write – although she was vague about that, telling him it was not yet clear in her mind. She surprised herself by even mentioning it, as it was something she usually kept to herself.

'Ideas, you know. They're coming together, but not clearly enough for me to give you a synopsis.'

'But it is not your first novel?'

'No,' she shook her head, 'it's my fourth. I write under a pseudonym. Really just to keep that side of my work separate from my academic life.'

He told her about his work, again in the vaguest of terms. A psychiatrist with patients, a forthcoming conference that he was chairing, a wife, no children, a busy life . . .

'You speak both English and French fluently – why? Or maybe I should ask, how?' she said.

'But you must know from my accent in English that it is not my first language,' he replied. It was true, his English was accented in the French manner, but she was charmed by it.

'You sound bilingual to me,' she said.

'Thank you. After I took my degree in Medicine and branched into Psychiatry, I spent a year in Quebec followed by a year in Ireland. My English was good to start with – it had to be or I wouldn't have got the position in Dublin.'

'In Dublin?' She appeared slightly startled.

'Yes. You are surprised?'

'No. Not really, please go on.'

'I worked in the university there – at that point I thought I would stay in the academic side of things, but later I decided my skills would be better used with patients rather than with students.'

'You prefer the one-to-one?' she suggested.

'Yes,' he replied. 'But you do not, I think?'

She smiled. It was true. It was why she was comfortable lecturing. She could dissociate from the masses and just give her best without being self-conscious. She had no problem answering questions on a podium, whereas with most people, on an individual basis, she felt vulnerable and often afraid. Behind a lectern her confidence waxed as she warmed to her theme, sure of herself within her own field, knowing her subject, knowing what it was she wanted to get across. She knew it was to do with power – that being in control gave her authority, and that that authority gave her both reassurance and status. But she was surprising herself now as she was enjoying sitting and talking with Jacob whereas usually she shied away from such a situation. But she knew that the previous evening had unnerved her – the loneliness in the apartment, the suffocating feeling of her own thoughts and the fear she had felt when the car had pulled up, innocent as that incident had been. The night had stretched long and empty before her with only her own thoughts for company. There was pleasure being with this man – his kindness and intelligence were clear to her. She felt herself relaxing for the first time since she had arrived in Paris.

Jacob was well aware of his own skills in getting someone to talk – that was his profession – but he found that he did not really need to use those skills to get closer to Esme as she seemed to be content sitting and conversing with him. He did not know what it was she was looking for, or, at first, why she wanted to sit with him and talk. But she seemed pleased to see him, comfortable in his presence, giving more of herself in their conversation than he suspected she usually did. He did not know why. Nor did he ask. But his curiosity was aroused. Her apparent openness intrigued him. He rightly suspected that she did not know many people in Paris.

She told him of her daughters. Three girls whom she called her flowers. Lily, Rose and Jasmine. Her love for them was apparent. They were twenty-two, twenty-one and fifteen. He reckoned Esme was about forty years old.

'You had them very young,' he said.

She nodded. 'Yes, in some ways I was little more than a child, although of course I did not see that then. But when I look at my eldest two they seem so young in many ways and I would not wish children on them yet. I want them to live – to fulfil themselves.'

'And did you fulfil yourself?'

She smiled. 'It's an ongoing process,' she said lightly.

Enigmatic, he thought.

He looked at his watch.

'You must leave?' she asked.

'Yes. But I often come here in the evenings after work – a recovery drink so that I don't take the problems of the day home. I should be here at around six thirty this evening, if you happen to be taking a break from your work,' he said. 'A Pernod and a Gauloise – it's a great way to end the working day, I find.'

She smiled again. 'You're tempting me,' she said.

'Maybe I will see you later,' he said, getting to his feet. He looked down at her. Her thin summer blouse was slightly gaping forwards and he could see above her breast a scar like a white star carved into her skin. It brought to mind the numbers tattooed on to his forearm, a scar of a different sort, he thought.

When he left her to go to work that morning, he thought of her with her green eyes, and her highlighted hair always neatly coiled on the back of her head, pinned with some expensive clip – a different one each time he had seen her. He recalled her neat and discreetly expensive clothing, her ankles crossed as she sat on a stool at the bar inside as she did that morning, or in a chair outside on the pavement, and the way her eyes sometimes darted away from his. Occasionally she gazed up at the sky, or looked down at her hands in her lap. He was caught between thinking about her as a man would, and yet aware that as a psychiatrist there was some turmoil beneath the surface. Here she was, this academic novelist, in Paris alone, presumably spending her days working, but dressed with such care and perfection. It was a veneer, he thought. A veneer to hide something. He thought of her poise countered by something – perhaps distress – that he could hear hints of in her voice, how she contained herself and pulled away in spite of herself.

On that first morning he could feel her need to talk, to communicate – was it to share something? Or was it loneliness? He was not sure. But as the days went by – and he and she kept meeting – he knew her need was to uncover her past while her fear of it stopped her opening up completely. He wondered at their friendship, and at the roles they had slipped into. He suspected that initially, after that first proper encounter in the foyer of the restaurant, and after they had bumped into each other in the bar on the street beside his rooms, she had tried, successfully, to direct their meetings so that they could freely talk.

He had no doubt that the attraction was mutual. But he was married and she was attached. But for some reason, in spite of this or, maybe, because of this, there had been freedom of speech between them right from the start. They had, quite simply, connected easily.

When they met that evening – she found him at his table with a drink and a Gauloise – he asked her if she was free to join him for dinner.

'My wife has gone to the theatre with friends,' he said. 'I have the choice of something sealed in plastic in the fridge, or eating out. So if you are free it would be a delight if you would accompany me.'

She was free. François was out of town again, working. The evening stretched ahead of her. She was pleased at the thought of company.

'I shall phone my wife and tell her where we are eating,' Jacob said. 'I can meet up with her and we can go home together.' He said this to reassure Esme that she was safe in his company and that the dinner invitation was just that – an invitation to dinner.

Initially, Esme was cautious talking about François until she had discovered that he and Jacob, despite knowing each other for a very long time, were not close friends.

'Merely acquaintances from school and university,' Jacob repeated to her. And she had said, 'Oh, I see.'

That information relaxed her, presumably because it meant she was not betraying one friend to another. Not that she did betray François in any way, but she let enough slip so that Jacob knew she was not happy. He wondered if she knew François was married, but he did not like to say. If she knew, then she would interpret disapproval. And if she didn't know, well, he did not want – at least not yet – to be the one to tell her. He felt a need to protect her, but feared in a sense being the messenger who might rue the telling of the truth.

'Tell me,' he said, as they sat at a table in a restaurant close to the café, 'let me get this straight. You have three daughters – these flowers, you call them. And they have three different fathers?' He kept his voice neutral. He intended no criticism but knew that the question was loaded for misinterpretation.

'Yes,' she said simply.

'Will you rewind this,' he said. 'Please. Will you tell me the story from the beginning.'

'The beginning?' she asked.

Was there a tremor in her voice? What was it he was hearing? Did the poise slip? Did the tiny smile lines around her eyes drop slightly? Was that grief he heard for a moment before she regained that composure with which he would always equate her?

'Which part of the story?' she asked. 'It is all made up of unconnected fragments.'

'But they interweave, don't they?' he said. 'Tell me about your childhood.'

'There was a child,' she said. It was the first time she had done this, moving from the first person to the third, as though distancing herself from the segment of her life with which she was about to acquaint him.

'And this child?' he prompted.

'Yes, well . . . this child was me. Happy, you know. Very happy. The sun always seemed to shine when she was little.'

He smiled as she said this. How often had he heard his patients saying that very thing, and not realising that it was not where they were in the past that they liked so much, but who they were. They simply preferred the person they had been before they took on the minutiae and the troubles of life that changed them.

'Was she an only child?'

'Yes. But she had cousins, aunts, uncles, grandparents, and doting parents. She had it all. She was born in Dublin. Raised and educated there. A wonderful house. And a garden with a tree house, and thousands of different flowers of every colour that had a perfume that carried on the night air.'

'And what happened to her?'

'When she left school she decided to study in Germany.'

'Germany? Why on earth Germany?'

'Well, she had studied German at school, done very well in her exams – she was good at school – you know, the swot who took home the prizes, the one who got top marks. Good at languages, a good thinker – you understand. It came easily. Anyway, her father died in her last year at school, and she wanted to get away. So she went to study in Germany.'

'But to leave her homeland and to go abroad? She was very young, I think – maybe eighteen?'

'She loved her father. Desperately. And he had died.'

'I see. And did she go alone?' He was both amused and bemused by the fact that he had slotted into her pattern of speech and the way she was telling the story. It was a long time since a patient had done that with him. Telling the story in the third person was an interesting way of distancing oneself from it as a way of handling it. It was also an easier way of telling it truthfully without getting emotionally involved.

'No. No. She went with her best friend. Jennifer. Perhaps not the best person to have gone with, as it turns out, but at the time, Jennifer was enthusiastic, and this girl thought it would be a good idea. She would have company. You know – someone to register with, to do the language exam, to share a place in the student residence . . . it seemed a good idea.'

'But it wasn't?'

'Well,' she smiled, 'I suppose it is a case of we will never know what would have happened if they had not gone together. Because you can't rewrite history, can you? "What's done is done." I'm rereading *Macbeth* at the moment – forgive the occasional quote I'm allowing myself.'

He too smiled, but he would not be diverted. 'You sound as though you are being fatalistic – but it is about the past you are talking, isn't it?'

'Yes. It is about the past. And I'm not fatalistic in fact. Not at all. Free will, et cetera . . . I believe in that. Completely. We are not preordained to do anything. Any act we do, we do by choice. Therefore the onus is ours.'

'And the knock-on effects?' he asked.

'I think we have to take them into account in so far as we can, before we actually do anything, but of course we can't always see what they may be. I suppose I try to live for today, but in such a way that I will not disturb my tomorrows, or indeed anyone else's.'

She believed in a morality by which she lived, he could see that. He was sure then that she did not know that François was married. Should he tell her? He knew that he would have to sooner or later, but he did not want to create an upheaval in her story.

He had wondered then, after their first deep conversation, what it was that made her what she was – that extraordinary mixture of composure and frailty. The vulnerability was there beneath the surface, but she carried herself in such a way that she appeared aloof, almost to the point of coldness, and yet she clearly carried such love for her girls – the flowers who peppered her conversation.

'Lily is my eldest, you know.' She said it firmly as though he might doubt this fact. 'I had her at the end of my first year at university.'

'In Germany?'

'Yes. In Germany . . .'

'But you've left out a bit. What happened before that, before you – before this girl – you – got pregnant?'

'There was this girl,' she said. 'And she was me. She was quiet and closed, keeping her own counsel in many ways, but strongly under the influence of Jennifer Delmont, once classmate, now confidante. They were in their late teens, teetering on adulthood, and they had gone to live in Germany.'

She gave him just the outline of the truth, avoiding the painful parts, telling him about two girls – two friends – who went to Germany. Jennifer had a German boyfriend whom she had met in Ireland. When she heard that Esme was going to study abroad, she decided to do so too. There was enough money in their homes to finance this venture, and both took jobs as waitresses when they arrived in Germany – a small steady income with a reasonable amount of tips gave them extra comforts.

Esme told Jacob just a précis of their time there. But in her mind she remembered details with a clarity that surprised her. The waters of the Neckar River flowed smoothly between its banks. The willows hung low across the gentle current. Along the towpath they walked – Esme and her friend Jennifer Delmont – in their summer clothing. Cotton T-shirts, flat sneakers on their feet, one in shorts, the other in a skirt.

'I'm not going back, you know,' Esme said to Jennifer.

Jennifer said nothing.

'I'm not going back,' Esme repeated.

'You don't have to go back,' Jennifer said. 'But you don't have to decide right now.'

Esme nodded. They moved on down the path.

'I wish we had rooms down in the town,' Jennifer said.

'Mmm, I know. Me too.'

They were living in student accommodation up on the hills above the German university town of Tübingen.

'Maybe next year,' Esme said hopefully. 'I'll stay on next summer and find somewhere for us.'

Jennifer nodded.

'I'm sure your mother misses you,' she said, reverting back to the previous conversation.

Esme did not answer. She doubted it. She wished Jennifer would not make pronouncements like that. It both unnerved her and irritated her. Jennifer knew nothing, but thought she knew it all.

Esme and her mother had parted on terms that were unclear, Esme's father having suddenly died of a heart attack. Esme, devastated, had hoped for something from her mother, but there was nothing forthcoming. Her mother had said, 'I did my grieving for your father months ago.' Her words seemed both harsh and unfair to Esme. That her mother should say that she had grieved for her father at any point seemed more than unlikely. After all, it was her mother who had called the marriage over, her mother who had asked him to move out, and when he had refused, it was she who had left, buying herself a mews house on a laneway not that far away, but closer to the city.

And Esme, lost, had drifted between the two, uncertain where her loyalties lay or if indeed she had any loyalties.

'I don't want to talk about her,' she said to Jennifer. 'Ever.'

If there was anger there, there was also despair. So much unthought, let alone unsaid. The past had become a forbidden subject as she and Jennifer started their new lives.

In their first tutorial, six of them around a table with their professor, Günter Wassermann, they carefully took each other in, while appearing to give all their attention to the words of the academic. Across the table Arjen van der Vloed caught her eye. They looked at each other. Neither smiled or showed any acknowledgement of the other – just the meeting of eyes.

He was tall and dark. Black straight hair enhancing the darkness of his eyes, his tan, and the smoothness of his skin.

Esme took in the straight neatness of his nose and the high cheekbones. His wrists were strong and slim. She looked back down at her notepad, knowing that he had seen her stare at him so intently. She tuned into Professor Wassermann's words.

The class, all foreign nationals, had to sit and pass a language entrance examination, although in the meantime they were permitted to attend the courses of their choice. Arjen's German was the best, with Esme a close second behind him.

Jennifer was struggling with the vocabulary and the grammar. She had only taken German as a subject in her last two years in school, and while she had done well enough in her final exams, it was quite different handling lectures and tutorials in the language. Esme knew that Jennifer was going to have to work twice as hard as everyone else. She had a spelling problem both in English and German, whereby she was never sure whether the 'i' came before or after the 'e'. Though mastering this in English, when she had eventually learned to list words into one of two columns, with Esme's help – like 'niece' and 'incipient' in one row, and 'receive', 'receipt' and 'seize' in another – for some reason it was not so easy in German for Jennifer.

'Go by the sound,' Esme said to her. 'When the sound of the word is "i" then the "i" comes last. Like in "*mein*" or "*dein*", whereas if the sound is "eeee" then the "e" comes last like in . . .'

Coming up behind them, Arjen van der Vloed said, 'It is a good thing it's German you're learning and not Dutch . . .'

'What's that supposed to mean?' Jennifer asked.

'Nothing really,' he said. His English was good, his accent slightly exotic. 'I was just making conversation,' he continued, politely, calmly.

'Well, don't,' Jennifer snapped.

He looked at her in surprise, and then he turned and walked away.

Esme stood there in the silence between the words and his departure and then she said to Jennifer, 'There was no need for that.'

She started after the Dutchman but he had strode swiftly off on his long legs.

'What's wrong with you?' Esme said, turning back to Jennifer.

'Nothing,' Jennifer said. 'He had no right to butt in like that.'

'I don't think he was butting in,' Esme said. 'I think he was being friendly.'

'Well, he can go and be friendly with someone else,' Jennifer replied. 'I don't like him sitting there looking at us during class.'

That was the crux of it, Esme knew. She was sure, well, almost sure, that Arjen had been looking at her and not at Jennifer, and that had annoyed her friend. She said nothing. Jennifer was difficult – always had been – but she was her friend. Jennifer had sought her out. Jennifer had stuck by her. Jennifer had been there when the walls closed in . . .

'I suppose we should go to the library,' Esme said, by way of changing the conversation. They found their places and worked silently, Esme moving, as ever, between complete focus on her work, and a sharp but subsidiary awareness of who was in the vicinity.

She liked to be seated with her back to a wall, but because of the shelving that was not completely possible. At any point, someone might walk behind her looking for a book. Her support factor was therefore Jennifer – Jennifer she trusted. When she was completely immersed in reading, she knew that if something happened – and what that might be she could not envisage – at least Jennifer would be there. To take down the number of a car? To follow the car to the ends of the earth? To hunt for her until she was found? No, she did not think those things so clearly, but they were there somewhere in the recesses of her mind. There was no such thing as safety, no place hidden enough for Esme ever to feel secure, but having run from home, she thought she had put as much distance between herself and her past as was possible.

There were no windows in the library. The shelving covered the walls and ran in rows at right angles into the rooms. The only daylight was from the skylights in the ceiling through which the summer sun burned down from above. In winter the heating brought a cosy comfort with it when the snow blocked out the skylights above, before melting on the thick glass. There among the books, Esme had found the safest place, deep in the room, Jennifer facing her across the table, and somewhere, not too far away, Arjen van der Vloed reading and writing and turning the pages of his books. She found comfort in Arjen's proximity but did not know why.

Fear had become instinctive to her. She protected herself with it. It would take half a lifetime more before she would realise that she had donned fear like a cloak, that she had absorbed it into her blood, that it had become part of the being that was her. If you learn to live with fear, if it becomes part of you, then it cannot come in as a shock. And Esme wanted to live shock free. She did not tell that to Jacob, though. She told him none of the details, just the facts.

Then she married Günter Wassermann before the start of her second year in university. Günter Wassermann, Professor of Linguistics in the university as well as part-time tutor and language teacher for the incoming foreign students. She had moved from her student accommodation to his apartment overlooking the Neckar River, where the oarsmen practised from early morning until the sun went down, in their sculls, fours or eights, with their coaches shouting to them from bicycles on the towpath.

Günter Wassermann was fifteen years her senior.

'I thought there was safety in his age,' Esme explained to Jacob. 'I had not taken into account that he had the libido of a one-year-old jack rabbit.'

Jacob laughed and she looked up at him with a grin, pleased but surprised that she had brought about this re-action.

'And should you have known this?' he asked her.

'Well, looking back – with the joy of hindsight – it seems completely obvious. But it wasn't then. I felt singled out – special, wanted, desired. What more could a nineteen-year-old girl want? Or so I thought. I had Lily the following year, and got my primary degree shortly afterwards.'

'That all sounds very successful, even if it wasn't planned.'

'No, it wasn't planned ... nothing was planned. Everything just seemed to happen. Although I would think now that if one forgot to take one's contraceptive pill, one was perfectly aware of the consequences on some level – but at the time I saw my pregnancy as an accident. But Lily was a joy – it was as if she filled a void. As if I had been waiting all my life to have her and to hold her and to be enriched by her.'

'And your mother? How did she take this?'

'I didn't tell my mother,' she said shortly.

Jacob watched her.

'My parents split up when I was eighteen. My father died shortly afterwards. I think I told you that. He died suddenly. He had a heart attack. I haven't seen my mother since.'

'That's interesting,' Jacob said into the silence that had quickly developed between them, despite the noise from outside on the street, the movement of cars and people, the chatter from a nearby table.

'Not really,' Esme said. 'She and I had less and less to say to each other. I could never please her, and I suppose, de facto, she could never please me. I always felt I had let her down.'

'And she had let you down?'

Esme nodded. 'Yes,' she said simply.

'And in what way had she let you down?'

'I suppose because I never seemed to fulfil her ambitions.'

'And how would she have taken your marriage?'

'She would probably have handled that all right. But my getting pregnant prior to the marriage would have wounded her sense of order,' Esme replied with a slightly sardonic smile.

'So you never told her.'

'No,' Esme replied after a pause. 'I think she saw children as something to be disposed of.'

'Disposed of?' He was startled. 'Did she dispose of you?'

'No, no, I don't think I meant that. I don't think she

disposed of me . . . I'm not sure. I don't think that's what I meant. Of course,' she continued, 'if one of my girls got pregnant or married and didn't tell me, I would be deeply hurt – probably irrevocably so – but I don't feel that my mother necessarily noticed that she and I were no longer in contact.'

'And what was the last contact between the two of you?'

'It was probably around the time of my father's death,' Esme answered carefully. 'I don't actually remember the last time I saw her. I moved to Germany to study, and I never really went back after that.'

'Did you and she write to each other?'

Esme shook her head. 'No, not really. She sent me money until my inheritance came through. After that there was no more contact. It's an awfully long time ago – over twenty years now. I don't think about her any more.'

'Is she still alive?'

'I assume so. I know I would have heard if she was not. I'm sure that Günter's wife would have found a way to tell me. He married Jennifer – my best friend – you know.'

'No, I didn't know,' Jacob said. She had slipped in the observation as if it were the most obvious thing in the whole world and yet it must have caused her grief.

'How long were you and Günter married?'

'Eight months, two weeks and three days,' she said, the explicitness of this making clear that once she had counted the days and that the details were still fresh in her mind, the numbers were never to be forgotten.

'That's as long as I lived with him as his wife, although the divorce took a further six months.'

It was here that Jacob put his hand on hers. 'That is painful,' he said. 'Tell me more – about Günter – tell me more about how you and he . . .' he said it gently, encouragingly, afraid that he was too clearly wearing the psychiatrist's cloak, but wanting her to tell him how this had come about.

And she did tell him. There may even have been a sense of relief in telling her story.

Esme's German was sound, and after the six weeks' intensive programme she sailed through the language exam, allowing her to register in a full-time course. Jennifer did not fare so well.

Although she passed, it was just that, a mere pass. It was recommended that she repeat the course to make things easier for her later. While Esme enrolled for a degree in Philosophy and Linguistics, Jennifer went back and repeated the six-week course, not so much because she saw any point in improving her German, but because she did not know what she wanted to study.

Esme was aware of characteristics in Jennifer that were unappealing. She felt that Jennifer had attached herself in school to Esme, partly because it made her feel good and partly because she liked the knock-on effect of being the friend of someone like Esme. Esme was aware of a mixture of jealousy and admiration coming her way. Little of this made sense to her, but she suspected that Jennifer had linked herself to Esme in the hope that some of the things that came Esme's way would rub off on her.

Now problems were arising because Jennifer found herself once again in the shadow of Esme, who appeared fulfilled by what she was studying and, on top of that, appeared more content in herself than she ever had been in the past.

Esme knew that Jennifer did not like the role into which she had allowed herself to be subsumed. Jennifer and the German boyfriend had broken up only weeks after she started at the university, and Esme was aware of a certain aimlessness in her friend. She could feel Jennifer watching her when she was busy studying in the library, and she sensed an irritation when she came back from lectures and tutorials. Esme was aware of frustration on Jennifer's part when she tried to discuss what she was learning. In an effort to comfort Jennifer and to boost her confidence, Esme began diminishing her own achievements, but she was conscious that for some reason, and for the first time, she was growing in a way that Jennifer was not. She tried playing this down in front of her friend but she knew that Jennifer was angered by it, even though it was meaningless and Esme knew it. She wanted to tell Jennifer not to be disturbed by the changes that were taking place, that they were normal – no, more than that, they were welcome. It was time that Esme was allowed to grow and not be a mere shade of a human being. But these were things that could not be said, and the more Esme grew, the more the roles within their friendship reversed.

And then, Jennifer went home for Christmas, and Esme was left alone. Esme went with her to the station to take the train to Stuttgart and on to Frankfurt to the airport, and Jennifer, kissing her goodbye on the platform said, 'I wonder how you'll cope without me.'

Esme could not help feeling that Jennifer's comment was unkindly meant.

It was then that Günter Wassermann invited her out. Günter with his somewhat flamboyant world-weary charm, who said, 'Come and have coffee with me,' one day while she was changing her books in the library. It was a long time later before Esme realised that he had, quite simply, been bored. He had parents down near the border with Switzerland but he preferred to spend his time either working or socialising with his colleagues or students. Term was over, everyone had gone home, and he had marked all the papers on his desk.

Coffee led to a drink.

It was cold and the streets were covered with snow, the

roofs of the houses looking as if they had been coated in thick pure white cotton wool. They walked down into the market place, Esme, too shy to tell him that she lived in totally the other direction, knew that she was going to have to walk all the way back to get a bus up the hill.

Down in the market, on the cobbled streets, he bought her a waffle with apple sauce on it from a stand where smells of cinnamon, vanilla and sugar wafted in the air. The icing sugar on the waffle stroked her nose. It was then he touched her for the first time – one finger wiping the tip of her nose while they both laughed, she with embarrassment, hoping that the tip of her nose had not been wet in the crisp and freezing night. A glass of mulled wine followed the waffle. She was light-headed – a combination of the sharp night air and the alcohol mingled with a sense of excitement. The loneliness of the Christmas holidays diminished. She slipped on an icy patch and he took her arm. By the time they reached the river they were holding hands. He pointed up to the turreted houses by the riverbank, showing her which one he lived in. They spent the following two weeks in bed, emerging only at night for dinner. She went back briefly to the student accommodation to fetch clothes and her contraception.

'Too late,' she said to Jacob. 'I appear to be one of those people who gets pregnant easily.'

They kept the relationship clandestine for the next three months, as tutor-student relationships would be frowned upon.

'I told Jennifer, of course, when she came back after the Christmas break.'

'And what did she say?'

'I think she was annoyed. Things weren't going so smoothly for her, and I appeared to have everything. Only an appearance, I know, but I think in Jennifer's eyes I was now someone to be envied.'

Three months later Esme found she was pregnant. Günter tried to convince her to have an abortion.

'I want this child, Günter. I need this child,' she pleaded. 'Please . . .'

He was adamant that she should not have it. She had a degree to finish, work to complete, and life choices to make.

'This is one of those life choices,' she said.

'But this isn't planned,' he objected.

'You can't plan everything in life,' she said. 'Why would I get rid of my baby just because I didn't plan on it? That seems unfair to me . . .'

'But there is a time and a place for all things – and this is not it,' he reiterated.

But she was steadfast.

He eventually relented. He married her in June when the academic year was over.

She flew home briefly to Ireland to get her paperwork in order. She did not visit her mother, although she did go out to the cemetery where her father was buried and she stood beside his grave, trying not to think.

'Trying not to think? Not to think about what?' Jacob asked.

'I don't know – the past, I suppose.'

He knew then that she had skipped something but he also knew from the way she was speaking that she was not going to tell him about that – not yet, anyway.

'I really must be going,' he said.

She nodded. He did not want to leave her then. There was sadness in her face and he knew that she was caught in the story she was telling him. But it was already late.

'I'll see you tomorrow,' he said. 'In the morning? The same time? Or earlier, if it suits you? I'll be there.'

She smiled at him then. 'Thank you,' she said. 'It was a lovely dinner. I've talked too much, though.'

'No,' he said. 'I enjoyed it.'

He called for the bill and paid.

'I'll catch a taxi outside,' he said. 'Naomi, my wife you know, she asked me to collect her at the theatre. How far is it to where you are living? I can walk you there or drop you in the taxi.'

'It's only around the corner,' she replied. 'I'll be fine. It's quite safe.'

None the less he insisted on accompanying her, and he hailed a taxi as soon as they reached the doors of her apartment block.

'*A demain,*' he said.

'*Au revoir.*'

CHAPTER THREE

'Tell me,' Jacob said. Then he paused.

It was the following morning. They were outside the café in the morning sun, at what had now become their usual table. Esme was wearing a white soft flowing skirt to her calves, and a matching white top, sleeveless with a scalloped neck. Her low-heeled brown sandals were suitable for walking and matched the simple brown leather belt on her waist.

She looked tired.

'You didn't sleep?' he asked.

She shook her head. The hands on the clock had crept around; seemingly endless minutes dragging into equally never-ending hours, until the dawn arrived. Her work would go better if she was not so tired, and she knew it. But she was not good alone at night. She liked – no, she needed – company.

'Do you have nightmares?' Jacob asked.

She nodded. It was easier now to avoid the truth – there had been no sleep, only recurrent fears that haunted even the lightest doze.

'Do you remember them?'

'No. Not really. Some images remain. You know – sounds

– footsteps on stairs. The cry of a baby.' She could not bring herself to tell the true awfulness of the night. Every time she closed her eyes, the monsters in her mind emerged. And the monsters had names. The Wolf and the Eyes. And it was their footsteps on the stairs that she could hear in the dark endless hours of night. She smiled gently. 'Just nightmares.'

'Tell me something that is puzzling me,' he said, reverting to the conversation of the previous evening. 'Why do you think Günter agreed to marry you? You made it sound like he was not at all keen, and yet he did agree.'

'It's interesting you should ask that,' Esme said. 'It's something I've thought about a lot. I was brought up within a guilt culture. Part of it came from within my family, part from my nationality. I carry guilt – guilt about things that are not my fault. And even though I can rationalise that, I still find it difficult to get rid of. Günter was different. I don't think he understood the concept of guilt at all, but he did understand shame. I think he cared how he would look among his colleagues. When it became clear to him that I was not prepared to have an abortion, I think that it was shame that made him agree. And I was too young, too foolish, too needy, I suppose . . . and instead of realising that that was no basis for matrimony, we married. And I thought I had got what I wanted. I thought I had found a home. A husband. A baby. I was busy trying to create a safe place. And of course, it was not safe at all.'

'Yes, I understand. But . . . but how did you and he fall apart?'

Lily was born in September – an event that Esme tried not to dwell on, because mixed with the complete and utter joy of holding this baby in her arms for the first time was the dawning realisation that there was still no sign of Günter. He brought her to the hospital when she went into labour at about seven o'clock in the morning, and left her there while he went to give his day's lectures and tutorials. Lily was born that night at around midnight and there was still no sign of Günter. The hospital tried contacting him by phone, but he had taken the receiver off the hook.

'Well, there was no point in both of us losing our sleep,' he said to Esme as she lay in the hospital bed the following day, feeling rather bewildered.

'Your wife has lost a lot of blood,' the nurse said to him. 'We were urgently trying to contact you during the night.'

He was shamed then into looking concerned, and being reassured that Esme's blood loss had been replaced, and that both she and her baby were doing well. He looked at Lily in her tiny plastic bed on wheels and agreed that she was perfect.

'When will you be coming home?' he asked. 'I'm asking a new colleague from the department for dinner at the weekend, and I was hoping you'd do your roast chicken for us.'

'*Herr Doktor*,' the nurse said with polite firmness to Günter, 'your wife nearly died in the night. We will not be releasing her at the weekend.'

And so Esme stayed in hospital for a full week until they were satisfied she was well enough to go home. And home she went, where Günter expected their life to continue just as it had before. He liked to entertain at least one night a week, and Esme did the cooking for that event, and sat with his colleagues as they discussed interdepartmental politics or world events. These conversations had excited her in the past, and had absorbed her interest. She used to be able to contribute to them. Now she was so tired she could hardly keep her eyes open.

She was torn between love for Lily – tiny beautiful white-haired Lily – and the realisation that she was missing out on life. She missed the joy of going to work in the library, of being able to read until three o'clock in the morning if something interested her enough, of walking to the pub to meet Günter after an evening's work. All of these things were gone now, and she would not have minded had Günter shared the burden of having a baby. But he was oblivious to her state of exhaustion, and had no interest in Lily unless they had friends over and he could carry her in to show her off.

It was nearly five months later. Esme was back in university, trying her best to juggle a baby, a husband and her studies. Günter seemed unaware of her activities. She was unsure if he had any preference as to what she did. She had tried discussing her return to studying but he had appeared disinterested in her actions, only saying that as long as there was no disruption in the running of their household, this particular decision was hers.

It was mid-afternoon and she had come home early with the baby in her arms, and let herself into their apartment. Lily was asleep, leaning in to her body, head turned inwards resting on Esme's shoulder. Esme's hand was on the back of her baby's head. She was moving very quietly, hoping to place the sleeping bundle in her cot and to get a rest herself before starting the evening meal. She was excessively tired and had picked Lily up early from the student crèche facility, cutting short her library time. The well-oiled lock turned silently and she let herself into the thickly carpeted corridor, easing the door closed behind her. She was about to slip her feet out of her boots when she feared the movement might disturb her baby, and so instead she started down to the tiny bedroom where Lily's cot stood waiting, the bars at the side pushed down, the covers neatly folded back so that she could lay the sleeping child down with the minimum of fuss.

But halfway down the corridor she heard a noise and

realised she was not alone. At first she assumed it was Günter on the telephone and then she heard Jennifer's voice. She wondered what they could be talking about, and why they were in the bedroom – she did not suspect for one moment what she would find when she opened the door. But she continued first to the baby's room and placed Lily in her cot, before heading back up the corridor and opening the bedroom door.

She took in the crumpled sheets, the entwined bodies, the look on their faces . . . a rising sense of disbelief gripped her with the true and utter horror of finding the two people she loved in such an embrace.

She said nothing. She just stood there trying to absorb on some level what was in front of her. There was a coat hanger on the wardrobe handle – she had meant to put it away that morning. She saw the pale wood of the hanger against the dark wood of the wardrobe as though in relief. The combination of the woods struck her as strange. The window was open and the low February sun shone through the room and she could see dust motes dancing on the sun beam and far below, in the crisp winter air, she thought she could hear the sound of the oars slipping in and out of the water, and the excited voice of a woman in the distance – although of course that might have been Jennifer's voice crying out in a mixture of ecstasy and of horror.

Or maybe it was her own voice. She had no idea.

But somewhere there was a voice and maybe it was saying 'yes yes' or maybe it was 'no no', she did not know, but a voice echoed in her head, and she stepped back and closed the door, and stood numbed in the corridor while she tried to take in her bearings, and tried to get her mind to think what she should do next.

Not this, she thought. Not this. Not here. Not my husband, not my best friend. Not all that I have . . . not in our bed in our apartment, in our home where all our hopes and dreams are placed . . . not this, please not this . . . But even as she thought it, she wondered what hopes and dreams she could have meant. They had shattered like glass in front of her eyes.

Günter appeared with a towel wrapped around his waist. He was saying something to her but she could not hear the words. She pushed past him when he tried to block her progressing down the hallway to the door. She left her keys and her bag and she ran down the flights of stairs, outside to the open air where she tried to breathe. She ran and ran along the narrow path, up into the old cobbled part of the town, her mind trying to close off a thousand images of pain and hurt and disbelief.

Not here. Not now. Not this.

But of course this was reality, this was real, this was her life changed again in the randomness of a moment, the randomness of her having come home early, of her being tired that day, of the library being too stuffy, of too many sleepless nights. And it was then she had bumped into Arjen van der Vloed. Arjen, whom she knew from Günter's tutorials from a whole year earlier, Arjen with his dark straight hair and his handsome face. They were no longer in class together, both having passed their language entrance exam on the first sitting, and now he was reading Economics and Political Science.

She bumped into him outside a craft shop and he reached out his hand and said, 'Esme, what is the matter?'

She may have already been crying, maybe she only started then, or maybe she did not cry at all. Maybe it was a howl of despair at what life threw at her. But he, undaunted, took her by the hand and led her back to his student flat down the next street.

He made her coffee and he poured her a glass of schnapps,

and she sat on his old brown corduroy sofa with him beside her, his knee touching hers, and she felt completely numb, even when he reached out and pushed her hair back from her face.

'Talk to me,' he said. 'Tell me what has happened.'

She gulped. She did not seem capable of swallowing properly. She could hear herself making strange sobbing noises, but she couldn't stop. He put his arms around her.

'It's all right,' he said. 'It's going to be all right. When you're ready, tell me what has happened.'

After a while the wild animal noises she was emitting stopped and she whispered, 'Günter . . . Jennifer . . . bed.'

It took him a while to piece together not just that Günter and Jennifer were in bed but that there had been something wrong in Esme's marriage for some time.

'Where is Lily?' he asked.

She was surprised he even knew that she had a baby, let alone the baby's name, and then his words penetrated her frozen brain.

'Oh God,' she groaned, getting to her feet. 'Lily . . . I must go back . . .' She could not believe that she had left the apartment without her. 'Lily,' she said aghast, only now realising that she had abandoned her baby and run. 'I should go home and feed her,' she added, getting quickly to her feet. 'I can't believe I did this. I just left her.'

'I think we should go and fetch her,' he said.

'Fetch her?'

'Yes. Now. At once. You can't leave her there. And you can't go back and live there.'

'What choice do I have?'

'You can either go back and live with the man who is having an affair with your so-called best friend, and bring your baby up in those circumstances. Or you can go and get your baby and make a new life.'

Esme looked at him horrified. Both options were unthinkable.

'Well?' he said. 'Shall we go and get Lily?'

And she agreed. She did not want to leave Lily there and yet she felt that taking Lily with her on whatever new journey she was about to embark on was going to be very hard on her baby.

'We'll bring her here,' he said, as if surprised when she said she did not know where she was going to go.

And it was that simple. He made it that simple. She could not imagine why he was prepared just to take her and Lily into his apartment and thought at first he was offering her refuge as a stop-gap measure, but it later transpired he was not like that.

'He loved me, you see,' Esme said to Jacob. 'It was that simple. I did not know what love was until I lived with him.'

The return to Günter's apartment was an ordeal. She climbed the stairs nervously with Arjen beside her, holding her arm and then her hand, reassuring her that there was nothing to be afraid of. She could hear their footsteps on the stairs as an echo in her head and she feared what they would find when they arrived.

'I can't do this,' she whispered as she stood before the door.

Arjen raised his hand and knocked firmly on it. 'Yes, you can,' he said.

Günter, now attired in full day clothing, despite the lateness of the hour, opened it.

'Where have you been?' he said by way of greeting. 'We're having trouble calming Lily.'

And what about calming me, thought Esme, as she looked in bewilderment at his face.

What she saw written across his cold handsome features

was selfishness. His only concern was for his own comfort, and she wondered that she had never noticed this before. She could hardly bear to think of Jennifer – Jennifer, her friend who had cooed over Lily and congratulated her, who had visited daily and helped with the shopping in the first week, and then who had somewhat withdrawn. But that was now no surprise as it became clear to Esme what had been happening. She kept wondering how Jennifer could have done this to her.

'I don't want Jennifer touching Lily,' she said briefly. It was the best she could come out with, and she could hear the feebleness of her words, and felt that he must despise her as she had no way of handling him – she never did have, but she only realised that now.

'Well, then, don't leave your baby here unattended,' Günter said.

The harshness of his words shocked her. It was as if this was all her fault, and yet she knew that it was not. It was also as if their baby had nothing to do with him. She could not take all the blame for what had happened. What had she done? What had she done that was wrong?

'Of course I know now what I did that was so wrong,' she said to Jacob.

He raised his brow as he waited for her to continue.

'I got pregnant.'

'It takes two to get someone pregnant,' Jacob pointed out to her.

'Well, Günter was never great on responsibility – at least not for anyone other than himself.'

'What happened then?' Jacob asked.

Jennifer had appeared then in the hallway, holding the wailing Lily, and passed the baby over to Esme without meeting her eyes. Lily seemed immediately soothed by being in Esme's arms. Whether it was the feel or the smell of her mother was unclear but she leaned in against her, her baby body relaxing, and her bawling eased.

Esme stroked her head and whispered to her, while Arjen suggested that they collect some things – items of clothing both for her and for Lily. The whole episode was bewildering for Esme. Günter was being excessively and self-righteously reasonable; Jennifer was hovering ruthlessly and purposefully on the edge of their marital breakdown; Arjen, who had nothing to do with anything, was in complete control and organising everything, while she, Esme, had the feeling she was hallucinating, probably brought about by the combination of exhaustion and shock.

'And Günter let you take Lily? Just like that?'

'Yes. I often think about that with a sort of sense of disbelief. First of all I abandoned her in the apartment and ran. And then when I finally remembered her existence, it transpired that Günter didn't want her. Why that should surprise me so much I don't know – but it did. For some reason it hadn't properly dawned on me. I think that I believed that after she was born, we were a unit – I didn't realise that Günter had not seen us like that. I sometimes wonder what would have happened if I hadn't remembered her. Would she have been forgotten? Unwanted?'

'But you did remember her. Don't forget that. This whole series of events must have been totally shocking for you.'

'I don't know how I would have coped had it not been for Arjen.'

The strangest thing about it was that Arjen had once been a student of Günter's, but now was giving orders like he was the mentor. He gathered together two bags.

'I'll be back for the rest of their things later,' he said to

Günter, who was standing in the corridor, looking uncertain. 'Is there a pram or a buggy for Lily?'

Günter looked as though he didn't know what either a pram or a buggy might be, and it was Jennifer who said that it was kept under the stairs in the lower hallway.

'Jennifer, can you put together bottles and diapers and whatever things Lily needs?' Arjen said to her as though it was the most normal thing in the world.

'I'll need you to carry these bags downstairs,' he then said, and surprisingly Günter moved into action and carried them down the long winding flights to the ground floor.

Then Arjen took Lily from Esme's arms, and said, 'Come along, Esme,' and they walked out of her old life.

He took them back to his apartment and they settled Lily down for the night in her pram. 'I'll go back and get her cot tomorrow,' he said to Esme, as he put on their dinner. And Esme sat there with a glass of wine in her hands and watched him.

When they had eaten he brought her back to the sofa and he stroked her hair. She sat there in a daze, wondering how any of this could be happening. She was wearing jeans with a blouse and cardigan, and he touched her throat with one finger while still looking into her eyes. She felt mesmerised.

He brought his finger slowly down the length of her throat to the curve of her breasts. 'I have thought of these,' he said. 'I thought about seeing them and touching them when you sat opposite me in class. I wanted to suck them and stroke them . . .'

His English was perfect in many ways, but sometimes slightly formal, and she closed her eyes and listened to him murmuring to her as he unbuttoned her blouse and slipped her breasts free.

She said nothing. She lay back on the sofa while one of

his arms held her, and his mouth latched on to one breast, while with deft fingers he pulled and teased the nipple of the other.

She had had no sexual urges whatsoever since Lily was born. First there had been the soreness and later just the endless tiredness as she tried to handle being a student, a mother and a wife all at once – crèches, papers, exams, shopping, endless things to be done and not enough time and not enough sleep. And Günter's interest in domestic chores was non-existent, his participation was zero and he appeared to have no comprehension of the word 'share'.

That anyone could possibly find her desirable in this state of exhaustion and sadness amazed her on one level, but it also excited her, and she closed her thought processes down and just let herself feel the enjoyment of being wanted for herself. There was a sudden and incredible pleasure of being touched by this man whom she had watched across a room but hardly exchanged more than a few sentences with over the year. Twice in the first semester when they were doing their language course they had had coffee together, but always in a group with the rest of their classmates. Once or twice she had been aware of him looking at her after she had married, but assumed it was with the same disinterest with which he appeared to look at the others in the library. Despite the fact that she knew he had looked at her with interest in the first semester, she really had no idea until that afternoon that he had in some way singled her out. She had felt neither wanted nor special while living with Günter. He had insisted that the normal routine of his life was adhered to, and despite her tiredness, their social life continued as though nothing had happened. He was uncomfortable when she fed Lily, asking her to keep her breasts well covered when they had friends over. That had upset her as she had always been very private in the feeding of her baby and she knew then what she had already suspected – that Günter found her pregnant and postpartum states unpleasant.

And this was different – this was Arjen, whom she barely knew, Arjen with his dark brown eyes in his handsome face, loving her just as she was, and for some reason, wanting her just as she was.

He made love to her on the sofa with a tenderness that moved her to tears. She had not known such gentleness, did not know that it could exist, that someone would stroke and caress her, putting her needs just above his own so that when they both came locked together, it would be as two people completely united – and yet they did not know each other. They had only ever really exchanged a glance.

Afterwards he lit a cigarette, which they shared, and the smoke spiralled gently upwards and away from them. He wanted her there – her and her baby, while already the cells that would become Rose were multiplying in her womb.

'It was that simple,' she said to Jacob. 'He loved me. He told me he had loved me for a long time. It made no sense at first, but later it did.'

Later it took on meaning, and slowly, as she learned about him, Esme realised that what Arjen wanted was to love someone – and to love that person unconditionally. She was not sure, despite her equanimity, if she would have been able to take on someone just like that – a fledgling student with a baby and with so much baggage that she could only survive by pretending she was someone else.

'Pretending to be someone else?' Jacob asked.

There was fear in her eyes then. He could almost smell it on her. He wondered if she actually knew what it was that she was hiding, and also how far she was prepared to go to uncover it.

'I meant there I was, having dissociated from my background, becoming this student and then this wife, playing roles, I suppose, not really having grown into "*me*". Do you know what I mean? All those doubts one has in one's teens as one emerges as an adult – I see it in my girls, my flowers . . . and I know that if one of them married now, before she became the woman she will become, she would either be stunted in some way, or it would take her longer to develop and mature. I think I was a pretence at being a human. Just half a person. I was nothing, just a shadow.'

But a shadow of what, wondered Jacob, as he made his way to his office. A shadow of a child, who had been well cared for, loved, doted on? It did not sound to him like it was the worst start in life at all. And he knew that she did not mean that. He knew she was not looking for pity. There was something too stoical and hopeful about her for that. He also knew that she was very manipulative. She had got this German lecturer to marry her so that she could have the baby, although it did sound as if she would have had the baby anyway. She had even implied that getting pregnant was no mere accident. I want this baby, she had said. I need this baby. And so she had it.

And then she had just slipped into the life of Arjen.

Jacob grimaced, realising how she was just slipping into his life.

When Jacob left for work, Esme left too. She walked to a park she had found the previous day. She would sit on a bench and read for a while before going back to the apartment. She would buy some fruit from the grocer's on the corner for her lunch, and she might lie down in the afternoon and try and nap because François had phoned and said he would come to her place for dinner. She had quite liked the idea of cooking for him – but that was before she moved to Paris. Now she was not so sure.

Part of leaving the apartment in London for a year was so that she would not have to do the mundane things like cooking, shopping, keeping on top of the girls' routines – although it was really only Jasmine, her youngest, she had to care for like that, as the other two were away at university. Jasmine was at boarding school, but quite often came to her for weekends, and once there was even one other person in the apartment, the level of work and everyday maintenance increased immediately. Esme wanted to avoid all of that. It was not really selfishness on her part, more the awareness that time spent preparing food, which she in fact quite enjoyed doing, and cleaning up and clearing away, which she did not enjoy, was time wasted. It was not that she did not have time to spend as she wanted – time was the one commodity she did have now – but she did not like the idea of spending it in boring repetitive non-constructive activity.

She was also aware that François's elusiveness over the previous days annoyed her as well as puzzled her. And she was less keen to make the effort to prepare a meal for him, fearing that he just might not turn up. His promises of phoning or meeting had so far all fallen apart. She had thought of asking Jacob about him, but decided against it as she didn't want one relationship intruding into the other.

She wondered what Jacob thought about her. A bit of her wondered what she thought about herself. She knew that she was behaving strangely, pouring out this story to someone she had only just met. But she felt driven to do so. It was self-serving of her and she knew it. Part of it was to do with being in a strange place and knowing virtually no one, and part of it was something else – something to do with Jacob. Perhaps the way he looked at her, or the way he listened . . . It was as if he had released a tap that had been too tightly closed, and all the water was now flooding out.

In the park, she pulled a white peaked cap from her bag and settled it on her head so that she was protected from the sun. She already had a high-factor protection on her face, but she was always careful, as she feared both getting burned and becoming light-headed from the heat.

She got out her copy of *Macbeth* and began to read, but the bench was uncomfortable, and she decided to go back to the apartment. In the grocer's she bought a pineapple, and then she decided suddenly, inspired by the layout of the fresh food in the glass cabinets beneath the counters, that she would cook for François after all, so she bought two steaks and a salad, bread and cheese, and she headed home. She settled in her leather window chair to read, the food now in the fridge. She was writing notes for her novel and, in the doing of this, was contemplating love and the true meaning of it, what people do out of love for someone else and out of love for themselves. What started as a philosophical thought to do with the morality of love moved on to thoughts about the duty of love.

We give what is due, what is *our* due, she thought, and then she wondered if one should give more. She did not know what that *more* could be. And yet she felt, she knew, she believed or maybe hoped that there was more than that. Love that would last, that would be real and balanced, that would not be taken away. Love that would be there when the sun rose in the morning and carried one through the day, that would still be in one's blood and bones during sleep and infuse one with warmth in the darkest of nights. The love a mother felt for her children was like that, except it carried a burden with it, the burden of getting the balance right, of not overindulging, not manipulating, not controlling but yet guiding and being there no matter what happened. She knew that, from a child's point of view, love – that particular love, maternal, paternal or both – was the linchpin of childhood. It was based on dependency.

Her thoughts had wandered. The love she wanted to consider was with regard to the characters in her novel. She was more interested at that moment in the love one felt for a spouse or partner. She thought real love must be tied in with safety – it would bring out the goodness in another person, someone to whom you knew you could give yourself completely and be safe within his love. But everything, including love, was transient and she knew it. As she perused her thoughts, her mind moved to the finite nature of life. When the sun goes down, she thought as she turned the page, then it is night, and when it rises then it is day. And if it stopped rising then there would just be eternal night. She supposed that that was what death would be. She was aware of the randomness of all things. The chance happening of meeting someone whom she might love and who might love her equally, the chance of being in a particular place at a particular time, the chance encounter of the sperm and the egg, the total and utter randomness of the Big Bang whereby she had come into existence at all.

She had no god, and no notion of one.

She had woken one morning and discovered that she was alive. Before that there was nothing. And she knew that one day there would be nothing more.

Now she worked each day, regardless of what day of the week it was. She put pen to paper, thoughts to words, pursuing the depth of her knowledge, examining her progress, developing her mind. Making up for lost time, she sometimes thought. At night she went to bed and during those sporadic hours of sleep, she dreamed of episodes in her life mixed with imaginings and fantasies that belonged to a world she never truly accessed. She was not sure that she wanted to access that world, although she knew she was touching on it with Jacob.

This thought made her think of him. She wondered about him, what it was that he was thinking – he did not give much of himself when they talked. His interest was so focused on her. She was not flattered by this, but she was aware that he was very different from the men she knew. She liked him. No, it was more than that. In some way she desired him – she wanted contact with him, both physical and emotional. When he had touched her hand she had felt something warm go through her blood – a *frisson* of excitement and of lust – but she had pushed that awareness aside. He was married. But she wondered if he had felt it too. And she was involved with François, even though she had no idea now where that involvement would lead, or if indeed she wanted it to lead anywhere.

She knew that she had been more honest than she usually was in the telling to Jacob the story of her first marriage.

Admittedly it was something she seldom spoke of but when she did, when, if ever, she spoke about the breakdown of that marriage, she gave the impression that she had remained totally intact, although she knew and did admit to herself that losing her first love through his deceit had diminished her and left her full of self-doubt. And while she knew that Günter must have fulfilled her in some ways while he had been with her, his deception had left her believing that she was not worthy of being loved. She found it difficult to remember what had been between her and Günter before it all fell apart. She had vague memories of endlessly talking about words and meaning, her hopes and her student life, her ambitions and her achievements. And she remembered she had felt so alive under his watchful gaze and his guidance in those early months. Was that love, she wondered.

She did not know. It had seemed to be love at the time. She had longed for his approbation, wanted to be in his bed, needed to be the centre of his attention. And she had been at the centre of his attention, but only for a short while.

But stoically she gave the impression of bouncing back, hiding the fact that the walls that protected her mind were paper thin.

Life is short, she had said to her children when they were old enough to comprehend. 'It is not a dress rehearsal,' she had added. 'This is it. This moment. This today. That is all we have. There are no guarantees for tomorrow. So you must seize this day.'

Carpe diem – that was her mission statement. And she adhered to it.

If there was something self-righteous in her approach to life, she did not mean it that way, and she genuinely believed that she did not deliberately hurt others. But there is always fallout. Perhaps she was aware of that on some level, but she tried . . .

She tried so hard to get it right.

Her children, Lily, Rose and Jasmine – they drifted away – schools and colleges, universities and trips abroad, holiday time spent between her and their respective fathers or the families of those fathers. But despite this drifting into their own lives, into the worlds that they were creating for themselves, they were still attached to her. Deeply attached. She saw this link as a lengthening of the umbilical cord that bound them to her for ever. It never failed to amaze her how they loved her. She never felt worthy or deserving of that love. But she both wanted and needed it. Her girls achieved or attempted to achieve their own ambitions, and she did not do anything to temper them although she sometimes tried to redirect them. She believed in the fulfilment of the self, but knew it must not be at the expense of someone else.

She saw abundance in her own life – the abundance of riches. Not of wealth, although she was more than comfortable in that regard. A prosperous father who had died saw to that, and an ex-husband who insisted that the home she lived in had the comforts befitting his daughter. And she was aware of the blessings of being comfortable, of being sound financially, of being secure, of not wanting. Her abundance, as she found it, was to do with the depth of her mind, her awareness of life and society, of politics and philosophy, of the balance a human being could find when born in the right place at the right time to the right people. Her daughters too, they were part of the abundance. She knew she was terrified of the empty space their growing up was creating. Before Lily there had been nothing.

Sitting now at the window, and thinking of the episode of her life that she had told to Jacob, terrible pangs of guilt pricked her mind. It was a guilt she had never managed to handle. The guilt of having run from that apartment and just abandoning her baby. She sometimes tormented herself by wondering what would have happened had she not bumped into Arjen. Would she have remembered that she had left the baby behind? Would she have gone back? Alone? Faced Günter's icy anger by herself? Would he have handed Lily over had she been on her own? She had no idea. She only knew that he did not want Lily. He never had. He allowed her in his life only on sufferance. Even now.

Lily loved animals more than people. Esme knew that. She also knew that that had come about because her father, Günter, had not shown the love a parent should show their child. Esme had no problem in Lily preferring the company of wild animals to that of humans, but she did fear that she personally might have contributed to that. After all, she was the one who had married Günter.

Esme had suggested to her eldest that she might like to study Veterinary Science, but Lily rejected this in favour of Zoology, in the hope that she would end up working with animals, but not in a confined way. Esme knew that Lily probably did not want to have to handle the owners of the pets she might end up doctoring. There had been talk of her staying on in an elephant sanctuary in Sri Lanka after a month's work there. However, not only was no money to be made there, but Lily actually had to pay to stay there and wash the animals. While Esme sympathised with her innate need to help animals, none the less she refused to continue to subsidise Lily's latest venture as she wanted Lily to find something to do that would both fulfil her needs and support her. And of course Lily's father would not finance her in any way that involved monetary outgoings beyond the basic maintenance, which the courts had decided upon.

Now Lily was tracking geese in Canada, on a government grant, and tying in the work with doing her master's. Esme wondered what affection Lily could feel from a goose.

She remembered Lily always befriending cats and dogs in Germany. 'Oh, it's purring because it loves me,' Lily had said as she stroked the neighbour's cat, or, 'He's my best friend,' as she let some dog in the park lick her face while both Esme and the dog's owner tried to separate the two. It wasn't that Lily lacked the possibility of friends, because people always wanted to befriend her. It was simply that she preferred the company of animals.

Esme feared that Lily's preference was because she was less likely to be let down by animals, and that she had not received sufficient individual love from her parents as a child. But Lily had been such an undemanding child that it had not been clear then that just maybe she should have been getting more attention. Esme worried that she might not be getting much attention now.

CHAPTER FOUR

Lily Wassermann, Esme's eldest child, unbeknownst to her, carried many of her mother's traits. She was rootless almost to the same degree as Esme. But unlike Esme, Lily kept seeking for a link while Esme ran from hers. Lily was drawn back to various places because of those links and ties to which she was so tenuously attached. Annually Lily spent a short period of time, usually a week or maybe ten days, with her father, Günter Wassermann, in Germany, and she enjoyed her trips to Jasmine's father in South Carolina. When asked where she was from, she was sometimes vague about it, in a similar vein to her mother's response to the same question. But while Esme's vagueness was deliberate, Lily's was sincere. It was as if she was not sure where she came from. When pushed she would say that she had been born in Germany, partially brought up there, in the States and in London, that her passport was European, but that she saw herself as a citizen of the world. She was aware that might sound like an affectation to the person who asked, but it was not meant that way – it was the truth. If they took it that way, well, she didn't care. She was totally unpretentious, kind and decent. She liked both animals and human beings but found animals easier to be around.

Twenty-two years old, with her mother's features but with her father's blue eyes and the blonde hair of her Aryan agnate ancestors, Lily Wassermann was engrossed in her work. She was part of a group that was tracking and tagging geese. The purpose was to study their breeding habits and migratory patterns, and her initial fears about the cruelty in putting bands on these wild birds was diminished as she realised that those she worked with really did have the birds' interests at heart. She sometimes felt that one day, somewhere in the future, some highly evolved species of human beings would tag lesser humans, ones like her, to follow their progress, their migration and their survival instincts. That thought horrified her, because with it came the fear of humans in zoos, humans in laboratories, humans being experimented on.

When she voiced this to her father, Günter just said, 'Is this not already happening, Lily?'

'What do you mean?'

'Human beings are already experimenting on other human beings. No animal knows how to use torture like a human does. And aren't prisoners on remand tagged?'

She hadn't thought of this. She had seen *Planet of the Apes* and it had frightened her. She had not realised what was already happening among her own species. What her father said shocked her to the core, and she longed to preach humanity and what it might mean if only everyone could be brought to a point where human compassion and kindness might be at the fore.

Günter had also said to her, 'Don't think so much, Lily.' Possibly this was both good and insightful advice from a man who scarcely noticed his daughter.

But Lily was a thinker. 'I can't help it,' she said to her parent.

'Well, endeavour not to worry so much,' he persisted, in

his somewhat stilted way. 'There are some things you cannot change.'

But with the optimism of youth, Lily still believed that you could change things. She protested outside embassies, she signed petitions; she helped wash elephants in Sri Lanka, and eventually found herself in the North Western Territories tracking geese. Her initial notes, to which she daily added, briefly and cryptically, referred to the family skills of the geese. The most sagacious, the most wary, the most family-orientated of all animals. If she felt any sadness in writing these words it was not on a conscious level. The scientist in her was to the fore when she was at work, but she could not help thinking that human beings could do worse than to try to learn from these birds.

Unlike human beings, the geese mated for life and, while on the ground, all their instincts were geared towards the survival of their family; in the air they changed and became part of a group, the individual becoming a cog in a greater machine. From a gaggle of geese, a word that somehow incorporated both their movement and the sound they made, they became a skein of geese in the air, and a wedge when they flew in V-formation. Their individuality, such as it was, faded into anonymity and they became part of a unit. She had not seen this yet and was unsure if she would be there when it happened.

Crouched with her binoculars, Lily had watched the hatching of the eggs of the Giant Canada geese in a particular nest, and the appearance of five goslings, closely guarded, herded and patrolled by their parents. Not for an instant were they left unattended from the moment of their emergence. Over the forthcoming days they were fed and cared for, and as the time approached when she and the team knew that the nesting days were numbered, they began to rise earlier and earlier in the mornings so as not to miss the moment of departure.

It was just before dawn one morning that she and Hugh Bonner, an English student with whom she had been paired, set off from the hostel. They had their backpacks with them in the four-wheel drive, as they had been doing over the previous three days, each day suspecting the imminence of the departure. And this turned out to be the day.

They left the SUV where they had been leaving it for weeks, making their way on foot across the rough terrain on a trip they were now well used to.

The word 'tundra' had initially intrigued Lily, until Hugh had told her that it came from the Finnish *tunturia*, meaning a treeless plain. And that is what it was. She could only imagine its bleakness in winter, its desolation and its silence. But now in the height of summer, despite its sparse and rough vegetation, it was alive with the chatter and movement of wild fowl.

With the female ahead and the five goslings in formation behind her, with the gander bringing up the rear, their family of geese started their journey across the boggy land. They could not be followed with any ease because of the dangers of the marshes scattered with lakes and rivulets, sedge-edged and damp, and it was with a sense of both wonder and sadness that Lily watched them go.

Hugh Bonner, older and more experienced, grinned at her.

'Wonderful, isn't it?' he said. 'And they'll be back. They'll lay their eggs here again and again, and their goslings will return exactly to this place to do the same. Awesome – tell me you agree that it's awesome?'

Lily nodded in agreement, smiling at his use of the word 'awesome', which she rightly suspected was an imitation of one of the Americans in the group. The weeks they had spent in this spot, watching and checking, noting all movement and all activity, had come to an end.

Lily, with her notebook out, marked the time and photographed the emptying area, as one by one the flocks of birds started to move.

'They'll keep moving now,' Hugh said to her. 'Through the wetlands until summer ends, when they leave for the south. And that you have got to see.'

'I won't be here then,' Lily said. 'I'll be back in Europe.' She had already told him this and wondered that he had not remembered it.

'You have to stay,' he said with enthusiasm. 'You can't miss the migration – it's the most amazing event – and after these last weeks recording every detail of their activity, there is no way you can miss what's to come.'

'But it's weeks away,' Lily said.

'We'll start the tagging next week,' Hugh replied. 'We'll be busy until it's time for their departure.'

Lily had admitted to him that she was scared of the tagging, even though she knew that all of the team really cared about the geese.

'We're so careful,' Hugh reassured her. 'When we net them we only tag the adults. We can't add to the stress levels for the goslings. We couldn't tag the little ones anyway, because they have still to grow and the tags would be too tight.'

They were both animated as they discussed the surveying that had just ended and the tracking that was about to begin.

'Was it last year you were here?' Lily asked.

'No. It was two years ago – but I think about it a lot and I can't wait for what's ahead. When were you planning on leaving, anyway?'

'I don't really know. I presumed I'd go as soon as the tagging was over. I don't know . . .'

She had originally supposed she would leave in early September when she would return to university to write up her notes before the start of the next term. Her tickets were booked for then, but the combination of what was going on between them, together with the forthcoming flight of the geese, had made her unsure of what to do. She let him convince her that it would be foolish to leave before the migration, and having decided to stay she found her whole attitude changing. Being part of this group had been a wonderful experience, and while she knew she would keep in touch with some of them, it would be so much better for her project if she saw the whole thing through.

'I'm really pleased that you're staying for the tagging,' Hugh said to her. 'We've been a good team – particularly you and me, I mean – and I'm looking forward to the next bit. It would be a shame if you aren't here for the end of this part of it.'

She liked him saying that about him and her. In a way she supposed it was inevitable, if one worked so closely with someone else, that a sense of involvement would evolve, an interest in each other, a caring and a consideration.

He told her then that he was intending to make his way down through the States. He planned on being in Illinois for the arrival of the first geese.

'Some two hundred thousand of them will settle there for the winter months,' he said. 'But my real hope is to go on down to Louisiana or Missouri. I haven't decided which. But I want to be there for the arrival of the others.'

'How many will go that far?' she asked. She knew the answer, because she had done the research, but she wanted to keep the conversation going. She hung on every word he said.

'Another hundred thousand.'

'I'm interested in the geese that don't return north after winter,' Lily admitted. It was part of her research, the part she was planning on putting in her final paper. While her initial study was following these birds from birth to their return to their birthing place, her interest was wider.

'I didn't know that,' Hugh said to her with surprise. 'I thought you were just doing what the rest of the team are doing – tracking and researching . . .'

Lily shook her head. 'That was the plan. But since then I've changed my mind. Grayson – my stepfather – he's been taking my sisters and me to the southern states on business trips over the years. Well, a business trip is a misnomer, but it's what he calls them. He has friends in both States. We've spent a lot of time in both Missouri and Louisiana. You know, in Missouri alone there are over one million resident geese. They are almost considered a pest – between their droppings, which are all over the place, and their proprietorial behaviour, which is amusing when you read of it, but not so funny when you are a resident. There are stories of geese in swimming pools, geese outside doors deterring people from getting in or out . . .'

Hugh laughed.

She was relieved. She could hear herself talking and knew that she was using her mother's vocabulary and that she sounded really uptight, but she didn't seem to be able to stop.

'In St Louis we stay with a friend of Grayson's – we call him Father Goose. Anyway, he has a really great lawn,' Lily continued. 'It stretches down to the river – and a flock of geese live in his grounds. He has befriended them and they act as guard-dogs. You should hear the noise they make when anyone approaches.'

'The honking?' he asked.

'Hmm,' she agreed. 'Like a dawn chorus that never ends.'

'And don't forget,' he said, 'it's half a pound of droppings per goose per day. That's a lot of shit.'

Now Lily laughed.

There was a great feeling of bonhomie between them, and Lily knew it was because of what they were sharing, every moment of every day, the patience required, the excitement in small changes in the environment, the physical tiredness and stiffness and the magnitude of what was happening. They had just shared the early departure of their nest – their personal nest, as she thought of it. She was glad they had come out early before the others.

'Let's go somewhere and get coffee,' Hugh said. 'We'll meet up with the others later.'

'Will they know where to go?'

'Oh, yes. Don't worry about them. They've been here before – they know their way as well as the geese do.' He reached out his hand and pulled her to her feet.

She suddenly was aware of how scruffy she looked. She ran a hand through her hair. 'I need a shower,' she said. 'I was too tired when we got in last night, and we left the hostel so early this morning.'

'Any regrets?'

'No, absolutely none.'

She brushed some damp mud off her knees, which adhered to her hands. 'I'm filthy,' she said in dismay as it dawned on her fully just how dirty she felt and must look. 'I can't go anywhere and have coffee like this.'

'Of course you can,' he reassured her. 'We can have a quick wash before ordering – and sometime later today, when we get to the next hostel, we can shower.'

They drove for an hour before finding somewhere for breakfast.

'Are you tired?' Hugh asked her.

'No, not at all. Even though I feel that I ought to be. But I just feel so exhilarated. Such a great feeling.'

'Yes, it's the best. But it is nothing as to how you will feel when you actually see them fly away.'

'I didn't think I could spend that long here,' Lily said. 'But I am going to,' she reassured both herself and Hugh. 'I was planning on going from here down to South Carolina, to my stepfather and sister, and then I have to return to Europe. I haven't seen my mother in months and I want to spend a week with her before going back to university.'

'Where does she live?' Hugh asked her.

Lily laughed. 'She doesn't really live in a particular place at the moment. She's always on the move. She has apartments in a couple of different locations but she's mostly drifting from one place to another.' It was not the most accurate description, but it was how Lily saw her mother. Esme was based in their London home, but was indeed always on the move.

'Why? Why on earth does she do that?'

'I don't know,' Lily admitted. 'It's just what she's always done. The longest we were ever anywhere was near Charleston, in South Carolina; we were there for almost eight years. I think that's the longest my mother has ever been in one place.'

'She sounds like she'd be as interesting to research as our geese,' Hugh remarked.

'Funnily enough I was thinking that the other day,' Lily replied. 'She is completely without roots. She travels fairly light. Her favourite possessions are her books, but as she says herself, they are almost all replaceable. So she just picks up what she needs as she goes along.'

'What does she do?' Hugh asked. 'For a living, I mean. Or doesn't she work?'

'She does a bit of lecturing and writes articles and books and things,' Lily said.

'Lecturing in what?'

'Modern philosophical thinking, critical analysis, the relevance of morality . . . that's one of her main themes of late.

Cultural differences – how a national psyche underlines accepted rules of morality. Anyway, you name it, my mother can talk about it. And she's written a few novels under a pseudonym.'

'Who is she?' Hugh asked with increasing interest.

'Oh, you won't have heard of her,' Lily said. 'Her name is Esme Waters.'

'I have heard of her,' he replied in surprise. 'And not only that, but I heard her speak in London last year. She was giving a lecture on the importance of constantly reviewing morality and moral philosophy in a changing world. If I remember correctly, she was speaking about the possibility of moral improvement. She's your mother? How amazing.'

'It's not at all amazing,' Lily said. 'She's just my mother. Just like your mother is your mother, if you see what I mean.'

She wondered if she sounded harsh. She had not meant to. She wanted him to see her just as her, and not as someone's daughter.

They pulled up into a highway filling station that was full of trucks and had a large restaurant.

Lily became aware that Hugh was staring at her. 'What's up?' she asked.

'I was trying to see the similarity,' he replied.

'What similarity?'

'Between you and your mother.'

'And can you?'

'I don't know. Your hair and eyes are different. You're probably taller than she is. But maybe your face – the bones, the mouth . . . I'd need to see a picture of her beside you to be sure.'

'We're alike all right,' Lily said. 'I don't know about in looks, but we're both driven by work and projects and plans. She always has something new that she's either working on or thinking about.'

In the 'restroom', Lily looked at herself in the mirror. What she saw was a long-legged girl in khaki trousers tucked into the thick socks around her ankles and hiking boots at the end of her slim legs. The fleece sweater she was wearing for protection against the early morning chill was scuffed at the elbows. She took it off and tied it around her waist, hoping that the blue T-shirt underneath might somehow enhance the blue of her eyes. She ran a comb through her white-blonde hair and then realised that she actually had mud on her face. She washed it off as best she could. She grimaced before admonishing herself not to behave like her youngest sister, Jasmine. After all, what did Hugh Bonner expect? A second Esme Waters? Just because they were related did not mean that she was Esme's clone, she reminded herself.

She felt none of the anger that both her sisters harboured towards their mother. Jasmine's anger was to do with the fact that Esme had left her father and rejected their life in South Carolina. Rose's anger was different, and far less clear. It was to do with Rose rather than Esme. Rose didn't know where she wanted to be and was torn between different cultures and different countries, and it was for this she blamed Esme. Lily, on the other hand, felt admiration for her mother. She had gone through the teenage years with the mixed desires of both wanting to resemble her mother and at the same time wanting to reject her. But with time and with Grayson's patience, she had come to see that she resembled her mother in so many respects that she might as well acknowledge that and get on with her life. And so she had. It had been a lot easier after she had made that decision.

Inside the diner, after they had washed, Hugh ordered coffee and sandwiches for them both and Lily pulled out her notebook.

'Oh, leave that for now,' Hugh said. 'Let's talk. There'll be time enough for work later. We're not going to see our geese for a few days because of the waterlogged terrain. We're going to have to wait until they reappear.'

'We won't recognise ours,' Lily said. 'I find that really sad.'

'It's not very likely,' he said to her. 'But let's not talk geese now. I want to know more about you.'

They had spent a couple of weeks in each other's company but had exchanged hardly any personal details. They knew certain things about the other – how they both were comfortable with silence, how they both liked to drink still water rather than sparkling, how Lily always returned her camera to its case after using it, while Hugh left his hanging around his neck for hours on end. They had developed a sense of companionability – a feeling of ease with each other. They had periodically checked that the other was all right, that the other was coping with the endless hours crouched on the ground or if the other needed a drink . . . They had developed a mutual understanding without knowing anything about the other. What they had in common was their work – their interest in the geese and dealing with the long hours of the surveying and coping with the physical discomfort. And as they passed time watching the geese they shared the same sore muscles, together with their passion and their interest. So that now, when they actually came to talk on a personal level, it was as if there was a firm basis of friendship between them already.

They had been accepting and supportive of each other while out in the marshes, and that friendship was there as a link to their now accepting each other as individuals on a different level.

Hugh told her of his career to date – his schooling and university in England, his research work, his papers for *National Geographic* and other magazines.

'You're at a whole different place to me,' Lily said. 'I'm still trying to get the basics done.'

'You've youth on your side,' he said with a laugh.

'That makes it sound like you are very old,' she said thoughtfully. 'How old are you?' she asked after a moment, wondering if that was too intrusive a question. There was always something difficult about asking people their ages.

'Five years older than you,' he said.

She smiled. She knew then that he must have asked someone her age, and that pleased her. It pleased her that he had wanted to know, and that he had gone to the trouble of finding out.

'What would you like to do now?' he asked her when they had finished eating.

'Sleep,' she said. 'In a really comfortable bed with the possibility of room service.'

He laughed. 'Right,' he said. 'Let's do that.'

Back in the SUV she knew that the dynamics between them had changed and she was not altogether sure when it had happened. She suddenly felt a shyness she had not felt before with him.

Like her, Hugh was wearing trousers and a T-shirt, thick ankle socks and hiking boots, but now for the first time she noticed the bones of his knees through the fabric, and she could not help but think what incredibly nice knees they were. She remembered him once unzipping his trouser legs one warm day, and removing the lower halves from just above the knee . . .

She looked up and realised he was looking at her and she knew that she blushed. He said nothing, just touched her hand lightly as the car sped up the highway. She was surprised again that he had not only heard of her mother but had actually heard her speak. It was the first time Lily had met someone who had known her mother. She was unsure how it made her feel. Proud? Embarrassed? Her mother was not famous; Esme Waters was a name known only in a small circle.

It also made her think how the Esme Waters Hugh had met was a totally different person from the one she knew. He had seen her mother as a lecturer and philosopher, whereas Lily knew her in a totally different way. She knew her as a mother who loved her daughters, who didn't sleep well, who was a bit too tidy, who had talked to her girls as equals in a sense, so that they, or at least she, Lily, recognised that her mother had a right to a life of her own.

Esme waited for François until nine thirty. At which point she was about to pour herself a glass of the red wine that was breathing in the kitchen, when he arrived looking slightly haggard and very tired.

'Apologies,' he said as he kissed her. 'One of those days.'

She felt then that her worries about his having another woman in his life were not just unfounded but also unjustified, and she settled him in her window chair while she griddled the steaks, and tossed the salad in the dressing she had already prepared. They ate at the dining table with two green candles in the strangely ornate candlesticks lighting up the room. She flambéed slices of pineapple in brandy and served them with vanilla ice cream. She was glad now that she had decided to cook for him. He seemed boyishly appreciative and she felt mellow and pleased that he was there.

Her earlier fears about her mistake in moving to Paris faded, at least for the moment. He talked about hospital politics and the general stress he was under, and she felt sorry she had doubted him.

At eleven o'clock he glanced at his watch.

'Shall we go to bed?' he asked her as she put the dishes in the kitchen.

'What time must you leave in the morning?' she asked.

'Oh, sorry,' he said. 'I forgot to say that I've another very early start. I would not want to waken you at six, so I won't stay over. I'll slip away as soon as you are asleep.'

She tried to bite back the hurt that was rising in her. He knew that she had sleeping problems, and that the only time she did actually sleep through was when she was safely in someone's arms. She had told him that, and he had seen for himself how soundly she slept when he was with her. She could not believe that he would not take that into account, and yet at the same time she felt she was being unfair, because he clearly was tired and had an early start.

'But if you sleep over,' she said, 'at least you will get an uninterrupted night's sleep, even if it is not for as long as you would like.'

'No,' he said. 'I really will have to go. Anyway, I didn't bring a change of shirt or socks or anything with me.'

This was all wrong, Esme felt. She also knew that she did not want him making love to her unless he was going to stay the night. It was part of how things should be. She did not do one-night stands. She wanted more. A relationship, no matter how remote – although she sometimes thought, the more remote the better – should satisfy both parties. And in her case, a large part of the satisfaction came from sleeping next to someone, knowing that they were there for her and because of her, and because they wanted to be with her.

It was clear that François, for whatever reason, did not want to spend the whole night.

'François,' she said, 'let's leave this until the weekend, when you are not on duty, and we can actually have some real time together. That will please us both.'

He did not seem to have the energy to argue with her, and then she felt sorry for him.

'You look too tired to come to bed for an hour or so and then to have to leave,' she said.

'I know. I am. I'm sorry. I'll make it up to you at the weekend,' he said.

She nodded. She knew what it was like to be too tired to function, let alone even to think. She was trying so hard to be understanding, the kind lover, the good partner. She kissed him good night and closed the apartment door behind him.

Tidying away the plates in the kitchen, she told herself it had been a pleasant evening, and even if it had not evolved as she had assumed, it was not bad. The truth, however, was that she had enjoyed the previous evening with Jacob more. This was not because they had dined out and she had not had to cook, but because there had been no expectations and no sense of feeling let down at the end.

One emotion that Esme had never truly learned was anger. She did not know how to be angry. When she felt irked by things, she was inclined to brush them off, feeling that it was a waste of time to dwell on them. She now thought that she should in fact be feeling anger at the way François was behaving towards her. He had, after all, agreed that she would move to Paris for the year so that they could spend more time together, and now that she was there he had only a couple of hours free at a time, and little inclination even to bring a clean shirt with him to her apartment so that he could stay overnight.

The night stretched ahead of her again. She poured a cognac and brought it to her laptop. Checking her email, she found there was one from Lily.

Lily was now clearly as absorbed in tracking wild geese in Canada as she had been a year earlier washing elephants in Sri Lanka. She was delighted because she had found two that had been tagged or logged the previous year in Ireland.

The colouring of the tag was apparently the method of ident-
ification. Esme thought of Lily, presumably finding some
internet café so that she could email her mother. She could
see her clearly, tall and healthy, with her blonde straight hair,
purposeful and intense. The email continued:

Ireland, Mum. ☺ Can you imagine? Ireland, where you
were born, but I have never been. They have travelled
so far. One of them is a white-fronted goose and its
journey would usually be Greenland through to
Northern Europe, but somehow it has arrived here,
looking very different from the Giant Canada geese
that we are tracking. Don't expect to hear from me for
a while as we are very isolated. ☹ More soon as I can.
   Love Lily.

Esme read this twice, amused at the emoticons.

It was good to think of Lily happy and busy, and also
actually being funded for what she was doing. It was important for Esme that her girls had direction and a meaning to
their lives. She knew that she had lacked that – and so much
of what she had done had been because of that deficiency.
But she didn't want to think about that now.

She got out her notebook and settled again at the window,
but the lights from the street as cars whizzed by were
distracting her, so after a short while she took herself to bed.
She settled on her pillows and switched off the light, hoping
that sleep might come quickly, but she had no sooner closed
her eyes than she thought she heard a creak somewhere
outside on the corridor. She lay there still and silent, trying
to concentrate on her breathing and on relaxing. She knew
the creaking sound was from the boiler in the kitchen – she
had heard it before on that first night when she listened to
all the sounds to customise herself to her surroundings. But

the creaking sound now reminded her of the footsteps on the stairs, of the door opening, of knowing that no one in the world could help her, that she was alone. She remembered crying out for her father and her mother, and the terrible realisation that they whom she loved more than anyone in the world could not hear her and would never find her.

CHAPTER FIVE

'I meant to ask you yesterday if your wife enjoyed the theatre?' Esme asked.

They were back in the café. The morning sun was already hot. Esme was breaking her croissant into small pieces, but not doing much about eating them. Jacob watched her crumbling it into flakes. She had her sunglasses on and he had the feeling that they were there to hide dark circles around her eyes.

'Oh, Naomi enjoyed it well enough,' he said. 'She loves the theatre but our tastes in it differ somewhat. Occasionally they overlap, but I'm not interested in musicals or burlesque.'

Esme nodded. She opened her mouth as though to say something, and then she changed her mind.

Two things occurred to Jacob, almost simultaneously. The one was to do with how she had spent the previous evening and if time was hanging heavily on her hands, because she appeared desolate. And the other was that he suddenly saw her as Scheherazade, who told the tales of *The Arabian Nights* – and he, like the King, was always coming back for more.

He wanted her to take up the story where she had left off, but she didn't look as if she was really there at all. There was something different about her this morning.

'If you would like to talk about anything,' he said gently, 'you know I will listen. But I'm also happy just to sit here and enjoy your company before I go to work.'

She nodded. 'Thank you,' she said. 'I'm just very tired. I need a night's sleep and I don't appear to be able to get it at the moment.'

'Are you afraid to go to sleep, or is it that sleep will not come?' he asked.

'A bit of both,' she said after a moment's pause.

'Do you have any medication you can take?' he enquired.

'Wine, followed by cognac,' she said with a slight laugh.

'I've heard of worse things. I won't prescribe for you, but I can send you to a friend who is a doctor, if you like.'

She shook her head. 'Thank you for the thought. I may come back to you on it, but I'm going to try not to. I heard from my daughter Lily last night. My eldest, you know.'

'Lily . . . she is the zoologist, is she not? Is she all right?'

'She's well. In Canada. She's tracking geese. It's part of some project.'

'Is everything all right with her?' He wondered if Lily had said something that had disturbed her mother.

'Yes, she's fine,' Esme replied. 'It's strange, you have children and you think the difficult thing is to raise them – all the worries attached to that. You know, making sure they are clothed and fed and educated and loved, and not forgotten about. And then they grow up, and you worry about them being grown up.'

He laughed. 'I can imagine,' he said.

'I had Rose, you know, only fourteen months after Lily.'

'That must have been hard going,' he said.

'Yes. Hard going,' she said briefly. 'Harder than you might imagine. I loved Arjen. That was love. He died . . .'

Jacob touched her hand, held it in his for a moment. 'You don't have to tell me if you don't want to,' he said.

When he released her hand, she reached for her coffee. At that moment a tiny spider crawled across the table. Esme put out her hand and, instead of turning away, the spider climbed her finger. She brought it closer so that she could see it. Suddenly she shook her head and, getting up, she carefully placed the spider on one of the potted bushes at the edge of the café, just as she had done the first time Jacob had seen her. She returned and continued talking as though nothing had happened.

'I do want to tell you. I think I need to tell you. He died before Rose was born. We were so happy,' she said. 'That was happiness. I think I knew that then. There was the turmoil of taking Lily from Günter, of leaving Jennifer with Günter, of not really understanding what was happening or why. I think I must have got pregnant that very first time with Arjen. We took Lily back to his place. He got friends of his to fetch her cot and all her things. I think I was in a state of shock for a while. I was riddled with guilt and despair, the notion that I could not possibly be a good enough parent, and despite my need to have Lily I felt like a failure, because I had left her there that night when I ran. To abandon your child . . . well, it shocked me that I had done that.' She had once suggested as much to Arjen in those brief months they had before he left her for ever and he had tried and tried to reassure her.

'Anyone would have reacted as you did,' he said. 'What were you supposed to do? Stay there and handle the pair of them in your bed? No. What you did was normal. You must not feel like this.'

But she wondered hauntingly how she could have left that tiny baby in its crib and how she could have put her own emotions before her responsibilities.

'I agree with Arjen,' Jacob said. 'What were you supposed to do that night? You were very young. You had just uncovered one of the worst acts of betrayal – your husband and your best friend. And you went back for her as soon as you got your mind around what had happened.'

Esme nodded.

'I must go to work,' Jacob said. 'But I will be here this evening. Are you doing anything? Will you join me? We can have a drink, and if you are free we can have dinner again.'

'Thank you,' she said.

'Will you be all right?' Jacob asked her. He was genuinely concerned. She was clearly less in control than she had been over the previous days.

'I'm thinking of going back to my place,' she said, 'and trying to sleep. Sometimes in daylight it is easier, for some reason.'

He walked her to the corner, and they went their separate ways.

Jacob wondered what had happened the previous evening to bring about such a change in Esme. She seemed more obviously disturbed, as though she had forgotten how to cover the cracks in the veneer. He sighed as he let himself into his rooms. His secretary was waiting with his first file of the day. He took it from her.

'Make sure I'm out of here by six today, will you please, Monique?' he said.

'Of course,' she replied. 'Oh, I've a note in the diary to remind you that the conference is next week and you're giving the opening address on the first day as well as the evening lecture. Don't forget.'

'I won't,' he said. 'But thank you for reminding me. I'll get on top of it at the weekend.'

He glanced at the file. 'Ah,' he said to Monique. 'Madame Junot.'

'Yes, she's in the waiting room.'

Jacob went into his own office and placed the file on the table. Madame Junot was here for what was to be her last appointment. She had had a breakdown nearly a year earlier, more than partially connected with her husband's philandering. She was a kindly woman in her forties who had taken an inadequate overdose and had ended up in the psychiatric ward in a hospital where Jacob helped assess incoming patients. He had spoken with her husband, who swore his womanising days were over and that all he wanted was his wife back – safe and sound, healthy, restored to what he had once loved. Madame Junot was very typical of his patients. He would piece her together – perhaps her husband would remain faithful to her. Perhaps not. Jacob feared not.

Esme walked slowly back to the apartment. She knew that tiredness blurred reality and she knew that she should not think about Arjen because it simply hurt too much. Even after all this time. She would tell Jacob in the evening what had happened, and maybe in the telling she would be able to let it go for a while. But they had been difficult times, and talking about everything did bring up the past more clearly in her mind than she had thought it would. She didn't seem to be able to shake it off. And Jennifer's behaviour had shocked her. They had never spoken of it again, but she knew that in some perverted way, Jennifer had got just what she wanted. Jennifer was clever. She had clung to Esme, giving the appearance of supporting her, but then taking from her . . .

Jennifer had seen that the things Günter could not bear were the trappings of family life. She had been jealous of Esme's relationship with him and she had closely watched the stress that the pregnancy and the birth of Lily had put on them. She saw that what Günter wanted was a regular companion in bed and someone to keep his place tidy and clean so that he could work undisturbed. Esme had even told her in the early days of her marriage that Günter hated her clutter in the bathroom, and that while he didn't mind her reading his books, he went mad if she did not put them back in the order in which he kept them. Yes, Jennifer had learned from Esme how to look after Günter. Esme suspected that there were no telltale traces of her in the bathroom or on the dressing table.

Jennifer had insisted that part of the divorce settlement was that they would see Lily once a month on a Sunday while she was a baby. That way Günter would feel he had not abandoned his responsibilities as a parent, but would also rejoice in Jennifer not having children and in the comfort of his home with her.

In due course they married and Jennifer kept things for him just the way he liked. They never had an undisturbed night and Jennifer was good to Lily, both when she was a baby on those solitary Sundays and then later when Lily was old enough to want to sleepover with them, and later still when she was in her teens and would go and spend a week with them during her school holidays. Yes, Jennifer was clever, and adroit at manipulating situations so that she was reflected in glory. The good partner, the good wife, the kindly stepmother. The thief.

Esme sighed. She no longer cared. She knew that she was so well off out of that situation, away from Günter's endless selfishness and his inability to bestow affection when it was needed. For some reason it suited Jennifer, but it had not suited Esme. She had not known that long ago, but she had learned it over time.

Esme sometimes felt caught in the webs of other people's lives. They were webs from which she could not disentangle herself. She no longer saw Günter and Jennifer. There was no need to, now that Lily was an adult. She had hidden her hurt and her disbelief in what they had done to her, in how Jennifer had stolen him, and how he had let Esme go so effortlessly.

It was easier at first because Arjen was there. He had carried her away from them, told her there was no need to have any contact. He would handle things – the legalities, the removal of her clothes from the apartment, the settling of her into his accommodation, meagre as that was.

They took it in turns to collect Lily from the crèche in the evenings when they had finished lectures. While one went to fetch the baby, the other hurried home to prepare something to eat and to quickly tidy the tiny flat. They took it in turns when their meal was finished to return to the library and work until it closed. Arjen . . .

Back in her apartment, she lay down on the bed and closed her eyes.

Arjen had sat beside her late at night or lay beside her in their bed with his hand on her swelling stomach. 'My rose . . .' he whispered as the baby's feet began to kick. 'I cannot believe how lucky I am.'

And Esme lay there beside him, wondering how he could think himself lucky to have her and Lily and the unborn Rose all leaning on him, all needing his time and love and affection.

He had left early one morning shortly before Rose was due to be born. He took the train north to go home to visit his parents and his brother, to tell them of the turn his life had taken, of the fulfilment he felt, of how he wanted to marry Esme now that her divorce had come through. He was going home to tell them all of this, of his love, of the baby Lily, and of his baby that Esme was carrying. He wanted them to come down to their wedding that was planned for a few weeks later, just before the baby was due.

It was unclear to Esme, both then and later, if Arjen had had some premonition of what was about to happen. Before he left, unbeknownst to her, he took out a life insurance policy with her as the named beneficiary. And on the train, although he was journeying to meet his parents, he wrote them a letter. She wondered why. Later his parents had shown her the letter, but it was in Dutch, in one of his notepads. It appeared to be more a sequence of notes than a constructed letter, as though he had been planning on what he was going to say to them. She did not ask them to translate his words; she knew from the way they behaved towards her that he had spoken of his love and that they were accepting of his wishes and plans. It had been given to them some weeks later, together with his rucksack.

His train had headed north in the autumn fog, speeding from Stuttgart to Frankfurt and onwards through fields already heavy with damp and cold. The first signs of early snow settling could occasionally be seen through the window as the brown fields turned to frozen white.

The train skidded. It seemed to slip on the tracks – a driver's error or an act of God, who knew? Who indeed cared, other than those who had to shoulder the responsibility? For Esme it made no difference. The outcome was the same. The train seemed to lift in places before buckling and falling to one side, rising from the tracks, hurtling across the bank, careering in great metal strips over and downwards, with the contents, both bags and people, thrown violently with it until all collapsed in screaming shards of glass, metal and steel in the frozen fields.

She could not bear to think of how Arjen had died. She would never know if it were quick or slow. If perhaps he performed some final act of courage before giving way to that endless sleep that surrounds life. Sleep was how she saw it. It was how she had to see it. A sleep of peace.

Ironically it was Jennifer who came to her with the news. Jennifer, who had got what she wanted and had taken Günter away for ever, turned up on her doorstep. Günter had been told in the university of Arjen's death and he felt that Jennifer was the person to tell Esme.

'I'm sorry,' she said. Esme neither knew nor cared what it was for which Jennifer was sorry.

Esme stood there with Lily in her arms, her stomach tightening with pain as she looked at Jennifer on the doorstep.

'Arjen is dead,' she said to her one-time friend.

Esme, standing there at the front door, had the strangest feeling that Jennifer must have gone mad, because Arjen couldn't be dead. She was sure of that.

And Jennifer, looking at her, must have felt something through the selfishness with which she had surrounded her whole life. Why else would she have come?

'Let me bring you back inside,' she said to her white-faced friend. 'Are you all right?' she asked. She did not mean was Esme all right in the general sense, as Esme clearly was not. She led her back into the apartment and Esme picked up two coffee cups off the table and brought them to the tiny kitchen.

'I think you should sit down,' Jennifer said.

Esme was thinking that maybe Jennifer had told her that Günter was dead.

'Did you mean Günter?' she asked after a moment.

It took Jennifer a minute to follow Esme's thought patterns, and then she said, 'No. Not Günter. Arjen.'

Esme went to the window and touched what appeared to be a very large web.

Jennifer couldn't help thinking that the place could do with a dust, as Esme vibrated her finger gently on the web.

A spider appeared, presumably thinking something had got caught in his web.

'My only friend,' Esme murmured, and Jennifer wasn't sure if she was talking about Arjen, the spider, or indeed about her, although that didn't seem likely after what Jennifer had done to her.

And then Esme sat down very suddenly, and the look of sheer pain on her face – both physical and emotional – startled Jennifer into action.

It was Jennifer who called the ambulance, but backed away when one of the crew asked her, would she take Lily.

'Oh, the walls, the walls . . .' Esme said to the nurse in the hospital. 'They are terribly thin.'

But she did not cry out nor make any noise as Rose was born. Her black-haired baby was placed in her arms and she held her close.

'Rose,' she said in response to someone asking her had she thought about a name. 'Rose van der Vloed.'

She knew Arjen would have rejoiced so she tried to do it for him. As she battled with a death and a life she struggled to find meaning.

Help came from strange quarters.

Christa Hoffmann, Arjen's landlady, lived across town in a large house. Once a week she came over to collect rent from the four separate apartments she owned, and in so doing had formed a particularly good relationship with Arjen. Sometimes when she came on a Friday evening, Arjen invited her in for coffee, and she had met Esme and knew of the forthcoming events in their lives.

Picking up the local newspaper the following morning, Christa had read of Arjen's death. Shocked, she immediately went across to Arjen and Esme's place. Knocking on the door repeatedly, she got no answer. It was quite possible that Esme had gone to the Netherlands to be with Arjen's family but she felt concern. She thought of Esme, eight months pregnant, and wasn't sure that Esme would have been up to the journey. She phoned the university and insisted on being put through to Esme's tutor. He checked with Günter, who checked with Jennifer, and she admitted that Esme was now in hospital.

'Where is Lily?' she asked.

No one knew.

Christa went to the hospital and she was the first person to put her arms around Esme and to both congratulate and to commiserate.

'I will help you,' she said to Esme, taking Lily in her arms and kissing her. 'I will help the three of you,' she said, looking into the cot. 'My house is large; my children have grown up and left. You will live rent free in the ground floor.'

'Why?' asked Esme, lying in the hospital bed with the new baby in a cot beside her, and Lily being held by this eccentric German woman.

'Why what?' she was asked.

'Why would you help me like this?'

And Christa smiled. 'Why not?' she asked in return.

'But how can I repay you?'

'You don't repay me,' the woman said. 'You pass it on.'

It was a long time before this woman told her a story. It was a story of a Jewish child hidden by Germans, taken into their home, reared by them as their own until the death camps closed and the living were set free.

'Yes,' she said to Esme, 'I was that child. And I could not repay that German family for what they did for me. They saved my life and I have no doubt of that. When I was old enough I asked them once how I could repay them. And they said to me, "Don't waste your life. Use it usefully." And later, when I was older still and I had employment and a reasonable income, I asked them again, could I do anything for them? And they said to me, "Pass it on." Pass it on. That's what I'm doing now.'

Esme often thought of that. She thought of one good act being passed on as another good act and yet another one. A world of spiralling good acts – spiralling outwards, encompassing more and more people. She wondered if she would ever be in the position where she could pass that act of kindness on. She didn't know. She knew it had not happened yet. She knew it might never happen. Oh, yes, she gave money to charity. She supported various groups. But that was not hands on. It was not what Christa had done for her.

To be there when her children needed her, that was the biggest demand she had to face.

'And this Christa,' Jacob said that evening when Esme told him that Arjen had died. 'What happened to her?'

'She helped me through that time. At first I had so little and two babies to feed. I have Christa to thank for keeping us going. My money came through after a while – both from my father's estate but also from the life policy Arjen had taken out.'

'But Arjen's family? Did they come to you?'

'They didn't know about me – not for some time afterwards. Arjen's things from the train were returned to them, and that was the first they knew of me. That must have been weeks after the accident.'

'But you didn't contact them?'

'Jennifer visited me in hospital and told me that the burial had taken place. Arjen was brought back to the Netherlands, and he was gone – just like that. I was really struggling, just to keep going. Christa carried me at first. She minded Lily while I was in hospital. Rose was born early and we had to stay there for some ten days, I think. But when they found out, they contacted me. The Van der Vloeds, I mean. Arjen's parents came to see me. They wanted us to go back with them to the Netherlands. They were just like Arjen. They would have taken me into their home and let me live as one of them, which is what he had done.'

'But you didn't go?'

'I was twenty years old. Scared out of my wits. I didn't speak Dutch. I had two babies. I had already run away from home – twice! From Ireland and from Günter. It would almost have been easier to take them up on their offer. But I knew that if I did, it would take me a long time to put the pieces together again. I was in the middle of my degree and I had Christa for support. So I stayed put.'

'And you got your degree?'

Esme laughed. 'Oh, I did. It took me twice as long as anyone else, though. Even with Christa's help with Lily and Rose, every day was a struggle. A combination of tiredness, grief and shock.'

'I'm impressed,' Jacob said. 'I've heard of people caving in under far less burdens. Tell me something I don't understand, though. Why had Arjen not already told his family about you and the baby?'

'It was silly really. He wanted to surprise them. We had thought of going up that summer when term ended. But he got a summer job in Tübingen, and I was struggling to catch up on study – and we let it go. They were going to come down in September to visit him, then his mother got the flu and that was postponed. And the longer he left it the more awkward he felt it would be to tell them by phone or by mail. So he decided to go up in the November.'

'And then he died,' Jacob mused. 'What kind of contact did you have with Arjen's family then?'

'Considering the distance we had quite good contact. Certainly more than with Günter and Jennifer.'

Esme told him how Günter and Jennifer took Lily for the occasional Sunday when she was little, but never for more than that. The Van der Vloeds had a farm and she and the girls would go there for a week at a time.

'It was difficult for the Van der Vloeds to leave the land, as you can imagine. You can't just abandon a farm for a week, so we went to them instead. They were lovely times, you know. Arjen's brother, known as Nop in the family, had a little girl the same age as Rose. Merel is her name. They became very close friends. I thought at one time I was going to have a problem, because the grandparents wanted to adopt Rose.'

'Did you consider it? After all, you were under the most incredible stress.'

'No. It wasn't up for consideration. I couldn't . . . I wouldn't.'

Jacob thought about that as he went home that night, having once again seen Esme to her door. It made him think of his own mother. He had only the haziest recollection of her in a pale yellow cotton dress, singing to him in a garden or a park – he did not know which. And a man in a suit, with a dark hat on his head – but he could not see the man's face any more. The memory was too vague. But he did remember the feel of the man's hand holding his. It was probably the only tactile memory that he had from those early years. And he was glad he remembered nothing else. That fleeting glimpse of his past was enough. After that there could only be pain and loss and he knew he was better off for recalling none of it. But then, of course, he had been very young. Esme's grief was closer to her. And she had her children as a constant memory of her past.

He wondered if Rose was better off with no memory at all of her father. Of course, there would be a sense of loss, of not knowing and yet perhaps having a need to know more about the dead parent. Whereas, he did not need to know any more.

He had gone to Auschwitz once with Naomi. It was a trip he preferred not to think about. It had been her idea, and she bought the train tickets without consulting him so he had little choice but to accompany her. He had found his parents' names on the wall. And he had stood there and looked at them because that was what you were expected to do. But he did not want the full tour, could not bear to know more about the gas chambers, the lime pits, the rooms full of shoes, or of hair, or of combs . . . the remaining belongings of human beings who had been slaughtered . . . the desolation . . . He had felt that Naomi thought this excursion, for want of a better word, must have done him the world of good. She had been very understanding afterwards, or that was the impression he got. He, however, had gone home and read a book, distancing himself as fast as he could from what they had seen. It was not like with his patients who had things they needed to uncover – indeed, like Esme had things she needed to work through. His past was different. The history of those years was written in blood, both in the soil of Europe and in the memory of the survivors, and he knew there was nothing he could do to make sense of it. He saw no point in dwelling on what he couldn't remember and ultimately would never be able to understand. Whatever it was that had happened to Esme he felt must have some meaning or more understandable context.

He wondered at how she had drifted from Günter to Arjen – it was as if she did not know how to make decisions. She appeared to take what was on offer without questioning.

And yet she said that it was love she felt for Arjen. Love that had grown on her part, although he had been in love with her for almost a year. It was clear that she had manipulated Günter, although ultimately he had outmanipulated her. But with Arjen it was different. She had fallen in with his desires and needs, probably because she had nowhere else to go – after all, the few real relationships she had – Günter and Jennifer – had ended in disaster. So she fell in with Arjen, and grew to love him.

Jacob wanted to ask her if her memory of her love for Arjen was real, or if it was something that had grown in her mind, but he had not wanted to suggest this. But then she had brought it up.

She had said, 'I sometimes wonder what would have happened if Arjen hadn't died. Could we have stayed so happy? I think so. I really loved him. It was a love that sort of grew and grew. He was a remarkable person. But then I think if I hadn't bumped into him that awful day when I found Günter and Jennifer together, would I maybe just have met someone else? Isn't that what happens? You meet someone, and if you give it a chance, maybe love grows?'

Jacob was unsure what she meant. 'You mean perhaps that you could love anyone?'

'Well, it's random, I think. I mean, if there was only one person on the planet for each of us – one perfect partner – well, then with my luck, my designated mate would be a member of a lost tribe and I would probably never meet him. No, I don't think there is one person only with whom we can fall in love. Do you?'

He didn't think so either. He thought of how she had referred before to her belief in randomness – the random nature of all things. He supposed that, like her, he believed in the randomness of love. You met someone with whom you had things in common. Physical attraction was there, the chemistry was right . . . and love grew.

Maybe that was what had happened with Esme and Arjen.

CHAPTER SIX

Rose van der Vloed, Arjen and Esme's child, had her father's dark hair and his eyes like pools that had once drawn her mother in and held her close for such a short period of time. She carried different baggage from her half-sisters, being the only one of the three who had no father. Somehow this factor seemed to her to be an insult and one for which she blamed her mother. That this had never been properly discussed with Esme did not help. Rose had made various efforts over the years but Esme seemed unable to talk about Arjen with any openness and these talks usually ended in accusations by Rose, and Esme clamming up, sometimes in apparent distress, which Rose either did not identify or which she saw as being unfair on her mother's part.

'Of course I love you all the same,' Esme had said when Rose suggested otherwise.

'You don't, Mum, you don't,' Rose had said.

'Darling, I do. I look at you and each of you comes from a special time of my life.'

But Rose thought she could see something in her mother's eyes – hurt or pain.

'Do I look like my father?' Rose asked, knowing full well that she did.

'Oh, yes, you do.'

'And you loved him?'

'You have no idea,' Esme replied.

But Rose wanted more. She wanted details and Esme would not give them.

Rose, now twenty-one, had moved back to the London apartment for the summer. She had returned there from her student accommodation just before her mother moved to Paris for the year. Esme had bought the apartment some eight years earlier, shortly after leaving Jasmine's father in South Carolina. It was a large, exclusive penthouse with four bedrooms and a river view. It had been bought with a combination of the money Esme's father had left her and money that Grayson – Jasmine's father – insisted she took as he wanted to think of her and the children in comfort.

After they moved to this brand-new and pristine apartment, Rose had made a point of writing her name over most of the walls, as if marking her territory like a tomcat. Esme had had the apartment redecorated immediately, but had left Rose's room as it was, telling her she could do what she wanted with it, but that she was to leave the rest of the décor alone.

In defiance, Rose, aged thirteen, had painted her walls black and, with luminous paint, had sprayed graffiti across them, then decided to leave her room as it was.

A variety of thoughts, both childlike and complex, emerged from these artistically constructed phrases.

'DEATH TO THE WICKED WITCH OF THE WEST' might or might not refer to Rose's childhood obsession with *The Wizard of Oz* and equally might or might not refer to her mother, Esme. Certainly her writing it on the walls was a throwback to her childhood.

'J'ADORE THE SISTERS' could have been sincere,

referring to her own sisters, but might equally be an allu-
sion to Sisters of Mercy. Rose's tastes were distinctly rock
and goth, and she regularly listened or bounced to their
hybrid of metal and gloom.

'THE CLOCK STRUCK THIRTEEN' could have been a
youthful but erudite reference to Orwell's *Nineteen Eighty-
Four*. But it might equally refer to the fact that when her
sister Lily was thirteen, a grandfather clock had fallen on her
in an antique shop.

There was nothing about Rose that was obvious – and
that was the way she intended to keep things.

Sometimes she dreamed – vivid stark dreams that made no
sense to her on a conscious level but she suspected they were
connected with her mother. She knew her mother dreamed
heavily. She had heard her cry out in her sleep and, when
she was little and sometimes slept in her bed, she had seen
her mother waking from nightmares, her body shaking and
her breath coming in frightened gasps. While her own
dreams sometimes startled her and left her feeling uneasy,
it was in a more remote way. Sometimes of late she dreamed
of looking out of a window and seeing leaves on the branches
of trees being blown in the wind. It was a recurring dream
and it puzzled her why she should be disturbed by it, because
the images in her fantasy should by rights have been
soothing.

Rose, like Lily, lacked roots. She had no idea where she
belonged or why. She had spent her childhood needing and
loving both her mother and Lily, but in due course the Van
der Vloeds offered her another angle to her life and another
sense of connection. While having two stepfathers had been
the norm for her as a child, her link to Grayson was very
much stronger than her link to Günter. She never felt she
had any bond whatsoever with Lily's father. And yet Günter

and his wife, Jennifer, always had their door open to her. Well, Jennifer had really. Günter did not notice much of what was going on unless it was of personal interest to him or likely to disturb him in any way.

Like Lily she saw herself as a European, but in her case it was because of her Dutch connection. The Dutch connection, which had initially seemed so tenuous, later evolved into something solid. A Dutch grandfather and grandmother, an uncle and an aunt and a cousin named Merel. Each of these relatives contributed in different ways to Rose's childhood. When she was nearly four, her mother had brought her to the Van der Vloeds' farm in the Netherlands for the first time that she actually recalled.

'Grootouders' – how she loved that word. They were her grandparents, her own personal ones – different from the Grosseltern of Lily's in the Black Forest, and from the Grandpa and Grandma of Jasmine's in South Carolina. The very fact that they existed made her special, as special to them as Lily was to her Opi and Omi in southern Germany, and as Jasmine to her Gramps and Grandma in Charleston.

They were people she could always go to, and the initial shyness she had felt on first meeting them when she was a little girl had quickly evaporated as they had all opened their arms to her.

Merel, her cousin, the daughter of Arjen's brother, even looked like her. They both had the same skin that tanned easily, both had dark eyes and very dark brown silky hair, and they had taken to each other with a reciprocal excitement that she still thought about with joy. Merel's name meant blackbird in English, and like her namesake she trilled and chirped most of the time, and when she wasn't doing either of those she was humming or singing.

Rose's first memory of being taken to the Netherlands was mixed with shyness and anxiety, unsure who these people were. Esme had told her they were her father's family, that they carried the same name as she did, and that they wanted her to stay for a week, and that yes, she had been there before. Each previous year of her life, in fact, Esme explained to her, although Rose had no memory of this at all. Clasping her mother's hand she had entered into their world – a world where the sounds were different from those in Germany and yet as grandparents they had similar names to Lily's grandparents in the Black Forest. They were Opa and Oma. And they were so accepting of her. There was no reticence in their greeting – their arms seemed open and they addressed her lovingly.

That Merel, her cousin, looked like her added to the ease with which Rose adapted. She had the feeling of coming home, but was too young to identify this. She listened carefully to the sounds they made when they spoke, wanting to learn them quickly so that she could be at one with them.

'*Kom hier, Roos en Merel,*' her grandfather called. '*Kom naar huis, kom naar binnen.*'

And they came running, she and her cousin, hand in hand from the fields. Here in the Netherlands she was Roos – '*mijn Roos*', her grandfather called her. They borrowed a bicycle for her while she was there. Around and around they cycled, two little girls with big dark eyes and straight dark hair, and the Dutch words danced in her head. '*Kom binnen, wij gaan eten. Binnenkomen, Roos en Merel.*' Bit by bit they made sense – first the meaning came from what happened after they were called, and then she found the words to repeat them. Her opa said something one evening, and she repeated the words after him, sitting on his knee.

'*Als mijn Roos bloeit, en mijn Merel zingt, vult mijn hart zich met vreugde,*' he said poetically and with love. She smiled up at him, as the sounds began to make sense. '*Mijn Roos*' – this is what Arjen, her father, would have said. It was how he would have called her, had he lived. He too would have said that his heart was full of joy as she blossomed.

Merel's father, Ome Nop, patted her head the way he did Merel's, and Merel and she snuggled down in bed together with Merel chattering away, the words pouring out of her in her effort to communicate. Rose felt as if she had found a new home. Merel was happy sharing her father and her grandparents, and Merel's mother, Madelief, took her as her own.

She was so happy there that, at the end of that week, Esme took Lily to Germany and left the four-year-old Rose for a further week. A phone call from Rose's grandfather five or six days later encouraged Esme to leave her for longer.

By the end of that summer Rose and Merel were chattering together with ease. Esme came back for her, scooping her up in her arms in the yard in front of the house.

'I missed you, darling,' she said.

'I missed you too, Mamma,' Rose replied. Even the way she referred to her mother had a Dutch ring to it.

'Oh, Rose, how you've grown and how tanned you are . . .'

'I'm Roos,' said Rose.

'You're Rose to me.'

And the dual world began – a parallel world in which Rose and Roos were contained in the same body, they shared secrets in different languages, they belonged in different places but were caught in time. Once a year, for the long summer holidays, Rose went to stay with her Dutch family. Time passed. The departures became more and more difficult.

'Ome Nop.' Roos, aged five, threw herself into her uncle's arms. 'I want to stay.'

But she did not want to stay alone. She wanted Esme there too. She wanted to live on the farm and have her mother ensconced by her side. She had missed her – terribly at first, and then in a slightly more remote way as though she was in some time warp in which her mother simply did not feature.

There was a discussion that she and Merel overheard one night. Their grandfather was talking to Esme, who had just returned to fetch Rose after a couple of weeks. It was now Rose who was translating for Merel.

'She might stay with us, Esme,' he said. 'We love her . . .' His voice was sad but firm. 'She is what Arjen left – she is his . . . ours . . . always a part of us . . . she might stay with us, and you come to visit us whenever you want.'

'I could not even consider that,' Esme said.

The listening Rose could not help wondering why no one asked her what she wanted.

'Esme, my dear,' her grandfather said, 'we only see her once a year. We would love her to stay . . . But you are young. So young. And so burdened with your children.'

Rose knew that Esme was contemplating his words. Her heart was pounding as she waited for her mother to speak. Her fate was in her mother's hands, and whatever the response was going to be, it could not be the perfect response, because perfection, whatever that was, was never to be. She thought about that later – what would perfection have been? Arjen alive, and Esme and she, walking in a field of tulips, laughing, holding hands; maybe they would swing her between them . . . Esme living with the Grootouders and she and Merel becoming sisters, and Lily there too . . . all of them living together in perfect harmony . . .

'I'm not burdened. I don't see my children as a burden. There is no way that I could not keep my girls with me,' Esme said. 'I will always make sure that she comes to you as often as is feasible. If she wants to come for the Easter break as well, and if it suits you, I'm happy for her to come. I want her to have your family in her life. I am grateful for your love for her . . .'

'That love extends to you,' the older man said. 'Never doubt that. Arjen told us . . . his letter, you know . . . never doubt it.'

And so Roos became Rose at the end of the summer. She was passed from one to the other, hugging and kissing them, before they left – her fingertips touching Merel's through the car window as the engine revved, and then they were gone.

Back to the other world.

And what was that other world? Now twenty-one, she was no longer sure. With Esme and Lily there had been three different homes – Europe, America, and back again – over and over during the years, and her trips to the Van der Vloeds' farm became the linchpin in her life. It was as if the Grootouders' home was the real world – the safe world where she knew exactly who she was.

'I realise,' Jacob said to Esme when they met for coffee the following morning, 'that these girls' home was with you in Germany, in the ground-floor apartment under Christa's place. That was their base. But it must have been strange for them having family elsewhere.'

'I know,' Esme said. 'I wanted them to know who they were – part of me and part of their fathers. I wanted them to be able to relate to their fathers' environments, I suppose. But at the same time it was very difficult. But what should I have done? Kept Rose from her grandparents? Kept Lily away from Günter? There were difficulties attached to this arrangement. But I didn't know what was really right. I had loved my father. I wanted them to love theirs. But it was very difficult. I think it explains what happened next.'

*   *   *

When Esme left Rose alone with the Van der Vloeds for the
first time, she took the train back to Germany with Lily. Lily
was going to spend one night with Günter and Jennifer. This
was to be Lily's first time alone as well, and Esme was both
nervous and excited about it. She was excited for Lily, because
it meant that Günter was in some way acknowledging her
existence other than in law. She knew that it was Jennifer who
had encouraged this event to take place, and she found she
had to admire her for her persistence. Lily was looking forward
to it, and whatever feelings Esme actually had towards Jennifer
she knew that for Lily to have some proper contact with her
father, she was going to have to bite those feelings down. She
replaced them with a form of pragmatism. Jennifer loved
Günter. Günter loved himself but somehow was happy with
Jennifer. Therefore it was a stable home for Lily to stay
overnight in. Esme was not sure that she actually believed all
of this, but it was the only way she could handle it. She also
feared that if she refused Lily contact with her father, later
Lily might choose to be with him. And she did not want
Günter Wassermann having any influence over their daughter.

She brought Lily to the turreted river apartment, climbing
the seemingly endless flights of stairs with her, carrying Lily's
small bag in one hand and holding Lily's little hand with
her other. Lily was clutching a teddy bear and looking hopefully up at Esme.

'Will we be all right, Mutti?' she asked in German.

'We will be just fine,' Esme reassured her.

She wasn't sure that this was going to be the case. It was
her first night alone in years – alone without a man or a
child – and she had vaguely planned the luxury of a long
soak in a hot bath, or maybe just sitting reading and not
having to worry if one of the girls was going to get out of
bed and come wandering in looking for a drink or a cuddle,
or another bedtime song.

She had finally got her excellent degree after six long years. Her perseverance had won out and the department had asked her if she would like to stay on.

She had not decided.

Esme was tired after she handed Lily over, kissed her and passed her bag to Jennifer – Günter was absent, of course. She noted how tidy the apartment was – Günter's books in neat piles on his desk, and those on the shelves in alphabetical order. As she passed the main bedroom door on her way out, she tried not to think of that day five years ago, but it was there in her mind enhanced even now by the sound of the oarsmen in the water below. She pushed the memory aside.

'I'll be back tomorrow evening,' she said to Lily, kissing the tiny upturned face. 'At six o'clock,' she said to Jennifer.

Esme and Jennifer looked at each other. This was the first time Lily was staying over, although these handovers took place approximately once a month. There was a tacit agreement that only formalities were discussed. Esme would say a time she would collect Lily, and Jennifer would agree. Esme knew that Günter was often not there at all during those monthly Sundays, and she knew that she could probably legally have objected to leaving Lily with his wife, everyone knowing that Günter would probably not see his daughter at all for several months at a time. But she chose not to object, because she wanted Lily to form a relationship of some sort with him, and not later to say that Esme kept her from him.

Having agreed a time, Esme wandered back up into the old town, to the square where she and Günter once had drunk mulled wine together with the snowflakes fluttering down, and where ironically, less than a year and a half later, she had bumped into Arjen when she had run from the nightmare scene in the flat.

This time she rounded the corner and walked straight into an American.

He was 'Grayson Redmond, of the Charleston Redmonds,' he told her after he had picked her up off the ground. 'I'm so sorry,' he said, in his South Carolinian drawl, even though it had not really been his fault.

'It was, I think you might say, a lightning love affair,' Esme continued. 'He bought me dinner – I don't really remember how or why. I was pleased to have company – my first night without the girls. He was lovely. The first man I'd really talked to since Arjen died. Five long years had passed. In that time I had only known motherhood and study. There had been no time for anything else – I was just a mother first and a student second. I wanted my degree as I knew it was the best way to get somewhere – also I was happiest studying, using my mind, I suppose.'

Grayson Redmond was in Europe with his parents. It was his idea of a wedding anniversary gift for them. He was already thirty-five, comfortable in himself, keen to please them in some different way as he knew that he had let them down in others. His mother despaired of him ever marrying. There were plenty of nice girls in South Carolina who would have done anything to share his life but Grayson did not want to settle down with the blatantly obvious – the golf-playing girls, the polo entourage, the debutantes and socialites of which Charleston boasted and with whom he was acquainted.

The plantation was his since the previous year, when his father had signed it over to him. His father and mother had then moved into Charleston to a residence that was only marginally smaller. They were 'doing' five countries in Europe. Grayson was aware that his mother had no idea which country was which and did not seem to know that they were hearing different languages in each. His parents were now spending five days on the Rhine and he had decided to depart on his own for those days and to tour some of the towns between Heidelberg and Freiburg.

And there in the cobble-stoned *Marktplatz* in Tübingen, he bumped into Esme.

'He said I bowled him over,' she laughed. 'Anyway, he was going back to the States about a month later and he spent most of that time with me. He took to Lily immediately, and she to him – well, that was not surprising. He was incredibly kind, and really loving with children. I had left Rose in the Netherlands for a couple of weeks, and Grayson took Lily and me on a *Kahn* on the Neckar. A *Kahn* is a punt, by the way. In all my years in Tübingen – and bear in mind we are talking six years – I had never been on the river. I had walked there with Jennifer in our first term, I'd watched it flow past the apartment where I lived with Günter, I'd pushed my babies in their pram along its banks, but I'd never been on it. It was like a taste of freedom. It was different from anything I had had before. I don't just mean punting on the river – I mean eating in expensive hotels, being driven out to the surrounding districts . . . it was wonderful. And Lily was happy. She adored him. We were so . . . I don't know . . . relaxed. Yes, relaxed. I'd finally finished my exams. There was the feeling of a new beginning.'

Grayson delayed meeting up with his parents after their cruise, and Esme left Rose an extra few days in the Netherlands. Grayson wooed her with flowers and dinners, and toys for Lily, who followed him around with adoration in her eyes. She sat on his knee and he would read to her endlessly. He was lovely to Christa upstairs and she in turn was charmed by him.

'Let me take you all out to dinner,' he said, hoisting Lily on to his shoulders, before fetching her teddy bear to accompany them. 'Frau Christa, you will need a jacket – we're eating outdoors and I don't want you getting a chill. Esme, leave the dishes. Life is too short for dishes. Let someone else do them.'

'They were the most fun-filled days I think I'd had since I was a child. Of course, I didn't realise that Grayson wasn't joking about the dishes. Anyway, he flew to Paris and said he would be back, and Lily and I took the train to collect Rose. Her grandfather started again about adopting her to make my life easier. I could hardly tell him I had just met someone else.' She smiled. 'I would not have left her anyway, but I think you know that.'

'I know that,' Jacob said. 'And so you married this Grayson?'

Suddenly with no warning, she reverted again to the third person. This she had not done in several days. And this time he clearly remembered the patient who had used this form of speech with him. It had been some ten years earlier – a woman who had spoken just like that, in the third person when she could not relate to what she had done or what had happened to her.

'Yes, she married him,' Esme said. 'This mother of two little girls, who had finally got her degree – she packed her bags and went to South Carolina with him at the end of the summer.'

Grayson Redmond was very possibly the nicest man in the United States, but his drawl was so slow that it was all Esme could do to keep her eyes open as he chewed the words, 'I do,' in their wedding ceremony as he might a Havana cigar.

She had closed her eyes as she waited for the vowels to be elongated out of all proportion and she had suddenly thought, my God, what have I done?

However, she had already said 'I do' and she found herself married and signing the register and thinking that at least there were a couple of compensations – Grayson Redmond made love as slowly and as deliberately as he spoke. He was also very good-looking – in fact quite an agreeable sight early in the morning. He was large and clean cut in an American way, with enormous shoulders and blond crew-cut hair, quite a number of years older than she, and for some reason that she never quite ascertained, he wore white open-neck shirts and jodhpurs, giving the impression he was always about to go for a ride.

Which, in fact, he was, as he pointed out in his Southern drawl. Only, not always on a horse. Esme had never been very good at understanding vulgarity, and it took her a while to comprehend his meaning. He had dressed in regular clothing in Germany and had kept this particular eccentricity hidden until he had lured her to South Carolina.

She had had a problem getting him to wear normal clothing for their wedding. Indeed, she had a problem convincing him that *she* wanted to wear normal clothing for the ceremony. He had thought it would be nice if she wore jodhpurs too. For a few moments she had thought that might be amusing, but then she thought of her father once saying to her to start things as she meant to finish them, and agreeing to wear jodhpurs for her wedding would have been acquiescing to something she did not want, and so she said that she had already chosen her outfit. She had worn an ivory summer dress, and Lily and Rose as her flower girls were both dressed in cream, Lily with a yellow-ribbonned belt, and Rose with a pink one.

* * *

There followed a period that in some ways made her ashamed. Eight years this period lasted. She had been briefly lulled into acquiescence by his lifestyle and his general approach to life. Jasmine was born that first year, and Esme had all the luxuries she had lacked before. Servants looked after everything. The only thing she had to do was bath and dress herself.

Laissez-faire and champagne, she realised, were a wonderful antidote to life as most people lived it. Combined, they had certainly blotted out a lot of things for Esme for a period of time.

Grayson had been like a drug – as long as she did not think about life, as long as she was prepared to play his games, drink his champagne, entertain his guests, and enjoy his sex. But once she found herself hiding from him, she was not able to stop hiding. She recalled one afternoon, secreted in one of the upstairs rooms between the curtains and the window, and, looking out to the distance through the glass, she could see the shagbark hickory trees on the upland slopes far out on the plantation, the same trees from which most of the furniture in the house had been made. She closed her eyes. Trees from windows . . . and she shuddered.

The girls took to South Carolina in different ways. Lily and Rose were very close, with Rose relying on her older sister and hanging on her every word. They went to school, Grayson driving them in the mornings and evenings when Esme was pregnant with Jasmine. Later Grayson still did the morning run, leaving Esme in bed with a cup of tea and a nanny tending to Jasmine until Esme felt like getting up. She felt indulged, luxuriating in circumstances that she had never even dreamed of. The plantation was a paradise for growing children, with its massive trees for climbing, fields for running in, horses for riding and servants to do the work.

*   *   *

They were indolent years. The only problems that arose were to do with the girls. Lily's affection for animals – an affection that had been apparent in Germany when she befriended cats and dogs – now took on a new direction.

At one point she collected alligator eggs from near the riverbank and put them in the linen cupboard. And it was little Jasmine who had opened the cupboard one morning to fetch some piece of clothing or maybe a towel and made the discovery. Some had hatched and were on the move. Jasmine closed the cupboard door, probably contemplated how to get the most attention, and then ran screeching down the corridor where pictures of the Charleston Redmonds gazed benignly or otherwise down on her.

'Nalligators, nalligators,' she had screamed, bursting into the master bedroom where Grayson and Esme were making love. Her scream suddenly silenced, she looked in amazement at her parents. 'What are you doing?' she asked, the discovery in the linen cupboard forgotten.

'I'm kissing Mom,' Grayson drawled. 'You're not supposed to come bursting in here like that, are you?' he said.

'I had to,' she replied, when she got her breath back. 'The nalligators are in the house.'

For a long time afterwards Esme worried that they had not all been found, and that maybe one or more had escaped and were living beneath the floorboards or hovering around a corner, waiting to pounce, despite Grayson's best if worried assurances to the contrary.

Lily had been admonished and eventually promised that she would bring home no more alligator eggs.

But there had been other animals, other wildlife – an owl that Lily had somehow enticed into the drawing room and which sat stony-faced on top of the curtain rail for two days and two nights as if in stunned amazement at its surroundings. This appearance of amazement evolved into an image of regal proprietorship. It flew away but then returned and this time stayed for two weeks. The girls sat on the sofa watching him and imitating his one-eyed observance of them – sometimes with his right eye open, sometimes his left.

Then there had been the tiger – Esme shuddered at the memory. For some reason it had been kept in a cage at the local petrol station, to Lily's consternation at the cruelty of keeping such an animal in such confined quarters in the brutal and oppressive heat. How Lily had released the animal without being mauled to death was a mystery, but release it she had, and the creature had disappeared in the swamp-lands to the south. Of course, Lily denied having had anything to do with Timothy, as the animal had been named, but Esme knew from the small satisfied smile on Lily's lips that Lily had somehow or other found a way to let the encaged animal loose.

'I'm glad it's free,' Rose said to Lily.

'Me too,' said little Jasmine, always inclined in her early years to imitate one or other of her half-sisters.

It was one of many happy moments shared between these three girls, in which all agreed that Timothy on the loose was preferable to Timothy in that tiny cage staring malevo-lently at them when Grayson went to fill the tank.

But then, a hunt had taken place, men with rifles, two helicopters, worried neighbours keeping their front porches closed and their windows locked. Lily had been distraught for days – but it came to nothing. Lily's distress clearly came from the fact that she felt guilty and that it would be down to her if the tiger were shot. Grayson tried consoling his elder stepdaughter by saying that Timothy would most defin-itely be better off dead than confined in that cage. But Lily, trying to hide the fact that she had released it and would be guilty of its death, combined with the horror of what her action had unleashed because everyone was so worried, was desolate all that week. However, the tiger had proved to have the same abilities at running and escaping as Esme subsequently portrayed. And later, Esme suspected that the tiger's absconding was a trigger in her own head for her ultimate run from the Redmond plantation.

It was a Thursday afternoon some eighteen months later, when Jasmine, a mere seven years old, was staying with her grandparents in town and attending a summer camp, and Lily was in Germany and Rose in the Netherlands, that the chatter in the drawing room suddenly proved too much for Esme.

They had invited fifty guests in for afternoon tea – a euphemism for champagne and canapés.

The conversation was about the temperature, which had risen to untold heights outside, the watering of the golf course, which many felt was inadequate, and the increasing number of alligators emerging from the rivers and lakes, two of which had been found near the eighteenth hole and, it later transpired, had actually filled the hole with their eggs . . .

Esme was glad Lily wasn't there – she might not have been able to resist a rescue operation.

All of a sudden Esme thought about the owl on the curtain rail and how it had finally flown out through one of the open windows, and Timothy, the tiger, roaming the swamplands to the south in freedom . . .

And at that moment, Grayson, bending down, whispered into her ear, 'When our guests are gone, I'm going to hunt you through the house, and I'm going to find you and carry you to bed. I'm going to tie you up and have my wicked way with you . . .'

Reality kicked in, and Esme stood there with cold rivulets

of perspiration trickling down her back despite the heat, and she knew that she could only stay there if she kept herself in a slightly alcoholic blur, and she could not bear the thought of the years ahead.

Having been once enticed by his charm and by all the material goods and the indulgent life that Grayson could offer her, she eventually ran from those very things. Grayson clearly could not be changed – he had been brought up to think of life in terms of one long spell of self-indulgence. And he had done nothing wrong. She knew that. He loved her and wanted to spoil her and make her happy. But standing there with a glass in her hand during one more party where the drink was flowing and the chitchat was more than she could bear, she looked out the open window and thought of the owl and the tiger.

Then, smiling politely at their guests, she had slipped out the door.

She left everything behind, taking just a handbag complete with passport, credit cards and cash.

Esme drove north through the night to Duck beyond Roanoke in North Carolina, where they had spent two consecutive summers. She walked on the beach in her white flowing dress and let the sound of the ocean wash away the noise inside her head. She knew she needed to plan, and that whatever she did she must take the girls into consideration. But she also knew there was no going back. She tried then to assess what had gone wrong, and why it had happened, but the only conclusion she could reach was that the problem was her – that she didn't fit, and that she never had. She had married Grayson for all the wrong reasons, although they had seemed right at the time. She had thought that maybe

it was love she felt for him, although the truth, she now saw
– and she hated herself for it – was that she had probably
just needed a holiday. Grayson had lifted her off her feet and
she had succumbed to his charm and his strength and his
need for her.

And she had wanted to be loved.

She spent the next night in the car, sleeping fitfully, with
the window open so that she could hear the waves, and the
following morning, tired but with a feeling of relief, she
bought a suitcase and some clothing. Driving further north,
a sense of direction and of destination becoming clearer with
every mile, she eventually abandoned the car at Richmond
airport in Virginia and flew from there to New York. A
further twenty-four hours passed before she felt sufficiently
in control to phone Grayson.

She felt a combination of guilt and nervousness as she
dialled the number. She could imagine him striding through
his mansion – she thought of it as his and not as hers even
though she had been living there for eight years – in his
jodhpurs with a white open-neck shirt, crisp and fresh
despite the ever-pervading heat. He would have called her:
'Esme, Esme, where are you, you wench?' A phrase that had
made her laugh in the early days, but later made her want
to run. And in fact she had run, from one room to the next,
finding places to hide while he hunted her. He had seen it
as a game, but she had not. She had stood behind long heavy
drapes, shielded from the room as she heard his footsteps
approaching and his voice booming, 'Wench, come to me.'
Motionless, holding her breath, she waited until she could
hear his footsteps fading into the distance.

She sometimes wondered, as she stood there with her
heart pounding, what exactly it was that she was feeling.
There was an element of terror that bore no relation to what
was actually happening. The feeling of panic made no sense.

After all, this was Grayson – charming, party-loving Grayson, with his open clean-cut face. Grayson who loved her, and had taken both her and her children on board with a lassitude and an equanimity that surprised even her. Grayson, who, if he caught up with her, would carry her Rhett Butler-style to their bedroom with its four-poster bed . . .

'I've left the car keys in the exhaust,' she said to him.

'And you're not coming back?'

'No. No, I'm not.'

'Esme, you've driven hundreds of miles – left the car two states away at an airport – abandoned it as far as I can make out. I'm to drive there and fetch it?'

'Oh, I thought you could get some lackey to do it,' she said, aware of the nastiness of her comment. She had been happy enough to let his servants run around after her and make her life so easy for the best part of eight years.

'You know, Esme,' Grayson said in his slow Southern Carolinian drawl, and she knew there was restrained anger beneath the surface, 'I think you should get yourself some professional help.'

'Help? Why?' She was playing for time, not sure if she wanted any more of this conversation.

'Because I gave you everything, and if that was not enough – then what will be? What will you do now?'

'I need to start working,' she said.

'You could have done that here,' he answered.

But she had not been able to. Their soporific lifestyle was not conducive to studying, teaching or writing, and that was what she wanted to do – and she had been swamped by his way of life. She wanted to tell him that but knew he would take it as an indictment on him, and she did not want to cast blame when she knew that he was right, the problem was her. It always had been, and she feared it always would be.

'I'm sorry,' she said suddenly, knowing how lame it sounded. 'This will be better for you. You should be with someone who appreciates more what you have to offer. You deserve better than me,' she added.

'Don't you think I can be the judge of my needs and wants?' Grayson said with slow pronunciation.

But he did not push her to return.

'I'm here if you need me,' he said. 'But we'll need to talk about the girls. Jasmine will be finishing camp at the end of the week, and I'll collect her from my parents and bring her home.'

Esme knew then that he had already realised that she was gone. He had been thinking and planning, and while she was glad that he was taking it as a *fait accompli*, she also felt an element of sadness, sadness that her absence was so easily accepted but mixed with relief that it could be that simple.

It did occur to her that there was a pattern forming, that three partners had come and gone in fourteen years, that she had run from him just as she had run from Günter, although under different circumstances, and for different reasons.

She had had no intention of abandoning the girls, though she knew that it might look like that on the surface. What she needed was a place of her own, a home she would create, and then her girls would be safe with her.

CHAPTER SEVEN

E sme had run and in doing so she made a thousand excuses, but inside her head she did not ever truly acknowledge the truth. She could not admit what she was hiding from or why. The monsters had followed her to South Carolina – they were there when the wind occasionally blew the leaves on the trees, when the stairs creaked at night, when Grayson hunted her and she hid and hid until there were no more hiding places. She had married Grayson thinking that maybe love would grow like it had with Arjen but it had not. The meaninglessness of life became intensified. Little things that she thought she had left behind caught up with her. Her girls meant everything to her, but she increasingly felt she was letting them down, and that one day they would stand like she did, staring out at the shagbark hickory trees and wondering what on earth they were doing.

Jasmine was content – she had everything she wanted. Lily appeared settled. Rose, however, was never really happy.

Rose did not grieve for Arjen. You cannot grieve for what you've never had, she once said to her mother. But it had not stopped her in school from crying for him. She had willed herself to do it to get out of trouble.

They were still living in South Carolina at the time. Seven years had passed. Years of events and action and learning to live in the brutal humidity.

Grayson's parents had reacted in different ways to the arrival of Esme in their lives – Esme and her two little girls.

'Well, well, well,' Grayson's father had said before telling Lily and Rose to call him Grandpa. 'I'll teach you how to work the stock market,' he added to the two little upturned faces.

'But a divorcée,' Grayson's mother whispered to Grayson. 'I wonder how she'll go down at the Club.'

'They will love her at the Club,' Grayson said, gazing across the room at his wife with a mixture of lust and delight. He had never met anyone like her. He was charmed by the blue-stocking image she portrayed, the seriousness of her conver-sation, and her love of her little girls. He loved how she cried out in her sleep and he could wrap her in his arms and nuzzle her neck until she slept calmly. 'Yes, they will love her at the Club.'

Everything circulated around the Club. The Redmonds' social life was what counted. At the Club, Esme was greeted with a mixture of enthusiasm, curiosity and jealousy. She sat on a sun lounger with her girls beside her. She was imme-diately approached and introduced and a piña colada appeared on the little table beside her. Lily was enticed into the pool with the other children. Rose stayed close to her mother, watching events with her large dark eyes. Esme smiled at everyone and let the action unfold as she tried to work out who was who and what was going on.

'You simply must come shopping with me.'

'You play tennis? Let's make up a team.'

'How did you manage to snap up Grayson?'

'Your little girls don't look at all alike.'

Initially she laughed. It was so trivial. All she had to do was smile and be agreeable, play tennis, bathe, go shopping, lunch, dine, drink . . .

She was busier after Jasmine was born as she insisted on bringing Jasmine with her and looking after her herself, despite her mother-in-law and Grayson's encouragement to leave her in the care of the nanny, who was so carefully procured after a series of advertisements in the local paper. And as Jasmine grew from babyhood she too, like Lily, was immediately integrated into the Club activities.

As the girls got older, Lily's energies were invested in whatever wildlife she could encounter. It was Rose who questioned more openly what was going on.

Rose did not mingle easily, and she hated going to the Club. After Grayson put in a forty-foot swimming pool behind the veranda at the back of the house, Rose had no more interest in going to the Club.

'But you have to come to the Club,' Grandma said. 'It's where you meet the right kind of people.'

'Who does she think she is?' Rose said to Esme.

'She's Grayson's mother,' Esme replied. 'And Grayson and his parents are very good to you. Let it go.'

'But that's snobbery or racism,' Rose had objected.

'I know, darling,' Esme had responded.

'Well, if you don't say it's snobbery or racism, even if it is your own grandmother – or in this case Jasmine's –' Rose continued, 'then the other person gets away with it. With being a snob or a racist, I mean.'

'I know,' Esme sighed. 'It's just that I think that with Grandma it might be easier not to argue with her because I don't think you will get anywhere.'

Rose restrained herself that time, but she wasn't always able to. She just did not fit in like Lily did.

In school, Mr Tyler had hauled her in front of the class because she had not done her math homework. Math, he called it. She hated that. It was maths or mathematics, not math. And he imitated her accent sometimes and she hated him for that too. Her English was perfect but there was the intonation of her early years in Germany in her speech.

'Rose van the man,' he said, thinking he was witty. Most of the class thought he was and they sniggered.

Rose looked at him with as much hatred as she could bring into her face. She hated him. Hated his ridiculous swagger and his stupid comments, hated the way he tried to get the boys in the class to laugh at the girls and to make them appear stupid.

She tried arguing with him and he tapped his chest and said, 'I teacher.' Then, pointing at her, 'You pupil.'

'You asshole,' she muttered under her breath, reducing the boy beside her to tears of hysteria way beyond any wit that might have been contained in her observation.

'What did you say?' Mr Tyler shouted.

She looked at him, looked at the class, looked out the window, and then she thought, what the hell?

'I said, you asshole,' she repeated clearly.

The class stopped sniggering and in the momentary silence before Mr Taylor went berserk, Rose told herself that whatever happened next was worth it just for the look on his face.

Before she knew it she was in the principal's office and it was there she decided to turn on the taps and she started to cry.

'My dad died,' she said to the principal.

Esme was called for. Mr Tyler went back to his class mumbling that he didn't know her father had kicked the bucket and Rose held her breath wondering for how long she would get away with this and the implication that her father had just died.

Not long, as it turned out. Esme and the principal had a talk in private and then Esme took Rose home.

'You weren't brought up to speak to someone like that,' Esme said to her.

'He's horrible,' Rose tried. 'He's always picking on me. He imitates my accent. He calls me stupid things and they all laugh . . .'

'Sticks and stones,' Esme said softly. It was an expression her mother had used. She knew it sounded dismissive, but the truth was she was beginning to worry about Rose. She could not bear any of her children to be unhappy.

'They hurt,' Rose cried. 'Sticks and stones hurt. AND names hurt. I hate them all.'

'It's all right,' Esme said. 'I know that names hurt. You have to be cleverer. You must not let them see when they get to you, because some people are so mean that when they find the chink in your armour, they will stick the knife in and turn it. That's human nature.'

'Well, it's not in my human nature,' Rose said.

'I know it's not.'

'Kids do things like that,' Grayson said.

'Mr Tyler does it. He's not a kid.'

'Some adults don't ever really grow up,' Esme said. 'The nastiness of childhood stays with them.'

'I hate Mr Tyler,' Rose said.

'Sounds pretty mutual to me,' Grayson contributed.

Rose was suspended for two days. She spent those days up the live oak tree with its Spanish moss hanging like cobwebbed haw beside the drawing-room window where she could hear every word that was uttered inside.

'You know, Esme,' Grayson said, his words coming through the window, 'you are very hard on yourself.'

Rose knew her mother was lying on the sofa staring at the ceiling as she so often did.

'It's not your fault that Rose said that to that dumb teacher,' he continued.

'That's not what's bothering me,' Esme said in a tired voice. 'It's the fact that Rose was crying because of her father.'

'But that's not your fault either. Anyway, I don't think it was grief that made her cry. I think things just got too much for her.'

'She's not happy in school,' Esme said. 'And if you're not happy in school when you're a child, life can look very bleak. Because when you're a child, childhood is all you have.'

'She's doing okay. Her grades are fine. She seems happy enough.'

'Does she? I don't think so. Her best friend is Lily. Her sister. She doesn't have any friends other than Lily . . .'

'What's wrong with that? She and Lily are very close. With just thirteen or fourteen months between them, it's not that surprising.'

Esme didn't reply. Rose knew that Esme was thinking and she wondered what was going through her mother's mind. It was interesting listening in, although she preferred it when they were talking about something else.

'She'll be fine,' Grayson said. 'She's not that difficult. I look at some of the people at the Club and I think we're doing fine with our three girls.'

Rose, outside the window, up the live oak, thought about that. It was nice to see herself as one of the three girls, three sisters. That made them close. Even though their fathers were all different. Grayson was nice that way. He liked pleasing them all. Whereas Günter didn't really even know their names. Lily had told her that.

'Now come here, my darling wench,' Grayson said, the texture of his voice changing. He had expressions that Esme feared had been amassed from trashy novels – the kind his mother read.

'Not now, please,' Esme said. 'I need to think.'

'You think too much, my girl,' Grayson said.

'I don't think you think enough,' Esme replied. It was not said sharply, but more with sadness.

It was true. Grayson didn't think enough. In fact, Esme once heard Rose saying that he didn't think at all.

'It was the summer she was thirteen when Rose was suspended from school,' Esme said to Jacob. 'Shortly afterwards Lily and Rose flew to Europe for a few weeks, and I found my sleep had gone again. I had been able to sleep at first with Grayson. But it was gone now. And I couldn't get it back. I spent most of the night either lying awake in bed, or staring out the window. I couldn't find any peace. I hated the fact that Rose was so unhappy. I felt I had let Arjen down. And I needed more.'

It was then that Esme left the plantation never to return. She knew that she was using Rose as an excuse. But she also knew that the whole picture was wrong. She wanted to explain this to Jacob, but she could not find the right way of saying it. She sat looking at him and thinking that whatever she said it would sound like an excuse and she did not want to excuse any of her actions. And Jacob, looking at her, thought of the dozens and dozens of patients he had seen over the years, both men and women, who had been trapped by circumstance and who simply did not know what to do and often could not see that the only way out was to open the door and walk. And yet Esme had seen that and had done it. Others stayed in their ill-fitting relationships both because they lacked the impetus to do something about them, but also because of the fallout. Who was he to say that Esme was wrong? He could not but admire her stoicism, her perpetual hopefulness as she moved through the years of her children's youth.

'I'm not a great mother,' Esme said suddenly. 'I know that. I admit that I used Rose as an excuse to explain my leaving the plantation. I left Jasmine behind that time when I ran. Not a great mother at all.' Her voice was full of sadness.

'Did Grayson let you keep the girls? Jasmine in particular, I mean.'

'Yes, he did. I half thought there would be a problem there, but Grayson wasn't like that. He was so easy-going, and he believed that the girls should be together. He made some stipulations, though, partly to do with his access to Jasmine, but more to do with where I lived. He insisted on giving me money so that I could buy a really nice place in London – that's where I went after I left New York. He flew over with Jasmine and they stayed in some luxurious hotel, and he worked his way through areas and estate agents and helped me find an apartment that was fitting for his daughter, but that was also safe. He knew I needed to feel safe and it was important to him to make things as right as possible. I could never have afforded the place I ended up getting. But Grayson was like that. He wanted things right for me and the girls.'

'I have to say, I think he sounds like a very decent human being,' Jacob said.

Esme agreed eagerly. 'He was – he is. That's the whole point. He was – he still is – a good person. But I wasn't the right person for him. Had I stayed there, one of two things would have happened – I would either have become like his mother, with my whole life circulating around the Club, and gossiping as a pastime, and being too interested in the minutiae of other people's lives. Or I would have lain on the sofa staring at the ceiling, being miserable and making other people miserable in the process. I wasn't happy, Jacob.'

'You mentioned something about Grayson wanting access to Jasmine.'

'Yes. He wanted her to fly to him at the end of every school term, unless she didn't want to. And the other two were to go with her if they wanted to.'

'Did you mind that?'

'Mind her going to stay with him? No, not at all. It was right for her and, quite honestly, it was also easier for me. I got part-time work in a university, initially just giving tutorials while I worked on my doctorate. The girls were in school. Obviously I was bringing Jasmine to and from school each day so the hours I worked had to slot into that, and I worked at night. There is a full seven years between Lily and Jasmine, so by the time Jasmine reached secondary school, the older two had finished, and moved to university. Jasmine is a boarder now – her wish, I might add. It wouldn't be mine. I liked having her at home and I miss her. But because of boarding school I decided I could take this year off. She says she might join me for the Christmas break, but I don't know if she will. She's in South Carolina right now – I had not wanted her to go there this summer. I wanted her to stay in London and to get some kind of a job.'

'But then you would have been unable to take your year off?'

'I would have postponed it until September. The girls are more important than my year off. We had a bit of an argument about it,' Esme admitted.

Jasmine, now on her summer holidays from boarding school, was spending what she called 'quality time' with her father in South Carolina. Jasmine's name had been taken from Jessamine – a South Carolinian flower. The blossom was like the yellowiest of daffodils but on a vine, and its delicate prettiness always cheered Esme. Jasmine was close enough as a name and as the description that her mother wanted for her.

Jasmine, now aged fifteen, going on sixteen, was going

through a 'phase', as Grayson called it. This 'phase' included arguing with everyone and thinking only about herself. She gave the impression that nothing much was going on in her mind whereas, in fact, she lived with an endless disorganised stream of consciousness. Like her sisters she was tall with straight hair, but hers was light brown. She had her father's broad forehead and his handsome good looks. Her smile made her appear prettier than she actually was, but of late she appeared morose and sulky, and exceptionally argumentative. She was the apple of her father's eye and enjoyed being indulged by him.

When she announced during a weekend home from boarding school with Esme that she was going to South Carolina again for the summer, Esme had tried for the first time to dissuade her, using the excuse that in July and August it was no place for a human being.

'I don't see why not,' Jasmine had said. 'We lived there as children. I've gone every other summer. And, anyway, slaves worked there in the heat and survived, and it's not as if I'll be working. And, anyway, there is air conditioning.'

'First of all,' Esme said carefully, 'back then when there were slaves, they were not considered human beings. And secondly, I thought we had agreed you were going to get a summer job. You need to be occupied.'

'I am going to get a job. But not this year. I'm going to spend the time with Dad.'

Esme hoped that once Jasmine got through this summer, she might grow up a bit and make some kind of plans or at least show some interest in what she wanted to do with the rest of her life. At the moment Jasmine's main interests evolved around quality nail polish, boys, wanting highlights in her hair and worrying about her skin and imaginary spots on her forehead. Both Lily and Rose had gone through similar phases but not to the same extent. Esme felt Grayson was at fault in this, as he was far too liberal, both with money and his only daughter. But while blaming Grayson, Esme also blamed herself. After all, she was the one who had married Grayson.

'I realise,' she said now to Jacob, 'I shouldn't have married him.' She sighed heavily. 'I'm not the best at relationships, you know.'

He nodded. He was quite aware of that by now.

Furthermore he wondered what was happening between Esme and François. He wanted to ask but couldn't intrude. While he now felt comfortable with her, asking her about the past, he was less sure of his ground with regard to the present.

At that moment, as though reading his thoughts, Esme said, somewhat tentatively, 'Look, may I ask you something? I know you have known François for a very long time, but I get the impression that you are not really close friends. That is right, isn't it?'

'Yes,' he said, wondering what was coming.

She paused now, looked away and then back at him. She raised a hand slightly and then dropped it back into her lap.

'Ask me,' he said. 'If I don't know the answer I will tell you. But you're right, we're not close friends. We were in school, less so in university, and nowadays I meet him at the occasional school reunion and that's it. Or indeed, if I bump into him in a restaurant!'

'I was wondering if you by any chance knew if he is involved with someone else. I'm asking because he's been very remote since I arrived. Absent might be a better way to describe him,' she said ruefully.

'Have you been to his home?' Jacob asked carefully.

'No.'

'Why not?' he asked now, knowing the answer only too

well. There was no way François could have taken Esme to his home. She would have known immediately there was a wife, even if François had brought her there at a time his wife was away.

'Well, it never really arose to date. Over the last eight or nine months there was never time. He lives a bit outside Paris, and it was easier to stay in a hotel on my flying visits in – and mostly we met in other cities.'

'And when you decided to move here for this year,' Jacob said slowly, 'you didn't suggest you moved in with him?'

'Well, no – I didn't. I want my own space. I didn't want to be in his place where I would feel like an intruder, there for a limited length of time. I wanted the freedom of being by myself. He then would have no one crowding his space either.'

There was nothing for it but to tell her the truth. He didn't really want to because he feared what it might unleash. He was not sure what he meant by that, but as she already said, she was not very good at relationships. In fact, she had had more misfortune in her relationships than anyone he had ever met.

'So, do you mean, other than his wife?' he asked. He could not think of any better way of putting it.

She put her hand to her neck. 'He's not married,' she said, the words sticking in her throat.

He looked at her.

'Is he?' she continued weakly.

'Why did you think he wasn't?' Jacob asked gently.

'I had asked him – it came up when I first met him. He said marriage was not for him . . .'

Clever François, Jacob thought. It was true in one sense, although he had lied by implication. She seemed really shocked. It was clear that she had ruled out that possibility.

'I'm sorry,' Jacob said.

'I didn't love him,' Esme said quickly. 'It's just . . . well, my judgement isn't great, is it?'

'My dear Esme.' He stayed sitting with her, getting them another coffee, waiting while she digested what she had just learned.

'Esme,' Jacob said when their coffees were on the table before them, 'I may not be able to see you over the weekend. I'm preparing for a conference. However, I'm giving you my card. Phone me if you need to. Any time over the weekend. And I mean that. And Monday morning, I'll be here . . .'

Esme nodded. 'I'll be all right,' she said, taking the card. 'Thank you for this. I really got things wrong this time, but better to find out now.'

'Are you going home to work? May I walk you to the corner?'

They finished their coffee and, getting up, Jacob took her by the elbow as they walked down the street.

'Call me,' he said.

Back in the apartment, Esme worked through the day. The notes she was making for the novel were beginning to come together. Occasionally thoughts of François came into her mind.

She felt a combination of anger and disgust towards him, mixed with annoyance directed at herself. Now that she knew the truth, everything fell into place and she could not believe that she had not seen it before. It was obvious. It had been from the beginning. Meetings in other cities, never being introduced to his friends or family – it would have been obvious to anyone, and she had problems understanding why it had not been obvious to her. She could only suppose it was because she had not wanted to see it.

It had suited her.

He had suited her.

She had no intention of fighting to hold on to him. She was not going to be some man's bit on the side. She wondered how long he was going to string her along, not telling her. If she felt anger towards him it was to do with the fact that he had lied initially by implying he was unattached. As a matter of principle she never got involved with married men – but, as she had found out the hard way, men were adept at lying.

'It's part of their appeal,' her friend Jennifer had once said to her. But Esme was not so sure. And yet she knew that honesty was not all that appealing either. But when she said that to Jennifer, Jennifer had shrugged. Like everyone else, Jennifer had her own agenda, and it had taken Esme a long time to see what that agenda was. But that was in Germany, and that was long ago. And Jennifer had got what she had wanted.

François phoned to confirm he was coming round to dinner.

'Let's go out,' Esme said evenly. 'I haven't had time to do any shopping. It would be nice to meet in a restaurant.' She had no intention of cooking a meal for him ever again, or for anyone else for that matter.

They arranged the time and the place.

At seven thirty she showered and washed her hair. She dressed in a neat low-cut black top with her tight cream skirt. She wound her hair up and set it with a clip. She spent time on her nails, cleaning them carefully and polishing them with plum-coloured lacquer. And she was in the restaurant at nine o'clock. He had already arrived and was being shown to their table, the waiter taking his small overnight bag for him.

For the first time since she had come to Paris, François was completely attentive. He asked her in detail about her week. She spoke about her work, and small routines she had

set up. She could see the irony in the fact that this night he
wanted to spend with her while now she had no more
interest. She was both polite and reserved, but she knew that
he did not see anything unusual in this. It was how their
relationship had worked.

They took a taxi back to her apartment.

'I think,' she said, taking the keys from her bag, 'that it
might be a good time to clarify something for me.'

'Yes, of course?'

'A straight answer, François?'

'Of course.'

'Are you married?'

The answer was written all over his face.

'You never asked before,' he justified himself, as she looked
at him coldly under the streetlight.

'I wouldn't let the taxi go,' she said politely, a moment too
late, as the cab pulled back out on to the street.

He hesitated. 'This need not come between us,' he said.
'You and I, I mean, we're special.'

'So special, that you lied about your marital status until
I was too involved to walk lightly away?' Even as she said
that she knew it wasn't true. She was not too involved. It
was inconvenient – but not really anything more than that.
She had decided after Grayson not to get involved with
anyone again – not really involved. It was not fair on the
other person. She was glad now that she had no real feelings for him. But there was an element of sadness. There
was a feeling of being wounded, but it was the type of wound
that would heal.

'Well, you have the apartment here for the year,' he said.
'And we do get on well, you know. And I do love you.'

'You loved me so much that you lied to me?' she asked.
There was no irony in her voice, but it was there in the
words. 'Come on, François. Tell me now how your wife

doesn't understand you, how I am the only one, that you would have left her but for the children . . . I think these are the things that men say under such circumstances.'

'May I not come up with you and explain?' he asked.

She looked at him carefully. 'François,' she said, 'I am many things that I don't like, but I would never ever have got involved with you had I known you had a wife. Please excuse me.'

'Just like that?' he asked. 'Just like that?' His voice was angry. But the fob on her key ring had released the catch on the glass doors of her apartment block, and she was through and had them closed before he realised what she was doing.

She walked quickly across the tiled floor to the stairs. She did not turn back.

She poured her nightly cognac and sat in front of the window. She knew she should be feeling something but she did not know what it was. She wondered what other people would feel in these circumstances. Anger? Hurt? Betrayal? She had no idea. She remembered reading in a magazine something about someone gorging on ice cream as an antidote to the end of a relationship. Weeping into the tub with a tragic film playing in the background on the television. It had made no sense to her.

She felt nothing. Not even a sense of loss. More the awareness of inconvenience. She knew this lack of feelings was not natural, but it was natural to her. She had no idea what the norm was, as she could not relate to it.

What she needed was to make a plan. A new one.

CHAPTER EIGHT

There was a crack on the ceiling. She tried to see through it. She reached her hand up but there was something holding her down. She smelled sweat and felt the rough rasp of wool against her face. She knew she was going to suffocate. She heard a long scream echoing round and round the room and she woke to find herself lying on the bed in her Parisian apartment. She was shaking as she pulled the quilt around her and lay there huddled into it.

She was at Charles de Gaulle airport by midday, her laptop in her shoulder bag, her suitcase beside her. During the night, sometime after the nightmare, she had decided to go to Nice, and early in the morning she booked a one-way flight.

Closing the door on François Artois, she knew she was doing the right thing but she was feeling regret over leaving Jacob. Any moment of uncertainty that she felt while cancelling the contract with the apartment's agency, losing her deposit and packing her bags and leaving Paris, was to do with him. She wasn't really sure what she was doing; she only knew that she could not stay there.

*   *   *

On another level, she knew, however, that in some way she had been making inroads – inroads into something as yet unclear. It was to do with her conversations with Jacob. And they had talked – talked and talked. She told him things she had not told anyone else, with an honesty that she feared exposed her as being cold and possibly selfish. This extraordinary relationship that had evolved between her and Jacob was totally unlike what was going on with François. It had a meaning she did not really understand. She only knew that she was talking to him in a way she had not spoken to anyone else – at least not since she had become an adult.

At one point she wondered if he was treating her as a patient or as an acquaintance, but as the relationship with François went on standstill due to his continuing absence, and her isolation in Paris intensified, she became more and more honest with Jacob. She remembered one morning saying to him that she feared boring him with her stories from the past. But he laughed and said, 'You have not tied me to this chair, you know. I choose to be here.'

She shivered when he said this. The idea of entrapping anyone and forcing them to do anything against their will was anathema to her. It was not what he had meant. He was only using a figure of speech. And she knew it. He chose to be there, just as she did. Why he would want to listen to her story had bothered her at first; later she simply didn't care. She needed desperately to offload it, and in a sense offloading it on to a stranger was easy – with that came no responsibility. But at the same time she knew it was more than that: there was some connection between them, some *frisson* that combined affection and possibly desire.

She also knew that in his own subtle and unobtrusive way, Jacob was forcing her to look back as though he knew there was something else she should start to tap. But it was time

to leave, time to move on, another city or town, another
start, a fresh base for this year off.

Having checked in her luggage, she took Jacob's card from
her purse and tentatively rang his mobile.

'Are you all right?' Jacob asked her when he heard her voice.

'Yes,' she replied. This was not completely true, but she
knew that it would be shortly. Because that was what
happened.

She would drift from the last relationship to the next,
covering herself, protecting herself, moving ever swiftly
onwards – so swiftly, in fact, that nothing and nobody could
catch her. She explained that she had packed and left Paris.

'You know,' Jacob said to her on the phone through the
background din in the airport and the synthetic voice
coming over the loudspeaker announcing the next flight,
'you know, if you need to call me, you may do so. Any
day. You know where I am early in the morning, and during
the working day, well, the best time is between five to the
hour and five after. I'm always free then.'

She feared that he thought she was leaving because of
their conversations and how much of herself she was
revealing to him. But she hoped he knew that she just needed
to move on, that the possibility of accessing the distant past
was of lesser importance than running from the immediate
past. Or so she saw it. She did not really see another link.
Her ability to compartmentalise things meant that she saw
them all as individual people, individual events, sections of
her life tied up in individual boxes, each one sealed and put
away, as she moved forwards.

She did not want to leave Paris, but knew that she must.
She knew that if she stayed, there would be long lonely nights
getting used to the emptiness in her apartment, and the
silence from the telephone, waiting to meet another man

who might, just might, give her what she needed. Although she knew that she had no idea what she needed. Love? Unconditional love? Was there such a thing? And would it satisfy?

Jacob would miss her. He was sure of that. But he knew that she had run for a reason. It was not just François Artois. It was more than that.

He put the mobile phone down on his desk, having saved the number on it. He was at home in his study, preparing for the conference. But he wasn't thinking of that now. He was thinking about Esme.

She was getting closer in her story to the present and the only place to access then was the past. He was sure now that her secret lay in the past. He thought of her and how he had seen her that first morning, and the spider she had so carefully lifted in her hands and looked at as if it were the most precious thing in the world. He wondered if she would phone again.

He had to get on. He pushed thoughts of her aside and started his plans for the forthcoming conference and what he needed to do. An opening address – simple enough. And then his lecture, which he thought Monique had said was in the evening. It was to do with memory, and that caused him some amusement as he clearly couldn't remember exactly when it was.

Naomi put her head around the door. 'Was that a patient?' she asked with curiosity.

He nodded. It wasn't quite true, but it was the easiest way to handle it.

'You don't ever give your phone number to patients,' she pointed out. There was no accusation in her voice, but her eyebrows were raised.

'It seemed the right thing to do,' he said.

'I'm going out.'

'Did I hear your mobile ringing too?' Jacob asked, as it filtered into his mind that he had heard something while he was talking to Esme.

'Yes,' she hesitated. 'One of my friends. We're going shopping. I need to get something new for next week.'

He could feel himself tuning out. Shopping, clothes, friends. Some he knew, some he didn't. Names – just names. They had one thing in common, though – they all liked to shop.

'Are you all right, Naomi?' he asked suddenly.

'Of course I am,' she said. 'I'll be home in the afternoon. I've something nice in for dinner.'

'I'll open a special bottle of wine,' he said. 'Enjoy yourself.'

It was all so polite, he thought as he heard the front door closing. Too polite. He didn't know why.

Was this his fault, he wondered. They really needed to talk, as he didn't know what was going on. He knew he was more preoccupied than usual, and that part of that was to do with Esme. But Esme was gone now. It would be breakfast alone in the café with his newspaper for company. He shrugged. When the conference was over he had a week off. There would be time then with Naomi to talk properly and to reconnect.

From the moment Esme had said *au revoir* to Jacob on the phone in Paris, nothing had gone according to her new plan. Her flight was delayed by two hours, so she used that time to book, by telephone, a month at an exclusive resort outside Nice. She emailed both Lily and Rose, saying she had changed her plans and was now on her way to the South of France. From their points of view it made no difference, but she wanted them to know where she was. They could still contact her exactly as before – either by email or by phone.

She telephoned the plantation in South Carolina. Esme had heard nothing from Jasmine in two weeks. She had phoned her several times. The first time she was told that Jasmine and Mr Redmond were in Arizona. The second time she had been told that Jasmine was out with Mr Redmond. The third time there was no answer, and although she had left a message and emailed Jasmine some five times, she had heard nothing more. This was not unduly surprising as Jasmine's main interest was herself. And Grayson, although very easy-going by nature, never replied to phone messages unless he had a particularly good reason to do so.

She would phone again later in the week, she decided. She was not worried, as she knew that she would have heard quickly enough if something had happened. She was quite sure that Jasmine would be out horse riding with Grayson early in the mornings, playing golf early in the evenings, and partying the rest of the time.

That was Grayson's existence. And she feared it was fast becoming Jasmine's. There was nothing to worry about and nothing more she could do on that front. She bought a salad and coffee for lunch as the plane was delayed a further hour. In the departure lounge she settled down with *Macbeth* and her pen and notepad and waited for her flight. She was conscious of the comings and goings of fellow travellers as they too waited for their flights. There was nothing amiss, she told herself. She could handle this. All she had done was to change her venue. She would be more comfortable in the South of France.

The resort boasted one of the nicest swimming pools she had ever seen. She had been there the previous summer with Lily. It had been one of those odd weeks, booked at the last minute when Lily had a little free time before heading for Sri Lanka and the elephant sanctuary. Rose, of course, had already left for the Netherlands and Jasmine for South Carolina.

It had been a lovely week. A combination of sunshine, swimming and nice food in a really excellent resort – and special time spent with Lily. In fact, the first time ever Esme had really spent with her alone.

She had suggested it tentatively, unsure if Lily would want to go. To her surprise Lily's face had lit up and she had quickly agreed. For some reason Esme had thought that holidays with either of the older girls were a thing of the past – they certainly showed very little interest in her as a person, just as a mother. She expected no more than that, and she had been delighted at Lily's reaction.

She remembered it now as an extraordinary time – like an island in her life. The two of them, not really as mother and daughter, but more as two people getting to know each other. She would have liked to have suggested doing the same this summer with Rose, but Rose had gone straight from term-time on a week's 'R and R', as she called it, with her rather odd boyfriend, and then began work at the hospital.

She hoped that maybe next year, just maybe, Rose might be interested.

Now, she would spend the day reading and making notes for her novel while lying in the sun. She would write for an hour or so before dining in the evening, and then write again until she went to sleep. It was going to be all right, she reassured herself. She just needed to regain her equanimity. She had done the right thing by leaving. If she asked herself why she had gone to Paris in the first place, all she could answer was that it seemed the right thing to do at the time. Her mistake had been in trusting François. But if you did not live by trust – trust of some sort, at least – what was left? Anyway, come September, Rose would be going back to university. The London apartment would be empty. She could always return there then and just write. She would make her mind up later. For the moment it was going to be a day at a time, she decided.

At last the flight was called and she settled on the plane, dozing, which is what she always did while flying.

The novel was coming together in her head. In it, the main character was the director of a company. His name was Macbeth. This eccentric egotist had a partner whose ambitions for him were even greater than his own. Ruthlessly they pursued his power, dismissing or even murdering those who stood in his way.

Greed and power, Esme thought in her semi-doze. She contemplated what a revolting combination these two characteristics were. There would be nothing autobiographical in her story. She was looking at a topic solely as an observer. She knew that what she should really do was to sit down and finish rereading *Macbeth* because she needed to settle on the structure for the second half of the book, but she also knew that she needed the distraction of actually writing. But she had not fully decided whether Macbeth's partner would remain strong or whether she would crumble as their crimes intensified. She would start writing that very evening, she decided. Just the first chapter. It would get her going, help her to visualise the background . . .

The plane landed and to her frustration Esme discovered her bag was not on board. She stayed at the carousel for some fifteen minutes after all the other luggage had been collected. Her laptop was weighing down her shoulder and she was feeling quite disorientated. There was that vague unease that maybe someone else had taken her bag but she told herself not to think like that. It was a useless exercise, and if it had happened, then there was nothing she could do about it. There was one other man at the other side of the luggage belt and that was reassuring. It looked like his luggage had not arrived either. In due course, she made her way to the Information desk to report her missing bag.

She was given a form to fill in and reassured that her bag would follow her as soon as it arrived.

The man she had seen waiting in the baggage collection area was there beside her. He nodded to her in recognition, and then glanced at the form she had almost completed.

'I'm staying there too,' he said with a smile. 'When we've finished with this, do you want to share a taxi?'

He introduced himself. His name was Peter Carew, an Australian lawyer who had briefly abandoned practising to re-enter the world of legal academia some years earlier, a period in his life, he explained, which coincided with the breakdown of his marriage. He was now back with a chambers in Sydney. He was holidaying in Europe for the winter, he said.

'Our winter, I mean – Australian winter. I like the sun and the sea, and it was one of the advantages of college life that I got long vacations. I used to travel a lot during that time – and I caught the travel bug.'

'That's nice,' Esme said politely.

'I saw on your form that your name is Esme?' he half asked, half declared.

'Yes,' she replied. 'Esme Waters.'

He mused over the name. 'Esme Waters,' he repeated.

For a moment she felt uneasy. Was he repeating her name as though he recognised it?

She sometimes wondered if Esme Waters had been the right name to choose. Although Esme was the name on both her birth certificate and passport, she had not been called that as a child. And it wasn't until she went to Germany with Jennifer that she had decided to use it.

In marrying Günter, she had changed her name to his. And when they divorced, and she was about to marry Arjen, she assumed she would change her name to Van der Vloed. But Arjen's death put paid to that. So she chose the name Waters and changed to it by deed poll. This name she felt represented the journey of life, where people were carried along on a flow of thought and event until most became inured to reality and lived in a cocoon. It was also just a short version of the translation of Wassermann, the name of Lily's father. Lily, her firstborn, born in hope and what she had thought was love. When she married Grayson, she did not change her name to Redmond.

She was momentarily uncertain if this Peter Carew had recognised her, but then she reassured herself it was most unlikely. There was no reason why he should have, as his legal world and her world of philosophical analysis did not overlap.

Arriving at the resort, he insisted on paying for the taxi.

'That seems a bit unfair,' she said.

'Not at all. Pay me back by having a drink with me this evening – well, it's almost evening now,' he added, looking at his watch. 'We'll check ourselves in. Say a prayer that our bags turn up, and we can head to the bar.'

It didn't seem like the worst plan. Esme had no change of clothing until her case turned up – she could not even go for a swim until she bought a costume, which she was going to have to do anyway as there was no swimwear in the items she had brought with her either to or from Paris.

There was some delay with Peter Carew's registration at the reception desk.

'You go ahead,' he said to her. 'Meet you in the bar in, say, an hour?'

'Right, well thank you again,' she said. 'I'll be there in an hour. In the same clothes probably, though.'

'Easier to recognise you,' he laughed.

She laughed too. He was cheery and jolly and there were no expectations. It would be nice to have company over a drink, and as long as she had understood him correctly, there was no one else he knew here in Nice, so she might well end up having company over dinner.

She made her way to the shopping area in the complex and bought a swimsuit and a bikini, a silver clip for her hair because she liked the look of it, and a long thin white shirt that she could use over her swimwear going to and from the pool.

They met for a drink. It was all so simple. They talked generalities, exchanged details about their respective children, their travels . . . life in general. A glass of wine led to another, and that led to his suggestion of their dining together. It transpired he'd already booked a table, in the restaurant extension, out on the terrace – a candlelit table with dancing coloured lights around the wooden fencing that separated them from a garden.

She smiled in delight.

'This is the very table my daughter Lily and I ate at last summer.' She remembered clearly Lily sitting opposite her and the two of them talking with a new friendship.

'This is the eldest daughter?' Peter asked her, as the waiter handed them each a menu.

'Yes, the one in Canada, tracking geese. She's going to be out of touch for a little, I think – they're in a very remote area and I think they'll be very busy for the next week or so.'

'Do you miss her?'

Esme did. She missed them all in different ways.

As she looked at the menu, she had the strangest feeling of *déjà vu*, or perhaps something more solid than that. It was to do with the repetitive nature of things. Here she was at a table having a meal with a man she hardly knew, learning a little about him, giving away a little about herself – eking out the titbits and the facts about their lives, passing time.

And with that idea came a feeling that horrified her – it was to do with life and how it was just the passing of time. It was something she already knew – knew only too well, in fact – but she did not want to think it now, nor to see so clearly the bleakness of her own perception of reality. It seemed to come down to this moment – sitting at a table with someone, some man, some woman, even her beloved daughter Lily, choosing, eating, drinking, over and over, passing time. She tried to stop her thoughts. She knew that the time with Lily here had not been like that, but in this instant it was as if the things she did to survive came down to this. She tried not to remember what it was like when her mouth was so dry that she could no longer swallow . . . the monsters were there, so close she could hardly breathe. She tried reaching for a glass of water but her hand would not move.

'Have you decided?' Peter was asking her as he closed his menu with the air of a man who clearly had decided what he was going to have.

She nodded vaguely. She couldn't speak – food? What did it matter what she ate? She could only eat it until she was full; its taste only lasted as long as it was in the mouth.

'You choose for me,' she said. It was unlike her to say such a thing, but she suddenly felt that any form of decision whatsoever was beyond her.

And she was afraid now. Not of him – he seemed quite happy to choose for her. She had the feeling she had given some kind of power to him – power over her by letting him choose her food. She hoped she wouldn't regret it later. She knew that what she had to do was to work through this bleak feeling. She would emerge the other side. She always did.

*   *   *

It had been there before, of course, in the distant past. After Arjen died that terrible feeling of emptiness had engulfed her. But in some strange way, his death had been strengthening. She had had to keep going. Her girls needed her.

She recalled one of the girls – Rose maybe, she wasn't sure ... It was one evening, a long time after Arjen's death. Drained of energy, Esme was sitting on the battered old sofa on Christa Hoffmann's ground floor with a child on either side of her, holding and cuddling them, catering to their every need in so far as she could but always looking as though she were going to cry. In those days there was sadness etched into her face, a grief beyond words, and yet she never did cry. And then one of the girls had asked her just that ...

'Mutti, do grown-up people cry?'

'Yes,' Esme had said. 'Adults do cry. They feel grief and pain just like children do.'

'I've never seen you cry,' Lily had said.

And Esme said, 'I know. It's one of those odd things. I don't know how to cry.'

Their food came and they ate. Esme had to force herself to concentrate on Peter's words, to try to give them meaning. She wondered what impression she was making on him. Did he notice that she was only half there? She did not want to be rude but feared she was poor company.

He was drinking and chatting, and he appeared very at ease with himself. She tried to loosen up. She was having a terrible problem in connecting. At the other tables the noise of talk and the clatter of knives and forks on plates seemed very loud.

'Are you all right, mate?' he asked her suddenly. 'If you hadn't said you'd flown from Paris, I would think you were suffering from jet lag. You have that slightly disorientated look I know only too well.'

'I think maybe I'm a little tired,' she admitted. 'I'm probably appearing churlish – it's not meant. I'm sorry.'

'No offence taken,' he said. She wasn't sure if he really
added the word 'sport' to the phrase, but she thought she
might have heard it. However, it could have been a parody
of what she expected.

'Will you have coffee?' he asked. 'Or will we have a couple
of brandies?'

'Brandy sounds good,' she said with a smile. 'But I'm
terribly tired. I'm afraid it is showing. I should probably just
go to bed.'

'Not at all. We'll be tired together. Let's go in to the bar.
It's lovely to have company so don't worry.'

The bar was packed and she could find nowhere to sit
while he got the drinks. She waited beside him. Someone
vacated one of the bar stools, and he suggested she sat down.
He leaned with one elbow on the bar and he looked at her.
She could not work out what he was thinking.

'I don't suppose your room has a balcony?' he asked. 'I'm
afraid I've got one of the rooms at the back – big windows
but no balcony.'

It was a moment of choice and she knew it.

CHAPTER NINE

Esme Waters sat in the shade, a parasol sheltering her from the burning summer sun of the South of France. Beside her on the ground lay several newspapers from the past few days – all with different dates. She was inclined to keep papers for up to a week to go back through them for anything she might have missed or to reread an article in greater depth. Her carefully highlighted hair was pinned up off her neck and face. Her peaked white cap gave her extra protection not just from the direct rays of the sun, but also from the glare of the sparkling blue swimming pool, beside which she was sitting.

She still had her copy of *Macbeth* with her. She had now read it twice and her notes were getting longer and more detailed each time. However, in the past few days she had done very little reading or indeed very little of anything other than lying in bed with Peter Carew or eating and drinking with him.

A shadow fell across her, and it was with a feeling of fear that she looked up from her book and tried to see who had interrupted her thoughts.

*   *   *

A young girl was blocking the sun from her bare legs. She was about twelve or thirteen, leggy and hipless in a lime-green bikini. Esme had seen her before, both in the restaurant and in the pool the previous day or the day before, darting about on her beautifully formed feet. Running. Smiling. Laughing. Balletic. The girl had straight blonde hair and clear blue eyes. She bent down and picked up the ball she had come over to retrieve. And spinning on her heels she turned and smiled at Esme.

'*Entschuldigung*,' the girl excused herself. Her voice was light and happy, a little smile on her lips, and she swivelled round on her heels and dived back into the pool, throwing the ball in ahead of her.

There was charm in her smile.

Esme watched her. Her dive was neat and effortless, the ball bouncing ahead of her on the water, splashing the face of another child who had then ducked and bobbed, before picking up the ball and throwing it back.

'Katarina,' a woman's voice called.

The girl with the white-blonde hair looked across at the table where a woman was sitting. The woman had a coffee on the table in front of her, and a glossy magazine. Katarina swam back to the edge of the pool.

'*Ja, Mutti?*' she said.

A conversation took place in which the woman explained that she was going back to her room to fetch something and that if she did not immediately return, Katarina was to meet her in the restaurant in an hour's time.

Esme, with *Macbeth* abandoned on her lap, listened and mused. The years she had spent in Germany had acclimatised her to the accents of different areas, different regions. These were educated people, possibly from somewhere near the north. She watched the girl nod in acknowledgement of what her mother had said, before disappearing back under the water and swimming strongly and cleanly towards the centre.

The woman finished her coffee, rolled the magazine up, put it into her bag and, standing up, she dusted some biscuit crumbs from her lap. She glanced at her daughter, Katarina, in the pool, and then she swung her bag on to her shoulder before slipping her feet into a pair of flip-flops and easing her way between the tables.

Esme watched her. She felt uneasy the way the girl was just being left. She glanced about. There were people lying on the sun loungers; some, like her, half-covered with parasols, some just baking in the sun.

There was something wrong. She felt it but could not see it. She looked carefully around, *Macbeth* now forgotten. Pulling herself up into a sitting position she checked the children in the water, trying to place which child belonged with which adult around the pool. A baby, neatly protected from the sun both by a parasol on its pram and by a larger umbrella, gave a cry. Its mother leaned over the pram with a feeding bottle in her hand.

A waiter appeared carrying a glass of beer and some fruity concoction that frothed at the top. Esme watched him progress to a couple who were staring vacantly ahead of them. Or so it seemed. It was difficult to tell what people were looking at when they had on dark glasses.

Esme sighed. She could not see anything amiss and finally she accepted that the general unease that had arisen in her mind was to do with the emergence of the monsters, and she tried to settle back into *Macbeth*. But her mind was wandering. It had been like that more and more since the time in Paris. The baby cried again. The children laughed and called from the pool, splashing around with their ball. The noise they made was now inside her head, and she was too distracted to read. The white-blonde-haired Katarina got out and climbed on to the diving board, jumping up and down on it before clasping her knees mid-air and hurling herself in to the water. She came down hard, sending spray in every direction.

A man came over and admonished her in French, and Katarina laughed and nodded although Esme was unsure if the girl understood what was being said to her.

They are a different generation, Esme thought. When she was a child, if someone told her off for misbehaviour, she would have been both ashamed and embarrassed. The children in the pool were still laughing, still splashing each other, overexcited and carefree.

In a sense Esme envied them the freedom that came with the self-confidence they had – a self-confidence that she definitely did not have at their age, and even now, although apparently completely self-contained, she knew was not there. She did have confidence – a certain amount – but not as much as she would have liked. She still balked at walking into a room, into a restaurant, into a party, preferring to wait and to enter with others. She appeared in control although, inside her, she sometimes thought there was nothing there at all.

Most of all, she feared being recognised. Not as she was now, but as she had been, long ago when she had left Ireland with Jennifer, before she started changing her appearance and her name.

The baby cried again.

She shivered. One of the people with the dark glasses had a white cane leaning against his chair. Blind, she thought. Momentarily she tried once more to think of Macbeth and his wife but then her mind wandered again. There was something there, something she did not want to think about, something she could not remember. It was to do with blindness. With eyes that could not see.

The baby cried again in its pram. A wail of longing, of need for its mother.

I could not see, she thought.

Maybe that was it.

The wailing from the pram did not ease.

She felt the need to leave the pool area. She did not want to consider herself in any way responsible for the children in the water, or for the abandoned Katarina. And if she stayed there, she would. There was a lifeguard, there were people around, other parents with children ducking and diving. This was not for her. She had done it in the past with her own and other children; she did not want this now. She stared at her watch until both hands were at twelve.

Now she could go back to the room.

Back to her room, back to Peter and his early morning stiffy, as he called it, although any other man she had ever known had been in that condition at seven or eight in the morning, not at midday. Stiffy was a word she did not like. It was crass. In fact, Peter *was* crass in some ways, but there would be safety in his arms and, getting up and putting her things together, she hoped he was in a gentle mood and felt like slow lovemaking, not the rough and tumble he appeared mostly to prefer.

Elegant low-heeled silver sandals on her feet and her loose white shirt hanging open, she made her way back into the hotel and along the corridor to the staircase, her footwear slapping on the tiled flooring, her book, towel and sunglasses in her hands.

The 'Do Not Disturb' sign was still on the door handle. She let herself into her room, leaving it hanging there. Peter was still there in her bed. He appeared to be asleep, flat on his back, tousled dark hair on the pillow, his erection apparent through the thin white summer sheet. Esme wondered if she actually felt like sex. Walking up to the room she had tried to think of something erotic to get herself into the right frame of mind, but whatever had disturbed her at the pool, whatever had distracted her from *Macbeth*, whatever had entered her mind had not truly left. The baby crying ... The blind man ... She might have been better going for coffee in the bar, or even a small beer as she had done the previous day to help her to loosen up, and to make herself more accommodating for sex with Peter. And it had worked.

But right now, what she actually wanted was to lie in his arms. Peacefully, silently, safe ...

Peter Carew seemed kindly but was certainly not given to introspection. He did not particularly take her needs into account, but Esme forgave him all of that simply because she wanted the company.

Now she could not bear to be alone at night – bad as it had been before, it was worse since Paris.

Peter stirred and opened his eyes. 'I thought you were never coming back,' he said.

'Well, here I am,' she replied, putting her things down on a chair and slipping off her flip-flops.

'Everything off,' he said. 'Hurry up. Hurry up. I want to see you.' His voice was deep with his Australian accent twisting the vowels.

She undressed slowly, pretending to fiddle with the buttons on her shirt, which were not fastened anyway, before dropping it on to the back of the chair. Her swimsuit was strapless.

'I wish you had your bikini on,' he said lazily. 'Wear it tomorrow, will you?'

'I could put it on now,' she teased him, knowing he wouldn't have the patience for her to change and to start over.

'No, no,' he said urgently. 'Just keep going.'

And she did. She peeled her swimsuit down slowly before easing it off her stomach and rolling it down her thighs, leaving it lying on the floor in a dark turquoise pool.

She stood there, saying nothing, waiting for his instructions. To date he had come up with different ideas for the moment.

He was smiling now as he looked at her. And standing there before the bed, the cold remote feeling that had encompassed her started to pass and she found herself half smiling at him.

After they had sex, and for some reason it was gentler than his usual morning sex if the previous few mornings were anything to go by, he kissed her quickly on the lips and got up to shower. She lay on her back with her arms stretched out as if crucified, wishing that he did not pull away so abruptly and yet knowing that as yet, he probably had never done anything else in his life.

'A shower and breakfast for me,' he said as he headed for the bathroom. She thought of saying, 'It's long past breakfast time,' but it did not seem worth the effort.

She rolled over on her side and pulled his pillow to her face so that she could both hug it and breathe in the smell of his head. She called in to him but he had turned on the water and could not hear her. She wanted to tell him that she had feared something at the pool, but then was glad that she had not. There were things about her that he did not know, that she did not want him to know and that she would never tell him. She would sleep after he left and they would meet later in the day at the pool. She would have company when she needed it, and that made up for the things that were lacking in the relationship that was developing between them, for the lack of perfection, for the lack of understanding and complete rapport.

*   *   *

Esme knew that she was being coldly pragmatic. She knew that she was using him just as he was using her. They both wanted company. She tried to keep her mind very still, tried hard to keep herself centred where she was, naked on a bed with just her knees covered by the sheet, as she heard the shower being turned off, and Peter brushing his teeth. She would shower too, but later – later after he had gone and she had slept with the sun high in the sky and the air conditioning keeping the room at an even temperature. She was already dozing when he came out. He rooted among his clothing to find his shorts before remembering he had left them on the balcony to dry. She heard the door slide open and knew that he was standing naked, stretching himself outside in full view of the pool and the other balconies. She would have smiled at the image had not sleep come in. She did not feel him pulling the sheet over her, nor did she feel his finger touch the star-shaped scar above her right breast. She had no awareness of his lightly stroking her hair, nor was she aware on any conscious level of him leaving the room. She may have heard the door click shut, but it was in her dream.

Her dream became a nightmare. In it, she could hear footsteps on the stairs and she waited, her breath held in terror for the door to open. There was a cry somewhere, echoing in the labyrinth of her mind.

She woke suddenly, startled, pulling herself to an upright position, clasping the pillow in her arms, perspiration streaming off her, her hair damp with sweat, her eyes wide open, her breath coming in short gasps. As she took in that she was awake, she recalled she was in the South of France, that the distant sounds were children in the pool and happy sunbathers chatting, and she breathed in and out as slowly as she could until she regained her equilibrium. The room was too warm, as Peter had left the balcony door open.

She lay there in the heat.

I am alive, she thought. Someone had said that to her once. He had said it came from Zulu – I am alive. She wondered what he meant and why he had said it, and indeed who it had been. And then she remembered. It had been another night, another hotel, another place. You are alive. It was François. He had said it to her, 'You are alive,' as she emerged to consciousness terrified from the nightmare. And with it came another memory, a memory from a different time, a different place – a woman dressed in a crisp white-buttoned shirt with white trousers, a badge pinned on her lapel. 'You are safe,' the woman had said. 'You are safe now. It is over.'

She got out of the bed and unsteadily went to the shower. Standing for ages under the water, soaping herself and washing her hair, she waited until those painful moments of semi-memory had passed and she forced herself to think about work. The water pounded down on her head. She kept her eyes tightly closed and tried to concentrate.

Coming out from the shower, she saw her laptop was open on the table near the window. She was almost sure she had left it closed. She hoped Peter had not been using it in her absence. She had not given him her password, despite several attempts on his part to cajole it out of her, but she feared that he might have found some way around that. She switched it on and then checked the time on it when it had last been used. She shook her head in irritation. She saw herself as being excessively suspicious of people and their possible actions. And the strange thing was that despite this tendency, she did not see the blatantly obvious. She sometimes hated herself for being like that, but she never seemed to get it right, no matter how hard she tried. She was inclined to trust the wrong people.

She went out onto the balcony, looking down, and thought briefly about phoning François in Paris. She missed the comfort of being with someone who knew her, even if it was only in a small way. There was something wearing about starting over, time after time. She was not given to regret, and she knew that she had been foolish in getting involved with François.

But she acknowledged now that what she really missed were her meetings with Jacob – Jacob Althaus, who, in those morning coffees and evening drinks, had managed to offer her something, perhaps some kind of stability. And yet, while it had sometimes been torturous talking to him about the past, it had to some extent freed her.

But freedom only went so far, or can only start at a certain point, and just when she was beginning to feel that she might talk to him about what had really happened, just as she started to feel a level of security unknown to her before, she had found out about François, and had finished their relationship.

Had she stayed, it would have been because she wanted her morning coffee with Jacob, and that did not seem reason enough for her to spend those long lonely hours working in the apartment and putting in time. And so she had packed, phoned Jacob from the airport and told him she was leaving.

Should she have stayed? She knew that she had been about to tell Jacob that her last real memory of childhood had been the celebration of her fourteenth birthday, and that after that there was really only a sketchy blur for the next five years, until she had woken up one morning and found herself in a German university with the first of the men who would people her adult life.

Back inside, she picked up her watch. It was five to five.

*   *   *

Jacob Althaus was sitting at his desk. One patient had left. He was waiting for the next. He leaned back and, with his fingertips touching each other, closed his eyes. The phone rang at two minutes to five, and he lifted the receiver. He knew who it was before a word was said.

'*Allô*,' he said. His voice was deep and resonant with an unidentifiable European accent.

'*C'est moi*,' she said. '*Esme.*'

'I know,' he replied in English. 'How are you, Esme?'

'I'm fine,' she replied, but he sensed immediately that there was something wrong. He glanced at the clock on his table. He only had seven minutes for her. He might have to delay his next appointment.

Keeping an eye on the clock, he leaned back in his chair and said, 'And where are you?'

'I'm in the South of France. I'm staying in a resort – I suppose that's the word.'

'That explains the background noise,' he said.

She moved to the glass doors and slid them closed. 'There. Is that better?'

'I wasn't complaining,' he said, hoping she could hear the smile in his voice.

'It seems ages since I left Paris,' she continued, as though trying to make conversation. He knew she was attempting to create an opening so that she could talk. In some ways it seemed a long time since she had left Paris, in others it was like yesterday.

'Are you alone?'

'I am at the moment,' she replied.

A cryptic response, he thought. Did she mean at that precise moment, or in general? The first, he thought. She was alone, but only at this moment. He knew her well. Knew her needs and some of her fears. But not all of them – she had not disclosed them all.

He also was quite sure that she had run from Paris because the truth was too close for her, even though she had disguised this well by suddenly asking about François's background, and then promptly finishing the relationship with him.

'And how have you been feeling?' he said into the silence.

'Oh, I'm fine,' she replied.

'Your dreams?'

'They're bad.'

He nodded. It explained the call. He knew her dreams were nightmares. He knew her struggle with sleeplessness, her need for sleep, and her fears of it. She had said to him once, '"Sleep shall neither night nor day Hang upon his pent-house lid." Or in this particular case, upon *my* pent-house lid.' She had half smiled as she said it, as though mocking herself, and then reminded him that she was in the middle of reading *Macbeth*.

He knew her desire for comfort and company in the night, how she feared the long hours until dawn, and how she made work the focus of her days.

'Do you remember what you dreamed?' he asked. He could feel her shrug down the telephone.

'Just the footsteps. The usual. On the stairs. You know. Perhaps a cry.'

'Did the door open?'

'I don't know. I heard the footsteps. I think I woke then.'

'You want to tell me something.'

She hesitated. His sentence was an observation, not a question.

'I thought of something I thought I might mention.'

'Yes?'

'You need to go,' she then said. 'It's time for your next appointment.'

'My secretary will see the light on the phone. No one will

164   MARY STANLEY

come in until I disconnect,' he replied. 'Tell me what you thought you should mention.'

'It's nothing,' she said. He could feel her withdrawing.

'Please say.'

There was a further silence.

'I should go,' she said.

'Tell me first what you wanted to mention.'

'I was going to tell you a name. I thought I would give you a name.'

'A name?'

'I have to go,' she said.

'Tell me the name first.'

The silence extended into a long minute.

'I really have to go,' she said. 'I was just going to tell you the name – Molly Kilbride.'

'Molly Kilbride?' he repeated, jotting the name down on paper in front of him. 'Who is she?'

'She's someone I used to know. A long time ago.'

'Did you know her well?' he asked, trying to hold her on the line. There was something about the name that reverberated in the back of his mind.

'Yes. Yes. I knew her very well once. But I have to go. And you have appointments. I'll call again.'

And the line went dead.

He did not hang up immediately. He sat at the desk looking at the name on the paper. He knew he had heard it somewhere before.

After a moment, he disconnected and then immediately dialled his wife.

'Naomi? Look, I'm sorry,' he said. 'I'm going to be late. Something has come up and I'm going to have to stay on after my last patient.'

Naomi's impatience was perfectly clear. He apologised again.

'We're meeting the Delmonts,' she said.

'Oh God, I forgot.' He felt bad. 'I'll meet you at the restaurant. What time is the table booked for?'

'Nine thirty,' she said. 'We're meeting for a drink in the bar on the corner between a quarter to and nine o'clock.'

'I'll make it up to you,' he said. 'If I don't make it for the drink go on to the restaurant, I'll catch you up there. I'll be at the table for nine thirty.'

'You'd better have a very good excuse if you're late,' she said. 'In fact you'd better have a very good excuse anyway.'

Oh, I do, he thought as he hung up.

It was an hour and a half later that his secretary left and he locked the outer door.

Back at his computer he typed in Molly Kilbride on his search engine. He sat in silence as up came six potential sites for the name he was seeking – there were many more, other Molly Kilbrides who had done different things, lived at different times, but he knew immediately which one he was looking for, and the vague memory he had had of half-recognition suddenly became clear.

It took him three different searches before he came up with a photograph. Black-and-white – the photograph was old and grainy. He glanced at the date at the top of the page. Going on thirty years old, in fact. How could he have forgotten her name? He had been in Ireland on a working exchange the year when that photograph appeared on the front of every paper, day after day, and then as the days slipped by, it had appeared inside the paper . . . Molly Kilbride. She was fourteen years old . . . the description said, brown hair, grey eyes . . . But Esme's eyes were green.

He wanted to phone Esme back, to ask her the connection and where Molly Kilbride fitted into her life. She couldn't be Molly, could she? God, he hoped not. Dyed hair? Contact lenses? He picked up the telephone and then thought better of it. She would phone again, when she was ready. She had given him something, the best she could do, all that she was able to do. He wondered if the name had come to her while she was asleep, or if it had been there all the time. He wondered what had triggered it. He read every one of the articles on the search engine, then, leaning back, he closed his eyes.

The story made him think of those days at Trinity College in Dublin. It brought to mind the cobblestones in Front Square, and the smoke in the Senior Common Room, the surface friendliness of the Irish and the difficulty in breaking through to the real people. He remembered the loneliness that his wife had spoken of back then, and he thought now as he had thought then, *but none so lonely as Molly Kilbride.*

A sense of the lateness of the hour brought him out of his reverie, and he took off his jacket, tie and shirt and washed briefly and quickly at the basin in the bathroom, before taking a fresh shirt from the cupboard and re-dressing himself.

Heading out of the building, he tried to hail a taxi before realising he couldn't remember which restaurant they were going to. He recalled a conversation with Naomi in which she had referred equally to Le Taillevent and La Coupole, but for the life of him the conclusion to the conversation escaped him. He had the feeling that she had asked him to book, and he had said back to her that she had more time . . . there might even have been an argument over his making that comment.

There seemed to be a lot of arguments over little things. He grimaced. She had mentioned meeting in the bar. Which bar? While still trying to get a taxi he phoned Le Taillevent to ask if there was a booking in the name of Althaus to be told quite firmly that no, there was not, and that they did not have a free table.

'I wasn't asking you for a table,' Althaus said. 'I was merely trying to enquire if a table had been booked in my name.'

'*Non, monsieur.*'

Mon dieu, he thought, with irritation. Surely it was Le Taillevent they had booked. The service was always attentive and discreet and the food excellent. They both enjoyed it. It really was one of the best restaurants.

He slipped his arms out of his jacket, and held it away from him in the heat of the Parisian night. In his air-conditioned rooms for the previous ten hours, he had forgotten just how oppressively stuffy Paris could be on a warm night.

It dawned on him now that the bar Naomi had mentioned was his favourite – the one on the corner of Rue de Gaité and Boulevard Edgar Quinet. No wonder she was irked. She had suggested there simply because of him. And it was close to La Coupole.

He finally got a taxi, but the traffic was slow and there was a build-up of cars ahead. There was nothing he could do but leave it in the driver's hands, so he sat back and stretched out his legs as far as he could in an effort to relax.

He removed his tie and, rolling it up carefully, placed it in his jacket pocket. He wondered how Esme was feeling. He suspected that she would be very nervous, having given him Molly Kilbride's name. She would know that he would have noted it, probably researched it, and that he would be trying to find a connection. And that if he did not find the link she would, in due course, have to tell him.

If she makes contact again, he thought. He knew her vulnerability, although he had not yet uncovered what had brought about that weakness in her. He now felt there was a very good chance that he might not hear from her again, and that she would run, as she appeared to have done all her life.

He pulled back from these memories as he stretched himself in the taxi.

Molly Kilbride, he thought. I wonder what happened to her.

He wondered if Esme knew, or was that what she was trying to find out? Was she running or was she searching? He wondered if she knew the answers, knew them consciously, that is, because he had no doubt that the answers were there, locked inside her.

'I'll get out here,' he said to the taxi driver. 'It will be quicker to walk.' He paid, and let himself out into the traffic, quickly crossing the road and walking the last four hundred metres.

The noise and clatter in the restaurant reminded him, as ever, of a railway station. It was art deco at its best, a place through which Josephine Baker once moved her long and elegant limbs, and where Henry Miller, Pablo Picasso and Salvador Dali had once dined. Looking around the enormous room Jacob realised he had no chance of finding Naomi and their friends. All of a sudden he saw Henry on his feet across the room waving to him, and he made his way to the table where the others were waiting. Naomi looked pointedly at her watch, while Henry Delmont, still on his feet, greeted him with enthusiasm. Jacob bent and kissed Sally Delmont on both cheeks, before trying to make eye contact with Naomi.

'My sincerest apologies,' he said. 'Having managed to get myself out of the office, I then had problems getting a taxi, and then the traffic . . . you know.'

'Why didn't you get a taxi?' Naomi asked in English.

'I did,' he replied briefly, knowing that once again she had heard nothing that he said, and also that she was trying to bring their problems and her irritation to the attention of the others by speaking in the language that was common to them all. It was symptomatic of their relationship now and he knew it, and yet he did not seem to be able to repair the damage between them despite his abilities to help other people with their lives. He was aware of the irony.

'Forgive me,' he said to her. 'It was one of those days . . .'

He knew there was no point in pursuing it, so he turned to Henry and asked him how he and his family were.

Although their history had briefly once overlapped many years earlier in the late nineteen seventies, the first time Jacob and Naomi had actually knowingly met the Delmonts was in New York some five years earlier at a conference. The women had become friendly and Jacob and Henry had met through them, and then Jacob realised that they had actually been in the same university at the same time. Henry had been a student at Trinity, while Jacob had been there on an exchange with another lecturer. Henry recalled attending Jacob's lectures, but Jacob remembered only the lectures, not the students.

They had since met at a further conference in Oslo, after which they had kept in contact. The Delmonts now lived in London. This meeting in Paris tied in with yet another conference in the university where Jacob would be speaking the following evening. The evening lectures were open to the public.

'I suppose you were working on your paper,' Henry said to him.

'I should have been,' Jacob replied, trying to get the waiter's attention. 'We should order,' he said. 'It could take forever for the food to arrive. They're as busy as ever.'

'I think it is wonderful,' Sally said. 'The atmosphere, the noise, the whole Frenchness of the place. It's exciting.'

'It is fun,' Naomi said, and for the first time that evening acknowledging Jacob's existence with any cordiality, 'but Jacob is right – we need to try to get our order in.'

'Tell me how the children are,' Naomi asked Sally. Sally's face lit up with pleasure as she pulled snapshots from her bag.

'Oh,' Naomi said, taking them and studying them carefully. 'How nice . . . how lovely . . . how pretty . . .' Jacob could hear her words and he also heard the sadness behind them.

And that, thought Jacob, is the problem. It brought him back to his thoughts just a few evenings earlier. It reminded him of his certainty in not wanting to have children. He did not want his gene pool to continue. He did not want his children to be part of one more cycle in history where he felt that ultimately the end would be the same. He knew of the random nature of things, of being in the right place at the right time, or indeed the wrong one, as he recalled Esme Waters saying to him at one of their earlier coffee encounters.

Esme had once said to him that she saw herself as a tourist on the planet – and the good tourist took only photographs, left only footprints. He had pondered that phrase later. He knew that she had given more than that, and believed that he too had done more than leave mere footprints, but when he pursued the observation with her at their next morning coffee, she smiled sadly and said, 'But when I am gone, what will I have left behind me? Maybe some books that will moulder in a library, and probably one day be removed and destroyed.'

'But you have also left children,' he said.

And she had smiled again at him with her glass-green eyes. 'Yes, that's what I meant. They are my footprints.'

Genetic footprints, he thought now. It raised the old question of the meaning of life, and, seeing Naomi across the table with her deep red lipstick, and the too-large stones on her fingers with their scarlet-polished nails, he felt an acute sense of sadness.

The arrival of the waiter interrupted both his train of thought and the ongoing conversation.

It was a good five minutes later and the wine was poured, when Naomi excused herself and Sally said she would join her.

'Any chance of meeting up tomorrow morning?' Jacob said to Henry. 'There is something I want to ask you.'

'Ask me,' Henry said, raising his glass to Jacob.

'Now is not the right time.'

Henry nodded. The women reappeared quite suddenly.

'Tell me, Naomi, where are the best places to shop here in Paris?' Sally asked. 'I'm going to have two full days to indulge, and I'm going to use every minute of them.'

Later in the meal, Henry said to Jacob, 'I was thinking that if you've time tomorrow morning, perhaps you'd like to meet for coffee. There are a number of things I'd like to discuss with you . . .'

Jacob knew that Henry was referring to the earlier discussion. 'That would be delightful,' he said. 'I've to do the opening presentation at twelve o'clock, just before our buffet lunch – so perhaps at ten thirty or eleven?'

They agreed to meet in the morning, and in due course both couples left to take a taxi, first to the Delmonts' hotel, and then on to the Althaus home in the suburbs.

Naomi was petulant and seemed keen to cause a row when they were on their own in the taxi, but Jacob sidestepped it with pleasantries about the evening, and the joy of seeing old friends.

'You look so much younger than Sally,' he said, and as he uttered the words, he wondered why he lied.

'Do I?' Her pleasure was evident, and he felt a surge of guilt rising in him. She did not look younger, she just looked more spoiled. She looked chic and expensive but there was a slight droop at the corner of her lips while Sally Delmont looked happier. He wondered, had he been aware of this before, or was it only now at the forefront of his consciousness because he had seen the two women together? Or was it because he felt guilty about his thoughts of Esme Waters? He held her hand as she alighted from the taxi, and she let him, as though her pleasure at his earlier comment was still ongoing, and again he felt guilt because he could not remember when he had last paid her a compliment.

Inside he poured them each a cognac, and flicked on the late-night news.

'Are you coming to bed?' she asked.

He looked up at her. 'I have an early start,' he said. 'Maybe you'd prefer if I slept in the spare room?'

'Whatever you like,' she said.

'Wait. I'm coming.' He tried smiling again, but he was tired and it was an effort.

None the less he pulled himself from the chair he had just settled into, and followed her up the stairs.

CHAPTER TEN

Having toyed over phoning François and finally realising that it was Jacob she wanted to speak to, Esme had dithered for a few minutes before dialling his number. The call left her nervous and uncertain. When she phoned she had not consciously intended mentioning the name Molly Kilbride, and indeed was not sure that Molly's name was anywhere in her mind as she made the decision to call and began checking for Jacob's number, until she recalled she had keyed it into her mobile.

And after she had hung up she was almost shaking. She had said it. Said it aloud. Told someone. She could hardly believe it was done. She had not uttered the name Molly Kilbride in nearly twenty-two years. She did not go there in her mind – not ever. At least, not when she was awake. She feared sleep because she knew she went there then. Now she must distract herself from the enormity of having given the name to Jacob. She went back and looked at her emails and reread the one to which she had given the least attention.

It was from Rose – Rose, her thorny child.

*   *   *

Rose was finally emerging from her goth phase and had stopped using the white makeup to which she had been addicted for the previous number of years. She had dark brown hair – so dark it appeared black. Her eyes were dark brown too, her face pretty, her skin smooth. Although sensible in her own way now that she was twenty-one, she was none the less the one who had said to Esme when Jasmine was born, 'Why did you have another girl? Were Lily and me not enough?'

'You are all enough,' she had said to Rose. 'Each of you is enough. I love you all.'

But Rose, then six years old and truculent, had sulked and looked at the baby crossly.

'Bad baby,' she had said, sticking her thumb in her mouth and leaving the room.

Esme had left the crying baby, and gone after Rose and tried to hold her close, but Rose was not so easily bought, not then and not since. Rose was her difficult child; the one who gave her due, but sometimes appeared to give it with effort.

Her email said, 'Hospital work still going strong. Am now working behind locked doors. Disabled, damaged, abandoned people. It would break your heart. Rosie.' It was a typical Rose-style email. It gave just enough so that Esme would know where she was and what she was doing, It also raised so many questions, but Esme knew not to ask those questions. There would be no answers. Once Rose had got her attention in any way she could, she would give no more.

Esme started to compose a reply, unsure at first whether to leave the message for a few days and then respond by asking a question or two, but knowing that she would get no adequate comeback. She decided to send her email anyway, filling her daughter in on the invitation to Japan that she had received the previous week, the weather in the

South of France, the ongoing nature of her work and saying she would like to hear more from Rose. She wondered why Rose's email had left her feeling disturbed. She read it through again. The fact that Rose had signed herself Rosie contained affection, so it was not that. Rose always signed her name in different ways and Esme knew that the signature reflected different aspects of Rose's character. Sometimes she was just Rose, other times Roos, and occasionally Rosie, which was what her sisters called her in moments of expressed affection. Disabled, damaged, abandoned – was Rose in some way trying to describe herself? No, hardly. Rose was no more disabled or abandoned than either Lily or Jasmine. Although Esme knew that having no father did make Rose feel somewhat abandoned, but Rose could hardly blame Esme for that. And as for damaged? No. Rose could not consider herself damaged.

Rose had finished her second year in university and this was a summer job tying in with her degree in Social Sciences. Her gap year after school had left her no more certain what she really wanted to do, and Esme was aware that Rose had wandered into a combined degree of Psychology and Social Science more because she had no clear sense of direction than with any vocation or future career in mind. What Rose ultimately intended to do was unclear, but being Rose she would try everything she could think of, and eventually find what interested her.

Time had passed and it was with surprise she realised it was already seven o'clock and the heat of the South of France was easing somewhat. It made her think momentarily of the long hot dripping nights of a South Carolina summer when any movement was an effort.

She wondered where Peter was and she went down to the pool for a last swim of the day. There was no sign of him,

and there were not many people left there. The children were
still swimming, although she assumed they had been and
gone many times, and had done other things since she was
there that morning.

Katarina's mother was back at her table, now with a man
in tow who looked much younger than she. Esme could
hear them talking – a mixture of German and English. The
man was proficient in neither and she thought at first that
he might be Scandinavian, maybe from Finland. It took her
a while to realise that they had only just met and that he
was from somewhere in the east of Europe – she did not
recognise his intonation nor the occasional words he used
in his own tongue. She wondered if Katarina's mother was,
like her, always hopeful that there would be someone better,
someone safer round the next corner. And she smiled wryly
as she had this thought, because in that moment she knew
that whatever it was she wanted, however she might try to
disguise it, either to herself or to others, it was not safety
that she sought – and then that thought horrified her
because if she did not seek safety, then maybe she sought
danger. And with that thought came fear – cold harsh fear.
She had had the chance of permanent safety – Grayson had
offered it to her, and she had rejected it. For her it was the
ultimate dichotomy – the boredom of routine and having
everything. These things did not offer happiness. She needed
adversity – goals and ambitions to make her life worth
living.

She had said this to Jacob over one of their morning
coffees in their Parisian café during the period she had spent
there. She said that what she had sought was safety, protection, somewhere out of the eye of the storm – and yet when
given that, it had been too dull.

Jacob had replied thoughtfully, 'You know, that is all right.
Our needs change. Sometimes, you know, certainty kills the

soul. At one point in your life it was exactly what was required. Later it was not.'

But she felt it was not all right – that it said something more about her than she wanted.

She slipped into the water and began swimming slowly up and down, avoiding the splashing children who were, in due course, called from the pool. Dripping and laughing, with towels wrapped around them, one by one they disappeared. She floated lazily, almost drifting off to sleep, while the pool emptied of people, as the sun edged down in the blue sky, and it was with a jolt she suddenly realised there was someone else in the water.

Before she had the chance to pull herself upright, she felt hands gripping her ankles, and despite her efforts to kick free she was pulled down firmly under the water. In her panic she gulped as she tried to release herself.

'You bastard. You fucking stupid bastard,' she said when she finally managed to pull herself out of the pool and had finished coughing.

'I thought you'd know it was me,' Peter said. 'And I thought you didn't use bad language.'

'Push me far enough and I will,' she said. 'You bastard. How could you do that?'

'I was only playing,' he said as he climbed the steel ladder beside her. 'I thought you knew I was there.'

'I didn't know there was anyone in the pool, let alone that you might be,' she said angrily. Her anger was mixed with terrible sobbing. 'How could I know it was you? And I'm claustrophobic,' she added.

'What's that got to do with it?' he asked.

'For God's sake, I could have drowned.'

'No you couldn't, I was there. I wouldn't let you drown.'

'I thought you were trying to drown me.' She was really shaken and his nonchalance was infuriating. 'I don't like going underwater. I told you that before. I'm afraid. I can't help it. I'm afraid.'

She had got her towel now and was wiping her face and wringing out her hair.

He tried to put his arms around her. 'I didn't mean to frighten you,' he said. 'I really didn't.'

The panic had eased. She was still shocked. She looked at him and could see that he was concerned.

'I'm afraid of enclosed spaces. I'm afraid of being trapped,' she said in an effort to explain herself. 'Under the water – it's enclosed . . . I feel trapped there . . . can't breathe . . . can't . . .'

'I didn't know,' he said evenly. He took her towel and wiped her face gently with it. 'I really didn't know. I know you'd said something about not getting your face wet, but I really did not realise. I wouldn't have done that . . .'

'You shouldn't do it anyway,' she said. 'It's dangerous.'

He bit back whatever he had been about to respond. She suspected he was going to say that she was overreacting. She didn't know if she was or not. All she knew was that he had terrified her.

'I shouldn't have done it,' he said, in an effort to reassure her. 'I apologise. Let's have a drink before we go up and change for dinner. I'm going to take you out tonight.'

He went to the bar to get a glass of white wine for her and a beer for himself. While he was gone her mind went back to the thought she had had shortly before he had pulled her under. Then she had been thinking it was fear that kept her living on a knife edge, and that she needed that fear. Now that was not as clear. If it was fear she wanted she had certainly just felt it, and it left her drained. For the first time it dawned on her with complete clarity that while fear was what kept her moving, it was freedom she wanted.

But she was free, and she knew that. She wished she could

talk to Jacob. Somehow some things had taken on a different meaning when she had shared them with him. Clarity had emerged from the darkness.

'I didn't know whether to get you a brandy or this,' Peter said, passing her the glass of wine. He was looking at her thoughtfully. She knew her hands were shaking.

'Why are you looking at me like that?' she asked.

'You're very pale,' he said. 'Are you sure you're all right?'

'I will be,' she answered.

She knew he had not meant to distress her like that, and that he had seen it as boisterous fun or something foolishly male. Grayson had been like that. He used to throw the girls into the pool and they had responded gleefully to his attention and to his sense of fun, while she had recoiled from it, fearing more for herself than for them, as she knew they were enjoying themselves.

'You don't have to take me out for dinner,' she said, regaining her equilibrium. 'I'm fine, really. We can eat here in the hotel.'

'I've already booked a table,' he replied. 'I found a nice place in town with music and I want to take you there.'

She sipped her wine. It filled the chasm of fear inside her. She knew that he had no idea how much he had terrified her.

They went to dinner and, just as he had said, it was a nice place. In a smoky corner on a small raised stage, a band was playing jazz. Even though Peter had booked the table prior to the unpleasant incident in the pool, he was clearly going all out to appease her, if appeasement was what she needed. She didn't think it was. As far as she was concerned, what had happened was over and she was trying not to think about it. Usually they talked generally, but this evening he seemed more concentrated on her as a person.

'Tell me about your name,' he said. 'Is Esme a family name, or who were you called after?'

'Oh, it's just a name,' she said. '*Es* means "it" in German and the *me* is me, if you see what I mean.'

'You mean it's a German name,' he said, misunderstanding her.

'No, that was a joke. I was being witty,' she explained, trying not to grimace. 'It's just a name.'

'It sounds like you chose it yourself,' he remarked.

And in a sense she had chosen it herself, but she was not going to tell him that.

'I lived so long in Germany,' she said. 'I've just made that bit up as an explanation for my name. It's just a name . . .' she added lamely, trying to think how to change the conversation.

'And Waters? Was that the name of your last husband?'

She wished she hadn't told him there had been three husbands – well, almost three. Her honesty had almost caught up on her.

'No,' she said briefly. 'I love the music.'

He turned and listened for a little. 'Yes, it's great,' he said, smiling at her. She knew he knew she had changed the subject.

'You know, Esme,' he said during a lull in the music, having just refilled their wine glasses from the bottle in the ice bucket beside him, 'when I looked you up on the internet all I got was the blurb that is on your books and a couple of interviews in which you avoided all personal questions – just the way you are avoiding them with me.'

'I didn't realise you were interviewing me,' she said, trying to keep her voice light.

He laughed. 'I'm not interviewing you, but you're very secretive about some things.'

'I've told you the things that are important – my daughters, my work.'

'You've told me what you've selected to tell me.'

'Isn't that all we ever tell anyone?' She wished the music would start up again.

'You're the most reticent person I've ever met,' he said. 'Your passport says you were born in Dublin.'

'My passport? Have you been going through my things?' she asked, startled.

'I looked at your passport,' he said. 'Is that a crime?'

'It's intrusive,' she answered shortly. 'I haven't gone through your things.'

'If you want to see my passport, I'll show it to you, but I've already told you that I was born in Sydney – it's not a secret.'

'It's not a secret where I was born,' she said sharply, trying to keep the agitation out of her voice. 'If you'd asked me I would have told you. You have no right to look at my personal things – ask if you want to know something.'

'And you would tell me the truth?'

'If it was important, yes I would – but it's wrong to pry on someone . . .' She was annoyed and perturbed, but she didn't know if these were normal feelings. She felt intruded on, her space invaded, her privacy impaired.

'It's normal to share things when you're having a relationship,' he said.

She had not thought of it like that. It did not seem like a relationship to her; it was more like two people putting in some time together because they were in the same place and were attracted to each other. She did not see it in terms of something ongoing, nor did she want to.

'I'm not sure I'm ready for a relationship as such,' she said.

'I wasn't asking you to marry me,' he laughed. 'What do you see this as? An affair? Is that not another word for a certain type of relationship? Is that not what we're having?'

Put like that, she felt that she was being silly at recoiling from the term 'relationship'. But it wasn't a word she liked.

'I'm in recovery,' she said, again trying to keep her voice light. 'I can't handle the concept of a relationship. Sorry.'

'So, will a fling do?'

She knew he was laughing at her. 'A fling is fine,' she said, 'but not if you go through my things.'

'Your reticence is enticing.' He was still laughing. 'It just makes me want to know more.'

'There's nothing to know,' she said, somewhat tersely. 'I wouldn't pry if I were you. You mightn't like what you find.'

She had a feeling that sounded threatening, and she had not meant anything other than to warn him off. It didn't work.

'Oh, good,' he said. 'I had a feeling there were things to be uncovered.'

'Even I,' she said almost coldly, 'even I do not pry into my life.'

He eyed her thoughtfully. 'Now that,' he said, 'is the most provocative comment you have made to date.'

'I meant that I move onwards. I leave the past behind.' She felt she was digging a hole the more she said, but it was true. She moved and tried to leave the past behind her.

'We can't leave the past behind,' he said. 'It's there all the time. We're the product of our past.'

'I leave it behind,' she reiterated.

'Do you? I think that is not possible. Like me, you have links with people in the past and with the child you were – we can't escape that.'

'This is a very heavy conversation for two people who are having a light-hearted summer fling,' she said, trying to move him away from whatever angle he was now coming from. She was feeling increasingly uncomfortable, both by his questions and by the earlier conversation on the phone with Jacob Althaus. Everything seemed to be connected.

'I heard from one of my daughters today,' she said, in another effort to change the conversation.

'See,' Peter said. 'You cannot escape the past – your daughters are part of it.'

'They are a part of my present,' Esme replied.

'But also part of your past. They link you with previous events, previous husbands.'

'Everything is linked that way if you choose to see it that way. And I don't.'

'Anyone would think you had something to hide,' Peter said.

'I don't,' she said, twirling her wine glass between her fingers.

He reached across the table and stroked her hair. 'You are very hard on yourself,' he said suddenly.

She shrugged. She did not really know what he meant.

'Tell me how you got that scar,' he said, nodding towards her breast. Her loose cotton top had opened somewhat, and glancing down she saw the scar he was looking at. She quickly fixed her blouse so that it was covered, and she turned away.

'I'm going to dance,' she said.

He picked up his wine glass and watched her.

She glanced around at other tables and at the small space for dancing near where the band was playing. And, surprising herself, she approached a table where four men were sitting talking and eating.

'I wonder,' she said, 'if one of you would like to dance with me?'

Two of them immediately got to their feet.

'Well, one of you will do,' she said lightly.

They looked at each other and smiled.

'We are both honoured to dance with you,' one of them said.

They were attractive, muscular men in casual smart summer clothing with open-necked shirts and dark cotton trousers.

It was only as they got on to the floor and nodded to the band that Esme realised they were connected with the musicians. The jazz stopped and the band burst into rock and roll, and Esme found herself spun around, moving between one and then the other as they twirled her under their arms from one of them to the other.

'I really asked the right people, didn't I?' she laughed, trying to catch her breath.

'Yes, you did,' one of them said.

'And we are glad you asked,' the other said.

When they finished, Peter had joined their friends at the table and Esme found herself sitting down between the two who had danced with her, her glass of wine in front of her on the table, and in the midst of a lively conversation. They were French and there were eight of them in all, including the musicians. It transpired that they all played in the band, different types of music on different nights in different clubs.

'And do you often ask strange men to dance?' one asked her.

'Oh, you're not that strange,' she said, unsure if he would get the wit behind her comment. But he did, and he laughed.

He introduced himself and then the others.

What had started as a jazz evening in the club turned into a singsong from different countries, with people at every table getting involved. The band was more than versatile, and appeared to know every tune that was suggested. Peter sang 'Waltzing Matilda', and Esme joined in the chorus along with several other guests.

'"You'll come a waltzing Matilda with me . . ."'

'How do you know that song?' Peter asked her across the table when he finished the last stanza.

'I don't know,' she said. 'It's one of those ones you hear along the way.'

'Now it is your turn,' said one of her dancing companions.

'Will you sing with me?' she asked. She usually shied away from anything like this, but the mood in the place was such that she was carried along with it.

The first song that came to mind was 'I Will Survive'.

She belted out the opening lines. It was a good choice because everyone knew it. She sang about her increasing strength and they all joined in. She could hear French accents around her as they sang with her.

Her innate shyness disappeared and she felt heady and happy as she led them, warm and uplifted almost to the point of fulfilment. She knew it was the wine and the men dancing and the feeling of belonging that was making her feel like that, and she savoured it, knowing also that it would pass and that she would be as she always was – slightly withdrawn, more than reserved.

'I haven't seen that side of you before,' Peter said as they walked, slightly the worse for drink, back to their hotel. He had his arm around her shoulder and she was feeling more relaxed than she had in days.

'That was such fun,' she said, laughing. 'I've never had my hand kissed by so many men.'

Even as she said it, she was embarrassed – was it so easy to please her? To be given a little attention – was that what she wanted? She didn't think so, and yet it seemed she did want that.

He spun her around and kissed her hard on her mouth, his tongue penetrating quickly and deeply. When he released her she couldn't open her eyes. She didn't know if it was the kiss or the drink but she felt weak in his arms.

'We should do this more often,' he said. And now she didn't know if he was referring to the kiss or to the evening, but either way it was all right. The moment was all right. She was all right. And she thought about the present, about the instant they were in, and how that was all that mattered. The past was behind her. Or so she liked to think.

They had another drink in the bar in the hotel as if to prolong the mixed sense of both comfort and tension between them before heading up to her room.

The following morning Jacob met Henry Delmont at the conference hall in the university and they brought their coffees to a quiet table in the corner of the restaurant nearby.

'It's a lot quieter here than in the restaurant last night,' Jacob said.

Henry smiled. 'I really enjoyed that place.'

'So, how are you really?'

'I'm fine. We both are, Sally and me. All is well. Now, ask me – you said there was something.'

'Yes. It is a coincidence that you are here at the moment,' Jacob replied. 'A coincidence because I was in Ireland at the time this happened, and you were there too. You might recall the name Molly Kilbride?'

'Of course I do,' Henry said. 'Who doesn't? I think anyone old enough to remember will never forget.'

'That's what I thought.'

'I should tell you now that you've come to the right person if you want to know something. I'm assuming this is a professional matter?'

'Oh, yes. It's to do with – well, a patient, I suppose,' Jacob said slowly. 'No, not quite a patient, but someone who has been confiding in me, and I am seeing this as a professional matter. She gave me the name Molly Kilbride and I believe she wants me to see something, although that something is not quite clear. What did you mean, I've come to the right person?'

'There are ironically two links here,' Henry replied. 'First of all my niece happened to have been Molly's best friend, and secondly I worked with Groucho. You do remember Groucho?'

Jacob smiled. Groucho was Harper Gumm, an American psychiatrist, who, for years, had been a leading light in the field in Ireland.

'I heard he died? Am I right?' Jacob asked.

'Dropped dead on a yacht in the Mediterranean in the middle of having sex . . . giving a whole new meaning to the term coitus interruptus.'

Jacob laughed again. 'Coitus terminus? There are worse ways to go,' he said.

'I'm damned sure there are,' Henry replied. 'But perhaps not from the partner's point of view. Groucho, you may remember, weighed a good twenty stone, if not more. A stiff on a ship,' he chuckled.

'Bit of a dead weight,' Jacob said, laughing again. 'How do you know all of this?'

'I was on the yacht,' Henry said.

'Where is this leading to?' Jacob suddenly asked.

'It's leading to Molly Kilbride,' Henry replied, spooning sugar into his cup and stirring it. 'Molly Kilbride was a patient of Groucho's. She was given the top dog way back whenever . . .'

'Oh, I see,' Jacob said. 'Groucho? Well, he was the best,' he added reluctantly. 'At the time.'

'And the reason I know so much about the whole thing is because Groucho left me his files,' Henry said.

'Did he? Why?'

'He always said he had many disciples but only one apostle – and I was that apostle.'

'I'm trying to decide if that is praise or not,' Jacob said.

'Well, it worked out as a bonus,' Henry replied wryly. 'At least as far as you are concerned – because I know everything there is to know about Molly Kilbride.'

'Do you know where she is now?'

'Sorry. I am grossly exaggerating. I meant I know everything there is to know about what happened to her – at least, to put that more succinctly, I know what Groucho pieced together.'

'But did he piece *her* together?'

Henry shrugged. 'Can you piece someone together after what happened? I don't think so. I'm curious, though. You said someone gave you Molly's name. Molly herself?'

'I don't think so. The person – woman – does not fit the description of Molly. My – let's call her my patient, for want of a better word at the moment – my patient has blonde hair and green eyes. The hair could be dyed . . . she could be wearing contact lenses. I'm hoping not. That's the best I can say. Now, tell me about your niece.'

'My niece, Jennifer – she is the daughter of my older brother – she was in class with Molly in school; they were friends,' he continued. 'They spent a lot of time together, and in fact the pair of them went to live in Germany.'

'Jennifer?' Jacob said in surprise.

Two representatives from the Danish contingency interrupted them at that point, and when they had finished the courtesies it was time for Jacob to prepare for the introductory remarks.

'Look,' Henry said to him, 'there won't be time now to talk. Maybe I should phone you when I get back to London.'

'I'm wondering, Henry, if I could have a look at that file you said Groucho left you?'

'I don't see why not,' Henry said slowly. 'It's a professional matter, you said. You were my lecturer once . . . You will treat it with full confidentiality?'

'Of course.'

'I'll send it to you.'

Jacob wanted to know more immediately, but there was nothing he could do, only nod in agreement and utter his thanks, and so Esme was put on hold while the conference got under way.

CHAPTER ELEVEN

Jacob Althaus had made his brief opening address, welcoming the delegates and inviting them to lunch. There followed a long afternoon before he came to give his public talk on the role of memory.

'I will tell you of an interesting patient who wanted my advice,' Jacob began. Such words had become his opening catchphrase over the years.

'He told me how he had made a very unusual time machine. His time machine could only go back in time, and never forward into the future. He had almost no control over where his time machine went, and no choice about when he stepped into his time machine.

'Put like that, it sounds like the stuff of science fiction. But we all of us have a time machine just like his, the time machine that is our memory.

'Just occasionally, we choose to commit something to our memory. It may be a phone number, or a name, or the date of a birthday. Indeed, I once met a man who could memorise the order of a whole deck of cards that had been shuffled and shown to him for a mere minute. But only a small minority of memories are formed in this deliberate way. The rest we just find there. Memory, like many of the powers that occupy the mind, is not under our conscious control. In so far as we possess a time machine in which we can travel back to the past, it is an unpredictable and unreliable one. Memory in that respect is much like expectation. When we see a series of events we do not choose what to expect will happen next – our expectation just happens to us, it just appears. And likewise, we do not often choose what to remember. Instead we smell a smell or hear a sound and are taken back, way back to where we were and who we were with when last we smelled that smell, or heard that sound.

'As psychiatrists, as doctors of the mind, it is critical that we understand as much as we can about the power of memory. Many patients have troubles based in their memories of the past, and, if we are to help, it will be by understanding the power of memory. A poet once said that God gave us memory so that we could have roses in December. If we can have roses in December, though, we can also have frostbite in June.

'To understand memory we must understand perception. It is widely accepted that our everyday perception does not consist in pictures of the world imprinting themselves on to our minds, as they might do on to a camcorder. Rather, our perception is theory driven. How we experience things depends not only on what things are there to be experienced, but also on the beliefs and expectations we bring to the situation. So when a patient speaks of their memories do not suppose that they are describing to you events that happened to them. They are describing their perception of events only, and your job as a psychiatrist often involves trying to separate what was really seen from the cognitively driven aspects of the experience.

'As psychiatrists we often encounter patients who are traumatised by memories of events past. We will, of course, urge the patient to forgive and to move on. But I wish to discuss today what that actually means. It does not mean that the patient can edit or delete some film they are carrying around in their mind. Forgiving does not erase unpleasant memories of the past; that would be to suppose the memory is under our conscious control in a way that it simply is not. A healed memory is not a deleted memory. Instead, forgiving what we cannot forget creates a new way to remember. We try and change the patient's memory of the past into a hope for the future.

'None of us can change our memories, and none of us can erase them. But it does not follow that there is nothing of value we can do. A memory, like any perception, is part theory driven but also part experience driven. If we as psychiatrists can discover which part is which, we open the possibility of changing the theory-driven aspect of the memory and neutralising it. The aim is never to erase painful memories; it is to reinterpret them as part of a new view of the world in which the patient might flourish. We help the patient to create a new narrative, and in this respect psychiatry is more artistic, creative and imaginative than many people realise . . .'

The human mind did select, but not always in the best interests of its owner. It was later, when he was going to bed, that Jacob found his thoughts going over his lecture and the subsequent questions from the floor.

'But the whole problem,' one delegate had said, 'is that if the unpleasant memories could be blended into a happier story courtesy of reinterpretation, the mind would already have done that on its own. Some memories just won't be reinterpreted in the way you suggest.'

'In that case, we must become better novelists and imaginers than the patient,' Jacob had replied with a wry smile. Whilst he meticulously avoided the personal in his responses, he did keep the cases to which he referred as anecdotal as possible. But, of course, the personal was relevant in his arrival at his conclusions. How could that not be?

He had been forced to come to terms with memories he would sooner forget while puzzling over events that must have happened but of which there was no memory whatsoever – like the number branded into his arm. But he did have memories of the transit camp in which he had found himself when the war had ended, unsure of how he had arrived there, unsure of anything prior to that other than sound and smell. God knew, if he could have just obliterated things, deleted them from his memory, he would have done so. Sometimes the smell of bleach conjured up a room filled with children – mostly silent, mostly staring vacantly or hopefully . . . he had seen that hopeful look on people's faces all his life and knew that the memory it conjured up was, in fact, the hope he had once felt, waiting to be selected, to be given a new start in his hitherto miserable life.

And he had been selected.

A long journey had followed of which he had little memory and then the arrival in Paris and the new life with a new family. A father, a mother and an older sister, Jacqueline. She, like he, had been adopted, though in her case she had come from Belsen when the war ended, a skeletal reminder of the callousness and brutality of human nature.

His adoptive parents were French and the household was multilingual, with French and Yiddish mixing easily, and a good smattering of English interwoven because his adoptive father had spent time in England during the war.

These parents were dead now, but Jacqueline and he kept in touch. She had married the boy next door, and he had grieved at her marriage because of the love he felt for her. Grieved – he thought about the word. Was it grief he had felt? Or a sense of loss or maybe rejection when she had started her new life? But then that was what it was all about – new beginnings all his life, starting in the comfort of a lavish German apartment, brutally taken from his parents and somehow surviving; then the transit camp with no recollection of how he had got there. Selection and adoption, then school, college, and university followed this – and there he had met Naomi.

He looked at her now asleep beside him in their large bed, and that sense of sadness he had earlier felt returned, and he slipped quietly from it and went to his study.

Settling down at his computer he wrote to Jacqueline, a short email asking her how she was and her children, hoping that 'the boy next door' was still behaving himself – he smiled as he wrote that because he had no doubt that Louis was behaving himself. He couldn't imagine Louis doing anything else.

And then he emailed Esme, which was the real reason he had got up out of bed. He had hoped that she might try to call him some time during that day but he had checked with his secretary and had also rung in to his voicemail, and there had been nothing from her.

'I was thinking about Molly Kilbride,' he wrote. 'I remember the story. Please make contact. My very best wishes, Jacob.'

Purposefully, he logged in to his search engine and brought up Molly Kilbride once again.

The photo gave nothing away. Just a little girl, in fuzzy black-and-white with a plain face, neatly attired in some school uniform. The description given was of a child with large grey eyes, and dark brown hair – a gentle girl, her school principal was quoted as saying. Intelligent, witty, sporty, full of fun . . .

He remembered those days when the autumn sun shone through the panes of his room in Trinity, and like many people long ago he had scanned the papers daily, following the trail to nowhere of the missing child. And he remembered too a further conversation with Naomi in their small Dublin flat when she had spoken about the kidnapping, and he had slapped his hand on the newspaper, with a sense of frustration at the awfulness of what had happened to the little girl, and said, 'One more reason not to have a child.'

He knew that what he had felt about Molly Kilbride back then had stirred other thoughts and memories about his own parents – what had they felt when they said goodbye to him, if indeed they had said goodbye to him? There was no memory of that at all.

It would have been different for Molly Kilbride. She would recall more, he thought. She would have difficulty forgetting what she would be better off not remembering. The grey-eyed Molly Kilbride.

He brought up Esme Waters on his search engine. There were a couple of photographs of her. Her green eyes were not clear in them, but her neatness was. It was the way he thought of her, that particular tilt of her head, the tidiness of her hair, pulled into some kind of roll on her head, her wide full lips. He flipped backwards and forwards between the photographs of Molly Kilbride aged thirteen, and Esme Waters in her early forties. It was the tilt of the head that was the only similarity. But it was enough.

Usually he was coldly and calculatingly removed from his work, from the cruelties he heard about, from the little or great abuses that destroyed people's confidence and sometimes their will to live. His childhood had been such that he was inured to much of what he heard. But not to this. Now he felt a sense of horror such as he had not felt before. He had to push it aside, this feeling of horror, and force himself to think about her in as detached a way as possible.

None of Esme's interviews contained anything of the personal. They were all related to her work, her castigation of the abuse of power and the innocent victims of crime, the need continually to review what amounted to morality.

Vociferous, he thought. She protests aloud about these things, she writes about them with what one reviewer referred to as 'enormous empathic insight'. He realised he saw her as a victim, as indeed all his patients were victims of one sort or another, but she was a victim who categorically denied victimhood. He remembered a conversation with her to do with the randomness of existence and the pure bad luck of being in the wrong place at the wrong time. He recalled noting her emphasis on the randomness of all things but had not pursued it. Now he wondered if there had been more to that comment than she appeared to have given.

Jacob recalled the first time he had seen Esme. He remembered her streak-blonde hair, her neat appearance in some expensive outfit, the expression of the utmost calm on her face, the care she took in not spilling the coffee she had brought out from the café, and then the moment she had seen the spider on the table, how she had abandoned both the coffee and her handbag while she took care of the spider. He remembered clearly the moment's animation as she looked at it in her hand.

And then later: 'I cannot sleep. And I want to.'

Of course she could sleep. But her sleep was so troubled that she often preferred to stay awake. Her nightmares were like demons that drove her to the brink of exhaustion, and when she slept she inevitably woke in a state of terror.

'There are monsters in my mind,' she said, and he knew

she was waiting to see how much she could expose, and how safe it would be to do so. He had no idea why she was telling him this, and could only assume that she had reached a point in her life when she had no further choice. And slowly her story had unfolded. He thought of that now, remembering how she sometimes spoke in the third person. It was as though she had disconnected from each of the people she saw herself as once having been.

He could not get her out of his mind.

In London, Rose van der Vloed was thinking about Esme too. She was thinking how she missed her. She was sorry now she had not gone with her to France, even for one week, because she would have liked the time with her. It would have been company during this rather long and tedious summer.

Coming into the apartment now after a day's work at the hospital, Rose checked her mail before putting on water to boil some pasta. She was tired and frustrated. Despite what she had implied in a previous email to her mother about enjoying her work, this was in fact untrue.

She was unsure if she had perhaps enjoyed it in the first few days before the sad reality of hopelessness sank in. She admired the other staff in the ward in which she was working – their enthusiasm and their optimism – and while she had gone into her summer job with both of these attributes, she felt they had been knocked out of her over the last few days. Her supervisor had reassured her that what she was doing was of value, but she was not so sure. The ward on which she was working was a psychiatric unit.

Some twenty men and women of varying ages and backgrounds were locked up there behind two heavy doors. No razor blades, no scissors, nothing sharp was allowed in. No shoe laces, no belts – nothing with any length or strength.

She now hated the work. She hated the combination of the neediness of the patients and their apparent uselessness, and the knowledge that anything she might do there would be fleeting. Most of it made her feel ineffectual.

It was difficult to tell the age of the patients. Some looked little more than children, some looked old beyond their years. She hated the knowledge of the bleakness of their lives, of their lack of prospects, of the fact that they would live this life and sooner or later would die, and their beds would be filled by others – other sick, disabled, tragic people. Some would recover and go back to the real world, but some of them would not stay the course. There was pointlessness to it all. They each had their own room, and sometimes in the mornings when she went in, the staff nurse would say, 'Suicide watch, room . . .' and would tell them which room or rooms contained the potential death-threat for the day.

Some of the patients moved through the days in a drugged daze; others were hyperactive, talking incessantly, appearing to be on the point of hysteria. Rose hated that.

She was quick to identify that what she liked was the peaceful equilibrium of the home Esme had created in the London apartment, where thick carpets absorbed the impact of their feet on the floor, and they were encouraged to talk but in a calm and thoughtful way.

Rose had, however, formed a bond with one patient, a man in his mid-twenties. His name was Roland Duval, and Rose liked him. There was an intelligent gentleness in his face and a hunted look in his eyes. She had tried talking to him, but he preferred to sit by the window and have her read to him in the afternoons. He hid his problems better than many of the other patients. He did not belong to either those who ranted or talked incessantly, nor to those who were so withdrawn that they could not be reached. She knew that he was in bad shape having tried unsuccessfully to overdose on a combination of drugs that had left him weak, shaken and sick.

Softly spoken, well educated, he sat by the open window in his room with a cigarette in his shaking fingers, listening to her read to him. He was thin, almost to the point of emaciation. Smoking was only permitted in the common area, but Rose said nothing when he pulled out his cigarettes in his own room. She went and found matches for him in the staff room. Twice that afternoon, he had looked up at her and she had stopped reading, sure that he was going to say something. Twice he shook his head, and leaned back in his chair.

He reminded her of her mother. They both had, at times, a look of the utmost sadness. Rose always assumed her mother's sadness was to do with Arjen dying, and she wished so much her mother would talk to her about it.

She hoped her mother was all right. She worried about her because she felt there was something slightly naïve about Esme.

Rose switched on the computer and was pleased to see there was an email from her. Then she read the email and saw that her mother had been invited to Japan to appear on some programme.

Rose looked at this in horror. Undoubtedly the programme would consist of putting the participants through some unspeakable torture. Rose's knowledge of Japanese television also included Samurai films and sumo wrestling, but neither of these seemed to be a likely possibility in her mother's invitation. She was about to write back to advise her under no circumstances to agree to participate in such a thing. But then, in a moment's change of heart, she decided to say nothing and to let her mother find out the hard way.

Rose wondered what her sisters would think of her decision and if they would find it uncaring of her. Lily would probably think that those programmes were unfair on the bugs and insects involved, because they had no choice in participation, whereas at least the contestants knew what they were getting into. Well, most contestants – perhaps not Esme.

Jasmine, on the other hand, would want to know what the prize money was and what you should wear if appearing on such a show.

'Get your feet off the table,' Grayson Redmond, coming into the drawing room, drawled at his daughter. It was as close to a holler as he was ever likely to come, but his general tolerance with Jasmine was reaching its lowest ebb.

Moving her legs off the table on to the floor, Jasmine did not turn her head to look at him.

'Look who's back,' she said, staring at the curtain rail.

He looked up and there was the owl, perched on the rail, apparently asleep.

'Lily will be pleased,' Grayson said.

'Well, she won't get to see it,' Jasmine said. 'She phoned to say she's going to stay up in Alaska or wherever she is.'

'Oh? Alaska? I thought she was in Canada. What's she up to?' Grayson asked.

'Oh, you're right. I think it is Canada. Anyway, she was all whispery and excited. I bet she's met someone.'

Grayson came over and tousled her hair.

'Don't do that, Dad,' she yelled. 'It took me hours to straighten.'

'But you have straight hair,' he pointed out, slight puzzlement in his voice. 'I don't know what the world is coming to . . . people with straight hair straightening it, people in the wilds of wherever, tracking geese, staying there, instead of coming back here. Never mind. Do you want to play golf later?'

'I don't know what the world is coming to,' she imitated him. 'People playing golf wanting to play more golf . . .'

'You sound like your mother,' he said with the mildest of annoyance.

'Well, how come it's all right for you to comment on me straightening my hair?' she asked.

'Maybe your mother was right and you should get a job for the summer,' he responded.

The owl opened one eye and stared at him.

'Maybe Mum was right and you should get a job,' Jasmine snapped at him, and getting up, she flounced out of the room, slamming the door.

He and the owl looked at each other and then he shrugged.

'I don't blame you for leaving your nest or wherever you live. I'd go and sit on a curtain rail in your home if it gave me a bit of peace and quiet,' he muttered.

The owl appeared to change the position of its shoulders and Grayson could not help wondering if it was shrugging.

Jasmine was infuriating of late. He had been through similar phases with both Lily and Rose. Lily's rebellion had been mild and had really only involved filling the house with animals. Rose's had been angrier, grumbling when she was going to the Netherlands to visit her father's family, and grumbling even louder when she came back to Charleston. She could never decide where she wanted to be. But it was Jasmine's insolence and indolence that was driving him mad. Silently he cursed Esme for letting Jasmine come to him for the summer, pushing aside the fact that Esme had not wanted Jasmine lying around the plantation, vegetating and thinking about her nails, which was how Esme had put it.

He forgot the conversation on the phone in which Esme said, 'She's at that awkward age. She should be doing something constructive, not being indulged by one of her parents.'

'Just because you don't want to indulge her,' Grayson had

said, 'it doesn't mean that I can't. She's my daughter too and she wants to come here, so why shouldn't she?'

This was probably the closest he and Esme had ever come to having a row.

He had forgotten Esme's reluctant adherence to his wishes and now blamed her for the disruption to his life. He had no memory of excusing Jasmine's behaviour by saying she was going through a phase. And Esme's somewhat sharp rejoinder, 'A phase that lasts for four years is a personality disorder.'

He loved Jasmine, enjoyed her company when she was having a good day, but those days were few and far between just at the moment. Instead, there she was, either with her feet up on the table staring at an owl, or else locked in her bathroom doing God alone knew what for hours at a time and yelling, 'Go away, Dad,' through the door when he tried to encourage her to go horse riding or to come down to the Club.

He was sorry Lily wasn't coming down from wherever she was. That girl had a modicum of sense, he thought, except for her interest in wild animals. Why she couldn't have a kitten or a puppy like other girls, he really did not know. He was damned sure no one in the Club had incubated an alligator's eggs in their laundry room or wherever the hell it was Lily had put them.

He poured himself a shot of bourbon from the decanter on the side table and sitting back on the sofa recently vacated by Jasmine, he put his feet on the table and surveyed the owl that was keeping a single eye well focused on him.

He suddenly remembered his mother was coming to dinner and he wondered what were the chances of her not noticing the new resident. He would have to say to Jasmine not to look up in case his mother checked to see what was there.

If it wasn't one problem, it was another. That his father was also coming to dinner did not perturb him in the slightest. Neither his father's eyesight nor his comments were anything like his mother's.

In her room, Jasmine kicked off her sandals and flung herself on her bed. She didn't know what she wanted to do. Golf had been fun the previous year but this year it held no attraction for her. The heat outside was unbearable, even in the evening. She felt she could hardly breathe, and any energy expended outdoors left her dripping with perspiration and just wanting to lie down. She envied Lily somewhere up in the north of Canada and Rose in London. Everywhere else seemed to be a better place to be. There was the added irritation that her mother had said to her that Charleston in the summer was not really the most comfortable place to be. She wondered where she would be when she was Lily and Rose's age, and wished her grandparents lived somewhere sensible like the Netherlands or Germany. She didn't think that Esme would be too pleased if she rang her and asked for rescuing although she felt that her father might not mind.

Everything she did irritated him. She could feel that. Why she couldn't sit quietly in the drawing room looking at the owl made no sense. She was doing no harm. Neither was the owl. It was years and years since the owl had mysteriously arrived one day and shortly afterwards left one night. They had come down in the morning and it was gone. She was quite sure it was the same one that had returned. And she couldn't blame it. If she were an owl she too would find a curtain rail in a large air-conditioned house and would sit there until winter.

She rolled over on her back. Time hung heavily on her hands. She thought of getting out her pet, but it meant getting off the bed and going over to the aquarium at the other side of the room.

She wished Lily were coming down to join them. Sometimes she hated Lily because Lily seemed always to know what she was doing. But once she heard Lily saying to Rose that she wished they were like other families. Although that now did not make much sense. What were other families like? Many of her friends at school had two sets of parents, although, as Lily had said, did they know anyone else with three sets? Grayson called Lily's father the Sour Kraut, which sounded wonderfully rude. He was careful not to say it in front of Lily, but Jasmine had told her. She was sorry afterwards, though. She had only been trying to annoy Lily. She had not meant to upset her. Sometimes she found that she said things that really upset other people even though that was not what she had intended. Lily had gone really pale and said, 'Did he really say that?'

She wanted to backtrack then, but couldn't think how. Rose said quickly, 'He wasn't talking about Günter. He was talking about food. Cabbage . . . pickled . . . you know . . . Saur Kraut.' But Lily must not have believed her because she got up and left the room.

Anyway, what did her sisters know about anything? It was all right for them. They were both in university and were allowed to make decisions for themselves. No one told them what to do.

Someone was always bossing her around. Like Grayson telling her she couldn't take the car, which was ridiculous. If you were allowed to drive when you were sixteen, what difference did a bit earlier make anyway? None whatsoever. He had rattled on and on about insurance as if she were likely to have an accident or drive hard into someone else's car. It wasn't her fault that Mr Kimble had such a large car that it stuck out of its parking place at the Club and she had clipped his wing. Mr Kimble wanted to report her to the police but didn't because he said Grayson was such an upstanding member of the community and a real southern gentleman, that he didn't see why his name had to be dragged through the mud just because Jasmine was out of control. Mr Kimble was President of the Club and thought that made him more important than other people.

Anyway, Grayson had paid for the damage, hidden the car keys from then on, grumbled at her until he was bright red in the face and refused to give her all of her pocket money that week.

Lily had once said that the problem about being brought up in so many different households was that the rules kept changing and it was difficult to remember what was acceptable in one place and not in another. Which was probably true, except that the rules on driving cars were pretty much the same wherever they were. Only in the States you could do it earlier. She wondered where her father had hidden the keys. She had not bothered to look for them because two weeks ago it didn't seem worth the trouble and she hated being shouted at. But now . . . well, now . . . she thought that if he went down to the Club he would probably take his filthy great Cadillac and she could take the convertible. If she knew where the keys were.

And on top of all her other problems, her grandparents were coming to dinner. Which used to be fun but wasn't any more. Gramps would give her twenty dollars probably, but would then give her a lecture on the stock market and she didn't really know what he was talking about, but then again Rose said he didn't really know what he was talking about either.

Grandma would ask when was Esme coming back, which always made Jasmine uneasy because her mother had never implied that she was coming back and it was years and years since she had left anyway, so it didn't seem very likely that Esme would have a sudden change of heart and think that hot old Carolina was the place to be. But Jasmine didn't know if Grandma knew that Esme was gone that long or if she was trying to needle someone – either Jasmine or Grayson, it was unclear which. Then Grandma would say in the next breath, was there any sign of the tiger, and that always made Grayson uneasy and he would shift in his chair and try to change the subject but you couldn't change the subject with Grandma as she stuck to it like superglue.

Jasmine hated superglue. She had once taken a tube of it from her father's desk, not realising that super meant super, and when she stuck her fingers together, having dripped glue on to his desk and then stuck her fingers to the desk, he had been really very annoyed. And when he finally got her fingers off the desk some of the surface was removed with them and he had to have something done to it called French polishing, which was really ridiculous because a bit of paint would have done the job.

She wondered what it was like tracking geese. In fact she wondered what it was like wanting to track geese. She had seen a photo of Lily in a pair of dirty shorts looking really very awful, which was surprising as Lily was so pretty and had such nice hair that she couldn't imagine why someone who looked like that would want to look so minging. But maybe really pretty people going around looking muddy sort of balanced things in the world a bit because it wasn't fair they were so pretty to start with anyway. And why Rose would want to work with people who were crazy was beyond her too. She imagined it was like being with Grandma only worse. Not that Grandma was actually crazy, but the way she behaved made you think that she might be because anyone normal would surely not wear a pale blue tracksuit when their bottom was so large, even if she was one hundred and four or whatever Gramps said when she had asked him how old he was. Gramps had said, 'I'm a mere seventy-five but your grandmother is one hundred and three,' and that was last year so she must be one hundred and four although she didn't look older than Gramps.

He had also said, 'Don't tell your grandmother I told you her age. She likes to be discreet about things like that.'

Why Grandma would want to be discreet about her age was another puzzling matter as she wasn't discreet about anything else.

Grayson had once said that discretion was nine-tenths of the law but Jasmine didn't know what that meant. But maybe that wasn't what he said anyway.

She wondered again where he could have hidden the car keys. The house was so big that she didn't know where to begin to look, but then it might be like playing hunt the thimble, which she had played at Darling Baby's party the previous year. Darling Baby was one of the kids at the Club. Anyway, it hadn't really been hunt the thimble, it was hunt the dildo, which was just like hunt the thimble, only it was teenagers playing it, and they weren't hunting for a thimble.

She wondered why someone would christen a child Darling Baby. Did they not realise that Darling Baby would grow up and be really horrible? Darling Baby should have been christened Nasty Teenager but then maybe her parents had thought that she would always stay as a darling baby, which is maybe what she was when she was born. But then they had christened their first child Skylark. What kind of a name was that? It might be okay if Skylark was a Native American because they had interesting names. But no, he was Skylark. She wouldn't call one of her children stupid names, if she had children. She wasn't sure if she would have children because she wasn't sure if she would know how to look after them properly. She didn't think it was right that she had two sisters with different fathers but then it was better than being Darling Baby and Skylark because they had the same father and he was awful. And so was their mother. Whereas at least she and Lily and Rose all had Esme as a mother and Esme was nice, even if she was a bit difficult to understand sometimes. And Grayson was a good dad except when he was shouting at her about her feet or the car. And Lily said her dad, Günter, was okayish – but only 'ish' because you couldn't talk to him about anything. And anyway, she was glad he wasn't her father because he had hurt Esme, whereas Grayson had never done that. She had heard Lily telling Rose about Günter hurting Esme. And Rose had said, 'That's awful.'

Rose had never liked going to the Club. Jasmine used to think that was silly of her because the Club had been great then, but now she didn't like it much – not unless Skylark was there. Skylark was called Thrush, Nightingale and Blackbird in school. Darling Baby had told her that. But Skylark said he didn't mind when she asked him once. He was sixteen. Sixteen was a nice age. She would be sixteen soon, but then he'd be seventeen. She wondered what it would be like being kissed by him. Darling Baby would be sixteen too. A really nasty teenager. Darling Baby would probably have a birthday party. Down at the Club. Maybe she would get to kiss Skylark then. At the Club. At Darling Baby's party. That was how she knew Darling Baby and Skylark. From the Club.

It was the problem about going to school in Europe, as Grandma called it. Really Europe was an enormous place made up of loads of different countries, not like America, which was an enormouser place but only made up of States. Grandma said she had been to Europe once and Jasmine had said to her, 'Whereabouts in Europe?' and Grandma had looked puzzled. 'The Hilton,' she'd replied, in a tone of voice that implied that was obvious.

Going to school in Europe meant that Jasmine didn't know many people in Charleston any more except from the Club, but Grandma said they were the right kind of people anyway. Rose said that there was no right kind of people because that implied there was a wrong kind of people. Esme had said to Rose that she was absolutely right but that it might be easier to keep certain opinions to herself when Grandma was around. Jasmine wondered briefly which of them was right – Rose for wanting to argue, or Esme for taking the quieter approach. Her mother never confronted anything. She always skirted around things and let other people get away with shit although she could talk for hours on topics of no interest whatsoever. Jasmine knew that her mother hated arguments long before Rose said it.

Rose didn't like Grandma. Jasmine knew that. But then Grandma didn't like Rose. You could see it sometimes in the way she said things. And she always said to Rose, 'What's that place you're from, honey?' Rose said that if there was any justice in the world Grandma would be sold into the white slave trade, whatever that was. She muttered it under her breath. Usually Jasmine repeated things that other people said to see the reaction. It was a good way of finding out the meaning of something by seeing how people responded. But she decided not to repeat that comment of Rose's. Not to Grandma, anyway. Rose really had enough problems with Grandma without adding to them. And Rose didn't have a father so Jasmine was kinder to her than she would otherwise have been. Lily's father, Günter, was an awful bollocks. Rose said that but asked Jasmine not to repeat it.

Rose had said to her that there were different types of people in the world and that she, Jasmine, would want to make an effort that she didn't fall into a particular category.

'What do you mean? That I'm a snob?' Jasmine said.

'No,' Rose responded vehemently. 'It is to do with worrying that you might end up like Grandma.'

Jasmine had looked at her.

'I'm sorry,' Rose said. 'I shouldn't have said that.'

There was a tacit agreement between the three of them that they would not tease each other about their different families, although it was sometimes difficult not to as they laid themselves open to comment.

'I don't mind,' Jasmine said. 'Anyway, I won't be like Grandma when I grow up.'

'You'd better not be,' Rose said. 'Because if you are I sure won't be visiting you.'

Jasmine looked mildly sulky because she liked being with Lily and Rose. She wished one of them were there now because if they were, it would diffuse dinner with Grandma and Gramps.

CHAPTER TWELVE

In the South of France, Esme lay at the edge of the bed, damp and silent. Peter had rolled off her on to his back and promptly started snoring, his body splayed in the position of the Da Vinci man, legs and arms stretched out, occupying most of the bed. Esme lay there for some ten or fifteen minutes, nothing really going through her mind other than the slightest feeling of rejection. She had tried telling him that she would quite like some post-coital charm, but he had laughed and said, 'A waste of time.' She did not see it like that. And wondered why men did. Why would any man think that it was adequate to woo a woman until he got her on to the flat of her back, or maybe her front, and then do with her as he wanted and promptly fall asleep, sometimes on top of her? Even a man with zero imagination must surely see that this was not necessarily the right way to get a woman to come back to bed with him again. Unless, of course, they had learned otherwise. And presumably they had. Because, of course, even when they did that, women kept coming back for more, enforcing their belief that it was perfectly acceptable to make love and then to pass out.

'Don't pull away,' she had said to Peter the second time they had made love.

'Just give me a moment or two of your attention before you fall asleep,' she had tried on the fourth or fifth occasion.

Then she had given up. She might as well be talking to a kangaroo, she thought, for all the attention he paid her after he had had sex.

Actually, she thought, a kangaroo might give her more attention afterwards because he would be so surprised. He would possibly postpone hopping off into the outback for at least two minutes while he readjusted his tail, or whatever kangaroos did. She would have sighed out loud but she was afraid of waking Peter. She wanted those silent moments now, having learned that he would not give her any personal time after he was finished.

Once in a newspaper she had read a report about a kangaroo that had been knocked down by two men in a Jeep. She remembered thinking they were probably drunk. Anyway, there was the kangaroo dead on the ground, and one of these fine men decided it would be funny to photograph the other with the kangaroo propped up against him. So they got out of the Jeep and they put a jacket on the kangaroo and, propping it up against one of them, the other took the photo.

And then the kangaroo turned out not to be dead, because it came round, took a look at them both and hopped off into the distance, still wearing the jacket, in the pockets of which was a wallet containing all their money, credit cards, driving licences and whatever else one travelled with in Australia.

The story had amused her then, and it amused her now. She wondered if by any chance Peter Carew might be one of those men. It wouldn't surprise her.

She decided to have a shower. She eased herself quietly from the bed and went into the bathroom, closing the door before pulling the cord that turned on both the light and the fan.

There were his clothes scattered on the floor just where he had left them when they had come into the apartment. She kicked them to one side of the bathroom floor. His wallet fell out of a pocket and, bending down, she picked it up.

Something made her open it, something to do with the kangaroo and other things. Maybe the fact that Peter had looked in her bag and checked out her passport. So she opened it, and slipped one card after the other out of its holder, glancing at them before returning them to their slot. The fifth card she pulled out caught her by surprise and in disbelief she sat down, holding it in her hand, the wallet, now forgotten, falling to the floor.

The card was for the Media, Entertainment and Arts Alliance and there was Peter's name on it. Another was an entry pass to a newspaper office. He was a journalist.

Why did he not say? Why did he leave her to believe he was a practising lawyer? Cold pinpricks of fear ran through her blood. He hadn't recognised her, she was almost sure of that. But the more she thought about it, the more uncertain she became. It was ironic that, having had a name that everyone knew when she was a child, she now had grown into someone whom people in a specific sphere instantly recognised. But she was sure it was nothing to do with the child she had been. It couldn't be. He couldn't have recognised her. Maybe he was just curious . . . she went out of her way to keep her privacy. She spoke only of her work when asked anything about herself. 'Only my work interests me,' she replied. She had once told a journalist to keep to the agenda, that he had no right to pry into her private life.

'My private life is just that – it's private,' she had said.

And that's how she kept it. Until now. It had been different for her as a child. She remembered too clearly the reporters when they reappeared just before her eighteenth birthday. Waking that awful day and finding they were outside the house, knocking on the door. She had seen them from her bedroom window and she had called for her father. 'Dad, Dad,' knocking on his bedroom door. And he wasn't there. She was alone in the house. And the fear that had dulled inside her was back. Where was her father? Why were the reporters there? And she had phoned her mother.

'I'm on my way over,' her mother had said. 'Just don't answer the door. Whatever you do, don't answer the door.'

Esme put the cards back in the wallet, briefly checking if there was anything more she should find there that might be of interest to her. There wasn't. She ran the shower and, getting in, she stood as the water washed Peter Carew off her skin.

She gave herself a few minutes to recover from the shock and then she started thinking about what to do. She feared that if she confronted him, she would get nowhere and he could write something about the time they had spent together. And yet if she did nothing, the situation would continue, and now she could not bear the idea of him touching her. It all seemed based on a lie.

She thought of how they had met at Nice airport, and slowly she realised that he had taken the lead from her. As she had handed in the address for her missing suitcase, it was he who had followed suit, expressing surprise that they were staying in the same place.

And when they arrived at the hotel, she now recalled vaguely there was some problem with his booking, but she had left him arguing this at reception while she went on up to her room. He, in fact, had encouraged her to go up to her room, asking if he could meet her for a drink later.

Oh, he had played her perfectly, she thought.

Now she needed to work out a way to handle him, so that he would not feel angry and rejected but compliant. She was always careful not to anger men.

*   *   *

Drying herself off, she put the wallet back in his pocket. In a moment of petty vengeance she dropped her wet towels on top of his things, but then changed her mind, fearing he might see that as being out of character, which, of course, it was.

Back in the bedroom she could not bear to get into the bed with him and she went instead and sat at the window. She wished they were spending the night in his room – that way she could just get up and leave. The chair was uncomfortable, but she found her eyes drooping with tiredness and she fell asleep.

In her dreams she feared the façade that covered her life would be undone. She dreamed tangled dreams wherein layers and layers of webs covered her and connected her to a myriad of other things. Clothing, apartments, furniture were all linked by this fine white gauze, so thin it was transparent, but so sticky it could never be disengaged.

Clammy and troubled, she woke in the morning to find Peter still snoring in the bed and her body stiff from the awkward position in which she had dozed.

Slowly, returning memory brought her back to the bathroom and the discovery in his wallet. In the cold light of day she contemplated how to handle him. She wished she were the kind of person who could simply stand up and shout, expose him for the fraud he was, yell at him for his manipulation, but in fact she was afraid. That cold edge of fear that had been with her most of her life was to the fore and she was aware of her inability to defend herself.

She needed to get away from him, but in such a way that he would not feel slighted. It disturbed her that she should have to approach things like that, but she knew no other way. She was afraid. Afraid of how he might expose her, what he might say about her, how she might appear. She was afraid of things that made no sense. She longed for safety, for comfort . . . for support. Had it ever been there, she wondered. In their own way, all the men had let her down, Günter by going off with her best friend, Arjen by dying, and Grayson – well, Grayson by just being Grayson. François in Paris – all these men, all her lovers – one way or another, they had slipped away from her or she from them.

She put on her swimsuit and a long white cotton dress over it, and slipped on her flat silver sandals. Quietly she put her book, glasses, and phone in her bag and let herself out of the room. She would stick to her behaviour of the previous weeks, give the appearance of there being nothing different, but she would be gone by nightfall at the latest. Now she needed coffee and a swim in the pool to clear her head and then she would find a way out of there, leaving it all behind her.

'Doing a runner', that's what Grayson would say if he were there. That's what he had said before. A runner. Well, who was he or anyone to judge what she should or should not do?

A double espresso ordered at the bar was brought out to her at the pool. She gave the appearance of settling on her sun lounger, as she did each morning. Everything was just as it should be if Peter happened to come out on to the balcony and look down at the pool.

After a while, she lowered herself into the water, and four lengths later her plans were made. She dried herself off. She would go to the airport and see where the next available flight was going – somewhere in Europe, with the sea, perhaps Italy. She was about to go back to the bedroom to tell him that she had been called back to London, when her mobile rang.

*   *   *

It was Lily. Lily, shaken and uncertain. Lily's voice breaking as she paused to catch her breath in between words. Lily with a sob in her throat.

'Mum . . . Mum . . .' She seemed to be searching for a way of saying something and at the same time trying not to cry.

'It's all right, darling, it's me. I'm here.' Esme's antennae were on full alert. There was clearly something wrong. All her maternal instincts were to the fore even as she felt, even as she feared that she would not be able to do anything. She could envisage her eldest daughter so clearly . . . Lily. Lily, tall and slim with her wispy fair hair, her long legs and strong but slender-wristed hands; Lily, with the courage to try out new things, to find new frontiers, to open locked doors; Lily, more comfortable with animals than with humans . . .

Her voice was shaky. 'Where are you, Mum?' she asked.

Esme, listening carefully to the voice, tried to find the emotion that was being hidden. 'I'm in the South of France,' she replied. 'But I'm about to leave here. Why? Tell me why.'

'Mum, I want to come home, but I don't know where to go to.' Lily's voice was biting back tears.

'To me or to your father?' Esme asked, still trying to ascertain what was wrong and how to handle it.

'To you,' Lily replied. 'He's away on holiday, in Hungary or somewhere . . . with Jennifer . . . Anyway, it's you I want to be with . . . if I may.'

'Of course you may,' Esme said. 'But please tell me what is wrong.' She tried to keep the anxiety out of her voice, gently trying to coax Lily into telling her what had happened.

'It's okay,' Lily said. 'It's nothing.'

She had retreated. Esme could feel it. She did not know whether to push a response from her eldest daughter or just to let it go. She knew she had heard real distress in Lily's voice, now carefully disguised. She also knew that if she put enough pressure on Lily she would crumble, but she wasn't sure if that was the wise thing to do with her daughter so many thousands of miles away. It might be better for Lily not to be pushed. Esme always feared that she did not know what was the best option, and now was no different. If Lily was on the verge of tears and frightened, should Esme be getting her help in Canada or waiting until they were together, by which time Lily might be all right again?

'I'm going to London,' Esme said, suddenly deciding.

'London . . .' Lily's voice sounded vague, as though the word meant nothing to her.

'Lily,' Esme was tentative, 'do you want to tell me what has happened?'

'I . . . I want to come to you.'

'You have tickets, don't you? For later in the summer. You need to change them. Can you do this?'

There was silence.

'Lily,' Esme tried again, 'I need you to listen to me. Whatever has happened – it will be all right. I can get Grayson to go to you immediately. He will be with you quicker than I can.'

'No, Mum.' Lily's voice was a little stronger, as though she was focusing better. 'I want to come to you. To London.'

'Can you give me your flight details and I'll get them changed?' Esme said patiently.

'No, it's okay. I'll be all right now. It'll be all right now . . .' Lily's voice trailed away. 'I'll go to the airport and do it there.'

'If you have any problem, phone me and I'll give them my credit card details,' Esme said. 'Lily,' she was cautious again now, 'have you been hurt?' She didn't know what she meant but it was the only way she could formulate the question to find out what had happened.

'It's all right, Mum,' Lily said. 'I . . . I got into a situation and I didn't know how to get out of it . . . I couldn't handle it. I know what to do now. I'll get to an airport . . . I'll come home. London.'

She would say no more, leaving Esme going over and over in her mind what might have happened to reduce Lily's voice to this quivering state. She felt it could not be to do with her work, because Lily had the tenacity and determination to stick with it no matter how gruelling or uncomfortable it might be. Tents and sleeping bags, stark hostels, lack of washing facilities – none of these things perturbed her eldest, whereas Rose liked to have access to at least the basics, and Jasmine needed luxury. Lily had no problem trekking with a heavy rucksack; Rose liked a case on wheels just as Esme did. And Jasmine, of course, would be more at home with a porter and a chauffeur.

That Lily had found herself in a situation she did not know how to handle was in itself worrying because somehow Lily always knew how to handle situations. She had an extraordinary equanimity and the ability to fit into unusual and new experiences without faltering. She did not think twice about trying something out, and entered into things, not so much with courage but with ease and zest. Esme knew that for someone else to do the things Lily did would require guts and audacity, but for Lily it was just part of her. So something must really have gone wrong for her to be on the verge of tears and wanting to come home.

It solved Esme's problem, though. Now instead of trying to find some lie to get herself away from Peter Carew, she could very legitimately say that she was needed in London.

She wondered what Rose would say when she found the apartment was not going to be hers alone any more. Rose would be glad to have Lily back, though. And whatever had happened to Lily, it would be better solved by being with her. It had to be. Even if she, Esme, could not help, Rose would.

Esme was heading towards reception to see about getting a flight out and to settle her account when the phone rang again.

It was Grayson.

Jasmine had found Grayson's keys. He had hidden them in the one place he thought she would not look – in her bedroom. Specifically in Taliban's aquarium in her bedroom. But he did not know she had an aquarium. Nor did he know she had a pet. Taliban was Jasmine's tarantula. A mouse-brown hairy fellow that she had found in Arizona and, thinking that it would equate her in some way with Lily, Jasmine brought it home in a box. Jasmine admired Lily's lifestyle, her predilection for wild animals, although she knew she would never have her sister's courage in that regard. But she hoped that a spider such as Taliban would attract Lily's attention and admiration when she finally met him. Having no real concept of how dangerous Taliban might be, Jasmine acquired an aquarium, collected crickets to feed him and kept Taliban in a style of which he had hitherto been unaware. Shredded cosmetic face pads and cotton-wool balls combined to make a comfortable bed. It was perhaps because of her complete ignorance of what she was dealing with, combined with the confidence of youth, together with being the sister of an animal lover, that Jasmine bonded with Taliban. And for whatever reason Taliban responded favourably to her attention.

Grayson, totally unaware that Jasmine had a tarantula in her bedroom, had gone in there looking for somewhere to hide the keys, assuming correctly that Jasmine would never look so close to home. Finding a large plastic container under a piece of cloth – Jasmine had the good sense to keep Taliban concealed whenever she was not in the room – Grayson dropped the spare keys into the box and covered them with a couple of stones. His fingers brushed against Taliban's back while he was doing this, but he did not know what he had touched and he left the room in ignorance. Taliban's reactions may not have been what they once were, due to too rich a diet.

Jasmine, having hunted for the keys for a while, was now bored. She took Taliban out to give him an airing. While he was sitting motionless on her pink bedspread, she decided to give the aquarium a spring clean.

It was then she found the keys.

Forgetting about Taliban squatting on the bed in surroundings where he was now fairly comfortable, Jasmine set off in the convertible, taking a spin in the direction of the hills and returning shortly after Grayson came back from the Club but in time for dinner with the grandparents.

Unfortunately, as Jasmine pulled back up the drive, she remembered Taliban sitting on her bed and wondered if she had closed her bedroom door. These thoughts distracted her and, as she pulled under the trees to park, she realised too late that Gramps's car was in her parking place. Despite putting her foot hard on the brake, she made contact, just as Grandma opened the door and had one foot on the ground.

Aaaargh, Jasmine thought. Jasmine often thought in onomatopoeic sounds to express her deepest emotions.

Gramps's car bounced forwards. Grandma, thinking that it was Gramps's bad parking and not realising that Jasmine had bumped them, screamed at him. Gramps, with reactions unusual for any man of his age, grabbed Grandma's arm and held her so that she did not fall out of the car.

Both were shaking as Grayson came running. His immediate concern for his aged parents was mixed with fury as he realised that Jasmine had been out in the car, which he had not missed as he had parked at the other side of the house.

A shouting match ensued, with Jasmine yelling that it was not her fault that Gramps had parked in her place.

'Your place? What do you mean, your place?' Grayson asked, bewildered.

'Gramps took my place,' Jasmine shouted back. She had never known how to accept being in the wrong and self-righteously stuck to her position. 'If he hadn't been there this wouldn't have happened.'

'If you hadn't stolen my car this wouldn't have happened,' Grayson reasoned as he hauled her out of the driver's seat.

'Now, now,' Gramps intervened, his voice a little shaky. 'No harm done.'

Secretly he was both proud and pleased with his own reactions. Grayson had recently been suggesting that he shouldn't be driving and this certainly showed his son that he was very capable behind the wheel.

'What happened?' Grandma asked. She seemed slightly dazed and also of late occasionally suffered from short-term memory loss. 'I thought we were going to visit Grayson for dinner.'

'You are, you are,' Gramps said. 'We're here. Here is Grayson.'

Grayson came around and helped his mother from the passenger seat.

'I'm so sorry, Mother,' he said. 'Are you all right?'

'Of course I am,' Grandma said, bemused. 'I'm well able to take a shower.'

'Mother, you're at Grayson's place,' Gramps said reassuringly.

'A drink is in order, I think,' Grayson said as he encouraged his mother to lean on his arm and walk towards the house.

'I'm not an invalid, you know,' she said, shaking off his helpful hand. 'I've no idea what is going on. I think it's dinner time.'

'I'll deal with you later,' Grayson called over his shoulder to Jasmine, who looked beseechingly at Gramps.

'I think you need some money to invest in the stock market,' Gramps said, reaching for his wallet in his pocket.

'I think she might need some money to fix your fender,' Grayson called again over his shoulder.

'He's so grumpy, Gramps,' Jasmine said to her grandfather, who was taking a quick look at the back of his car.

'No harm done,' Gramps said again. 'Well, not much, anyway. Nothing that money can't fix. Now, did you see how I saved your grandmother's life?' he asked proudly, as he flicked open his wallet and gave her thirty dollars. 'Now, that's for the stock market. And here's a couple of hundred towards the fender. That'll appease your father. Give it to me during dinner and say you're sorry and it will all be all right.'

Jasmine took the money and rolled it up, putting it into her shorts pocket. No way was she going to put any of it into stocks or fenders.

'Whatever you do, don't you look at that owl,' Grayson hissed at her as they went into the drawing room.

Jasmine scowled at him. She had had no intention of looking at the owl. In fact, she had forgotten the owl was there until he mentioned it. Now it was all she could do to keep her eyes off the curtain rail. She glanced quickly and sure enough, there it was sitting, one eye open surveying the proceedings.

Grandma sat back on the sofa. She was dressed in a champagne-coloured top over white trousers. Just above her enormous right breast was a decoration in the same dusty brown colour. It looked a bit like a large flower with wisps and tendrils spiralling in all directions. She took her glass of martini from Jasmine and sipped it gingerly.

'Is this dry?' she asked her granddaughter.

'Yes, Grandma,' Jasmine said, not having any idea what

type of drink Grayson had given her to pass to Grandma.

There was the slightest movement on the top of the curtain rail as the owl readjusted his position.

'I'm furious with you,' Grayson hissed at Jasmine.

'It's not my fault you put the keys in my room,' she objected. 'I assumed you wanted me to take the car out.'

'What's this? What's this?' Gramps asked. 'You put the keys in the child's room, Grayson. What do you expect?'

Grayson sighed. He despaired of the lot of them. Grandma, whose memory occasionally disappeared so that she had no idea where she was or what she was supposed to be doing, was now back, fully *compos mentis*, although she appeared to have no recollection of what had happened out in the yard.

'One of the great things about getting old,' she said re-assuringly to Jasmine, 'is that the boring bits of the day disappear. I have no idea how we got here, which is probably just as well as your grandfather drives the car like he would a helicopter.'

Jasmine laughed. She had an image of her grandfather hovering then speeding before some kind of crash landing, which is more or less what had happened.

She looked again at her grandmother and wondered for a moment if she was seeing double. Because there on her grandmother's ample bosom appeared to be a second large flower with tendrils.

Grandma at that moment reached up her hand, as though aware that there had been some change, and she adjusted her flower slightly before reaching for her martini glass again.

Jasmine's eyes opened wider in disbelief. Taliban was sitting on Grandma's shoulder, one long hairy brown leg reaching down to touch the tendrils of the flower, which might briefly look like something with which he could mate.

She was afraid to breathe. Grayson might not be too keen

on sharing his house with such a large spider. Grandma might have a heart attack. Gramps would, of course, go on talking about the stock market. She didn't know what to do. She was clutching a glass of Coke in her hand and she didn't dare to move in case Taliban was startled.

'What's that, honey?' Gramps asked, peering at his wife's blouse.

'My flower,' she said proudly. 'I thought you'd never notice it.'

Eeeek, Jasmine thought as Taliban moved an inch closer for further inspection.

Grayson said, 'What?' It was unclear to what he was referring. Jasmine wondered if she had spoken aloud.

At that moment the owl, whose vision was clearly better than any of the adults', raised his wings, let out an almighty shriek and flew with amazing speed towards Grandma. The martini went flying and it hit Taliban, who retreated at equally startling haste back over her shoulder and disappeared. The owl made a desperate attempt to remove the flower from grandmother's chest, momentarily mistaking it for the tarantula.

Grayson leaped to his feet to protect his mother.

Gramps said, 'I'd put my last dollar into oil if . . .'

Grandma screamed as the owl, puzzled and perturbed, returned to his curtain rail.

Jasmine realised she hadn't breathed since the event had started and suddenly exhaled.

Grandma happily suffered one of her senior moments at that point and said, 'What was I saying?'

Grayson looked at Jasmine and whispered aghast, 'For God's sake, did you see that?'

Jasmine, suddenly realising that there was no reason for him to connect her to the tarantula, tried to decide quickly if it would be better to deny having seen anything, or to admit to a shocking incident having just taken place. Unfortunately the look on her face gave her away.

'Do you know anything – ANYTHING – about that large hairy THING that was on your grandmother's shoulder?' Grayson asked. He was on his feet now. He kept his voice as low as possible as he didn't want to disturb his parent, who seemed oblivious to what had taken place.

'My word,' Gramps said. 'Is this an owl I see before me?'

'No, no,' Jasmine said. 'But I did see something. What was it, Dad?'

Grayson stared at her.

'It was an owl,' Gramps said with satisfaction. 'And it's now sitting on the curtain rail.'

Grandma said, 'Heavens above, I could have sworn something tickled my neck.'

A cautious inspection by Grayson reassured her there was nothing there. He looked apprehensively behind the sofa on which his mother reclined, empty martini glass in hand. There was no sign of anything.

'I think maybe if you go inside to the dining room . . .' he suggested uneasily. 'Jasmine, get my gun,' he added as he helped his mother to her feet from the comfortable depth of the sofa.

'Your gun?' Jasmine was aghast. 'Who are you going to shoot? You can't shoot the owl.'

'I'm not going to shoot the owl,' he said. 'I'm going to shoot that "thing".'

'Taliban? You can't shoot Taliban. He's mine.'

All three adults stopped and stared at her.

'You've joined the Taliban, dear? Now isn't that interesting,' Grandma said.

'What's going on?' asked Gramps, sensing a situation of which he ought to take control.

'Taliban!' Grayson croaked. 'Taliban!'

Jasmine ran to the sofa. 'You can shoot me first,' she yelled. 'You're not shooting Taliban.'

'No one is shooting anyone,' Gramps cried, leaping nimbly for one so elderly in front of his granddaughter, as Grayson abandoned his mother and produced the gun with amazing speed from his recently French-polished desk.

'Stand back, all of you. In fact, get out of here,' Grayson shouted.

'Son, put that gun down,' the old man said.

'Take my mother out of here,' Grayson replied. 'Get away from the sofa, all of you.'

'You're not shooting Taliban,' Jasmine wept. 'Let me find him. He's mine. He's my spider. He didn't do anything wrong.'

'Jasmine, he's the goddamnedest biggest spider I've ever seen,' Grayson roared. 'And he's not sharing my house.'

'Please, please let me find him. I'll put him back in his house,' Jasmine pleaded.

'What's for dinner?' Grandma asked, heading out the door.

'Grayson, put the gun down,' Gramps said in parental tones not to be ignored. 'Let the child look for her spider.'

'He's no mere spider,' Grayson shouted.

'Never mind,' Gramps said, pushing the muzzle of the gun aside. 'He's Jasmine's pet and he's done nothing wrong.'

'Nothing wrong!' Grayson shook his head in bewilderment. He wondered if he were mad or if they all were. 'That thing could kill her,' he said.

'It hasn't killed me yet,' Jasmine said. 'I've been caring for him since we went to Arizona – that's at least three weeks ago. He knows me. He's mine.'

'You can't own a wild animal.'

'Lily bred alligators in the cupboard off the kitchen,' Jasmine reasoned.

'But we got rid of them. Every last one of them. There are some things you can't have in a house.'

'We have an owl . . .'

'So you see,' Grayson said to Esme on the phone, 'it would be better for us all if Jasmine was with you for the rest of the summer.'

And that, thought Esme, was just what I suggested at the beginning of the summer. That, or that she got a holiday job.

'I'm on my way to London,' she explained. 'Send her there. I'll try and get her some kind of summer work. Hanging around the house is no way for a girl her age to be passing the time.'

'And the tarantula . . . ?'

'Tell her to release it over near the hills. I'm sure it'll thrive. I'll be in London by tomorrow, if not tonight. Rose is in the apartment there. Just get Jasmine on a flight. And might I suggest you calm down, Grayson.'

Esme had not followed the whole story as Grayson was both irate and inarticulate, and, like Gramps, she was amazed that he would hide the car keys in a tarantula's aquarium in Jasmine's room.

Jacob Althaus pushed his chair back into reclining mode and tried to get to sleep. He did not want to go back upstairs to Naomi and their bed, and he knew that if he went to the spare room she would be irked at what she would see as rejection. This way he could say he had fallen asleep at his desk. The images on the computer screen were still on his mind.

He wondered how Esme was, wondered what turmoil was in her mind now, or was she sleeping peacefully. He thought about her as they had sat outside the café beside his rooms and he missed the smile that lit up her face when he approached. He missed hearing her voice, her gentle questions, and her reminiscences. He closed his eyes.

When he woke it was to the phone ringing. It was Monique, his secretary, calling. She was concerned because he was running late. Glancing at his watch, he realised to his horror it was already a quarter to ten.

Racing upstairs, he wondered why Naomi hadn't woken him. There was no sign of her in the bedroom. He showered quickly and was out of the house in twenty minutes, trying to remember if Naomi had said where she was going that morning.

His secretary was waiting for him at the conference room in the university.

'Don't worry,' she said. 'Everything is running smoothly. They're in the middle of the first paper. I explained to anyone who asked for you that you were delayed in your rooms with a patient.'

'Thank you,' he said. 'I don't know what I'd do without you.'

'Mrs Delmont was looking for your wife.'

Now he remembered Naomi and Sally were going shopping.

'Did my wife turn up?' he asked.

'I don't think so. I didn't see her. Mrs Delmont went for coffee and said she would be back.'

That was odd. Naomi was the world's greatest shopper and it was surprising that she would miss the opportunity of showing a friend around.

'If Mrs Delmont comes back and is looking for Naomi,' he said, 'please tell her that my wife left before me this morning and that I'm not sure where she is. But if Naomi doesn't turn up, ask Mrs Delmont to join us for lunch. They will be breaking at one o'clock.'

*   *   *

The conference finished that evening at five and there was still no sign of Naomi. Jacob excused himself and went home early to find a note from her on his desk.

> I'm going to stay with my sister. I need time away from you. You might think I have that time all the time, but I don't. I'm always waiting. I'm tired of waiting. I'll be in touch.

He could hear her voice in the words, and the irritation, which of late was always so close to the surface; but reading deeper he could sense her sadness, and he despaired.

CHAPTER THIRTEEN

Now motivated and with her excuses ready, Esme organised a flight for herself for that evening. She went back to her room and began packing, moving swiftly and silently about her room, keeping one eye on the tousled heap in the bed. She had almost filled her bag before Peter awoke.

He looked surprised as he took in what she was doing. 'Going somewhere?' he asked.

She nodded. 'I've to get back to London,' she explained. 'One of my daughters – well, both in fact – but one in particular is in trouble and I've to get home.'

'I thought you didn't have a home,' he said, pulling himself up in the bed to watch her.

'I told you I've a place in London. It's where the girls are going. Rose is already there.'

'Rose is the Sociology student?' he asked.

'Yes, but she's not the one in trouble. Unless, of course, she is and I don't know.'

'That sounds like you're expecting the worst.'

'Of course I'm not. It's just that Lily, my eldest – the one who was tracking geese – she needs me.'

As she said it, the words surprised her. She did not think of her children needing her. She loved them with all her heart but was sure that they were who they were in spite of her, not because of her. That one of them might actually need her came as a surprise.

'What's happened?'

'I don't know. She wouldn't say, but she was distressed.'

'You said "both",' he prompted.

'By both I meant the two who aren't in London. I meant Lily and Jasmine. Jasmine is giving her father a hard time and he can't cope with her. So he's sending her to London.'

'Teenagers, huh!'

She thought of telling him about Taliban but changed her mind, as she did not want to give him any more insight into what was going on. There was something about Grayson's description of the tarantula checking out the flower on his mother's blouse that made her blood run cold, but she suspected if she heard the same story from Jasmine she would end up laughing. She did not want to tell any of this moment to Peter. She wanted to share nothing else with him. It was done. His deception left her cold.

'Have you time to come back to bed?' he asked.

'No,' she lied. 'I have to leave for the airport now. My flight is in two and a half hours' time. I have to get out of here.' And as far away as possible, she thought.

'Do you want me to come with you?' he suggested.

'No. I have to do this alone.'

'Am I going to see you again?' he persisted.

'I don't know, Peter. I just don't know. Right this minute I can't think further than getting to the airport and then to London to be there for the girls. Will you stay here?' she asked, as she put the final things in her case and went to check the bathroom for anything forgotten.

'I don't know what I'll do,' he said. 'I enjoyed being here because of you, you know.'

'But you were coming to stay here anyway when we met,' Esme said.

'Yes, but its attractions aren't quite the same now that you are departing.'

'Oh, you'll probably pick up someone else,' she said.

'Excuse me? What does that mean?'

'Just teasing,' she said lightly.

He had lied to her. She knew it. It was written all over his face in that one second before his usual comfortable mask reasserted itself. She thought of the journalist's card in the bathroom in his wallet and she wanted to confront him but could not think how to without having to handle some kind of argument that might get out of hand. She knew how good she was at fielding questions from the floor of a lecture theatre but how useless when things went wrong in her personal life.

It reminded her of that time when she had found Günter with Jennifer in their bedroom all those years ago and how she had run.

She left Peter, saying that of course they would keep in touch by email and that she hoped he would continue to have a good sabbatical. She avoided answering him when he asked for her address in London, saying she wasn't sure how long she would be there, then changing the subject. She knew that he was watching her closely as she eluded the question, but she didn't care. She was nearly gone now and the only way he could hurt her would be . . . she paused in her thoughts. Would be what? By the words he wrote? The way he portrayed her? Publicising the intimacies of their shared bed? But he wouldn't do that. Would he? It would end up saying more about him than about her.

She let him kiss her on the cheek and bring her bags down to the taxi, hovering while she checked out, and waving as the taxi pulled away from the doors. She glanced out the window at him, and what she saw in his face made her think momentarily of Grayson. There was kindness there, and also concern.

'I'll email you,' he called.

And then the taxi pulled away.

Long hours awaited her in Nice airport as she had lied about the time of her flight. Long hours to sit with her book, half reading, half thinking, pondering she knew not what – Lily upset in Canada, Jasmine undoubtedly argumentative in South Carolina, Rose in London, working in the hospital.

The time passed slowly. In the early evening she rang Jacob's office number on the off chance that he might be there. She got his voice mail. But he must have checked for messages because shortly afterwards her mobile rang, and it was he.

'Jacob,' she said. Her voice faltered and she could hear overtones of Lily's voice in her own – an echo of someone looking for help although not sure if help was to be had.

'Esme,' he replied. 'I got your message. How are you? In fact, where are you? That sounds remarkably like an airport in the background again.'

A flight was being called and Esme waited until the sound abated before admitting that yes, she was, once again, in an airport.

'Where are you going?'

She explained about Lily and how she was needed. Then she told him about Jasmine and the tarantula.

Jacob laughed. 'I'm sorry,' he said. 'I can see that this tarantula only adds to your problems, but it is funny. Did he manage to shoot it?'

'I really hope not,' Esme replied. 'Jasmine is the most unforgiving sort. Anyway, I don't think he did shoot it, because when I suggested she released it out near the hills, he grunted and sort of agreed, which implies that Taliban – can you believe the name? – was alive and kicking.'

Jacob laughed again. 'You are making this all sound like a very funny tale but – forgive me if I'm wrong – did something else happen?'

She told him then about Peter Carew and the Media, Entertainment and Arts Alliance card in his wallet and how he had lied to her.

'Is there any chance that he is a member of this Arts Alliance, and has access to a newspaper office because he does a bit of legal journalism?' Jacob asked after a moment's thought. 'You did say he was a lawyer or some kind of legal eagle, didn't you?'

'Yes. He is. And I did think of that,' she said. 'But the more I thought about how I met him, the more I felt that there was something not quite right about it.'

'He could have lied in the airport when you both lost your cases simply because he saw the opportunity to seduce a beautiful woman.'

'I'm not beautiful,' Esme said.

'It's in the eye of the beholder, remember,' Jacob said.

'I'm just me,' Esme said.

'I know,' Jacob replied. 'That's what I meant.'

There was a pause. He wondered what she was thinking – whether it was to do with what he had said and, if so, had it unnerved her, or was it about what lay ahead of her? He wished he could see her face. That calm that she maintained most of the time in public disappeared when she was with him and he could see the movement of thought in her head through her eyes. What he meant by that he was not sure, but he knew that she came to life in some different way when she was with him. Of course he had seen her with François once, and also that first morning in the café, and there was something both isolated and aloof about her then. A self-containment that dissipated when he and she drank coffee together of a morning, and when she let him inside the protective armour behind which she lived most of her life.

'You gave me a name,' he said.

There was silence from her although he could clearly hear the busy humdrum background noises in the airport.

'Are you still there?' he asked.

'Yes.' She could be replying to either observation or question.

'I remember the name,' he continued. 'Molly Kilbride. I was in Dublin at the time . . .'

'I see.'

'You regret giving it to me?'

'Regret?' She mused on the word. She did not usually regret things. She saw no point in looking backwards at all, for the past could not be changed. She said as much. 'The past is as it is. We can't change it.'

'Change it? No,' he replied. 'But understand it. The past can be understood.'

Another flight was called. There was increased background noise as people shifted from their seats and hurried each other along.

'It's difficult to talk here,' she said. Someone had just come and sat beside her.

'I don't suppose there is any chance of you coming through Paris?' he asked.

'I can't,' she said. 'I had difficulty enough getting a flight to London today, and I need to be there for my girls. I should go,' she added.

'Go with one thought,' Jacob said. 'The amount of times you have said to me that you think you are not a good mother – just remember, they called and you went running *to* them, not from them. I'll talk to you soon.'

It was the most encouraging thing he could think of saying to her, because he was aware that in running to her daughters she was in fact running away yet again.

His words resonated in her head. She longed to see her girls. Yes, she was really pleased that it was to her they wanted to come. Well, Lily anyway. Lily had sought her out and was coming to her for whatever reason. That in itself was rewarding, although the thought of Lily in trouble was very upsetting. But it was comforting to think that Lily needing help was seeking her out. It made her feel that she must have got something right somewhere along the way.

She allowed herself to think of Lily as a baby, tiny, soft, sleeping in her arms, and Lily now, long-legged, serious, and confident – a credit to someone somewhere, but God alone knew whom. No one had any claim on Lily. Esme felt that nothing she could do now would reverse the damage she had done to Lily by abandoning her years before, even though Lily had no knowledge of that event. She felt she had no right to be proud of anything Lily achieved, but could only rejoice for her.

Günter, she knew, had no claim for pride either. He would not ever have seen Lily again had Jennifer not insisted.

She was glad now to be older, to be away from all of that. At least when her daughter called for her now, she was there for her. And she would come running for her, she would be there for her in London, she would do whatever she could to help her.

'I'm not coming back,' Naomi said to Jacob on the phone shortly afterwards.

'Reassure me that you are all right,' he replied after a pause.

'"All right" in what sense?'

'Naomi, whatever it is you are thinking or going through, I will be here for you.'

'I'm filing for a divorce,' she said. 'Will you contest it?'

'You may have whatever you want – you only have to ask.'

'I only wanted you,' she replied.

This was not true but there was no point in him telling her so.

'You have me,' he answered, and as he said it he wondered if that were the absolute truth. Clearly Naomi did not think so.

'I don't have you,' she said angrily. 'The whole world has you, but I don't. You are remote and busy with your work. You're permanently preoccupied. You're late for everything. Your patients – your all-consuming insufferable patients – are your priority. I've had enough. Do you understand? Enough.'

He could hear the fury in her voice. This time he did not respond as he let her words settle. He had thought that he was the good companion, the faithful husband and the hard-working breadwinner. But perhaps she was right. Perhaps in his own way he had been as selfish as Esme's Günter Wassermann. He did not really think so. He thought that he gave and gave and was there for her when she needed him. He knew that it rankled when he was running late for dinner or when he occasionally went back to work at the weekend. He knew too that she was selfish but felt that that was at least partly his fault. If he had given her the children she wanted, her time would have been occupied differently. And he knew that she saw it that way.

Although the truth was, if they had had children they would be grown up now and Naomi would have had a feeling of redundancy that she would probably not have been able to remove. She would have lived through her children and would have been waiting for them all the time. But then her demands on him would have been reduced because they would have been spread evenly across a family. But he also knew that she would never see that because she had not found something with which to occupy herself – be it children or a career or a hobby; she would still have reached this point of feeling inadequate. He would not hurt her now by saying to her that she should have found something to do with her life other than to shop and socialise. It would be too cruel. He had hurt her enough.

'Say something,' she said. 'Just say something – say you miss me. Say I had a meaning in your life.'

But what could he say?

'I love you, Naomi,' he tried. 'I'm sorry that is not enough.'

She put down the phone.

He wondered if their relationship would have worked had he retired early. She had certainly suggested it often enough, as though it were the answer to everything. They would have gone on cruises and beach holidays, bought an apartment in the South of France or Spain or maybe in Tuscany; they would have shopped and ate . . . the thought of it made him despair. It might have brought her happiness but it would have been the death of him. And he knew it.

He supposed they had grown so far apart but he did not know how he could have changed that. He had worked hard, genuinely believing that that had been understood between them as how he both wanted and needed to live his life. He believed he had spelled it out clearly in the early days. Maybe she had thought he would come around to the idea of children, and have a child with her. Maybe she thought that having a busy and successful husband would fulfil her. He no longer knew what she must have thought. He could see how she perceived he had let her down, but could not see how he could have done anything differently. There was a certain inevitability about the phone being put down on him.

He sighed. He knew he would be all right, and was quite sure he would survive. His work would keep him busy. He wondered if he would miss her. It was a cruel thought but he pondered it carefully until he realised that he would miss the comfort zone that she offered. The knowledge that she would be there for him when he came home from work, that she would have arranged various social events, different parties and dinners, restaurants and theatre bookings . . . he had failed her.

And it grieved him.

Love dies somewhere, he thought. Somewhere, somehow, the bonds that had tied them so closely for so many years had disintegrated. He could not be precise about when it had happened, probably because he had been so engrossed in his work, while she – she had had little else to think about. The nutrients for a happy marriage were occupation and sharing. Good open communication was vital. But what you shared had to be of interest to the other person. His work was so private that he shared only generalities with her. And what she shared with him really had not interested him. He now felt shock that it had ended so suddenly, but knew that it was not a sudden ending for her.

And now he was tired. Tired to the marrow of his bones.

He went to bed and his last ironic thought before falling asleep was that she would never again berate him for being late for anything.

When he woke it was the following morning and, arriving at his office, he found a file waiting for him.

'It came by courier this morning,' his secretary said.

He picked it up. It was still sealed in its envelope. He put it in his briefcase to bring home and read in the evening. At some point during the day he opened it and found a short note from Henry Delmont:

This is what you were looking for. I glanced through it before sending it on. It's fairly complete although I seem to remember there was something more to the story. Call me if I can be of further help. It was a good conference. See you soon, Henry.

It was kind of Henry to have responded so fast. He could not have been long home and yet he had found the file, packaged and sent it immediately. He wondered what Henry meant by there being something more to the story, and if that something would be clearer after he had read the file.

He also considered the possibility that it was unethical of him to be researching the background of a friend. But then Esme had given him the name, and she had only done that so that he could help her, even if she did not consciously know it.

It was Friday afternoon and Rose was finishing up her work in the hospital for the week. The wind blew gently and the leaves on the trees beyond the window moved softly. Rose looked back to the book she was reading. Roland Duval liked Shakespeare and at his request she brought in various plays from home. At the moment she was reading him *Macbeth*. She had picked up the copy that her mother had accidentally left behind when she went to France early in June. Esme had first asked Rose to post it on to her, and then had changed her mind, saying she had picked up a copy in Paris.

As a style of reading aloud, Rose found it difficult – first saying the character's name and then the words – but it did not seem to bother Roland. He listened, occasionally nodding. Sometimes as she read she felt uneasy.

Nothing in his life
Became him like the leaving it: he died
As one that had been studied in his death
To throw away the dearest thing he owed
As 'twere a careless trifle.

'Will you have any visitors this weekend?' she asked him,
before leaving that Friday evening.

He shook his head.

'No family?'

'There is no family.' His voice was acutely sad.

'If I can,' Rose said carefully, not keen to make a promise
to which she could not adhere, 'I will try and come in over
the weekend to see how you are. Would that be okay? We
could read a bit more then, if you like.'

He looked up at her, surprised. 'Thank you,' he said.
'Thank you.' His voice acknowledged the thoughtfulness
of her gesture, and for a moment his sad eyes almost
smiled.

She glanced at his hands. They had always attracted her.
At first she had thought that he kept his little finger on each
hand tucked into the palm in some strange contorted way,
and then she had realised that he quite simply was missing
these fingers. His hands were perfect but for this deformity.
Long and slender, beautifully formed but missing what
everyone else took for granted. She had had a problem in
keeping her eyes off them in the beginning, but now when
she looked at them it was not with curiosity but with admiration. She thought they were beautiful in their uniqueness.
They seemed longer and more elegant than any other hands
she had ever seen. For some reason they made her feel defen-
sive of him. Why should three fingers and a thumb be any
odder than four fingers and a thumb? She would have liked

to have drawn them or photographed them and stuck them on her bedroom walls with her other bits of strange memorabilia.

Rose came home from work.

Roland Duval was on her mind as she checked her email. There was nothing there. Nothing from Esme in France, or Lily in Canada, or Jasmine in South Carolina.

Thinking about Jasmine made her think about the States. How she had hated living there, hated the wet dripping heat of the rolling seasons, but as a child, of course, she had not known that she hated it. It was just part of her life, and a part that she happily left to go to the Netherlands come summer each year, where the weather, although variable, offered seemingly eternal relief. She was never sure now if home was London or the Netherlands. This was her first summer not staying for at least a few weeks with the Van der Vloeds and she missed them.

The phone rang, interrupting her thoughts. It was Merel.

'Hey, Roos. I miss you,' Merel said.

'Hallelujah,' said Rose, an expression she had picked up from her cousin. 'I was just thinking about you. I miss you too. I've made the mistake of a lifetime in spending the summer here. The job is awful. It's the most depressing thing imaginable.' They knew each other so well that pleasantries were bypassed as they filled each other in.

'Mine isn't much better,' Merel said. 'I'm putting some kind of spare parts into something or other that I haven't yet identified in a factory.'

Rose laughed. 'Trust me, it's better than what I'm doing. I'm dealing with death on a daily basis.'

'This is death,' Merel said.

Merel's English had improved just as Rose's Dutch had.

But somewhere over the years she had fully acquired Rose's language and, as Rose admitted with mild irritation, Merel's English now seemed better than her own.

'I've two new piercings,' Rose contributed to this diatribe of complaints.

'Ear or elsewhere?'

'I'm still sticking to the ear,' Rose answered. 'I had to remove the one in my navel – don't ask. Well, I'll tell you anyway. Some sick bitch in the hospital where I'm working yanked it out last week . . .'

'Au! What bitch? Why?'

'To be fair to her, I don't think she did it deliberately. She was being sedated and she was thrashing around the place like an octopus and I got in the way.'

'That sounds terrible,' Merel said.

'How are my Grootouders?' Rose asked, changing the subject. 'And my Ome Nop and Tante Madelief?'

'They're fine. We're all fine,' Merel said.

All fine. Rose felt a pang of envy. Everyone seemed to be doing something or being with people they liked while she hated getting up in the morning to go into work, and hated coming home to the empty apartment.

After the phone call, she made something to eat while contemplating the weekend. All her friends were away for the summer or had stayed up at university to complete projects or whatever. She wondered if she could get to the Netherlands at the end of the summer, even for a week, ideally before Merel went back to her music college. The balcony stretched around two sides of the apartment so it was possible to follow the sun for most of the day. Around the corner, on the widest part of it, the sliding French doors opened up and there Rose sat down to have her meal. She had the doors open and the television turned towards it so that she had the benefit of the warm evening air combined with the screen. There was a table with six chairs, but she chose to sit on one of the lounger-type seats, with her feet up, holding the saucepan of pasta on a towel. The area around her naval was hurting, and sitting upright was uncomfortable. She realised she didn't feel hungry, and that she had cooked simply because it was what she did each evening. She put the saucepan on the ground. She had turned the television on and now she let the images she was watching wash over her and take over from the day she had had at work. That Merel had phoned was great. It had been the highlight of the day even if it had been a mere ten minutes. Merel and she would have fun if only Merel was there in London.

Rose had a boyfriend – a biker called Billy whom she had met in Cambridge one afternoon a year previously when Esme had gone there to give a lecture, and Rose had accompanied her.

While her mother shared her philosophical views with some one hundred odd students and a handful of her peers, Rose sat in a coffee shop on King's Parade with one cappuccino after the other frothing in its cup on the table in front of her. It was there she met Billy, a leather-clad student who appeared to be wearing mascara. It was his only affectation, he told her when she asked him if it was indeed mascara.

'Is your name Charlene?' he asked her. 'I don't like that name.'

She shook her head. 'No. Rose.'

'Ah. A rose by any other name is still a rose,' he misquoted. He was studying English.

'What will you do when you are finished?' she asked him.

'I will speak the language,' he replied.

She grinned.

They went for a walk down to the river. He biked up to

London at the weekend to visit her. She took the train down to him the following weekend.

And so began their relationship. But he was gone now for the summer, leaving behind only a pair of boxer shorts that for some reason, possibly to dry them, he had nuked in the microwave. Crisp and unidentifiable as to their previous molecular structure, the plastic buttons having melted into the fabric now appeared as bulbous globs on a tartan background, Rose had pinned them to her bedroom wall.

She missed Billy and his odd ways. She was lonely now, and there was no one around and she was feeling really fed up.

She was supposed to work for another seven weeks in the hospital, although hospice, she thought, would be a more appropriate word. It was a hopeless situation and she was not sure that her going in and out on a daily basis was in any way going to contribute anything in a positive sense. But for Roland, whom she cared about, she would have liked to hand in her notice but she refused ever to give up on anything she had started. She was aware of this as one of her traits, and following a psychology lecture she had attended at university, realised that she behaved like this simply because she felt that Esme did the exact opposite and she did not want to emulate her mother. Once she tried sharing this with Lily, but Lily's response was that Esme did not give up on things, and that it was just Rose's perception that she did.

'But she walked out on your father,' Rose said.

'On Günter?' Lily said. 'Well, I think she was right. Grayson said she found Günter in bed with her best friend. With Jennifer. You know. What should she have done?'

'Grayson told you that?' Rose was surprised, surprised that Grayson had said such a thing, that Lily was so calm about

it and that indeed Günter could have done something so
horrible.

'Yes, he told me. He said I was better off understanding
why she had left Günter. And of course he is right.'

'It's a pity that she doesn't tell us these things herself,'
Rose said.

'She wouldn't betray Günter,' Lily said. 'And I like her for
that. And you should too.'

'Well, she walked out on Grayson,' Rose tried again.

'Rosie darling,' Lily said. 'It's fine for us staying in
Charleston for the holidays, or vacation as Grayson calls it,
but quite honestly I couldn't bear to live there.'

'But that's not the point,' Rose objected, knowing that Lily
was right. 'When you marry someone, it is supposed to be
for life. It says it in the wedding script.'

'Well, I'm not going to judge her on that one,' Lily said.
'I don't like being judged when I do things or change my
mind or whatever. I do my best. I think she does her best
as well.'

'But it doesn't really take us into account, does it?' Rose
asked.

'Rosie, you have to give her a break. She's entitled to happiness too. You wouldn't want a miserable mother, would you?
A stay-at-home boring mother who got her kicks out of
going to the gym or gossiping on the phone or whatever it
is some mothers seem to do? Now would you?'

Lily was so easy-going, always seeing everyone else's side
of the story. What Rose envied here was Lily's clarity. Rose
had such muddled memories of when and where she had
been happy other than in the Netherlands. If asked, she
would have said that they had lived outside Charleston quite
happily until Esme had suddenly done a runner. Maybe Lily
was right, Rose thought. But it had been difficult for them
all then. The plantation had become their home. Rose had

learned to love to climb the big trees with their cobwebs of haw, hiding high in the branches while Lily and Jasmine looked for her. Rose wished she didn't know that Günter had betrayed her mother like that. It was such a cruel thing to do. Esme didn't talk about it. She only said that Günter was happy with Jennifer and that that was good. Once Rose had asked her if she had ever been happy with Lily's father and Esme had sat thoughtfully for a moment and then said that yes, yes she had been happy.

'I was happy when Lily was born. I was young and prob-ably foolish – full of hope.'

'You don't have hope now?'

'Oh, yes, I do,' her mother replied. 'I have hope every day. There is always something new, some new thing every day. I am full of hope.'

'Tell me about my father,' Rose said.

'Your father was the loveliest man in the world,' Esme said. These were words that she always used when speaking of Arjen. 'And it was my joy to know him and to be part of his life.'

Rose often brought up the subject of Günter simply to lead her mother on to speak of Arjen. She loved hearing about him, but Esme was always reticent, giving little and even then always just saying the same things. There was a time when Esme could not talk of him, a time when Lily and Rose were brought to the crèche on a daily basis and Esme went to university and finished her degree and started her post-graduate work.

Rose remembered how her mother had once said she did not know how to cry. It had puzzled her as a child. How could you not know how? Was crying something you learned how to do? Had her mother never cried? What did it mean? Had she learned it or unlearned it? What were tears and how come her mother did not know how to shed them?

'I don't know,' her mother had said when Rose asked her. 'I must have just grown out of them. I have you two. Maybe that's why I have no need for tears.'

Rose thought maybe it had to do with her father. With Arjen, who had died long ago. On a cold grey morning when the grass was covered in snow and even the rivers were frozen, a morning before Rose was even born . . . long ago.

CHAPTER FOURTEEN

R ose sat on the balcony now staring down at the River
Thames while in three different airports around the
world her mother and her two sisters checked in their
luggage.

Rose was now feeling very restless and dissatisfied, alone
and lonely. She wished so much that she had gone to the
Netherlands. The skin around her navel hurt where the
patient had pulled the stud from it. Rose knew she should
change the makeshift dressing she had put on it, but she
could not be bothered. It was Friday night and she needed
to shake off the week. She decided to go out. There were
two nightclubs not so far away. Three stops on the underground and she would be there. She was cool about going
alone. It would not be the first time. She would go and dance,
letting the music take over her head and vitalise her blood.

In her bedroom she thought briefly about repainting her
walls and decided she might do that the following weekend
if nothing better occurred to her. It was an idea she had had
on and off over the past few years, but had done nothing
about as she liked the comfort of the familiarity of it. But
now, she thought, maybe she was growing out of the black-
ness of the walls with their luminous painted writing.

She rooted in her wardrobe for a top that would conceal her stomach, as she did not want the plaster on view. A skin-tight black micro skirt and high-heeled black sandals were the start of her outfit. She wandered into Lily's room and looked in her cupboard for something to wear on top. Lily, being taller, had a couple of possibilities there. She settled for a skinny halter neck in a thin material that just about reached the top of the skirt that sat on her hips. Its pale blue colour enhanced the tan she was building up in the evenings on the balcony. She brushed her hair before spraying a pink streak on one side and then mussing it up. She checked the six rings in her right ear were hanging evenly, and then with a spray of her mother's perfume in Esme's room, she was ready to go. Slipping a thin-strapped bag on her shoulder, she was about to leave the apartment when she decided on a shot of vodka for a combination of luck and confidence, and a possible antidote to the pain in her stomach. Her naval was now throbbing and she promised herself she would look at it in the morning in the shower and would put on a clean dressing.

She left the television turned on so that there would be a welcoming sound when she returned.

It was ten twenty when she let herself out of the apartment and walked down the long carpeted corridor to the elevator.

At the same time Esme's flight finally took off in Nice airport, tearing down the runway before lifting up and becoming airborne. Esme closed her eyes and, verging on sleep, she wondered what her girls were doing.

Lily had just handed in her rucksack, having managed to change her tickets. It would be two flights and, with the time difference, a full twenty-four hours before she would arrive at Heathrow. She was feeling less weepy and more in control as long as she had something practical to do. She kept saying to herself that she was going home and that somehow she would pull together what remained of her dignity.

Jasmine, in her bedroom on the plantation in South Carolina, was packing and wondering if Taliban would survive the flight in her suitcase. In the end she decided that she had read somewhere that the hold on an airplane was very cold, and so she would have to bring him with her in her hand luggage. She had coaxed him out from under the sofa with a live cricket and then told Grayson that she had brought him out to the yard and that he had scampered off in the general direction of the distant fields. Grayson seemed relieved and questioned her no further. She got her small wooden jewellery box and put him into it, jamming the lid slightly ajar with a necklace that her grandmother had given her. She put this in her shoulder bag with a magazine, some cosmetics, and a handful of crickets in a large matchbox.

'Jasmine, get a move on,' Grayson called from outside her door.

A last look in the mirror and Jasmine was ready for departure.

'Will you take my case, Dad?' she yelled back.

'Isn't it on wheels?' he said, putting his head around the door.

He saw the empty aquarium and shivered as he remembered how he had so carefully hidden the keys in it.

'No more tarantulas,' he said to her as he lifted the case off the bed.

'No, Dad.' She sulked a little, thinking that would be the best way to convince him that she was grief-stricken over Taliban's departure.

'I mean it, Jasmine,' he said. 'And you're to give your

mother no trouble – well, at least not any more than you've given me.'

'No, Dad,' she repeated. 'I swear I won't get another spider.'

She wondered what Lily would think of Taliban. Esme liked spiders. She knew that. Esme was always rescuing them from baths and sinks, carrying them carefully to a place where she said they might have a better life. Why spiders always headed for baths was a puzzle to Jasmine. Presumably many, if not most, of their relatives and ancestors had been washed away in baths, and yet they always went there. Did they like the idea of a big white empty space? Or were they like elephants? Lily had told her that elephants visit the grave-yards of their relatives. Could that be the case? She wondered if anyone had thought of that, and if not, might it be a new idea. Something for Lily's thesis? Though Lily was doing her paper on geese. But maybe she could change it to spiders.

Grayson had told her that Esme said that Lily was now on her way home to London too. Lily was going to be so impressed with Taliban.

It was working out better than she had hoped – the fact that Lily would be in London too, and Rose was already there. She wondered how Esme would react to having the three of them all at once – not something her mother had encoun-tered in some time. Grayson was travelling with her to Atlanta because, as he so bluntly put it, he didn't bloody well trust her. Which she felt was scandalous, as when, if ever, had she done anything untrustworthy? This flight from South Carolina meant that she would miss Darling Baby's birthday party and any chance she had of kissing Skylark, which prob-ably wasn't very high anyway, as every girl in his year was, according to Darling Baby, hanging on his every word. It didn't sound very likely to Jasmine, though, because it was not her experience that American girls hung on anyone's word – well, not if Darling Baby was anything to go by.

Jasmine was now sorry that she hadn't said goodbye to her grandfather the previous evening but there had been such a row going on and she'd been sent to bed – although of course she had not gone to bed. Having rescued Taliban from under the sofa she had let him sit on the bed instead while she considered what was in his best interests. After all, he was her responsibility and she didn't want him staying in the house underfed and undernourished, because who would look after him in her absence? And she couldn't bring him out to the hills like Grayson had ordered because he was now house-trained and his outdoor survival instincts might be diminished.

The owl had flown. Sometime during the night, it had taken to the window and was gone. Grayson said it was a good thing, because now he could reset the air conditioning to normal and not have it going at full blast to counteract the high temperatures permeating through the open window. Jasmine had not thought of that. She hadn't realised that he had done that so that the owl could stay indoors. She thought it was nice of him. It made her worry, though, what it would be like to be an adult because there were so many things to think about when you were an adult and she did not like the idea of that at all.

They flew from Charleston to Atlanta where Grayson saw her through to her next flight to London. He gave her some money, which was decent of him under the circumstances as he was still quite cross about Taliban although he had clearly forgotten the damage she had done to her grand-father's fender, so between his money and the money Gramps had given her anyway, Jasmine had quite a tidy sum. He also gave her some sterling so that she could get a taxi from the airport. Despite the fact that her hand luggage was checked before going on to both flights, no one discovered Taliban. Jasmine would quite have liked to have taken him

out and let him stretch his legs on the plane and to tell him
he was about to make his first trip to Europe. Not to the
Hilton, as Grandmother thought of Europe, but to their
apartment on the Thames. During the flight she took her
bag to the toilet and fed him another cricket. He seemed
happy enough and she went back to her seat and watched
the movie.

Rose spent a couple of hours in the nightclub. The strobe
lighting flashed and flickered and she danced wildly and
freely, unleashing all the pent-up energy from the week past.
Occasionally the pain from the tear in her navel penetrated
through and she went and got another vodka, keeping herself
one step ahead of the ache. The throbbing from it now seemed
to be in perfect timing with both her heartbeat and the music.
At two in the morning she decided she should head home.
She was still fairly alert when she went to the door of the
club and called for a taxi on her mobile, but once she had
done that she felt a wave of nausea and raced back inside to
the toilets where she threw up repeatedly. Staggering back to
the door of the club she went out on to the street, aware of
the bouncers watching her as she got into the back of a car
parked outside. The pain now was suddenly stronger than
the numbing effect of the alcohol and she felt extremely
unwell and decided to lie down on the seat. Before doing so,
she gave the driver her address, unaware that there was neither
a driver nor anyone else in the car with her.

Meanwhile, Esme's plane had landed in Heathrow.
    She had phoned Rose shortly before the plane left Nice
to say that she was on her way home, but had got her voice
mail and left a message. She knew she should have phoned
Rose earlier to say she was coming but she had put it off as
she did not feel like dealing with whatever emotion Rose's

voice would contain. It wasn't that she felt that Rose would be unreasonable. It was more that she was so concerned about Lily and bothered about Jasmine that she was afraid to phone Rose and to find out something further had happened.

At the back of her mind there were other thoughts. One was that she might have been unfair to Peter Carew.

Perhaps Jacob was right and Peter was simply a legal journalist and she was being paranoid. The more she thought about this the more reasonable it sounded to her.

And then there was the issue of her work. With the three girls in the apartment she knew that the silence she needed was simply not going to be there. Pushing these thoughts aside she made her way to the carousel from where, this time, she collected her bags safely, and then she walked out to the taxi rank.

Arriving at the apartment block, tired and feeling dirty from the hours spent in Nice airport, she wheeled her bags to the elevator, and on the fifth floor she went quickly to the apartment. She let herself in as quietly as she could before realising that the television was on. She checked briefly to see if Rose was up, but her bedroom door was closed. She turned off the television and the lights, and then brought her bags into her own room. She had a shower and went to bed.

She slept until ten, waking to her phone ringing. It was Grayson, saying which flight Jasmine was on.

'I flew with her to Atlanta, and I saw her through to the London flight. She's definitely on it.'

'Good,' Esme said.

'Well, I'm off to bed,' he said. 'Talk soon. And good luck with her.'

Esme went to the kitchen to make coffee and saw then that Rose had left the place in a pretty shocking state. She went to check the voice mail on the house phone, before remembering she had had it disconnected some time earlier because it had rung continually for each of the girls, even when they weren't there, and was just too distracting. When they were all there, they had spent their time shouting to each other to take a call. She was unsure if Rose had got her message or not. She went to her bedroom door, knocking gently, not wanting to frighten Rose, who might well not know that all of her closest female relatives were either in or on their way to the apartment. There was no reply.

She opened the door and found Rose's bed empty; most of the contents of her cupboards were strewn on the floor. Had she not known Rose, she would have assumed that the apartment had been burgled. However, knowing Rose's propensity for untidiness, she had no doubt that Rose had simply left the place in a rush the previous evening. She wondered where her second-born was.

She told herself not to feel irritated at the state of the place. After all, Rose had not known that they were all coming home. Had she known, she would probably have done something to make the place look more like she had found it at the end of her university term.

Esme began by clearing the dishes from the balcony table and a saucepan that was full of congealed pasta from the ground, and then stacking the dishwasher. Anything of Rose's she put inside Rose's bedroom door, and then tidied the rest of the lounge and the small study area off it where she, Esme, usually worked. She made herself coffee and went and sat outside. The sun was shining and the water of the river flowed smoothly past below. One sightseeing boat after the other drifted by and she sat at ease thinking about a variety of different things. She felt comfortable there, but always reminded herself never to feel too comfortable. She feared complacency. It made her think of the easy life with Grayson, when year after year had slipped by and she had done nothing. This London apartment had given her a sense of position, of security and of wellbeing. The girls had taken to their new surroundings very quickly, each making a room her own. She organised schools for the three of them, informing Günter of the new arrangements for Lily. Günter did not care. He paid her school fees and gave some money towards her maintenance, and beyond that he really showed no interest. Rose's grandparents in the Netherlands were glad that Roos, as they called her, was back in Europe. She was closer to them now, could visit more often, and they were pleased. But while Rose's paternal family were happy, Grayson, she knew, must have been devastated.

Esme remembered a conversation with him.

'You are making me feel ashamed,' she said.

'All I ask is that you think of me with kindness,' he said. 'I probably should not have married you, but I did. And I don't regret a day of it. If I am sad about anything it is because it wasn't enough for you.'

'You know, it's not your fault – what happened, I mean,' she said.

'Oh, I know that,' he said. 'I do know that.' He kissed her on the forehead. 'Let's stay friends and do what's best by the girls.'

Esme sighed as she thought about those early days in London.

Grayson had been true to his character, just as Günter had to his. It made her wonder about her own character, because she wasn't really sure who she was at all. And if she wasn't sure back then, it really was not much clearer now. Despite her work, her sense of purpose, the raising of her daughters, she knew that there was always a feeling of loss and an aching lack of completion.

Work alone filled that gap in her. By studying, writing or

lecturing she could keep the monsters at bay. She knew she was going to have to start work as soon as possible, and she hoped that when Lily arrived from Canada, whatever the problem was, it could be quickly sorted. She knew that she must give Lily all the help and attention that was required, more if necessary, but she also knew that she just wanted to get back to her work.

She wondered vaguely where Rose could be, but she was not concerned. There was no reason for Rose to be at home. Rose had not known they were coming and it had been a Friday evening, so she might have gone to stay with friends.

She dreaded the arrival of Jasmine, even though she was looking forward to seeing her just as much as the others. But she knew that with Jasmine would come some kind of trouble or unrest – some disturbance anyway – there was no doubt about that. The problem was that if Grayson could not handle Jasmine, there was really no reason to think that she, Esme, would be able to.

She looked at her watch. It was already midday. She rang for a taxi to collect Jasmine from the airport, and wondered at what time Lily would emerge. There was still no answer from her phone. And still no sign of Rose.

The driver of the car into which Rose had so heedlessly entered in the early hours of the morning had returned to it with his own daughter, who was the worse for drink. He got her into the passenger seat, strapped her in and headed home to Hampstead. At this point he thought of leaving her in the car but then changed his mind and, not noticing that he had a second unconscious passenger on the back seat, hauled his daughter out and half lifted, half dragged her into their home. He left her asleep in the living room and went to bed. At ten in the morning he and his wife went to do the weekend shopping and it was then they found Rose.

Their initial surprise turned quickly to anxiety as they realised that she appeared highly feverish and could not be woken. They took her straight to hospital where she was whisked away, leaving them to try to explain how she had come to be in their care. Her strappy shoulder bag revealed who she was and her address on the south bank of the river was unearthed. It was going on three o'clock in the afternoon when the police knocked on the apartment door.

Esme was now working, engrossed in her reading and making notes, a cup of coffee beside her, laptop open on her desk, the washing machine working away in the kitchen. She was startled from her involvement by the buzz of the in-house intercom. She was surprised to see what time it was as she answered the call. It was the concierge below at reception, saying that a member of the Metropolitan Police wanted to speak to her. She wondered briefly if Jasmine could have arrived and was already in trouble. There was a sharp tap at the door, and she ran her hands quickly through her hair before opening the door and encountering the police-woman.

She looked at her in surprise, having checked first that Jasmine was not with her. Her mind was racing as she first of all assumed it was some routine call, or a mistaken address, and it was only after a couple of seconds that she took in what the woman was saying.

'Is this the residence of Rose van der Vloed?'

Esme stood stock-still in horror. It was like her worst nightmare from her waking hours. It was not how Arjen's death had been told to her, but it might have been. It was what every parent fears somewhere in the recesses of the mind – that knock at the door . . . the police . . .

'Yes, yes. I'm her mother. Is something wrong? Is Rose all right?'

It was quickly apparent that Rose was not all right and that Esme needed to get to the hospital as fast as possible.

The policewoman offered to drive Esme in the direction of Waterloo station, where she would quickly and easily catch a cab, which assistance Esme gratefully accepted. She had only partially unpacked, and her handbag still contained her passport, airline ticket stubs and various other paraphernalia that she would normally not carry with her. As she slipped shoes on her feet she looked in despair at her room, completely indecisive as to what to take with her. In the end she grabbed a cardigan and her wallet, phone and keys and said that she was ready.

Blood poisoning, she kept thinking. That was what the policewoman had said. Blood poisoning. She couldn't imagine how you got blood poisoning, let alone the process from acquiring it to ending up in hospital. The police car used its siren on the way to Waterloo, adding to Esme's anxiety. She thanked her escorts and got into the taxi they had kindly stopped for her.

She suddenly remembered that Jasmine would arrive at the apartment and would have no way of getting in, but there was nothing she could do about that now. She tried contacting her on her mobile and then remembered there was something odd about Jasmine's sim card, and that she possibly had two – one for the States and one for Europe. But she could not really remember. She tried to call Grayson but his phone was turned off, and although the house phone in South Carolina rang, she could imagine it echoing downstairs, heard only by a tawny owl.

At the hospital, there was, at first, no time to think. She could hardly take in what the nurse said to her. They had operated on Rose's naval and had removed a piece of broken ring and were now draining the poisoned wound. She was in the intensive care unit and was clearly very ill.

'Is . . . is she going to be all right?' Esme asked, almost afraid to utter the words aloud.

'It's too early to say,' the nurse said. 'If she responds . . . we're doing our very best . . . septicaemia . . . it's really too early to say . . .'

Rose was still unconscious. Dressed in a clinical gown and with a mask on her face, Esme stood by the bed and stroked her daughter's hand.

'You're safe now,' she whispered. 'It's going to be all right now. You're safe.'

But as she uttered the words, she was not sure if she believed what she was saying, was not sure that Rose was safe, was not sure if she would survive. She tried saying it more firmly, as if some strength behind the words might endorse them. Rose lay there still and silent. Safe, she thought. A word she remembered from long ago. The promise made at birth to a baby, a promise that could never be kept . . .

After a while, the nurses asked Esme to leave.

'Go and have coffee. Get something to eat,' she was told. 'Come back in an hour. We're just going to change the drips and the doctor is going to look at her.'

'I don't want to leave her,' Esme said.

'Is there anyone you would like to phone, anyone who can come in and be with you?'

Esme felt frozen. The words frightened her. It was as if they felt she was going to need support. She could think of no one who would come and stay with her during this ordeal. She went downstairs and outside, where she stood leaning against a wall. She couldn't leave the hospital. It was too far to get back home and return again – she needed to be close to Rose. She tried both Lily and Jasmine's phones, but there was no reply. Jasmine's was dead. On Lily's she left a message. She felt guilty because she knew that Lily was coming home for some kind of help, and yet there was nothing she could do for her now. She felt as if there was nothing she could do for any of them. Rose needed her the most and yet she was powerless to help her. She did not know what message to leave on Lily's phone, as she was concerned about alarming her. She just said that when Lily got to the apartment, could she look out for Jasmine and let her in, and that she would phone them as soon as possible.

It was only then she thought of the concierge in the apartment block.

She rang him and asked him if he would see if Jasmine had arrived, and if so, had she been able to get into the apartment, as she did not know if Jasmine had brought keys with her from the States, or indeed if she had had them to start with.

She went back and sat in the intensive care unit, and an image of her mother came to mind. Susan – that was how she had addressed her mother, which was very unusual back then in her childhood. All her friends called their mothers 'Mum' or 'Mummy'. But Susan had been different from other mothers in an indefinable way. She was a mixture of an old-fashioned parent and a very modern mother, involved in her religion, an unquestioning believer, which was the type of worshipper Esme now disliked the most, though as a child she had not seen that, and had merely taken her mother's eccentricities on board. Now sitting there with Rose fighting for her life, it was Susan she thought of, and for the first time ever, she thought of her mother with compassion.

Jasmine had arrived in London, identified her waiting taxi driver by a board he was carrying with her name on it, and arriving at the apartment block, she had got in without any problem, attaching herself to two other people who were entering the building. She got herself and her case as far as the apartment door and then discovered there was no one inside. She plonked herself down on the floor and sat there, having checked on Taliban. She was both hungry and tired now, and couldn't think what to do.

Jasmine was not given to lateral thought. Her phone would not work, and she was getting more and more annoyed at her mother for leaving her sitting on the floor outside the apartment. Initially she reassured herself that Esme was out buying food and would be back shortly, but two hours later she was getting very cranky.

It was at that point that the concierge came up in the lift and found her on the floor, about to settle down to doze on her case.

'Are you Jasmine Redmond?' he asked.

She opened her eyes and looked at him. Experience had taught her to deny everything.

'No,' she replied.

He looked at her carefully. He was relatively new to the apartments and he did not recognise her. He had seen her coming in with a couple a while earlier and assumed she was in their company.

'Well, I'm sorry, but you can't stay there,' he said.

'I'm waiting for my mother,' Jasmine retorted.

'And her name is?'

'Esme Waters.'

'And you're not her daughter Jasmine?' he asked again.

It dawned on Jasmine that maybe he had a message for her.

'I am,' she said.

'Do you have anything to prove it?' he asked patiently.

Jasmine dug her passport out of the pocket of her jeans and gave it to him.

'Right,' he said. 'Your mother asked me to unlock the door for you.'

'Sorry,' Jasmine said, now slightly embarrassed at how short and rude she had been.

'That's quite all right,' he said, as he unlocked the door for her.

He carried her bag in for her and she thanked him.

Lily arrived late that night. Unlike Jasmine, she had a key to let herself in. She found Jasmine eating pizza, looking at the television.

'Hey,' Jasmine said, looking up. 'I thought you were Mom. What are you doing here?'

'I'm fine, thank you, Jazz,' Lily said in reply, coming over to hug her. Her face was very pale, and her hair hung limply down her face. 'What are you doing here? And what is that doing here?' She jumped back in alarm.

Taliban was sitting beside Jasmine on the sofa, watching *Big Brother*.

'That's Taliban. My friend. And just as well I have him, as I don't know where Mom is. I'm all alone.'

'You don't look very alone to me,' Lily said, pulling further back and carefully eyeing the tarantula. She was dazed from tiredness, travel-weary, sad, and now Esme wasn't here, and Esme was all she wanted.

'Don't touch Taliban,' Jasmine said, as Lily fetched a bowl from the kitchen, which she placed over him.

'I have no intention of touching him,' Lily replied in as reassuring a voice as she could muster. 'In fact I'm trying to make sure that he doesn't touch me. Are you out of your mind?'

'Where's Mom?' Jasmine asked, settling back to the show on television.

Lily shook her head. She was starting to feel like she was hallucinating. 'I have no idea,' she replied. 'Have you tried her phone?'

Jasmine didn't answer.

'Jazz, when did you get back?' Lily tried again.

'Dunno, some time ago.'

'Have you seen Mum since you got back?'

'No. The concierge had to let me in. And, before you ask, I don't know where she is. And even if I did I wouldn't tell you.'

Lily looked at her in amazement. She couldn't work out if Jasmine was being serious or not.

'Do you know something, Jazz? You are the most spoiled rotten horrible kid I've ever met. I'm being perfectly reasonable, and friendly, and actually I was quite pleased to see you. What's going on? All you think about is you.'

'Yeah . . . well . . . just as well that I do, 'cos no one else does.'

'They don't need to think about you,' Lily now snapped. 'They know that you will think about yourself, enough for all of them. So why should they think about you? Why are you here, anyway? I thought you were in South Carolina for the summer. In fact you were in South Carolina. I spoke to you there just a few days ago. Why are you here? Oh, great . . .' It suddenly dawned on Lily that Jasmine had probably been deported. 'What have you done now?'

'Nothing. And it wasn't my fault anyway,' Jasmine sulked. Then in a flash of brilliance, 'It's all *your* fault. The owl came back. Your owl. And you let the tiger go, that's why I got Taliban . . .'

'Jazz, if I weren't so tired . . . Jazz, please. Your tarantula and my tiger have nothing to do with each other. Now, where is Mum? This doesn't make sense. And Rose. Have you seen Rose since you got back?'

Jasmine shook her head. She had forgotten how irritating Lily could be. Like a dog with a bone. Never knew when to stop and leave other people alone.

'Jazz, listen to me.' Lily tried very hard to be gentle. She felt close to tears with tiredness and with everything else that she was biting down inside her. 'Don't you think there is something a bit odd that neither Mum nor Rose are here and it's a quarter to midnight. At least I think it is. And you've been here for hours . . . and they haven't been around.'

'I thought Mom had gone shopping,' Jasmine said.

Lily looked at her in despair. She could never quite believe how Jasmine's mind worked – or in fact didn't work.

'What time did the concierge let you in?'

'Dunno.'

Lily checked her phone but it wasn't working. She had no idea where her English Sim card was. She took her rucksack apart in her bedroom, noting how Rose had rooted through her closet and chest of drawers. She decided to go down to the desk and see if she could phone her mother from there.

'Look, Jasmine, I think if you have the energy you should unpack. And if you don't, maybe you could just put your bags in your room. The place is the most awful mess. I'm going downstairs and I'll be back as soon as I've checked where Esme is.'

She had reverted to calling her mother Esme. She usually called her Mum, although when she was little and they lived in Germany, she had called her Mutti then. She often called her Esme, though, when pulling rank with her younger sisters. Her own problems were pushed aside. All her instincts warned her something was wrong. Esme always told them where she was and where she was going.

Downstairs she tried phoning her mother, but there was no answer from her mobile and none from Rose's when she tried that.

She left a message on each, saying that she and Jasmine were in the apartment and that both were fine.

*   *   *

Jacob Althaus spent the day reading the file on Molly Kilbride. He drank endless cups of black coffee. At some stage during the day he removed a meal from the freezer, thawed it in the microwave and then cooked it. Twice he tried calling Esme and both times her phone was off. Close to midnight he booked a flight to London for the following day. He considered the hour and then decided that it would be preferable to phone Henry Delmont at that time, late as it was, rather than first thing in the morning. Either way he was likely to waken him, but he needed to talk to him.

'Sorry about the time, Henry,' he said when his friend answered the phone.

'No problem. We haven't gone to bed yet.'

'I'm coming to London in the morning. Any chance we can meet?'

'Come and stay,' Henry said. 'I think I've been expecting your call all day.'

'Thank you. My flight is at eleven. Can you give me directions?'

Henry checked which airport he was flying into, and then gave him details of how to find them.

'You'll be with us in the early afternoon at the latest. We'll have lunch then. Is that okay?'

It was fine. Henry said they could have the afternoon together and that Jacob was welcome to stay for as long as he wanted.

Jacob took the file to bed with him and started reading it over again, trying to piece together the bits that Esme had told him about her background with the notes of Harper Gumm.

CHAPTER FIFTEEN

Since Jennifer Delmont had betrayed her, Esme had never let herself become too close to anyone. She had learned the hard way not to trust. But now, as she sat on a lone chair in a corridor in the hospital, she wished that there were someone she could call, someone who would drop everything and come and help her. It was with practicalities that she needed assistance. She was not looking for comforting – she never looked for comforting.

Esme had no way of knowing if Jasmine had got into the apartment, or indeed if Lily had yet arrived and if one or both girls were worried about her absence. Further phone calls to the concierge proved useless. He either wasn't answering or had gone to sleep. She wished now there was a landline in the apartment but, at the time, having it disconnected seemed the right thing to do. She did not know the names of her neighbours. The anonymity of a large apartment block suited her.

Her editor was on holiday. Günter and Jennifer were somewhere in the east of Europe. Grayson was too far away to help. She had no close friends, only acquaintances. She thought about Jacob. She knew that he would help if he could. She was sure of it. But she also knew he was in no position to help her now. She had thought she needed no one to rely on. She had thought that her own resources would carry her.

Sometime during the night, Rose's condition worsened and Esme was allowed back to sit by her bed, where she held her daughter's hand and came as close to praying as she had allowed herself to over the years.

It was to Arjen she prayed, beseeching him for help.

That she might need company did not occur to her. Her only concern was Rose, attached to a variety of monitors and drips, and the whereabouts of Lily and Jasmine. Every so often the thought of Lily and her distress would come to mind, but in her very pragmatic way, Esme pushed those thoughts aside. There was nothing she could do, not yet. Lily must be somewhere over the Atlantic now, on her way home, and Esme would be there for her just as soon as she could.

As she sat by Rose's bed, listening to her breathing, she knew her father and mother had once sat by hers in a hospital just like this one. She knew they must have watched her as she was watching Rose, looking at the drips on the stand beside the bed, waiting, hoping, fearing . . .

She identified so strongly with Rose lying there that it actually felt as if it was she lying there, as if she no longer knew the difference between herself and Rose, where one ended and the other began. She knew what it was like to lie on a bed close to death – so close that it seemed to be one breath away. She hoped that Rose did not want death as she, Esme, once had. She hoped that Rose knew that life had a lot to offer and that she, Rose, had a lot to give. She knew that if she could, she would willingly swap places with her. Even though she did not want to lie there, drugged, attached to drips and monitors, she would do that because she would do anything for her girls.

Anything.

Her daughter's hands were exceptionally clammy, her face suffused with an unhealthy pallor, her breathing uneven. Rose normally reminded her of Arjen – the same skin, lightly tanned all year round, the same brown eyes – a smaller female version of Arjen. She thought now of the many times Rose had tried to ask her about him, and how she just said that he was the kindest man she had ever met. Now she felt guilty. There were times she could hardly look into Rose's face because she saw Arjen mirrored there and it was simply too painful.

She wished she had told Rose a thousand tales about him – but what was there to tell? How could she have told of those eight months of love? What could she have said that would have fully explained it all? What words could she have used to tell of the magic and the disbelief? What image would Rose have wanted anyway? Would she have cared to hear how her father, Arjen, filed the divorce papers on Esme's behalf just days after she moved in with him, and how within six months Esme and Günter were no longer man and wife? Would she really want to know that the Friday before he died Arjen had applied for their marriage in the local town hall and was on the way to the Netherlands, both to tell his parents and to invite them to their wedding?

Would Rose want to know that Arjen and she were so concerned that Rose might be born early because the marriage ceremony was booked for the day before Rose's due date of birth? Would Rose laugh at Arjen's fantasy that she would be born in the town hall during the short ceremony?

Or would Rose prefer to hear how Esme used to hurry home, and while she prepared their supper, she would half listen through the open window for the clickety-click of the wheels of Lily's baby pram on the cobblestones – but only on those days when Esme had brought Lily to the crèche.

Arjen carried Lily in a sling on the days he was doing both crèche journeys. They never had one argument in the whole of their eight months together. There was nothing but gentleness and love.

'When our baby is born,' he once said to her, 'we will take both our children to the Netherlands, and my parents will care for them and you and I will spend a whole day alone. We'll cycle by the canals, we'll walk in the fields, we'll spend a whole night in bed undisturbed.'

How could she have told Rose any of that? It occurred to her then that maybe that was what Rose wanted to hear – all those tiny fragments of memory that captured what could be caught of Arjen's life with her.

But how could she have told her anyway, Esme thought. Would words have captured the love she and Arjen had shared? From the moment she had heard of Arjen's death, she had not allowed herself to think of anything other than how to cope – how to look after Lily and Rose, how to pass her exams and how to forge a life for them.

Sometimes back then every moment of every day was a struggle. The endless effort of waking in the morning and facing the hours bereft of Arjen, struggling to keep her head together, struggling to hold on.

But she had known then, quite clearly, that that was not a real struggle for survival. It might have seemed like it, but she knew better. She knew what trying to survive really meant – and so when her peers watched her in amazement as she went from lecture to seminar and then to the library and back to her babies, stunned at her strength, she knew they had no idea that by comparison with the past, this was easy. Easy? No, easy was not the right word. But she had known that she must keep going. Not like in the past. She knew that all she must do was not look back and not think.

She inherited her father's money in due course. Arjen's

life insurance policy, taken out the day before he left her, came through. But before that, there was nothing. No money. Nothing. Christa, her landlady, had helped her all the time, often taking the babies to the crèche for her, giving her dinner when she came home exhausted in the evenings. Yes, Esme knew that that was not struggling for survival – it was simply learning how to live again.

How could you tell that to a little girl? And yet now, she wished she had. Rose had deserved more than to hear that her father was a wonderful man. Somewhere during that long night by Rose's bed, Esme knew that if Rose survived she would tell her. She would tell her that there were men like Arjen in the world – good men who knew how to love, and that . . . and what? Her mind faltered in its tiredness, she felt her eyes closing.

And now again, an image of her own mother came to mind. Susan sitting once upon a time beside her bed, her eyes red-rimmed and her face drawn. No, it was unbearable. She would not think about it. She could not think about it.

'You need rest,' a nurse said to her, coming and crouching in front of her.

Esme opened her eyes and looked up at the kindly face, hearing the compassion in her voice.

'I can't leave her,' she said, nodding towards the bed. 'She might need me.'

'She's better than she was,' the nurse said. 'And you, ill with exhaustion, can offer her nothing, you know.'

'But . . . what if . . . I . . .' Esme could not find the words. She could not finish a sentence. Her fears were making her inarticulate. She was afraid to utter the words, as if, by doing so, she might make those fears reality.

'She's stable now,' the nurse said.

A doctor, who had appeared seemingly from nowhere,

looked at the chart on Rose's bed. His sudden appearance made Esme realise just how tired she really was. He could have been there for a while and she would not have known. Her tiredness was making her disorientated and gave her a surrealistic feeling that made it impossible for her to connect to anything.

'Stable?' she asked. It was all so cold. They were talking about a patient, and she knew that they cared in so far as they could, but it was different for her. This was not just a patient. It was Rose, her Rose, her baby born on a day when it was snowing and even the lakes had frozen.

'Yes,' the doctor replied. 'She's fighting the toxins very well. If she's this good later in the day we will be thinking about moving her to a ward.'

'Really?' Esme said. 'I had no idea she was getting better at all.'

'It's slow,' he said. 'But she's fighting hard. Obviously the alcohol she had consumed didn't help, but that's gone out of her system now – well, almost. We think she may have vomited most of it and that has assisted. She's young and healthy, apart from what happened to her. She may have been sick for days. Certainly the plaster we removed appeared to have been on her wound for some time. But the nurse is right. You need rest now.'

Esme wondered how she must look that they both appeared more concerned with her than with their patient.

'I'm just tired,' she said. 'But shouldn't I stay until you do move her to a ward?'

'I think . . .' he glanced at the chart, searching for the name, and then finding it, 'I think Rose would like you with her later rather than now when she doesn't know what's happening. And for you to be able to comfort and care for her later, it would be better if you got some rest.'

'Go home,' the nurse said. 'Don't worry, we have your number, but I don't think we are going to need it.'

Esme hated the idea of leaving Rose, but knew that they were right. She was now so tired that she could hardly think clearly.

'You'll get a taxi at reception,' the nurse said to her. 'Rose is safe.'

Safe, safe, safe . . . the word buzzed in her head as Esme sat back in the cab. She wanted to close her eyes but knew that if she did she might not waken, and now there was Lily to face. Indeed, she could only hope that there *was* Lily to face – and Jasmine too.

Although it was early, the traffic was already heavy and the journey home took forty-five minutes. It would have been quicker on the underground, but Esme was too tired to face the walking that would involve. As the taxi pulled down the Embankment and drew up outside the apartment block, she realised she must have momentarily dozed off. Praying that she would find the girls in the apartment, she paid the driver and let herself into the reception area. The concierge was asleep at his desk. She could not blame him. What else should you be doing at six o'clock in the morning? Opening the apartment door, she knew immediately that Jasmine had arrived. Her bag was open on the hall floor, clothes strewn all over the place. In the living room it was not much better. Esme half remembered having cleaned the place when she had arrived from France – was it merely a day ago? But now it was worse than the way Rose had left it.

There seemed to be quantities of pizza slices in various places around the room as though its eater had taken a bite from each wedge and then abandoned the remains. Esme looked around in momentary dismay before shrugging off any irritation. It wasn't worth it, she thought. What did such things matter?

She checked that both Lily and Jasmine were in their rooms.

Lily's room was tidy. Her rucksack lay empty on the floor, leaning against the wall, her possessions already taken out and sorted, either into the laundry or into cupboards. Lily lay curled up on her side, her knees pulled towards her chest. Wisps of white-blonde hair fell across her cheek. The way the light shone into her room from the hallway it seemed as though her eyes were surrounded by dark shadows. Esme wanted to go and touch her, but she pulled back, not wanting to disturb her, knowing that she must be suffering from jet lag. She gently closed the door and checked on Jasmine.

Jasmine was sprawled on her back, sleeping very much as Grayson did. One arm on the pillow behind her head, the other stretched out so that her hand dangled off the bed. She pouted in her sleep. Her bedroom appeared to have been ransacked, with everything she possessed heaped and strewn across the floor. The light caught the glitter in the polish on her nails and Esme stepped forward to look at her more clearly. Her hair looked like it had been streaked, and Esme could not decide whether it was from the sun in South Carolina or that it had been dyed. She was about to close the bedroom door when some small movement on the floor distracted her. She looked again carefully but there was nothing. Closing the door, she thought of Rose lying so ill in her hospital bed, and any frustration that Jasmine might evince in her evaporated. At least she was healthy and at home, and what more could a parent want?

Lying down on her own bed, Esme set the alarm on her mobile for midday, before inserting its battery charger. She had left her door open so that if the girls woke before her, they would see that she was there. She was asleep within minutes. Her sleep was haunted by the sound of a child crying. Through a window in her mind, the leaves on trees fluttered in the breeze.

Jacob Althaus landed in London at midday and made his way to Henry and Sally Delmont's house where lunch awaited his arrival.

Sally hugged him before standing back to look at him carefully. 'Is everything all right?' she asked. 'Naomi . . . ?'

'Has she been in touch?' he asked.

'I see . . .' she said thoughtfully. 'I see. Have you left her?'

'No . . .' He hesitated. 'It's the other way around. She's left me.'

She grimaced. 'I hate prying,' she said. 'But did you see this coming?'

'If I had given it enough thought,' he replied, 'then, yes . . . I suppose I did. I just didn't expect it, though.'

He was reticent. He did not want to talk about Naomi – it was not why he was there. And yet he knew his friends were concerned, probably both for him and for Naomi.

'She had hinted that there was someone else,' Sally said gently. 'So I suppose it is not that big a surprise for us. But when you phoned and said you were coming to London, I think we thought that you had left her.'

'Oh, there isn't someone else,' Jacob said. 'My interest in this other person is only as a friend and possibly as a patient – it's a professional concern, that's all.'

Sally looked at him in bewilderment.

And as he looked back at her it suddenly dawned on him that she was not talking about him having a relationship with someone else. It was Naomi she was referring to.

'Naomi . . .' he said. 'Naomi has met someone else?' He could hardly take it in. 'How stupid of me,' he said then. 'For some reason that never occurred to me. I thought she had just had enough . . .' He was silent for a moment, and then he shook his head.

'Come,' Henry said gently, interrupting his thoughts, 'we'll have a sherry in the garden. Mind the step, though. It's crumbling. We're having it rebuilt this week.'

With a sherry in his hand, Jacob sat in their patioed garden and let the afternoon sun warm his face. It felt good – just being there with friends. The salty bite of an olive in his mouth felt clean and sharp. For some reason that he could not immediately ascertain, he felt an enormous sense of relief that Naomi had found someone else. And that made him feel guilty, because in his heart he knew what that meant. He was glad. Glad that he did not have to worry about her, glad that he did not have to make any more excuses in his mind for staying late at work, and finding other things to interest him than the empty shell that had become their once loving home.

Henry looked at him. 'That came as a bit of a shock, I think,' he said.

Jacob nodded. 'There is none so blind . . .' he replied, leaving the quote open-ended.

'I'm going out,' Sally said. 'I'm leaving you boys to have your lunch together and to talk.'

'So discreet as ever, Sally,' Jacob said, getting to his feet and embracing her. He smiled. 'For a long while I have assumed that Naomi was spending a lot of time shopping. I did her a disservice.'

Neither Henry nor Sally said anything. He realised it was awkward for them. Naomi must have hinted that evening when he was late for dinner . . .

'Anyway, I'm off,' Sally said. 'We've given you the bedroom overlooking this bit of the garden,' she added. 'And you are to stay for as long as you want. Understood?'

'Understood, *chérie*,' he replied. 'And thank you.'

After she had left and they went inside to eat, Henry fetched a bottle of wine from the fridge, slicing around the foil top with a penknife before pulling out the cork.

'I always feel under pressure with wine when I'm dining with you,' he said with a grin. 'No mere bottle of white plonk for you.'

'This looks lovely,' Jacob said, surveying the salads, pâtés, cold sliced meat and nutty grainy bread on the table. 'And a chablis to go with it! Well, you do honour me. Thank you.'

'Now if Sally had stayed, she would have insisted on lighting the candles,' Henry said, looking at the silver candelabra on the table.

'May I?' Jacob reached in his pocket for his lighter. 'This lunch deserves to be eaten in true style.'

He was aware they were both just talking, filling in time until they sat to eat and would then discuss why he was there at all.

Henry poured the wine into the crystal glasses, before sitting at the head of the table.

'I take it you have not come to us because of Naomi,' Henry said as he served up the food.

'No,' Jacob replied. 'It is to do with the conversation we had in Paris and the file you sent me.'

'Ah, yes. Young Molly Kilbride. Now a patient of yours?'

'No. I cannot truthfully say that,' Jacob said. 'But my interest is professional.' As he said it, he wondered again if he was being honest. 'I met someone – more by chance than anything, I suppose. And she has been telling me her story in small snippets. And then she gave me the name Molly Kilbride . . .'

'You implied the other day you didn't think she was the same person. Do you still think that?'

'No. I don't think that any more. I think she is the same person. And I believe she wanted me to know that. I would never have guessed – I had no reason to. She gave me the name so that I would have a link with the past at which she had hinted. No, let me put that clearer. She had told me bits about her past and occasionally expressed regret that she could not remember all of it or perhaps that she had not pieced it all together.'

'And now?'

'Now, I would like you to tell me the story. Yes, I know, I've read the file. But you know more, both because you were there as Harper Gumm's apostle, as you so succinctly put it, but also because you implied that there was more that you knew.'

'Yes. There is so much more than is in the file. You see, Groucho, in his efforts to help Molly, spoke to everyone who was involved. Her parents, her parents' friends, their son, his friends, the police – everyone. He put together a complete picture. And then, of course, Molly herself. She told him her story – how she survived, both physically and mentally.' Henry paused. 'Linking the present and the past is difficult,' he continued.

'Indeed. I know. Let me start by telling you this . . . There is a woman. Esme Waters is her chosen name. She appears serene and gentle, with eyes like clear-cut green glass. When she smiles, they smile too. But deep within her there is something that is hurting her so badly. She has described herself as being only half a person.'

Henry nodded. He sipped his wine.

'There was a child,' he said . . .

CHAPTER SIXTEEN

There was a child.
Molly Kilbride.

Dark brown hair and a happy smile. Harry Hastings held this child, his child, in his arms, bounced her on his knee, remembered with clarity the moment of her birth, his feelings of bewilderment followed by the burst of emotion that flooded his veins, and the knowledge that he could hold no more joy – that this was the ultimate in human emotion.

He told Molly these things so that she would know of his love, and they were words she remembered, words she carried through her childhood.

Clever in school, loved by her parents, bubbling and cheerful, given to bursts of introspection and serious reading, followed by outbursts of laughing and dancing and excesses of energy – she was a contradiction in many ways, like most children. A good child. A decent child. Wanted. Protected. Secure.

The world she knew included a large back garden, a tennis court, and a tree house. Her upbringing included music and art and all the warmth and nourishment that a child could want.

Her mother, Susan Kilbride, taught her of God – a God of righteousness and power who smote the wicked with

His sword, and raised up the good and brought them to a place in puffball clouds of bliss – a paradise where they existed in perfect joy. Molly knew of nothing else – just the promise of comfort on earth followed by perpetual happiness.

These notions had not made her smug – she knew she had to work to achieve that perpetual paradise but knew also not to dwell on it. It was something for old age when her hair was grey and she was like her grandmother, with skin too thin to hold her mottled tired veins, and when the need for peace was more important than climbing trees or reading books. While she was aware that some things are kept for old age, she did not ponder on them or think about them excessively.

Decency and kindness, a moral conscience – they taught her these values and guided her through her childhood.

Her clothes, new or old, were clean and fresh, the food on the table was carefully chosen for its nutrition.

If there were moments of anger between her parents, moments that upset Molly, they passed because Molly knew her parents loved her. Her father kissed her in the morning and tucked her in bed at night. He read her stories – the ones Susan skipped in her books. She liked the sounds of words long before she ever knew what they meant. They echoed in her head as she drifted safely off to sleep.

Her mother, rather less demonstrative, controlled Molly's progress in school, insisted on her piano practice, brought her to the dentist, drove her to church. God looked out for her. God was on her side.

Or so she thought.

Love is shown in different ways. And Molly's world was full of it.

Mozart was playing on the stereo while Molly did her homework. Music for the brain, her mother said.

Fish was served three times a week. Food for the brain, her mother said.

Bedtime was early. Sleep enhances your performance, her mother said.

Prayers before bedtime – so God would know she held Him in her heart.

'Don't overdo the God thing,' Harry said.

Molly heard him.

Susan replied, 'The God thing! Harry, what do you mean? God is God.' Her voice was cross. Molly moved back from the doorway. She went up the stairs to her room to read. Her room was quiet. There it did not matter who walked in which paths of which lord god. There the magic was in tales and myths – different countries had different stories, each special to its origin. Fairy tales from different countries – different regions. The word 'religion' sounded a bit like 'region'. Perhaps religions were region based. She was not sure. She just knew that her mother's god and her father's god did not exactly overlap. But it did not matter. Their morality was the same and it was that which was at the core of her being.

Yea, though I walk through the shadow of the valley of death, I shall fear no evil – they said that in her mother's church. It made no sense. She did not know evil. The most she knew was that God had cast the devil out from His Heavenly Kingdom, and evil was banished.

Molly Kilbride's world was a cocoon of warmth within which she grew. From newborn baby to child, from child to girl, as puberty came in, it seemed to have been an easy ride.

Budding breasts emerged from the child's flat chest, her bones elongated to a slight gawkiness, her open smile still lit up her face and her eyes sparkled with delight. Her growing-up was embraced. Molly had her fourteenth birthday.

It was an old-fashioned party, with a mixture of the generations drifting through the rooms. Grandparents, uncles and aunts sat around the garden with glasses of champagne and finger food on silver platters, handed around by reluctant cousins who had been encouraged to mix with the adults.

'Dancing Queen' was playing, and Harry winked at her. It was their song. His and hers. Sometimes when it played he took her hand and they sang it together. Now a wink sufficed.

Indoors, with the French windows open, cousins, school friends and neighbours' children ran in and out, coyly checking each other out as mingling with the opposite sex was not a pastime with which they were yet familiar.

Boys and girls clambered up and down to the tree house where a tray of toffee-coated apples lay alongside a bowl of crisps. The mixing of the generations was startling for some of Molly's school friends. Small cousins rolled on the grass, chattering with each other, while the boys in the tree house looked at the girls with interest.

Molly was at ease – she knew this world. If there was jealousy directed towards her, she was not aware of it – it was not an emotion she knew or understood. She glanced at one of her classmates, trying to read the expression on her face – was she enjoying herself? Would she be nicer to Molly because of this invitation? And she wondered what was going on in Jennifer Delmont's head. In a moment of insight Molly knew that the only way she could ever really know what someone else was thinking was if she could access someone else's mind – but just for a moment . . . not to stay there . . . just to see the world through that person's perspective, albeit briefly. And then, of course, she wanted to return to the safety of her own mind, which was where she would always be most comfortable, because she had grown with it and in it. That was security.

Or so she thought.

She was that child who danced and sang and it was her fourteenth birthday.

Everything was hers for the taking. That was what Harry, her beloved dad, said. 'The world is your oyster,' he had smiled. That had been the evening before, when he and Susan had taken her to a hotel in town to eat her first oyster. She had felt grown up that evening as a door into an adult world had briefly opened and she had partaken of those things that would be hers. They had walked around the front of Trinity College on the way to Wicklow Street and the oysters.

'Here is where you will come to study,' Harry said to her. 'Here you will use that brain of yours and we will be even prouder of you than we already are. Isn't that right, Susan?'

And Susan, who so often looked into the depth of everything, surprisingly enough said, 'Yes.'

Molly Kilbride undid her seat belt. It was the day after her birthday party and it was hot in the car as her mother, Susan, suffered from some extraordinary temperature disorder that meant that she was cold when other people were not, and hot when others were freezing, or so it seemed to Molly.

'Put your seat belt back on,' Susan said.

It was one of those erratic days as summer ended and autumn had not quite decided to begin, when the sky was slightly overcast, and a morning chill was suddenly being replaced by heat.

'I'm just taking off my coat,' Molly explained. 'It's very hot.'

'I'm freezing,' her mother replied, just as Molly knew she would.

Molly struggled out of her coat, threw it into the back seat, and refastened her belt. It was the early days of seat belts but Susan Kilbride was a stickler for detail.

'If we went to the library first,' Molly suggested as she looked out the window at the passing houses, 'I could read while you're in the bank.'

'No,' Susan said. 'Bank first, then we can spend as much time as you want in the library.'

It was a reasonable argument, as Molly would have complained had they been rushing in the library.

'And I want to get rid of this money as fast as possible,' Susan added.

The money was in a bag locked in the boot, and Susan, who hated these occasional trips to the bank with so much cash, was uneasy. Her husband, Harry Hastings, engineer and nightclub owner, sometimes gave her a bag with a slip of paper. 'Lodge it for me, Susan,' he said. 'I don't have time this morning.'

They pulled in at the bank and Susan looked unsuccessfully for parking in the spaces reserved for the bank, before pulling back out on to the road and parking on the double yellow lines. She did not notice a car pulling in directly behind her.

'Come in with me, Molly,' she said.

'Do I have to?'

'No, you don't have to do anything,' Susan said.

Molly had recently started to bicker, niggling over tiny points. Susan's initial reaction had been to argue back, stating her case and insisting on obedience, but her sister, Jane, whose children were older, pointed out to her that it might be easier just to fight for the important things and to find compromise on the others.

'Oh, all right,' Molly said, as if Susan had just insisted. 'I'll come in with you.'

'Put your coat back on,' Susan said as they got out of the car.

'I'm too hot,' Molly replied.

Susan said nothing.

She went to the boot and unlocked it, lifting out the heavy holdall as Molly joined her on the pavement.

'Molly . . .' she began.

What happened next happened so fast that later Susan was at a loss to explain it with any clarity or sequence.

One moment they were alone at the back of the car, and the next moment there was a man beside them with one arm around Molly.

'Give the bag to your daughter,' he said to Susan.

She stood motionless, taking in with horror his balaclava-covered head, the startled look on her daughter's face, the flash of something in his hand . . . She opened her mouth to scream, but if she were capable of uttering any noise it was unclear because he immediately said, 'Don't do that. Act normally. Hand it to Molly.'

He knew her name.

In a dream she handed the heavy bag to her daughter, and Molly took it. The man half lifted half dragged Molly back to a Mercedes, and he threw both the bag and her daughter into the back seat, leaping in after them, and the car took off.

Susan, standing on the road beside the open boot, then screamed and screamed.

Molly Kilbride, in the back of the car, heard that scream somewhere in the depths of her mind. She took in the bald head of the driver and black leather upholstery, before a strip of rough material was bound across her eyes, blinding her to any other visual observation.

'Please,' she found her voice and whispered, 'please . . .' before a gag was put around her mouth and she found herself pushed down on to the floor. She crouched there, gagged and blindfolded, while the car sped down the road, weaving through traffic and across the city.

The smell of the leather interior was fresh in her nostrils at first until she got used to it. It reminded her of Harry's latest car, bought a month earlier, and that lovely smell of newness that only a car could have. She remembered her mother commenting on it the day it arrived.

Molly called her parents Susan and Dad, because Susan liked to think of herself as a woman ahead of her time, even though she was caught in her past, in her upbringing, in her religious beliefs, the mythology of her own childhood and a single-minded conviction in her rights. Harry, on the other hand, had equilibrium and gentleness, also learned in his own childhood. These attributes embraced Molly in a way that was just as comforting as her mother's approach but were possibly more appealing.

While Molly loved them for the parents they were, she admired them because they were what she was not – tall, talented, successful, or so it appeared through her childish eyes – but she had of late discovered that they annoyed her.

Things they had done in the past, things she had done with them, pronouncements they made, their certainty of their own worth – all these things she had started to question, making her irritable and querulous, often against her natural instincts.

Doubled up on the floor of the car, all she could think was how much she loved them and wanted them, how much she needed them and relied on them. Her immediate mental reactions were that they would come and get her back, that they would find her with that confidence they always displayed, that any minute she would hear the siren of police cars, and they would be surrounded and she would be returned home to their large comfortable house in the suburbs, and that Susan would fetch her library books, and she could curl up in bed and read.

*   *   *

The car was belting along now – she did not know if it was on a main road or some side road; it was impossible to tell. The gag was tight around her mouth and she tried moving her jaw up and down to loosen it, keeping her head tucked down so that she would not be seen.

'Fifty or sixty thousand,' she heard her captor saying. His accent was different from Harry's educated city voice, and she surprised herself at the thought – surprised at the fact that she could take in something like that while feeling terrified. She was less aware of the discomfort and the fear while she was contemplating what had happened and what was going on. She tried to remember what she had taken in, in those seconds between him grabbing her and being pushed into the car. The windows of the car were dark. She had not been able to see into them, and did not know there was a driver until she was actually inside. She wondered if Susan had seen his face. The man who had lifted her was wearing a jacket; she could remember its texture as his sleeve brushed against her face. She shifted uncomfortably on the floor. It was difficult to breathe in that position, and she lifted her head for air. Her hands were still free but she was afraid to use them to shift either the blindfold or the gag in case he then tied them too.

'It was black,' Susan Kilbride was saying. 'A Mercedes. I think a Merc. I'm almost sure a Merc. A large car. Black. Yes, I think black. Or maybe dark blue. Maybe not a Mercedes – but large . . . I couldn't see through the windows. There must have been someone else driving it, because the man who . . . the man who . . .' Her voice broke. Her gabbling ceased momentarily, and one police officer guided her into his car.

'You've got to go after them,' Susan started again. 'You have to. Molly is wearing a red jumper. It's not warm enough. It's definitely not warm enough.'

'It's all right,' the officer said. 'We're going to get you down to the station. Your husband is on his way. It'll be all right.'

'But aren't you going after them?' she asked, perplexed.

'We already are,' he said to her. 'Someone thinks they got the number, or at least part of it. Cars have already been dispatched. Now, just sit in the car, and go through it slowly in your head. Anything you can think of, no matter how small – it could be useful.'

Susan held on until they arrived at the police station, but the sight of Harry running across the reception area towards her reduced her to the tears she had been fighting.

'Don't cry,' he said, putting his arms around her. 'For God's sake, stop crying. You can't help Molly while you're in this state. I need you calm. For God's sake, Susan, stop crying.'

She gulped and tried to stop as they were ushered through into an interview room.

'She's only wearing a red jumper,' she said. 'She's going to be so cold.'

'What else is she wearing?' a female officer asked her.

'What do you mean?' Susan asked.

'Tell me what Molly's wearing,' the woman repeated.

'Jeans. Blue ones. No . . . no, she's not. She's wearing a skirt. No . . . I can't remember.'

'Of course you can,' the woman said to her gently. 'Just sit down, and we'll go through everything.'

'He knew her name,' Susan suddenly said. 'He called her Molly. I'm sure he did . . .'

'Are you sure?' Harry asked. 'Really? He called her Molly?'

'Yes. Yes, I'm sure he did. He said something like, "Give the bag to Molly."'

'Had you addressed her before that? Had you used her name?' she was asked.

Susan sat quietly, now thinking carefully, trying to piece together those last few minutes before Molly was taken.

'I don't know,' she replied eventually. 'I may have said something to her. I may have used her name. I don't know. I can't be sure.'

'What do you think you said to her?'

Susan thought again. It was difficult to be sure of the sequence of events. 'I think I told her to put on her coat,' she said. 'I may have said, "Put your coat on, Molly." I don't know. If only I had insisted she came into the bank with me . . .'

'How do you mean? Was she not going in with you?' Harry asked.

Susan ran her hands through her blonde hair. Both hands were shaking.

'You know how she is at the moment, Harry,' she said. 'If I tell her to do one thing, she goes and does the opposite. So when she said she didn't want to come into the bank, I said she could stay in the car, so she promptly got out of the car to come in with me. You know what she's like . . .'

'How old is Molly?' one of the officers asked.

'She's fourteen,' Harry said. 'Her birthday was yesterday.'

'Going on eighteen,' Susan added. 'You know what they're like at that age. Everything – everything I do is wrong.'

'Just in her eyes,' the woman said to her. 'It's perfectly normal,' she added reassuringly.

'I know it's normal,' Susan said. 'If only I had insisted she stayed in the car. Or if I said to her that she had to come into the bank, then she wouldn't have got out of the car.'

'Stop that, Susan,' Harry said. 'That's going to get us nowhere.'

'How much money was in the bag?' he was asked.

'Just over fifty-four thousand,' he replied.

'I have the slip of paper you gave me,' Susan said. 'It's in my bag.' She rooted in her handbag, and pulled it from her wallet.

'Fifty-four thousand three hundred,' she said.

'Why have they taken Molly?' Harry asked. 'They have the money. Why did they take her?'

'Probably as collateral.'

'Collateral?'

'Security. If something went wrong in the getaway, they have her to bargain with.'

'But now what?' Harry said. 'They got away. Surely they will let her go. They got what they wanted.'

'Yes,' he was told. 'She may well be dropped off out of the car somewhere on their journey to wherever they are going.'

'The car number?' he said. 'Did you say that you got the number?' Harry asked Susan.

'No, I didn't. But someone else did.'

A bystander had taken the number, and was almost sure it was correct. Even as they were talking it was being checked.

A different detective joined them. 'The car was stolen last night. It was taken from outside a nightclub sometime between midnight and two this morning.'

'One of my nightclubs?' Harry asked.

'No, a different one. In a different part of the city.'

'This was all planned,' Harry said slowly, as pieces of the story started to come together.

'It certainly looks like it. There may be an IRA connection . . .'

'What? God no . . . Why do you think that?'

'We don't know it for a fact. It could be IRA or it could be some gangland operation. We're not sure at this stage. We think your wife must have been followed this morning. Otherwise it is all too random. They must have known that she was carrying the money. Now, how would they know?'

Harry thought carefully.

Harold Hastings was, first and foremost, an engineer. His main claim to fame, not known to the general public, was that he had designed and constructed a road to link with a motorway in a Middle Eastern country, but he had got the calculations wrong and the motorway had to be rebuilt to accommodate his error. Harry got paid, the taxpayer paid for the reconstruction, and life went on. But his confidence was disturbed and he bought the first of several nightclubs so that he would have something to fall back on should it all come out.

Harold Hastings and Susan Kilbride came to parenthood quite late. They were both in their mid-to-late thirties when Molly was born.

Susan insisted that Molly take her surname, saying that Harry's family name made her think of battles and it was inappropriate for such a tiny baby. Harry expressed surprise, as he had never seen his name other than just that – his name, his heritage – and had assumed that it would be passed to whatever offspring he might have in life. Susan was adamant that it was unacceptable for a baby, and lying there in her private room in the hospital, recovering from an emergency Caesarean section, nothing would dissuade her. Susan was stubborn about strange things.

Her older sister, Jane, took him aside in the hospital corridor and said to him, 'Let her have her way on this one, Harry. There will be other more important battles to handle later – things really worth fighting for.' This was Jane's approach to everything in life, and while Harry had thought that his was something worth fighting for, he now supposed he was in shock from the suddenness of the whole event, as little Molly had arrived three weeks early and was duly ensconced in an incubator, where, it would turn out, she would have to stay for some ten days.

And so he conceded, and Esme Molly Kilbride was accordingly registered, and Harry wondered, if they had another child, might he be able to insist on the use of his name. However, there were no other children.

'She's all we have,' Susan said to the officers, as if having another child might make Molly's absence more bearable.

'We're doing all we can to get her back,' she was reassured by a voice that might have held a certain amount of hesitation, because the car that had taken Molly had disappeared in the traffic, and as yet there was no trace of it.

'Tell us about Molly,' the female officer said. 'What's she like? Will she keep her head? What's her health like?'

'Her health?' Susan seemed startled. 'She's fine. Why?'

'No, I just wondered if she might have asthma, or if she is on any medication.'

'No, nothing. Molly is fine. Healthy. There's nothing wrong with her,' Harry said, as Susan did not seem able to grasp the meaning of the question. 'Molly is special,' he added. 'If any child can keep her head, it will be her. She is a thinker.' He was trying to reassure himself. His voice was not as calm as his words.

They went home to find a recent photograph of Molly. Susan toyed between the one the school had taken the previous term, and the portrait photograph that had been done in a studio in town for Molly's grandparents, a copy of which was framed in their living room. The police took both photographs.

The headlines in the evening papers read, 'Child and Money Taken', 'Woman Robbed of Child', 'Molly Kilbride – Gone Without a Trace.'

And Molly Kilbride was gone, seemingly without a trace. Days passed and stretched almost into a week. Dark days, dark as in a world with little light or hope. Days of torment for Susan and Harry as their world fell apart, and Molly – the light and dream of their lives, their reason for being, their fulfilment – had disappeared into the darkness.

And while they waited, sleepless, frightened, their child was trying to pull down shutters in her head to bolster the thinness of the walls of her mind.

Sticks and stones, she thought, as she lay on a bed, tied to the iron bedstead during those long days and nights. Sticks and stones may break my bones, but names will never hurt me.

That was what her mother had said when Jennifer Delmont called her an ugly fat toad because she had got first place in class and Jennifer was annoyed, some six months earlier.

It had hurt – those words had hurt no matter what Susan might say.

Molly feared she was ugly, was sure she was fat, and as for a toad . . . well, a toad was a toad. It was fine for a toad to look like and to be a toad, but it was not one bit fine for a human being to look like and to be a toad.

But she remembered Susan's maxim, and she thought about it when lying on the bed, her hands bound to the bedstead. For some reason now, those words took on a different meaning.

She did hurt. She hurt more than she had known she could hurt. But it was the fear – the terror that she could not handle. That terror was there when they were in the room and when they left. It was there when the light was on and when the light was off. That terror encompassed her. She struggled to contain it.

The walls of my mind are very thin. I will let no one in.

At first her eyes were blindfolded, and then they removed the tape.

The curtains were drawn. A little light filtered through a triangle at the top of them, and through the sides she could see through a tiny section of windowpane. There were trees blowing outside in the wind. The leaves were brown and red and yellow. The leaves were falling.

There was a crack on the ceiling.

She watched it.

It spread from the centre ceiling-rose in a jerking line across the breadth of the room. It took on significance as the hours went by.

Was it elongating? Was it extending? Had it shifted imperceptibly while she blinked or dozed or slept?

Her geography was little more than adequate. She roughly knew the continents and where they were positioned in relation to each other because she had travelled with her parents to three of them – three including Europe. Europe she knew. But there was no coastline in Europe that looked like the crack. She thought it might be like the continent under the United States of America. Or as Harry, her dad, called it, Americay.

She couldn't remember what that country was called. It had a long coastline with a different ocean on either side. It was the far side of that continent she thought the crack might look like. Brazil was somewhere down there. But she wasn't sure which side. Nuts and coffee – she remembered that from a coloured book of maps she had had when she was little. She wondered what had happened to those books – all the books of her childhood. Had Susan thrown them out when she was finished with them, when she grew out of them, or were they somewhere hidden in their home? A crack had appeared on their kitchen ceiling once. A little plaster fell off. Harry fixed it. Her dad. He did such things. But after the plaster had dried, he painted it, and somehow the paint pot fell off the top of the ladder. She had been watching him. She rushed forwards to catch it. An arc of white paint splashed across her. It was sticky and it smelled. At least it's only emulsion, he said, as he wiped her face.

'For goodness' sake,' Susan said, 'you are so incompetent.'

'It was an accident,' he replied reasonably.

Sticks and stones, Molly thought. Next time some repair work needed doing, Harry got in a decorator.

'And what's that going to cost?' Susan said. 'Can't you do it yourself?'

'I'll leave it to the experts from now on,' Harry said. He winked at Molly. 'Sure, it's only money, Susan,' he added. 'And we have plenty of that.'

Plenty of money.

Over fifty thousand pounds in that bag, and it was not enough to buy Molly freedom.

Molly wondered what freedom meant.

Freedom was being able to go to the library. It was . . . she paused in her thoughts. What was freedom? At that moment freedom was not being tied to that bed, with her wrists chafing and a knot of fear that at first had been confined to her stomach and then to her head, but was now all-reaching. There was no part of her that was not afraid.

South America – it came to her in a flash and she was back in her thoughts.

The walls of my mind are very thin, but I will not let them in.

She could hear the footsteps on the stairs.

South America. There was a mountain range there – she could see the little triangles in her mind, the triangles in her coloured childhood book that signified mountains. Not pyramids. Pyramids were in Africa. She had seen them. They had gone on horseback. She, Dad and Susan.

The mountain range in South America sounded like Andy.

Andrew Mortimer was the son of friends of her parents.

Richard and Bluebell. She wondered, as she had done in the past, was Bluebell really Bluebell's name, and if not, how had she come by it? The names of flowers were lovely. Each evoked a different image. Lilies – they sowed not, neither did they spin, or was it reap? Did lilies not reap? She did not know. Heather on the mountainside. Roses blooming red and white. Harry brought Susan roses sometimes. Big bouquets. Bouquet had two meanings but she didn't know if they were spelled the same. Sometimes it meant a big bunch, and sometimes it meant a smell. A nice smell. Names were interesting. Her name was Esme. But she was known as Molly. She couldn't say Esme when she was tiny, it was too difficult, and somehow she became known as Molly – Molly had been her middle name. She quite liked the name Molly. As names went, it was not bad. There were no other Mollys in her class. She knew no one else with the name Bluebell.

The walls of my mind are very thin – but you can't get in. I won't let you in. Andrew Mortimer was twelve years older than she. He was very good-looking. They had nothing in common.

Sometimes the Mortimers came for dinner – Richard and Bluebell. They came smartly dressed and bringing wine and chocolates and flowers, and Molly came in to say good night. Sometimes they went to the Mortimers' on a Sunday after-noon for a barbecue. Once Andrew was there.

'Entertain Molly,' Bluebell said to him.

Molly felt embarrassed. How could he entertain her? She was eight years old. Andrew was nearly twenty. He was going to start university the coming term. He had been abroad for a year. He was going to study Physics. Molly knew nothing about physics. And Andrew knew nothing about what eight-year-old girls liked. Dolls. Books. Horses. These were the things that interested her.

'Come up to my room,' he said to her. 'I have some great board games.'

The walls of my mind are terribly thin . . . I will not let you in. That's what the little pigs said to the panther. I'll huff and I'll puff and I'll blow the house down, the panther said. The little pig said something . . . something . . . she couldn't find the words . . . but it ended, 'I'll not let you in.' The panther . . . no, the wolf . . . it was a wolf . . . she thought.

It was not like that with Andrew Mortimer.

'Aren't you very hot in those shoes?' Andrew Mortimer had said. 'Take them off. Make yourself comfortable. We'll play cards. I'll teach you poker.'

She unbuckled her sandals, and slipped off her socks and sat on his bed. Andrew pulled a pack of cards out of his desk drawer.

'We could play in the garden,' he said.

She thought he looked so nice. She wanted to stay in his room. She didn't know what to say.

He got up and went to the window and looked out. Down below, Richard was putting charcoal on the barbecue. The Mortimers had lived in South Africa. Barbecues were the norm. Bluebell was carrying out gins and tonic for Susan and Harry. They were sitting back on old-fashioned deck chairs. You had to be careful of your fingers with deck chairs. That's what Susan said. You could catch them if you weren't careful.

'What little feet you have,' Andrew said as he shuffled the cards.

Molly looked at her feet. She didn't know if they were big or little. They were just her feet. They were small in comparison with Susan and Harry's. Small in comparison with Andrew's feet. But probably just about the right size for her.

'You have a cut on your knee,' Andrew said. 'A scar. What happened to it?'

'I fell.'

She had fallen while chasing a cat in the garden. She had run out of the kitchen to chase the cat away because the robin was eating . . . he was pecking at the ground. She had known she was going to fall from the moment she left the kitchen. Her momentum was all wrong. She was going too fast and she misjudged some aspect of the steps. She had kept going until she cleared them but then she went forwards and landed on her hands and knees, not quite making it as far as the grass.

'Not too much damage,' Harry had said. He was making an omelette for her in the kitchen. 'What a brave little thing you are.' She didn't cry. She smiled at him, biting back the tears. He cleaned her knee. Only one knee was cut. He picked bits of gravel and dirt from her hands and soaked them in the sink.

'I bet that was sore,' Andrew said as he dealt the cards.

The walls of my mind – please don't – don't don't don't – don't come in.

Through the gap in the curtain she could just see out the window. She could see the rain. Through her tears she could see the rain. Water through water. What was rain? Where did it come from? What were tears? Where did they come from? Was rain some natural phenomenon? Some emotion of nature? Like tears expressed some emotion on her part? Or did they? Is that what tears were? What did they express? They were pointless. When you cried your nose got bunged up. Better not to cry. Difficult to breathe with a bunged-up nose. Mustn't cry. Must stop the tears. Tears won't help. Andrew, she thought. Andrew, Andrew. Andrew come and find me. She had given up on her parents. She could not bear to think about them. She had tried in her mind to call them. Mummy, Dad, Susan, Harry. She had tried so hard to concentrate on them that they would know by some kind of telepathy where she was. Andrew Mortimer was so nice. He shuffled the cards and he explained what she had to do. It was so easy. You either had a pair or a three or a flush. Or you didn't. He said he would teach her how to bluff.

That was nice. That was safe. That was Andrew. Andrew Mortimer. When she grew up she wanted to marry him.

There was a mirror on the wall by the door.

The door opened. She could see through the mirror out the door.

Molly screamed. The scream was not out loud. It was in her head. The tape across her mouth made sure of that. And the scream echoed and echoed round and round the walls of her mind.

Oh, so thin, so very thin.

There was a mirror on the wall. She could see someone in it – she could see part of a face, two eyes watching.

'No . . .' she screamed. That was aloud. The tape was off.

The wolf's hand was over her mouth now. Her scream was suffocated inside her head. The eyes still watched. She could see 'him' in the mirror. The Eyes. She called him the Eyes. The Eyes did not look in the mirror. They looked through the mirror. The Eyes watched. The Eyes could stop it happening. She willed him to look in the mirror at her face and he might see her pleading with him, pleading with her eyes to his eyes. The man – the wolf – the man with the balaclava on his head kissed her. Black black, just his eyes showing. Cold eyes, emotionless, hungry, frightening – she did not know how to view them. They were terrifying. He had moved his hand and his mouth was on hers, rough woollen material rubbing against her face. She couldn't breathe.

*   *   *

'Did you enjoy the game?' Susan asked.

'What were you playing?' Bluebell said.

'He taught me poker,' Molly said.

'Poker?' Susan said.

'Never too young to learn it,' Harry said with a laugh.

'Andrew has always liked numbers,' Bluebell said. 'He says poker is a great help for numbers. Or is it numbers are a great help for poker?'

Molly listened avidly. She liked words. She was all right at numbers, but they didn't have the same interest as words. Numbers to her were symbols of quantity. Words had a depth of their own.

There was lemonade with ice and a slice of lemon and a straw. There was a tiny umbrella sticking out of the glass. Molly needed the straw so that everything would remain intact, and the tip of the parasol would not touch her nose. The parasol was yellow. So was the straw. The cubes of ice bobbed slightly when she sucked.

She looked up at Andrew from her drink. He turned his face away. Her smile stayed transfixed on her lips. *Oh, the walls of my mind . . .*

Bluebell had kissed her when they left after the barbecue. She would have liked Andrew to kiss her, but he was busy carrying plates in from the garden. 'See you, Molly,' he called as they went out the door.

Molly Kilbride had been a very self-contained child. A serious little thing, enthusiastic and loving, who tried to please. And usually succeeded. Harry was not difficult to please. He adored her. Susan was a little more demanding. She liked things just right. She liked ceilings painted as soon as the plaster was dry. She liked clothes folded neatly in cupboards, sorted into categories. She liked perfection.

'I hope that doesn't leave a scar,' she had said about Molly's cut knee.

'It'll be grand,' Harry said. 'It just needs to heal. And even if there is a scar, sure, it's only her knee. It will fade as she grows.'

'I wonder if it should be stitched,' Susan said.

Molly did not want stitches. It had hurt enough. It was time to leave it be and let her get on with things. Leave the cut alone. Let it heal. Dad knew these things in a fatherly way. Susan liked things just right, in a motherly way.

When Molly was thirteen, Susan and Harry had a dinner party. They invited Jeremy Coyle. He was Harry's nightclub manager. He was from the North of Ireland. He was thirty-three and he had a girlfriend whom Susan called the Blonde Bimbo and Harry called the Bombshell. Her name was Lola.

'Hello-allo, Lola,' Harry sang when they came to dinner. They came to dinner with the Mortimers. Andrew wasn't there. Andrew had gone to university and Molly hadn't seen him for at least two years. Lola's legs seemed to go up to her armpits, and she wore a dress that was so short that when she sat down and Molly came in to say good night, Molly could see she was wearing black lace knickers. Molly went to bed after she had kissed Bluebell and Richard, and shaken hands with Jeremy and Lola.

Jeremy looked at her. 'You look like your mother,' he said. He touched her cheek. She didn't like the way he looked at her.

'Come now, Molly,' her mother, Susan, said abruptly. 'Bedtime.'

Bluebell interjected, 'Andrew sent you his love, Molly.'

Molly smiled politely. She wasn't sure that Andrew had sent her his love. It didn't seem likely. She felt that Andrew would not have mentioned her. She thought it was the kind of thing an adult might say, thinking it would make the recipient feel good. She was not sure if it did make her feel good. She liked to think about Andrew.

'What a little poppet,' Lola said.

A poppet. It sounded like a type of sweet. A sweet that you sucked. She tried to think it was a sweet in her mouth.

The walls of my mind are terribly thin . . .

The crack on the ceiling was her friend. When she turned her body, in so far as she could turn because she was trapped by her wrists, the crack seemed to turn too. She called it Andy. A tiny chip of plaster fell off it on to the floor. She knew that Andy had let that piece of plaster fall to make contact with her. She was sad that it had fallen on the floor. It had been meant to fall on to her on the bed. The walls of the ceiling are very thin, she thought. They will fall in.

No. Andy would not let that happen. He would hold on tight to the plaster. That's what you had to do. To hold on tight. To something. If she could just remember what to hold on to.

A spider appeared. Black. Thick-bodied. Long-legged. She named him Jericho. He walked on walls. The walls of Jericho.

In Brussels, William Murphy, trader, banker and investment whiz kid, got a phone call from a friend of his in Dublin.

'That you, William?'

'Yes. Who is it?'

'Christy.'

'Well, hello, Christy. Haven't heard from you in a long time. Are you coming over?'

There had been an ongoing invitation, not yet accepted, but both were sure that at some point Christy would go over, stay with William Murphy, paint Brussels red, and return to Dublin with an almighty hangover. It was the story of their relationship.

'No,' Christy replied. 'I'm too busy at work. Look, Will – have you rented the house out or something and not told me?'

Christy lived next door to William Murphy's mother's house on the canal, outside Dublin – isolated houses with few neighbours. William's mother had died earlier in the year, and the house had been left empty awaiting probate.

'No, why?'

'There's been a light on in there over the last few days, and I went to check it out. I don't have a key. Remember, the estate agent took it last month, so they could move in as soon as the will was cleared? Anyway, I knocked on the door, but there was no answer.'

'Don't worry,' William said. 'I left a couple of lights on so that it would look like there was someone there in the evening.'

'I know that,' Christy said. 'But I'm not talking lights on all the time. I mean sporadically. I came in at three last night and there was a light on upstairs behind the curtains, and I'm sure it wasn't on when I went out in the evening.'

'That's odd,' William said thoughtfully. 'I wonder if there has been a power failure and when the electricity returned, the lights just went back on?'

'I suppose it's possible,' Christy said. 'Anyway, I just wanted you to know.'

William Murphy hung up. There were a couple of ways of handling this. He could ring the estate agent and have someone call at the house to check that everything was all right and to reset the timer. Or he could pop over himself. It was ages since he had been home. He could catch up with some friends. A few drinks. Irish pubs . . . He checked his diary. No point in going over without some other reason so he wouldn't have to pay for the flight. He rang his secretary and then got two meetings set up in the bank in Dublin for

two days later. His secretary organised his flight. He rang his
girlfriend.

'Marian, I've to go over to Dublin for a day or two. Want
to come too?'

Marian said no, she did not want to go too. She was busy
with her art course, and Dublin held no attractions whatsoever at that moment.

'I'm going out the day after tomorrow,' he said. 'So if you
change your mind, there's still time to buy a ticket.'

Marian said she would see him for dinner later, but that
she did not think she would be changing her mind.

William vaguely wondered if there could be squatters in
the house, and if so, how he would get rid of them. He had
a feeling that there were something called squatters' rights,
but was unsure what that might mean.

He made a mental note to take the keys with him. Then
he picked up the phone again.

'Hey, Andrew,' he said, when the call was answered.

Andrew Mortimer, now twenty-five years old, was writing
his doctorate. He had transferred from Physics to Pure
Maths, and was working on something to do with the relation between prime and non-prime numbers. Or so Bluebell,
his mother, explained it to her friends. She really did want
to understand his work and his interest, but it was exceed-
ingly difficult because he explained it so badly to her. Some
four days before William Murphy phoned him, and on the
same day that Molly Kilbride was lifted outside the bank,
Andrew, who rented an apartment in the city centre, had
left college early to change his clothes before meeting his
parents for dinner in a restaurant off Suffolk Street. It was
his mother's favourite place and, not being particularly good
at cooking, he was looking forward to it.

Walking to the restaurant an hour later, he passed

someone carrying an evening paper. The man was walking down the street towards him with the paper open. Andrew saw both the headline and the photograph of Molly Kilbride on the front page. He had not seen Molly in a couple of years, although his mother occasionally mentioned her. He remembered her as a little girl who learned very quickly how to play poker.

He had liked Molly, enjoyed her intelligence, and what he remembered as a not-so-bad Sunday.

He changed his direction, went to a newsagent and bought a paper. He read with disbelief what had happened earlier in the day. He kept thinking, wondering where he had been at that moment when little Molly had been taken. He wondered about the word 'kidnapping' – wondered if that was what described what had happened to her, but it didn't read like that. It read more like she had been in the wrong place at the wrong time. Hurrying to the restaurant, he found Bluebell already at the table with a drink to hand. He kissed her and showed her the paper. She read it with horror, her eyes widening in shock.

'We can hardly sit here and enjoy dinner,' she said. 'I'm going to phone Harry and Susan and see if Molly has been found. Those papers go to print early in the day.'

Molly Kilbride had not been found. Her abduction was now being treated as kidnapping although no ransom demand had been made.

The days passed and Andrew Mortimer followed the non-event of finding Molly Kilbride. He picked up a newspaper every morning on his way into university and he phoned his mother daily to keep abreast of what was happening. Even though nothing was happening. The black Mercedes had been found in County Westmeath. A shoe of Molly's was discovered on the floor of the car under the driver's seat. Her parents were offering money. They would do anything to have their daughter back. But nothing was happening.

Then, four days later, William Murphy, school and college friend, rang from Brussels.

'I'm coming over the day after tomorrow,' he said to Andrew.

'That's great,' Andrew replied.

'Are you all right?' William asked. There was something in Andrew's voice that made it unclear if he was or not. Andrew was reading the paper at the time. The picture of Molly was small. She was mentioned on page four in a tiny column, that just said, 'Still no trace of missing schoolgirl.' There was something so dismissive about it, and Andrew, who had not thought of her in several years, found that he was now thinking about her all the time. He could remember her large grey eyes with the tiny flecks of colour in them looking at him with shy interest as he explained the rules of poker.

The photograph did not do her justice.

'Sorry, Will,' he said. 'I was looking at a picture in the paper. The daughter of friends of my parents has gone missing. She was taken during a bank raid. Actually, that doesn't really describe what happened, but never mind. Go on.'

'Do I know her?' William asked.

'No. She's only a kid.'

'Sounds like you like her.'

'Sure I do. Why not? I can't imagine what has happened to her. Her parents must be going out of their minds. Mine are. Anyway, what was that you said about coming over?'

'The day after tomorrow. Can you put me up? The mother's house will be damp and horrid. And I've rented out my flat.'

'No problem. The spare room is empty.'

'Empty? You got rid of the bed?'

'No. Idiot. I meant there is no one in it.'

Andrew's flat overlooked the river. Two bedrooms and a comfortable living room with a small kitchen. The view from the living room was at its best at night when the city lights sparkled in the water as the tide ebbed and flowed, even if the Liffey sometimes smelled to high heaven.

'How long are you staying?' he added. 'Not that it matters. You can stay as long as you want.'

'I'm coming in the day after tomorrow and leaving the following evening. I've got two meetings lined up for the afternoon.'

'Come by my office when you're finished and we can go out for dinner.'

'Will do. There's something I have to do while I'm over – but I should fit it in before the meetings.'

As it happened the plane was late leaving Brussels and William had no chance to go to his mother's house. As it was, he only just made it to the Central Bank in time for the first of his meetings. By the time he had finished it was already seven o'clock. He rang Andrew.

'I'm running late.'

'So I gathered. I was just thinking of leaving here.'

'We can go and get something to eat. God knows, I need a drink. There's something I have to do afterwards.'

They arranged to meet in a pub on Baggot Street, and it was going on eleven thirty by the time they had finished eating.

'I've to check out the mother's house,' William said.

'Check it out?'

'Oh, long story – boring,' William said. He had drunk too much and he was tired. Glancing at his watch, he continued, 'Look, it can wait until tomorrow. I need my bed.'

'But if we don't do it tonight . . .' Andrew said.

'Yes, but if there are squatters, which is what Christy, the next-door neighbour, thinks, then we're in no state to be calling the police,' William said. 'Best leave it until tomorrow.'

They walked back home to the riverside flat. And in so doing they postponed Molly's rescue by a further twelve hours.

Oh, the walls of my mind . . . the walls of . . . the walls . . .

Molly could no longer form a sentence in her head. Andy, stretching across the ceiling, dropped a little more plaster in empathy – and Molly Kilbride scoured the inside of her mind to find something to hold on to . . .

Jericho smiled at her. He had long lashes on his eyes. He was a friend of Andy's. He had climbed the walls and joined Andy on the ceiling. They were her friends.

Friends . . .

Molly had lots of friends, girls who asked her over after school, but Susan was not enthusiastic about after-school visiting. Friends were for the weekend, when piano practice was done, when the week's work was checked, when Molly had tidied her room. Friends . . . Jennifer Delmont. Molly liked Jennifer but was not sure what Jennifer really thought about her. Jennifer was so competitive. Jennifer always seemed to want what Molly had. When Molly wore her hair in plaits, Jennifer did too. When Molly wore clear nail polish, Jennifer did too. Jennifer wanted to be first. But Molly was first.

Molly liked being first but Harry's attitude of doing one's best being the best one could do stood her in good stead. To work hard and to enjoy it, that was Harry's approach. Molly liked languages. Latin she had been learning for two years, and she had recently started both French and German.

Unlike some of the girls in her class she did not muddle the two up. She could hear so clearly the different sounds, and saw immediately the links in vocabulary between French and Latin, and in structure between German and Latin. Everything interconnected clearly for her, and yet the differences had equal clarity. Other girls sometimes used a German verb mistakenly in their French homework, or twisted a French noun to make it sound German – but not Molly. It just came easily to her. *Jericho, tu es mon ami*, she thought. *Du bist mein Freund.* She wondered if Harry and Susan would let her take up Italian. Unfortunately Greek wasn't an option. She had once borrowed a book from the library on Greek mythology. It had opened up doors in her mind. Molly liked links.

Another piece of plaster fell from the ceiling. She remembered her Bible stories. The walls of Jericho came tumbling down. She thought of Samson. And Delilah. Delilah did not interest her. Delilah got a servant to cut off Samson's hair. Samson interested her. Samson wreaked havoc as he brought down the walls of the temple. Was it a temple? The walls of something. Not Jericho. Samson shook the pillars when his hair had grown. She supposed her hair must have grown, but there were no pillars for her to shake, there was no escape. She watched Jericho on the ceiling. He was standing motionless beside Andy.

'Join us,' Jericho said.

Molly listened intently. She was sure she heard him speak. She stared and stared at him as the unspeakable, the unmentionable, the unbelievable was happening. She closed the windows in her mind – oh, the walls were so very thin, and then . . . then . . . Molly's soul left her body.

Molly was on the ceiling with Jericho and Andy. They held her hands. They said, 'Don't look. Just don't look down.'

And she did not look, although she knew that some ten

feet below her on the bed something terrible was happening to Molly Kilbride.

'I had a good lunch today,' Jericho said.

Andy smiled.

'We are all linked,' he said. 'Caught in time and space. You, me and Jericho.'

Molly looked at them both. She had never known such friendship in her life. 'You, me and Jericho,' Andy said. It was a threesome. A triumvirate. She knew that from Roman history. They were close, so close – as close as a child, a spider and a ceiling crack could be. They were outside time and space.

'You are my friends,' she said to them. It was tentative, nervous, uncertain. She was unsure if they spoke her language. She tried it again . . .

She looked shyly, carefully at them. 'My friends.' She tried it in French: '*Mes amis*'; in German, in Latin.

'Yes,' said Jericho. 'We are friends. You, Andy and me. *Philos*. That's Greek,' he added.

'It's certainly Greek to me,' said Andy.

Andy blinked. A piece of plaster fell from him towards the bed. Her eyes followed the plaster. It landed beside the child on the bed. She could see the child's face – the scream on the face in the silence of the room. The Wolf pulled the woollen hat off his head and he was doing a terrible thing. She knew it would be rubbing her and hurting her if she were there on the bed. But she was not there.

She had separated.

She was with Jericho and Andy. Her spirit was floating high, high above the anguish below.

'My name is Andy,' said the crack.

'I know,' she said. She couldn't remember when he had introduced himself, but it had been some time earlier.

'I'm named after the Andes,' he told her.

Yes, that made sense. That was the name of the mountain range. She remembered now. The Andes in South America. She smiled at him. Jericho took her hand in his.

'I don't know who named me Jericho,' he said. He had long eyelashes. She had thought that she had christened him, but now it did not seem very likely. He seemed older, wiser, more established than she. He must have been named a long time ago.

'I am the way,' he said, 'the truth and the life.'

'He that believeth in him,' said Andy, 'will never die.' He sighed. 'It makes for a long life which isn't much fun when you're just a crack on a ceiling.'

Jericho laughed.

'You can still have a lot of craic,' he said. 'You just have to know the right people to have it with. Like Esme here.' He smiled at her again.

'I'm Molly,' she corrected him gently.

He laughed a spidery laugh. 'Now now,' he said. 'You were born Esme and to Esme you will return. That's Molly below. You are Esme.'

'I hurt,' she said to him.

Jericho held her hand tighter.

'It's all right,' he said. 'Leave Molly behind, Esme. I will lead you over the Andes into a world unseen, full of coffee beans and a mighty river.'

'I hurt,' she whispered again.

'It's all right,' Andy said. 'I giveth and Jericho taketh away.'

A tiny piece of plaster slipped from him and fell downwards.

'Concentrate, concentrate, concentrate on me . . .' Jericho said. 'I spin my web and catch you in its structure. I am the word. I am Yavay.'

'Yavay?'

'Yes. I am God.'

'Long ago,' said Andy helpfully, 'the people of Israel feared to take the Lord's name in vain, and so they stopped saying it altogether and its pronunciation was lost.'

'But Yavay?' she asked again.

'JHVH,' Andy explained. 'Who knows how to pronounce it? Maybe Jehovah. Maybe not. I call him Jericho.'

'But I called him Jericho,' she said.

'Of course you did,' said Andy. 'That's his name.'

'I wish . . .'

'What do you wish?'

'I wish . . . that . . . I had not been born.'

'It is going to be all right, Esme,' said Jericho.

'Trust him,' said Andy. 'He knows everything.'

CHAPTER SEVENTEEN

The light was different. That was the first thing she became aware of. The second thing was that there was the drip in her arm. Her hand was bandaged and she could see there was something attached to it. Beside her bed there was a bag of some clear fluid hanging from something that looked like a clothes stand. Slowly Molly pieced together that something had changed. She was not tied to the bedstead. Her hand hurt, but she was warm. Her head was on a pillow and the pillow did not smell. The bed did not stink. She did not itch and hurt. Someone was speaking to her.

'Molly.' It was Susan. Susan was sitting by the bed holding her hand. Not the hand with the attachment. Her other one. 'Molly, it's me, it's Susan,' she said.

Molly looked at Susan. Susan was her mother. She rather wished that she called her Mum. Mum or Mummy – they would be nice words to say now. And there was Harry. He was standing behind Susan. And there was a nurse. A round face with nice eyes. Looking into hers, holding her wrist, taking her hand from Susan, checking her pulse. Looking at a small watch in a pocket on her chest. Looking into her face again. Her mouth moving. Something being said. Molly knew she was expected to listen. But she did not know if this was wise.

'It's all right, Molly,' the nurse said. 'It's all right now. You're safe.'

Safe . . . Molly thought about the word. Safe. It was something you put money in. She listened to their voices. Reassuring sounds, although the words meant nothing. They had no meaning whatsoever.

'You're in hospital,' Susan said to her. 'It's all over, you're safe now.'

Molly closed her eyes again. She closed her eyes, wondering what her mind would bring to help her through this fantasy of rescue – of being safe, of being free, of existing in a world where the torment was over. She opened her eyes to see if it was a dream. She looked at the ceiling – there was no crack. Andy was gone. Andy . . . her friend. It made her think about Andrew . . . Andrew Mortimer.

She said, 'Andy.'

'Yes,' Harry said. 'Thank God for Andrew. He rescued you. We will never be able to thank him enough . . .' Harry's voice seemed to break.

Andrew Mortimer had woken at five in the morning with a knot in his stomach and the onset of a hangover that would take at least ten minutes to kick in. He wondered what had woken him. It was some thought. Something had triggered in his brain. Something he had read . . . He got out of bed and went into the kitchen where he ran the tap and drank two large glasses of water. Then he went rooting through the drawers looking for some painkillers. Finding a packet of something or other – he couldn't even read the name on it – he pushed two capsules through the foil and swallowed them, and took himself back to bed. He was just about to fall back into sleep when he remembered what he had read in the papers. There had been a request to the general public to be on the look out for something different in a neighbour's house, for someone not behaving as normal, for something just a little out of the ordinary – and he recalled William saying something about the light being on in his mother's house on the banks of the canal. He almost got straight up out of the bed, and then he reassured himself that nothing could be out of the ordinary in a place so public, a house on the canal.

The car in which Molly Kilbride had been taken had been found in some county miles away from Dublin. There was no reason to think that Molly could be in William Murphy's dead mother's house. His mind hovered on the verge of sleep as a headache, dull and heavy in his head, kicked in. He thought of getting out of bed and fetching two more painkillers, working on the basis that the more he took the quicker they might work, but there was now a mild feeling of nausea on top of the headache, and so he fell back on the pillows, and waited for sleep to return.

But sleep would not come back. Just suppose – just suppose Molly was in William's mother's house . . . He got up again and woke William. At first he did not say what was on his mind, just encouraged William to get up, saying that time was running out and that William would have to get his plane back, and asking did he not have things to do before then. William resisted. He too was suffering from the effects of the previous night. But Andrew now was not to be thwarted.

'We ought to check out the house,' he said to William. 'I'll make us some coffee. But we've got to get up.'

'Oh God,' William said. 'I think I'll phone the estate agents and have them look into it. I don't think I can handle it.'

'Then give me the keys and I'll go and look for you,' Andrew said.

'They're in my jacket pocket,' William said. 'Now, let me

get back to sleep.' He rolled over in the bed and pulled the pillow over his head.

Andrew went and found the keys and brought them back to the spare bedroom.

'William, wake up, you lousy bastard,' he said. 'I need to know which key it is, and I don't know how to find the damned house. I haven't been there in years.'

William groaned and reluctantly opened his eyes. 'I've a plane to catch later,' he said. 'I'd better get up and come with you.'

Reluctantly, Andrew waited as William showered and gathered his things up, throwing them into his bag. He seemed to take for ever, insisting on drinking his coffee before they left. At the last moment Andrew went and took a sharp knife from the kitchen. He wrapped the blade in a handkerchief and stuck it in his jacket pocket. They flagged a taxi down and made the journey out of the city.

'I hope you're paying the bill,' William said, looking at the taxi meter. Andrew Mortimer did not have much money, and could only hope he would have enough to cover it. If the worst came to the worst they could find a bus or train to get back to the city.

The sky was grey and ominous, thunder rolling some-where in the distance behind them, as the taxi pulled up in front of the house.

'Wait for us,' William instructed the driver, as the two got out.

Opening the front door, they found the house empty and quiet. They stood there silently, as William fumbled for a light switch, as the hall curtains were drawn and the lights were off.

'Hey, William,' Andrew whispered. 'Go carefully.'

William looked at him puzzled. 'What?'

'Sssshhhh.'

William went to the kitchen as Andrew headed for the living room.

'Someone has been here, all right,' William called in to him. 'There are signs of occupants of some sort – cups in the sink . . .'

Andrew made for the staircase, taking the steps two at a time, his hand on the knife in his pocket. All the doors upstairs were closed and he started towards the first door – throwing it open to reveal a bathroom with a couple of towels strewn on the floor.

He swung open the first bedroom door and stood for a moment in horror as he tried to take in what was in front of him.

'William, William,' he shouted over his shoulder, 'call the police quickly,' and then he made for the bed where he could see a child lying, her hands taped to the bedposts, her mouth bound, her body motionless in the dim light filtering through from the side of the closed curtains. Her eyes were looking towards the ceiling and he was unsure if she knew that he was there. He tried to unpick the tape but his fingers faltered as his nails scratched at the edge, endeavouring to lift it sufficiently that he could pull the binding off. He remembered the knife.

He heard William gasp in disbelief behind him. 'Jesus Christ,' he heard William say. 'Jesus Jesus Christ . . . ?'

Molly Kilbride's eyes never flickered. They stared blindly at the ceiling as though she were engrossed in something up there.

'Is she alive?' William asked.

'Call for the police and an ambulance,' Andrew shouted. 'Hurry up.'

William was down the stairs before he realised that the house phone was long since disconnected. He ran out of the front door and down the steps to where the taxi was waiting.

'Call for the police, quickly,' he said to the startled driver. 'And an ambulance . . . fast. Now. Quickly.'

The driver, taking in the wildness in William's face, immediately reached for the handset in the car.

'It's that missing child,' William said, jerking his head back towards the house. 'Quickly.'

They were there in minutes – sirens blaring. First on the scene were two policemen on motorbikes, then squad car after squad car and an ambulance, and Molly, lifted from the bed in someone's arms, was carried limp down the stairs and into the ambulance. Tiny, helpless, brutalised, filthy, unaware, she was wrapped in a blanket and held tightly as she was passed into the waiting vehicle. Her eyes were closed now. Someone thought they heard her say something about the walls of Jericho, but her voice, dry and cracked in her throat, was less than a whisper. She curled, foetal, on her side as her wrists were massaged, a vein was found, a drip was inserted, and the ambulance began its journey at full speed through the traffic with the police on motorbikes escorting it to the hospital.

She had thought the walls of Jericho might be a dark yellow or mustard colour. That was what she had imagined, but the room had been pink with a white ceiling, and Andy had been grey. Jericho was . . . she looked again. The ceiling was smooth, uncracked, newly painted. There was no sign of Jericho. She felt alone and frightened, like she had been before Andy had sent her the plaster and Jericho had invited her to their lofty heights. She closed her eyes and slept. When she opened them again she was unsure what was real – she only wanted Andy and Jericho but an apparition of her mother was in front of her again.

She wanted Susan to go away. Susan could not help her,

neither in real nor in ghostly form. There was no hope if
Jericho did not call her back – but the ceiling was unlined
and the walls of her mind were so terribly thin.

Harry, her dad, appeared in front of her. She began to
wonder if perhaps he was real. She could feel his hand
holding hers. It felt like her dad's hand all right. Large and
strong. Protective. She looked again. He was still there. She
moved her head and Susan was on the other side of her. Her
hands could move. She was almost sure they were not tied.
They hurt, though. She looked down the bed. There was
something attached to one of them and a white bandage
over it. She could see a tube coming from it. She followed
the line of the tube. It was not Andy. It was attached to something that looked like it had a clear liquid in it, and the liquid
was dripping down it. She closed her eyes again.

She thought she could hear a voice, maybe Jericho's. The
voice said, 'Sleep now. You are safe.'

It was over. She knew that sometime later. It was all over
and she was in a hospital bed. One of her parents was there
all the time. She had no idea how long had passed. Time
was meaningless. It was wakefulness and then sleep. The
wakefulness was full of sleepiness. Nothing had any meaning.
It was a while before she let herself hear the words that were
being spoken.

'You're safe, Molly.' Harry's voice sounded almost
pleading. 'I promise it is over and you are safe.'

She thought she might have heard her voice asking him,
was he sure, was he absolutely sure, that it was over?

But where would there be safety again, she wondered. She
had thought that her childhood was safe. It had seemed a
safe place with two parents – a place where she was loved
and was allowed to grow and laugh and be . . . be what, she
wondered. Be Molly Kilbride.

That was what the doctor said when she asked him who she was.

'You are Molly Kilbride,' he said. He had dark-rimmed glasses. His eyes were brown and his face was lined. His hair was black with streaks of grey. 'They cannot get you again,' he said.

She had no idea what he meant or to whom he was referring. She wanted to know where Andy and Jericho were. They were the old reliables. They alone could really help her.

She found spiders in the oddest of places, and she rescued them all, lifting them carefully on to the palm of her hand and bringing them to places of safety.

But they were in her mind only, they were not real. Nothing was real. It was a long time before she could begin to make anything connect.

'A return to normality,' the doctor said. 'And the sooner the better.'

Susan was shaken, that was clear. Molly had seen her red eyes when she got up that morning from her hospital bed. Molly looked out of the window. She had little or no idea what was going on. There were words she heard spoken, some had meaning, some had not. This conversation now was meaningless.

'Reality,' the doctor said.

Molly wondered if they knew she could hear. She was sitting in the reception room outside his office and the door was partially open. She wondered if it had been intentionally left open. She rather thought not, but she did not care. She looked around. There was a small spider underneath the radiator. She got up and went to look at it. It wasn't Jericho.

'Does the word Jericho mean anything in particular?' she heard the doctor ask, as if he knew she had been thinking about Jericho.

'Jericho,' Harry said. 'Jericho? Well, no. Why? The walls of Jericho,' he mused.

'Go on,' the doctor said.

'Molly had a book with stories in it – old Bible stories. She liked the one about Daniel and the lions,' Harry continued. 'There was one about Jericho. About the walls crumbling . . . Is it important?'

'I don't know. Possibly not. But sometimes she refers to Andy and Jericho.'

'Andy is the boy who found her,' Susan said. 'Andrew Mortimer.'

'I know,' he said. 'She told me all about him.'

Molly stood up and looked down at the car park several floors below the room she was in. The cars looked like toy ones, all in different colours, all tiny, moving in and out of parking spaces like in a game.

'She has mentioned Jericho to us as well,' Harry said. 'The Israelites circled the walls of Jericho, and on the sound of trumpets the walls fell, destroying the whole city, except for the house of Rahab.'

'Rahab?'

'A prostitute who had given shelter to the spies Joshua had sent into the city. There was probably an earthquake – that's what caused the walls to fall,' Harry continued.

'So Jericho didn't survive?'

'No. It was never rebuilt. It was left as it was, as a sign of God's anger against those who took false gods.'

'Does Molly know that Jericho was never rebuilt?'

'She knows the story,' Harry replied.

'You know a lot about the Bible,' Susan said to him, the surprise apparent in her voice.

'You gave her the book,' he responded. 'I just read it to her. The stories you skipped.'

They looked at each other.

They could not reach each other either.

They were separated now, not just by different interests, different pursuits in their lives, but also by their daughter, who was the one thing that they had had in common. They had come together and clung to each other like frightened children during the period that Molly was kidnapped. But now, now that Molly was back, they could agree on nothing.

'What happens now?' Susan asked the doctor.

'Molly does not appear to recall what has happened. She only refers obliquely to events. It's her way of coping. I think now she should return to school, back to her peers, back to normality. And then we see what happens.'

'The court hearing is tomorrow,' Harry said.

'Are you going to it?'

'We haven't decided.'

'There is no point in Molly being brought to it. I understand from the police reports that she is not needed, and it is pointless to put her through that experience. What have you told her?'

They had told her that the men had been caught and that they would be put away for a long time and that Molly would never see them again.

Molly wondered whom they were talking about when Harry and Susan told her of the arrests. She asked if Andy and Jericho were safe and was told that Andrew was fine and that the Mortimers sent her their love. Harry had asked her what she meant by Jericho, but she had turned away, closing down the conversation.

She slept badly at night. Sometimes she felt she could hear someone breathing in the room with her, another heartbeat quickening, not quite in unison with hers.

Sometimes she woke thinking she had felt rough wool

rasping against her face and she opened her mouth to scream, but no scream came. She remembered the moment he had taken off his balaclava – that moment when she knew that she was not going to be left alive. She knew as she looked into his face that she had always known who he was. She remembered that moment in her own home when he had touched her face and she had recoiled.

She turned on her bedside light when she dared move and she sat up in her bed, shivering. There was no one else there.

Just her.

One night Harry came into her room after she had turned on the light.

'You can't sleep?' he asked her, coming to sit on the edge of her bed. 'I saw your light on. Talk to me.' He looked into her face, noting the guarded look in her eyes. 'The bad men are gone,' he said to her. 'They won't be coming back.'

She looked around then, checking the walls of the room – there was nowhere they could be hiding. And as she looked, she remembered that there were bad men – two of them, somewhere outside in the night.

'Bad men,' she said softly.

He was unsure if it was a question or a statement. 'They caught the bad men,' he said. He knew he sounded as if he was speaking to a much younger child, but there did not seem to be a better way to communicate with Molly now. 'There was a court hearing last week and they have been detained. The trial will be later. They won't be let out for a long, long time. You are safe now. We are all safe now . . .' his voice trailed away.

'Is anyone safe?' she asked.

'Yes,' he repeated patiently. 'You are safe now. Such a thing will never happen again. You came home to us and we will look after you. You are safe.'

But there was a world out there, outside her window, and she knew that if you went out into it, you took a risk. Every moment of every day was a risk.

It was a while before she told that to Dr Gumm.

'We have a choice,' he said to her. 'We can choose to be defeated by the bad and evil things on the planet. Or we can fight them.'

'I'm not strong enough to fight anyone,' she said sadly, taking his words quite literally.

'I didn't mean that you should go into physical combat with them,' he explained. 'I meant that by facing life, by over-coming fear, by living, you can fight them and what they did. You are in control of your life – no matter what it may seem like to you. And as you grow up, you will be more and more in control of your own life.'

Molly shuddered. She felt wave upon wave of nausea.

Home in her bedroom, with its shades of lilac and pink, her furry toys sat neatly on their shelf. She remembered clearly that moment of walking into her room when she came home from hospital. That sense of expectation that she used to have when coming home from holiday simply wasn't there. That moment of coming into her room and seeing all her possessions with a sense of joy and renewed optimism after two or three weeks abroad with her parents now was void.

Coming home from hospital, there was nothing.

Her room seemed to belong to someone else and she could not remember who that person was. She looked at her things and wondered at what meaning they might have. The comfort she had got in the past from them did not rise in her. Her bed was freshly made and her pillows plumped up, and she looked around with a sense of dismay – she did not know what was expected of her.

Susan was looking encouragingly at her.

'It's good to be home, Molly, isn't it?' she said hopefully. When Molly did not respond, she tried again.

'It's good to have you home.' Susan's voice was trying to be firm, but Molly heard the quaver in it, and knew that something was expected of her.

'It's good to be home,' she replied. They were empty words, and Susan knew it. But it was a start.

Susan knew from what the doctor had said that if Molly could start to behave normally and to react reasonably or rationally it would be a step forward. But she herself did not know what rational meant.

She looked at her daughter's pale empty face and she wanted to scream. But she had no idea what noise she might emit, nor what words to howl, and so biting back her distress and anguish, she hid the agony one more time. What Molly needed was for her parents to be strong for her, to support her, to coerce her back to normality, and that was what Susan was determined to do. Dr Gumm had advised that.

Susan was essentially a pragmatist and while she had lost all contact with reality when Molly was missing, she knew now what was expected of her and she had no doubt in her ability to bring it off. Molly must be reintroduced into her old world and in some way rehabilitated so that the pieces of her life prior to the event could be picked up. There were things that could not be fixed and she knew that. She felt the only way forward was to obliterate what had happened.

But it was not that simple. She had no idea how to talk to Molly. She felt that if the psychiatrist and the doctors could not talk to her daughter, how could she? Molly's eyes frightened her. They seemed dead most of the time, and the rest of the time they were frightened. She could see the fear in them. She could smell the fear in her child. She did not know how to connect with her.

'Look,' she said to Molly. 'All your teddies are sitting waiting for you.'

'Yes,' Molly said politely.

It was that politeness, Susan decided, that was so unnerving. Prior to the kidnapping, the old Molly would have said something else, something like, 'So what?' or 'What do you mean? They are just teddies. They are not waiting for anything.'

But this Molly looked blankly at the bears as if she were unsure what, if anything, she should do.

'Shall we put one on your bed?' Susan asked.

Molly continued to look at them and Susan could not be sure if she was even seeing them.

'You always liked this one best,' she said, picking up a very old cuddly bear that had a pink bow around its neck. She placed it on the bed with its furry head and its little round ears resting on the pillows.

'Let's unpack your things,' Susan suggested as she unzipped the holdall Harry had placed on the floor at the foot of the bed. She carefully lifted out the clothing she had folded and packed earlier in the hospital, nightwear, another pair of jeans and some tops. She took out the washbag that she had put together two weeks earlier after Molly had been rescued. The hairbrush she put on Molly's dressing table. The small pink and white spotted bag she brought into Molly's small bathroom off her bedroom and she placed it on the shelf.

'Will you unpack this, Molly?' she asked.

Molly nodded.

'Molly,' Susan said tentatively, 'Dr Gumm said that if we do all the little ordinary things that are normal and part of everyday life, all the other things will fall into place.'

Molly nodded again.

Her father brought her out to the garden, a place where she had always been happy.

'We're going to give it a proper clean-up this weekend,' he said, looking around at the flowerbeds. 'A last mow of the grass for the winter. A bit of a tidy-up. You will help, won't you?' he asked hopefully.

Molly looked at the beds. She felt a terrible sense of dismay. Even here there was something wrong. It was now early winter, and any late autumn flowers were drooping on their stalks. But there was no colour, no smell. It wasn't that they looked brown, as they should have in their withered state. They were grey. The whole garden appeared in varying shades of grey, as though colour had evaporated. She looked up at her tree house, painted in a bright yellow, now exposed in its tree as the foliage had fallen in her absence. She shivered. In the corner of the garden the peony roses, always the last flowers to die because of the sheltered place they were planted, were still blooming. She walked over and put her face down to them. There was no scent. They were usually a deep red, now they were grey. Even the leaves on the ground, which should have been the multicolours of autumn, were grey. She remembered the leaves on the trees – she could see them from the window, through the side of the curtains – they had been red and gold and yellow, and over those days they had fallen. Fallen from the trees. And now on the ground they had no colour. Nothing had any colour. It was gone. There was nothing left.

'Let's go back inside,' Harry said. 'Susan is making hot cocoa. Look, she's waving to us.'

Molly obediently looked at the kitchen window.

*   *   *

Molly Kilbride, with her large grey eyes in her hopeful face, with her wavy brown hair hitting her shoulders, had returned to what had been the safest, most secure, happiest place in the world. But now it was empty.

She went to the library with her mother, and she wore her coat when she was told to, and when Susan suggested, she even buttoned it. She fastened her seat belt and did not undo it until they got to the library, and she only released the clasp when Susan said to her, 'Come now, Molly, let's go in.'

There was a four-week charge on the books, because a month had passed since Molly had disappeared, but the woman in the library waived it aside.

'It's good to see you back, dear,' she said.

Molly wondered what she meant, but did not ask. With her large grey eyes, she looked at the librarian, and the woman smiled kindly back at her.

'She's looking well,' she said to Susan. 'What a terrible time it has been.'

Susan nodded. What could she say? Molly looked like Molly. She looked like she had looked before the 'kidnapping', as it was referred to. She looked like the photographs that had been in every newspaper on a daily basis.

But the essence of Molly was different. The walls of her mind had become impenetrable. She blanked when she was not reading. She blanked when they spoke to her at the breakfast or dinner table. She blanked when she sat in the doctor or the psychiatrist's rooms and she moved in silence inside her own head.

The walls of my mind are very thin. I will let no one in.

It was five months afterwards that Susan, sitting straight-backed, her face steadfast, faced Harry in their dining room.

'I'm taking Molly to England.'

'What?'

'I'm taking her away. She'll recover away from here. I will look after everything,' Susan said.

'I can't go with you,' Harry said. 'I can't leave my work.'

'It doesn't matter,' Susan replied. 'I've booked our flights. We're going. Maybe you can join us the odd weekend. Maybe not. But we have to go now. It's the only thing we can do for her.'

Harry was sick of fighting, sick of the endless argument about what to do with Molly. He loved her more than his life and he did not doubt that Susan did too. They just could not agree on how to proceed.

'She's given her statement. She remembers nothing that is of any use. There is no way she can appear at the trial. She has to get out of here as fast as possible,' Susan said – words that he had heard over and over the previous days.

Upstairs in her bed, Molly lay looking at a spider on the ceiling.

'I'm going away for a while,' Molly said to him.

Jericho, if it was he, did not answer. He disappeared into a newly formed crack by the ceiling rose.

Molly closed her eyes. All she wanted was to be back with Andy and Jericho and far away from everyone and everything else.

'You see,' Henry said, 'she couldn't relate to anything.'

'Let me understand this – I know I'm back-tracking, but I want to get a proper picture,' Jacob said. 'They left her there to die?'

'The police reckoned they hadn't finished with her. They had removed her blindfold, possibly on the third day. She told Groucho that she knew then they were going to kill her. They left her there, tied up, and went out on another job and then they were picked up during that robbery. They kept silent about the kidnapping, needless to say. They were questioned about it, but they said not a word. And she was left abandoned in the house on the canal.'

Jacob sat silently taking this in. 'If she hadn't been found . . . ?' he said thoughtfully.

'She would have died.'

Both men were silent now with their own thoughts. A child left tied to a bed, filthy, frightened, forsaken, unable to escape.

Jacob shook his head, trying to clear the horror of the image from his mind. 'What happened then?' he asked.

'She didn't settle back into school, despite Groucho's best efforts and hopes. And then her mother took her to England, I think. They stayed away for the rest of the academic year, not returning until the following September.'

'Did Molly have to repeat a year in school when she got back?'

'No. I think they may have got tuition for her in that year away. She came back sometime just before the term started and then went back to school. I think that is what happened. She caught up quickly enough, I imagine. She was very intelligent and industrious. Sally and I were visiting my brother – for dinner, I think. And Jennifer, their daughter, had Molly over. I remember thinking that Molly was sort of an ideal child – ironic, isn't it? What had happened to her made her one of the most damaged children imaginable, and yet there she was – polite, helpful, quite sweet, in fact. She helped clear the plates from the table. She spoke nicely. A gentle girl . . . yes, gentle. That sums her up. Quiet, reserved . . . but that was not surprising. She had been kidnapped the previous October during the mid-term break. It was now early September, maybe. Almost a year had passed. I gather that she was quite a celebrity in school. My brother told me that it bothered him that Jennifer seemed to envy her – Jennifer appeared to him to be riding high on the status attached to being Molly's best friend. It irked my brother, because, as he said, how could anyone envy her? She had been kidnapped, raped, scarred, left for dead . . .'

Jacob thought about that for a moment. 'Human nature is very odd . . .'

'Especially teenage girls. They can be quite vicious. However, my sister-in-law was quite proud of the fact that Jennifer stood up for Molly in school. Apparently some of the girls gave her a hard time, wanting to know what it had been like – oh, they had read stuff in the newspapers and had heard stuff . . . a load of rumours and gossip – and instead of letting Molly try and find her place again, they questioned and teased her. Goading her, in a way. Jennifer stood up for her, became her best friend, gave her support.'

'The same Jennifer then went and slept with Molly's husband,' Jacob said drily. 'And subsequently married him, you know.'

'Yes, we weren't even invited to the wedding,' Henry said. 'Probably just as well, I suppose. I imagine Jennifer must, on some level at least, have felt a sense of guilt or embarrassment. I mean – to run off with your best friend's husband. It's not quite the thing, is it?'

'What happened to the two men – the kidnappers?' Jacob asked. In the back of his mind he was thinking of Esme saying to him, 'I'm only half a person.' Her words were now explained. Yes, she felt herself only half a person, although she was a completely full person as far as any observer could see. But like her, he too had no memory of a period of his life and knew that what she meant was as much to do with the lack of memory as to what had happened to her. He feared that he had made Naomi only half a person by not giving her exactly what she wanted. And yet he knew that no human being could or should rely on another one to make him or herself complete. A sense of fulfilment or completion could only come from within. If he had his time over again, perhaps he could explain that to a younger Naomi so that she would not live her life waiting for him to give her whatever it was she needed. It was to do with being diminished by life and events.

What a façade human beings create, he thought.

'Unfortunately it was not like it is now, with DNA, et cetera,' Henry was saying. 'Same with lack of video link, though I remember Groucho saying that there was no way Molly could have given any kind of evidence anyway. Not only was she completely traumatised, she contradicted herself over and over about what she saw. She referred to a man with a bald head – he was the driver of the car. She said she saw his eyes for an instant in the rear-view mirror as she was thrown into the car. She also said she saw him in a mirror on the bedroom wall – but she had no more recollection of him. And the other one – the one she called the Wolf – well, she said he removed his balaclava and that was when she knew he would never leave her alive. And at the same time, she said that she never saw him at all. Groucho suspected that she may have tried to convince them that she hadn't seen him or that she wouldn't tell if they let her go. She couldn't give reliable evidence because sometimes she was absolutely sure she hadn't seen him – and yet, she very clearly did. She would have been torn apart in the witness box. Molly called them the Wolf and the Eyes. You saw that in the file. Anyway, one of them – the one she called the Wolf – his name was Jeremy Coyle, he was a manager in Molly's father's nightclub, IRA links, an out-and-out thug, you can imagine. He got fifteen or eighteen years for armed robbery, and I think ten years for the kidnapping and rape. The judge was so shocked by the crime that the sentences were run consecutively rather than concurrently. He ended up with about thirty years. And the other – the Eyes – got eight or maybe six years for driving the car, being an accessory, you know. He was never connected with the rape, and he gave evidence to reduce his connection with the kidnapping. He said that it was not part of the plan. Anyway, under pressure he caved in, spilled the beans, so to speak, and the other chap, probably justifiably, got the full whack.'

'And that's justice, is it?' Jacob said angrily. 'What an insult. Esme – Molly carries the memory of what happened for the rest of her life, and those two bastards . . . they must both be long out of prison now?'

Henry looked at him thoughtfully. 'I see you don't know what happened next. Anyway, in Molly and Jennifer's last year in school, the one who was charged as an accessory – the Eyes – he was released early – good behaviour or whatever.'

'No time off for good behaviour for Molly Kilbride, though,' Jacob said, an element of bitter irony in his voice.

'No. No time off for Molly. However, the Eyes – the one who was released early – well, he didn't last long. Harry Hastings – Molly's father – picked him up within hours of his being released from prison and did a job on him.'

'Did he kill him?'

'Oh, no. He said death was too good for him. However, the only problem was that now Molly's father was charged with grievous bodily harm and the poor bastard had a heart attack the day he was charged. And he died.'

Jacob digested this in silence. 'I see,' he said eventually. 'I think this explains a lot about her – about Esme, I mean. She never went back to Ireland after leaving school. I suppose it is no wonder. What was left? A mother she couldn't relate to, and not much else.'

'Yes, starting over was probably the best thing she could do. Only the marriage didn't work . . .'

'And so she starts over again and again. A cycle she can't break . . . keeping herself as detached as possible so that it is easier to pick up the pieces and begin again . . .'

'How much of those events does she remember?' Henry asked.

'I really don't know. I do know that she has nightmares – her sleep patterns are erratic. Mostly she is afraid of sleeping. I think she looked for protection in getting married over and over but she wasn't very lucky there either. Between a German who ended up with her best friend, and a Dutchman who was killed in a train accident . . . and finally an American who suffocated her – figuratively, I mean. Since then, she has travelled light. Well, lightish – she has three daughters but they make her feel inadequate. She has very mixed feelings about herself as a parent. On the one hand she would do anything for them and would protect them any way she could, and on the other hand feels that they might be better off without her because she feels she can't protect or help them enough. She writes novels as a pastime.'

'Published?'

'Yes. She uses a pseudonym – H. Hastings. Her father, I presume.'

'Interesting,' Henry said. 'I've read two of her books, not knowing, of course that they were hers. Sally took them on holidays last year or the year before. They were good. They're in the guise of quick easy-to-read thrillers, but in fact they deal with issues of how crime leaves the victim. Insightful is how I would describe them. In the light of all of this, it is not surprising really. Where is she now?'

'She's here in London,' Jacob said. 'A problem arose with one of the daughters and she has just flown in.'

'A bit like yourself,' Henry said. 'I see.'

And Jacob knew that Henry did see.

'You said Molly was scarred – you meant figuratively?'

'No – no, I didn't. Well, scarred figuratively as well, but apparently the one she called the Wolf – the one who got the thirty years – he carved a mark on her shoulder or her breast.'

'What?' Jacob was horrified. He had seen the scar. He had no idea how she had got it, but it had never occurred to him that another human being had inflicted it on her.

'Why?'

'I don't know why. I'm not sure that there was a clear reason for it. Groucho said it was a power thing – he was showing who was in control and leaving his signature.'

'I don't know why that bit shocks me particularly – not on top of everything else.'

But he did know why. In that moment of hearing that the star had been carved into the child's skin, Jacob remembered the instant the numbers were branded on the inside of his arm – a moment of white light, excruciating pain, and the smell of burning flesh. And he thought of the child, Molly, and what she must have felt. He closed his eyes in an effort to blot out not just the image of Molly but the horrifying memory from his own past.

As Jacob unpacked his bag in his bedroom with a view of the garden, he stopped what he was doing and stood at the window.

His feeling of being intrigued with Esme he now admitted to himself was love.

He loved her.

It came to him with surprise.

He loved the way she walked and the way she sat. He loved the silence of her face when she was in thought and the depth of her green eyes, even though he now knew that she was wearing coloured contact lenses. He wanted to see her grey eyes. He wanted her to know that she was safe. He wanted to be that person who made her feel safe. Even as he thought that, he knew that she must already know that on some level, because why else would she tell him her story? He felt that she had chosen him. He wondered how and why. Had he just been in the right place at the right time? Wasn't that what she had said to him once – something to do with randomness, the random nature of being in the right place at the right time, or indeed the wrong place at the wrong time. Her whole life was propelled by her need to run, to get away from the past . . .

He was caught in her history and her lack of memory, although he wondered what it was that she did not remember. He was quite sure she knew about the kidnapping – why else would she have given him the name Molly Kilbride? She wanted him to find out about Molly so that she would not have to tell him of the fear she had once felt and maybe still did. He knew that she loved her girls but feared she could not be a good mother.

He thought of the things she had said about her own mother. She had once said, 'My mother let me down – over and over.' Another time she had said, 'My mother blamed me.'

Blamed her for what? For being kidnapped? For the break-up of her marriage to Esme's father?

Esme had not mentioned any of that. Just that their marriage had ended and that her father had died. Had she meant that the marriage ended *because* her father had died? It was a lot for anyone to carry, let alone someone who was trying to pick up the pieces after being kidnapped and raped.

Then he thought of Esme's mother. Susan. He wondered what she had felt. He thought of the trauma she must have gone through when her daughter disappeared – the anxiety of that awful week in which Molly Kilbride was front-page news, the fear of thinking of her daughter dead, of the endless and painful waiting, putting in time, unable to do anything constructive to get her child back. What must that poor woman have gone through?

And then, when she was old enough, that child disappeared out of her life for good. No contact, Esme had said. How must that have made the mother feel? She ended up losing everything – the husband she must once have loved, and the child who no longer loved her. Such grief . . . to say goodbye to a child and not to know if you would ever see that person again. Presumably his own mother had felt like that . . . unbearable.

Looking down at the garden he smiled as he suddenly realised that among the many flowers he could see from the window were lilies, roses and jasmine. The jasmine creeper covered almost the whole wall on one side. He now remembered smelling it when he was sitting out on the patio, but its identity hadn't registered. Opening the window, he could smell it again. The lilies stood tall and beautiful in one of the flowerbeds, and the roses were of every colour. He wondered if Rose identified herself with any particular colour. He had seen photos of the three girls, individual passport-type shots as well as several pictures of the three of them together at different ages. He knew from Esme that they were not together much now that they were older.

He thought of her, and her three girls – all named after flowers. The flowers in her childhood garden had no colour and no smell any more, she had said to Groucho. So she made her own flowers, wove them into her life – a valiant effort to give meaning? And now they were growing up. They were leaving her. Perhaps it was that that she could not bear. Perhaps it was the feeling that she had no more meaning despite her desperate efforts to create a life for herself.

Sally had now returned and she came and knocked on his door.

'Are you settling in, Jacob?' she asked him. 'Is there anything you need?'

He invited her in and, standing with her at the window, he mentioned Esme and told her about the flowers.

'Are you going to see her?' Sally asked.

He admitted that he was, but that he would leave it until the following day.

'I'll make contact tomorrow morning,' he said. 'Hopefully she'll have time during the day to meet up.'

'If you would like I could cut some of those flowers for you to take to her,' Sally suggested.

'Thank you. That would be lovely.' He had been thinking that very thing but knew that he could not have asked her, and had wondered if he might find similar flowers in a florist's shop on the way to Esme's place.

'We'll cut them in the morning,' Sally said. 'That way they will be fresh. I'm not sure how long the jasmine will last, though, as I've never cut it before. But it smells wonderful, doesn't it?'

He agreed. Its fragrance permeated his room, and the evening sunlight coming in shone on Sally's face, and for a moment he envied her the comfort of her home life and her love for Henry. A marriage that had worked, he thought. Rare enough. What expectations could people have any more? He thought of Esme saying, I suppose I try to live for today, but in such a way that I will not disturb my tomorrows, or indeed anyone else's. It wasn't the worst maxim. There were no guarantees, though.

'Come down and join us in the garden when you're ready,' Sally said.

CHAPTER EIGHTEEN

Esme woke from a deep sleep to her alarm sounding, thinking at first that her mobile was ringing. She reached in a panic for it before realising that it was simply a wake-up call.

Lily put her head around the door and then came in to kiss her.

'Lily, Lily,' she said as she hugged her eldest. 'I was so worried about you, but there was nothing I could do. Rose . . . Rose is in hospital.'

Lily's pleasure at seeing her mother evaporated from her face, as did her own personal pain, while she listened to Esme's story about Rose.

'How is she now?' she asked.

'I'll ring the hospital straight away,' Esme said. 'I never thought I would sleep so solidly or so late.'

'Jasmine,' Lily called, 'put on coffee for Mum and me, will you?'

Jasmine too put her head around the door.

'Hi, Mom,' she said. 'Look what I have.' Taliban was sitting on her arm.

Esme sat up abruptly in the bed. She had been about to hold out her arms for Jasmine to come to her.

'Goodness,' Esme said with interest. 'Let me see.' Jasmine brought Taliban over and put him on the bed and Esme gazed at him carefully. After a moment and a slight shake of her head, she said, 'Are you sure that's safe? Hang on, I thought Grayson told you to release that into the wild.'

'He wanted to come with me,' Jasmine said.

'Well, sometime today you are to take him to the zoo. Understood?'

Jasmine looked at her and then at Taliban. She wondered why her mother wanted her to take him for an outing to the zoo but decided not to ask.

'I don't even get a hug?' she asked her mother.

'Of course you do, darling.'

Jasmine went and put on the coffee while Esme rang the hospital and Lily joined her in the kitchen and explained what had happened to Rose.

'It's not fair,' Jasmine said. 'I wanted to get some piercings, other than my ears, and neither Mom nor Grayson would let me.'

'Jazz,' Lily said reasonably, 'this isn't about you. We all have problems. But this is about Rose ill in hospital. Could you stop thinking about yourself just for once?'

Jasmine scowled. Lily had no understanding whatsoever. If she had been allowed to pierce her stomach this would not have happened to her. It was typical that Rose, who was older, was allowed to do what she wanted and then when something went wrong with it, everyone had to drop everything and just think about Rose. It wasn't fair. Nothing was fair and, of course, Lily couldn't see that because Lily was perfect.

'I think,' Lily said, looking around the living room, 'that either before or after you take Taliban to the zoo you might like to tidy this place up. Mum's got enough problems today without having to handle this.'

'What's wrong with it?' Jasmine asked. 'It's just clothing and my things – I'll put them in my room later.'

Lily got the cups out of the cupboard and fetched milk from the fridge. Jasmine was staring at the boiling kettle, wondering again why they wanted her to take Taliban to the zoo. They could hardly expect her to hand him to a zookeeper. Taliban needed careful attention. He was now back on the sofa under the glass bowl that Lily had taken out the previous evening. Well, she would take him on a trip to the zoo if it made them all happy. She would be able to say afterwards that she had done what they'd told her. At least it would get her away from them all for a few hours, and from listening to how poor Rose was doing in hospital. She was probably fine anyway. It was just Rose looking for attention.

'You do understand, Jazz, that that tarantula can't live here. Don't you?' It was Lily at her again. Perfect Lily, who had freed a tiger and could do just what she wanted.

Jasmine nodded. It seemed the easiest thing to do because they wouldn't let up.

Lily brought two cups of coffee into Esme's room.

'Can I get in beside you?' she asked.

Esme nodded. She was preoccupied. She had just come off the phone.

'Rose is much better,' she said after a moment.

'I'm sorry. I didn't ask. I'm glad,' Lily sighed.

Esme looked at her closely. 'You haven't got into bed beside me since you were about ten years old, have you?'

Lily shook her head.

'No, I haven't. And I don't even remember the last time I did. And yet it must have been momentous.'

Esme smiled.

'No, it wasn't momentous the last time you did; it was momentous the first time you didn't, if you see what I mean.'

'Do you remember?'

'Remember what?' It was Jasmine in the doorway.

'Jasmine, do me a favour,' Esme said gently but firmly. 'Would you go and have a shower and get dressed? I want to talk to Lily for a little.'

Jasmine looked at them both. Esme's bed looked an awful lot nicer than her own but she reluctantly turned on her heel and went back to bed.

Esme and Lily looked at each other and both raised their eyebrows before smiling.

'Do you remember when I stopped getting into bed with you?' Lily asked again.

'Yes, I do. It was after the alligator episode and I told you that we are responsible for our actions, and that if you let alligator eggs hatch in the house you were responsible for what then happened. You were furious with both me and Grayson – in fact you were furious with Jasmine too because she had found them. You must have been about ten and after that you never got back into bed with us.'

Lily laughed. 'Yes, I remember now. I felt that if you thought I was so grown up that I was responsible for my own actions then I was too grown up to get into bed with you. And the only loser there was me . . .'

'No,' Esme said. 'I was the loser too. I missed you. And Rose, because she copied everything you did back then, stopped coming into bed as well. So I really lost out.'

'Did you hate me?'

'Hate you? Why would I hate you?'

'I don't know. I hate me . . . I suppose.'

Esme put her coffee down and laid her head back on the pillow.

'Do you want to tell me what has happened?'

*   *   *

Lily Wassermann, with her white-blonde hair and her blue eyes, went to bed with Hugh Bonner in the first motel they found. Four stars it had not, but it was a long way from the hostels and the wooden sheltering they had been using. She was in the shower when he opened the door and stepped in with her. His body was hard and rough and tanned, and he nuzzled her neck with his lips before shampooing her hair. When they were both clean of the mud and dirt of the previous weeks, he took her on the floor of the shower with the water cascading down on them both.

'Oh, I love you,' she moaned aloud in the heat of the moment, but she meant it. She loved him. She loved the time they had spent together. She loved his greater experience. She loved every single thing about him, and now they were together. He was hers on the floor of the shower, locked into her as she crouched on his thighs, his head buried between her breasts.

And then it was over.

They dried themselves and got into bed. He slept solidly for some eight hours, while she dozed and watched him, thinking of all the loving things she would tell him when he awoke.

But when he woke it was as if nothing had happened. He had her up and out of there as fast as he was able.

'We have to join the others,' he said.

'I thought we didn't have to find the group for a couple of days? I thought you'd said—'

'No, no,' he hurried her along. 'The others might be looking for us.'

And that was it. It was over before it had even begun. The following days were a complete torment as he ignored her unless forced to speak to her and even then it was cursory to the point of rudeness.

*   *   *

'Mum, I was devastated. I couldn't believe someone would treat another person like that.' She was crying now.

'I hate asking you this, but was he your first?' Esme was relieved to hear what had happened. It was so much less than what she had imagined, but she knew that she must not let Lily know this, at least not yet. There might be more to come.

'Yes. No. Yes. I had a boyfriend briefly in university, but it was only fleeting. I'm . . . cautious, I suppose.'

Esme knew that was true. Lily was cautious when it came to emotions, carefree when it came to animals, adventurous when something new came along – but not boys.

'Did you actually love him?' she asked.

Lily nodded.

'Why did you come home?' she asked.

'I needed to get away from him. He was so nasty to me. He either didn't speak to me or sneered at me. I felt used. Humiliated. I wanted to be with you. He even said that the geese don't remain faithful to their partners – that they sneak away to . . . you know . . . do it with other geese.'

The hurt in her voice was intense, and any desire Esme had to smile at the image of these philandering geese immediately evaporated. Somehow this man had managed to hurt Lily to the quick.

'You know I can't make this better,' Esme said. 'You know there is no quick antidote to love.'

'But you have loved and lost and bounced back over and over,' Lily said, and Esme knew that her daughter had thought that she had the answers.

'I don't have any answers,' she said slowly. 'I may give the impression of bouncing back – but I really only pick up the pieces each time, and try again.'

Esme felt bewildered as to why Lily had come home. She knew she had no answers for anything and wondered that Lily thought she did.

This was Lily heartbroken. What had happened did not seem such a terrible thing to her. She knew that this was life – men hurting you. It was what they too often did best. But she knew she must not put it like that to Lily – on the one hand because she wanted Lily to have hope, and on the other because there was always the wonderful possibility that maybe Lily would be lucky sometime or another in love, and she would not want to deny that as an option.

'You pick up the pieces so well, Mum,' Lily said tentatively.

'That's just the impression you get,' Esme said. 'The truth is . . . oh, I don't know what the truth is. Of course I've been hurt . . .'

'Grayson told me what Günter did to you,' Lily said quietly.

'Grayson told you? What did he tell you? Why?' Esme was shocked. She didn't want her children knowing anything bad about their fathers.

'I was complaining about you once,' Lily admitted, 'and Grayson said that I had no right to judge you for leaving Dad. I had always thought you had just up and left him like you did Grayson, and that Jennifer had been there to help him at that time. But Grayson told me the truth, a couple of summers ago, when Jasmine and I were staying with him. That must have hurt, Mum. Your best friend and your husband? Was he your first?'

'He was the first man I loved,' Esme said. 'And, yes, it did hurt, but we recover from hurt – we have to, otherwise there is no way forward.'

'Did you love Grayson too?'

'Grayson was different,' Esme said. 'He offered, dramatically speaking, respite from the storm.'

I should not have married Grayson, she thought. It had not been fair on him nor on her, and of course when she had run from him, it had seemed to be unfair on the girls. But, she sighed, thinking to herself, we do what we do to survive. We can have everything in the world, but we are nothing without peace of mind. Yes, we need adversity to achieve and to feel fulfilled, but peace of mind comes only with reconciliation within the self . . . and what reconciliation have I reached? What reconciliation can I ever hope for . . . ?

'Will I ever be happy again?' Lily asked her, interrupting her thoughts.

'I promise you will,' Esme said. 'In due course you will see this Hugh for what he is – a user, a taker. You need to find a giver . . .'

'Grayson was a giver.'

'I think I meant that you need to find someone who knows the balance – maybe that is where there is love. Love that can last.'

'Is our whole life spent looking for love?'

Esme smiled at her. 'Now you are being dramatic. You are far too much like me to think that you are going to waste time looking for love and love alone. You will fill your days with many different kinds of happiness, and when love comes along – and it will – you will seize it and enjoy it.'

'It's like the song says, love hurts,' Lily said. 'Do you love anyone right now?'

'Apart from you and your sisters – well, I don't know. I've to get up and get into the hospital. Rose needs me now too.'

'I'm sorry,' Lily said.

'Don't be sorry. You needed me – that's all right.'

Esme was still surprised at the conversation they had had. Lily coming to her like that was unusual. Lily needing her as a person – a friend – a confidante . . . that was something she had not ever expected. It gave her the strangest feeling.

'I felt despair,' Lily said suddenly.

'Oh, darling,' Esme said, putting her arm around her again. 'That's part of life, you know. Those feelings of despair, they come, but you have to remember they pass too. And then life returns to us. Hope . . . it springs eternal. You mustn't forget that.'

'You have felt despair too?' Lily asked.

'Yes,' Esme replied. 'I know despair.'

In her heart she knew that the despair she had felt once, long ago, was the deepest, worst despair there was. She remembered that she had wished for death or for not to have been born. She also knew that in some deep recess of her mind, having survived, she had decided that she was not going to let life destroy her. She knew each day was fleeting, that it must be seized, that somehow having survived what happened to her as a child, she would not let herself be ground down again. And with all the other blows that had come her way – each devastating in its own way – she had somehow managed to pull the tattered pieces back together. Günter had helped her put the past behind her. Arjen had helped her put Günter behind her. Grayson had helped her move on from Arjen and his perfect love. And after that she was on her own. Somehow she became stronger. Holding her girls close to her. Drifting first, then finding a place where she could live using her mind, forcing it to think forwards and not backwards. Creating a place where her girls would be safe. Her flowers. Her flowers that she would protect until the end of her life, whom she would watch bloom and fulfil the promise of their existence . . .

'You're very brave, Mum,' Lily said.

'No, I'm not brave,' Esme said. 'Trust me. I'm not brave. There was a time . . . no, it doesn't matter. But I am not brave. The only thing I know is that life is a gift.'

* * *

Lily insisted on coming to the hospital too and Esme was glad of the company. Rose was being moved to a ward when they arrived and Lily hugged her as the bed was wheeled down the corridors.

'I can see you are pleased to see each other,' one of the orderlies said with a laugh, 'but could you hold off until we get her to her destination?'

'Sorry,' Lily said, reluctantly letting go of her sister.

Esme hung back, watching them. They were so close and so loving to each other. Maybe that was one thing she had got right. Yes, the girls bickered and fought, and sometimes the noise was unbearable, but they also loved each other. Jasmine, over the previous few years, had driven the older two to the brink of fury at how spoiled and selfish she had become, but the bonds were still there – strong, loving, forever connected. Esme wondered, as she had often wondered in the past, would life have been different had she had a sibling – a sister or a brother, someone who would know what it was like to be you, or who would at least have a better understanding of you, whose love would be unconditional like it was between her flowers?

Esme leaned down and kissed Rose. She was now just attached to a single drip. Her face was pale under her tan. The unhealthy colour that had flushed her cheeks the previous day was gone and she looked almost gaunt.

'They told me you stayed with me all yesterday and all night,' Rose said to her.

'I wanted to be here when you woke up,' Esme said. She did not add that she had thought Rose was going to die and she was not going to leave her. She was going to be with her to the end. She would never abandon one of her children again. 'But they sent me home late last night, once they knew you were going to recover.'

'What do you remember?' Lily asked her.

'Nothing,' Rose said. 'Absolutely nothing. I remember my stomach was hurting and I decided I'd have a shot of vodka before going to the club – but I don't even remember going to the club, or anything else for that matter. The nurse told me . . .' Rose closed her eyes. She felt exhausted.

'She needs to sleep now,' the nurse said.

'Can I stay here beside her?' Esme asked.

'I'm glad you were in London, Mum,' Rose said, her eyes closed.

Esme and Lily stayed beside her until she was asleep, and then Lily decided to go back to the apartment.

'One of us had better see that Jasmine takes that thing to the zoo,' she said.

'That's not like you to call a living creature a "thing". I'm very fond of spiders,' Esme mused.

'Mum, that's not a spider. It's a tarantula. Do you really want it living in the apartment?'

'No,' Esme said, with a slight air of distraction. 'Especially with the mess in the apartment at the moment. Far too many hiding places.'

'I'll go back home, and after I've sorted Jasmine out, I'll sort out her mess. Don't worry, order will return.'

Esme was glad to hear that. She hated lack of order.

Rose was asleep. The drugs had knocked her out again. The place in her mind was cold and alone. She thought she could taste the burned and bitter flavour of strong coffee, or maybe she smelled it. The taste changed and it became acidic and metallic and she was sitting with Roland in front of his window, looking out, with the trees moving softly outside in the summer breeze. She was reading *Macbeth* to him and she looked up to see if he was still smoking and all she could see was the colour red. A crimson slash across her mind and then just red. Red. Red. Red.

'No, no,' she murmured, and Esme clasped her hand and told her it was all right. It was going to be all right.

It was a long day, sitting in the hospital on a chair by Rose's bed. Esme occasionally went down to the canteen for coffee; the rest of the time she sat by Rose, talking to her gently when she was awake, just watching her when she was asleep. While Rose was now clearly recovering, Esme was aware of certain emotions that she had fought the previous day. There was a terrible frustration attached to sitting beside the bed of your child, not knowing if she was going to recover but knowing that there was nothing you could do to help, other than to sit there and wait. And that wait was both exhausting and terrifying.

In her cool logical way, Esme worked through those thoughts, and with them came an ever-increasing awareness about her own mother. She had thought of her mother the previous day, had thought at one point that to have her mother there would have been real support, but she had sworn to herself never to see her mother again. Now, in the light of the previous day and sitting beside Rose watching her breathe, she was forced to think of Susan yet again.

It occurred to her that once Susan must have sat beside her bed and must have felt the same terrible feelings that Esme had been feeling – despair, frustration, fear, trapped by circumstance with nothing left but prayers.

The afternoon and evening seemed interminably stretched. The hospital staff let her stay as long as she wanted but at ten in the evening it was suggested again that she go home for the night.

'Rose will be released probably the day after tomorrow. Maybe even tomorrow. She just needs sleep now . . .' Kind and reassuring. Rose was going to be fine.

Esme looked at her daughter.

'So soon?'

'As soon as we know she is through this. She will be on medication for a week. She will need rest and more rest, which is what you need right now.'

'I'll be back tomorrow,' Esme said to Rose, leaning over to kiss her again on the cheek.

'I'm fine now, you know,' Rose said. She had been given toast and tea, and, although weak, was clearly greatly improved. 'I'm supposed to be at work in the morning – do you think you could tell them what has happened?'

Esme wrote down the name of the hospital and reassured Rose that they would be contacted.

'Mum, there's a man there – in the hospital, I mean, on my ward – I told him I'd drop in over the weekend and I didn't, as you know. I'm concerned about him. Please, can you ask them . . . no, can you tell him . . . ?'

'Tell him what?'

Rose thought a moment. She was unbearably tired but Roland was now on her mind.

'Mum. I promised I'd come in and see him. He's called Roland. He's so alone. I feel I let him down by not going in to see him. I was going to read to him. We're in the middle of a play. Reading it, I mean . . . Mum, if you can get to see him, will you tell him I'll be back. I promised to come back. Tell him . . .'

'I'll tell him,' Esme said. 'Now you get some more sleep.'

When she got home the apartment had returned to its usual tidy state, which was the way she liked to keep it.

'Lily, thank you,' she said, looking around.

'Thank me too,' Jasmine interjected. 'Lily made me clean up the whole place.'

'Thank you too, Jasmine,' Esme said.

The evening was cool. She put on a shawl and sat out

on the balcony, a coffee beside her that Lily had made.

'I've to get up early in the morning,' Esme said as both girls came out to join her.

'You look like you could do with a lie-in again,' Lily said, looking at her mother.

'I've been trying to find this place through the telephone directory and then through Directory Enquiries.' Esme tapped the piece of paper in front of her. 'It's where Rose is working and I need to let them know that she is in hospital.'

'I'll do it,' Jasmine said. 'If you know where it is, I'll get up early in the morning and go there and tell them, and you can have a lie-in.'

Lily and Esme looked at her in amazement.

'Why would you do that?' Lily asked.

'Why not?' Jasmine frowned.

'Well, it's very nice of you,' Esme said.

'And you think I don't know how to be very nice?'

'No, that's not what I said.'

'It's what we thought, though,' Lily said teasingly with a grin.

'That's horrible. I was just trying to be helpful.' But she smiled back at Lily.

'You are helpful,' Esme said slowly. It was the most out-of-character thing that Jasmine had ever suggested. 'Well, if you mean it – then thank you. The problem is, although Rose has given me a name and very precise directions, I think the name she gave me is either the name of a ward or of a larger group or something like that, and that's why Directory Enquiries can't find it. Look, Jasmine.' Esme had the A–Z open on her knees. 'It's really very close by. Are you sure about going there? You've to get there by nine – that's when Rose is supposed to be there. Is that all right? Are you sure?'

Jasmine nodded.

'Oh, I promised Rose I'd leave a message there for a patient. Roland is his name. Can you get someone to tell him she's ill but will be back soon – maybe next week?'

'Sure. I'd better go to bed now,' Jasmine said. 'Seeing as I've such an early start.' She planted a kiss on top of Esme's head and waved at Lily as she went back inside.

'What's got into her?' Esme asked. 'I can't help feeling there is more to this altruism than meets the eye.'

'I've no idea. She's been in a funny mood all evening. She went to the zoo, apparently, and found a new home for Taliban. When she came home she was really quite helpful – and now this – going round to Rose's work place in the morning! Whatever next?'

'Are you feeling any better?' Esme asked her.

Lily shrugged. 'Mum, I'm fine. In the light of Rose being ill, and the state of the rest of the world, my problems are really minute. Yes, it hurts. I hurt because of what Hugh did to me. And I hate myself for not seeing the banding of the geese through to the end. I might do that next year somewhere else – I don't know. I shouldn't have run – I know that, but I couldn't bear the way he treated me.'

Esme nodded. Throughout that day her thoughts had returned to Lily and how she must be feeling. While she was glad that Lily had felt that she could come running to her, it did evoke other emotions. On the one hand it hurt that she had had no one to run to years ago, or so it had seemed back then. And on the other, she was concerned that Lily should run when something so trivial happened. Then she had to remind herself yet again that it was not trivial to Lily. It was real hurt, real grief, a real feeling of despair and humiliation.

Glancing through the large terrace windows, Esme noticed Jasmine sitting in front of the television, looking as if deep in thought. She almost called in to her to ask what was wrong, but then restrained herself simply because she really did not want to know.

Jasmine was deep in thought. She was hoping that by going to Rose's place of employment in the morning, she would make herself feel better. She would atone for all the wrong things she had done. By her getting up early, both Esme and Lily could sleep in; even if she was as jet-lagged as Lily, or as tired as Esme, she would be doing something helpful. She was also reassuring herself that it was not her fault what had happened to Taliban. She had done her best – her very best. She had taken his wellbeing into account. He had been the most important thing, and she had done her best – she really had. She told herself this, over and over.

She had gone to London Zoo as ordered by both Lily and her mother. She had bought her entrance ticket, Taliban safe in the jewellery box, jammed open with Grandma's necklace so that he would have enough air, in the bottom of her small shoulder bag. She had made her way to the house of spiders and had looked around at various specimens. There were all kinds of names for them like *Aphonopelma chalcodes*. They belonged to the spider family *Theraphosidae* – order Araneae. Jasmine didn't know if this was a surname or what. It also said they had eight eyes. She didn't think Taliban had, but then she could be wrong.

Suddenly she spotted Taliban's identical twin behind glass. She had looked at it with interest and wondered if this would be the right place for Taliban to live. She read what it said on the small notice beside it. It was only then she discovered that Taliban and his identical twin were among the most dangerous creatures on the planet. She was completely shocked that Taliban could be considered dangerous. For some reason that had not occurred to her. She had thought that Timothy the tiger was dangerous, and the alligators, but not her little pet. She looked at the notice again. It said that tarantulas sometimes had a bald patch on their abdomen, and they got that by flicking irritating hairs from it into the eyes of their enemy. She could hardly ask if she could hand him in and have him put in with this other tarantula. He wouldn't last five minutes, she thought.

There was no way she was leaving Taliban here.

And anyway, the notice said that tarantulas lived alone. She thought of him in the bottom of her bag and wondered if she should take him out so that he could have a look. She knew that she would know immediately if he liked his new surroundings, but there were a lot of people around the place and she remembered both Grayson's reaction and how he had reached for a gun, and also Lily's shock on seeing Taliban, and she changed her mind. She did not want to be responsible for what might happen. And someone might hurt Taliban.

Now she didn't know what to do. Bring him back home? Lily would be cross. Esme might not mind, though. She wondered if she could cajole Esme into letting Taliban live with them in the apartment. But then what would happen? At the end of the holidays – and she did not want to think that far ahead – she would either have to leave him behind her, or else take him back to school with her. But if the school found out they might kill him. After all, Grayson wanted to shoot him, and he was her father and knew that Taliban was her pet. The school might not be so considerate. She decided to wander around a bit more and then to bring Taliban home with her. She would ask Esme what to do. Esme would know. She knew how to handle things. That was what mothers were for. They dealt with problems. Esme would decide where Taliban would be safest.

She took the underground back home. When she arrived back at Waterloo, she checked her bag to see if he was all right, and it was then she discovered he was gone. Somewhere, somehow along the way, Taliban must have escaped. Now having read how lethally dangerous he was, she was more cautious as she put her bag down on the platform, and carefully lifted out various things. On the ground she placed a comb, her wallet, a bottle of water, an envelope with a stamp on it that she had liked and had filched from Grayson's desk, the spare set of car keys from the convertible that she had brought with her from South Carolina so that she wouldn't have to go hunting for them the next time she was there – if indeed her father ever allowed her back – and then the jewellery box. The lid was open. Grandma's necklace was in the bottom of the bag, as she discovered when she tipped the bag over on to the ground. But there was no sign of Taliban.

'Are you all right?' someone asked her. 'Have you lost something?'

'I'm fine,' she mumbled, glancing urgently around to see if there was any sign of Taliban on the platform. There was not.

Having checked carefully that Taliban was not hiding in the bottom of the bag, she scooped everything up and tried to remember when she had last checked on him. She was pretty sure that it was as she was leaving the zoo.

It made no difference. He was gone.

Now she became aware of her mother watching her though the balcony window. She tried waving and smiling. She decided the best thing to do was to go to bed. She would think about Taliban tomorrow – not that she could imagine where or how to find him.

She hoped he was safe.

*   *   *

Not long after Esme went to bed, the weather broke. It started
with a roll of thunder in the distance and then lightning that
lit the sky over and over. Finally the rain came down. Lying
on her back, curtains open, with the lights from the city glis-
tening in the dark wet night, Esme listened to the drum-
ming of the rain on the windowpanes and on the table and
chairs outside on the balcony. For the first time in several
days she allowed herself to think – this was her first opportunity to contemplate anything clearly, without the worry of
Rose, or indeed of either Lily or Jasmine dominating her
thoughts.

So many things sparked off different fears and added to
her sleep problem. Little things that would be inconsequen-
tial in other people's lives took on a meaning in hers that
shook her to the core of her being – the sound of a baby
crying, the creak of a staircase, a footstep in a corridor, a car
pulling up abruptly, blind people at a swimming pool . . .
There was no escape. No matter how hard she tried to restart
there were things she carried with her. It was as if her life
was a sentence from which there was no parole.

She supposed that by falling in love with Günter
Wassermann she was trying to find a way to live that was
free of the past, but between Günter and Jennifer that potential façade had been destroyed. Dear Grayson. François . . .
and now she regretted her recent brief interlude with Peter
Carew. He had been another mistake, a rebound reaction
after her hurried exit from Paris. Perhaps she had got into
bed with him just to prove to herself that she did not have
to be alone, but it had been a foolish thing to do. She thought
now about Jacob suggesting to her that she had perhaps done
Peter an injustice by assuming that he had befriended her
for journalistic reasons. She felt now that her reaction
bordered on paranoia. Who was she anyway for anyone to
want to interview? Unless, of course, she had been identified

as Molly Kilbride and she was quite sure she had not been. Molly and the past – they were so long ago that she felt safe from recognition.

There had been a time when journalists had knocked on her parents' front door on an hourly and then a daily basis. She remembered her mother, Susan, saying, 'Will they never leave us alone?' And Harry had replied, 'Don't forget we owe them. If it hadn't been for the publicity we got after Molly was kidnapped, no one would have known to look in the house next door . . .'

But Susan was right. It had been so intrusive. No, it had been more than that. It was invasive. They had done their best, Esme thought. She thought now about her own three girls and she wondered at how she had been able to have children after all that had happened. She knew that she had feared that something as awful might happen to one of hers, even though she felt that statistically it was highly unlikely. And, of course, nothing like that had happened, and yet other things had. It was all relative. She sighed. She was tired but knew that she would not sleep. Her mind was working too fast. She got out of bed and stood at the window, looking through the rain. She wondered where Jacob was, and if he was asleep in his Parisian home. She had not had the time to phone him since she had arrived in London. She would do so the following day. Glancing at her watch, she corrected the wording of her thoughts. She would phone him today, maybe mid-morning or, depending on whether Rose was released from hospital, later in the day.

She had fed him the name Molly Kilbride. She wondered now why she had done that. She had never said the name to anyone – not even to Arjen – not ever. Jennifer knew, of course, but Jennifer had been sworn to secrecy. She wondered briefly if Jennifer would ever have told Günter, but then she decided it was unlikely. Jennifer had wanted to remove Esme from Günter's thoughts. Telling him the true story of his ex-wife might not have done that quite so successfully.

The pretence had begun when she and Jennifer had moved to Germany. She had talked it through with Jennifer, initially saying that she just did not like her name and then admitting that she couldn't live with it and with what it meant to other people. Leaving Ireland had been part of the scheme of things. It was in her last year of school, when her father died and the papers were once again full of Molly Kilbride, and the journalists were back, waiting outside her home or her school to ask her how she felt. Then it was that she had said to Jennifer, 'I have to leave. I need a clean start and I will never get it here. I will always be poor little Molly Kilbride.' She saw then that the only way she could countenance recovery or rebuilding a life was by discarding the vestiges of her past.

Jennifer had listened, had nodded and had understood. Jennifer had been there with her from the beginning, even though Esme did not know what the beginning really was. It had been easy to discard the name of Molly. Her passport identified her as Esme Kilbride. And that was the start of her change of identity. It had been that simple. In the changing of her name, she had walked away from the past, and no one knew other than Jennifer.

When Jennifer betrayed her by sleeping with Günter, Esme wondered briefly if she had felt that she had the right to do something like that, as she had protected Esme and participated in Esme's abandonment of the past. Had Jennifer seen it as some kind of payback time?

These thoughts were disturbing her. Bit by bit, everything was coming back to her own mother. What had once seemed so clear-cut, now no longer did. She was so aware of the parallels over the past forty-eight hours, parallels between herself and her mother, the sitting waiting by a hospital bed, praying for a child to survive, to pull through, to return to normality – that must be what Susan had gone through all those years ago. She now felt empathy for her mother. Back then she had not. Back then she had felt nothing, not for a long time, and then she had felt blame.

Was that fair? Probably not. And she knew it. She knew that for some reason both she and her mother had blamed each other.

There had been a time in the initial period of the kidnapping when all Esme – or Molly, as she had been back then – could think about was her parents, and her undying need for them. That period had faded and been replaced with a long anguished cry for help directed at humanity in general, and later at Jericho and Andy. And later still, when it was over and she was released and found herself in hospital, it had been a long time – if indeed ever – before she could relate to her parents again. She could see now that they must have been desperate, but of course she had not understood that then. But now, as an adult, knowing how they had stayed by her bedside over days and nights and days again, she knew they must have been out of their minds with worry.

It was already two o'clock in the morning. She went to the kitchen to make tea and she allowed herself to think about Jacob. She tried to keep her thoughts concentrated on his friendship and on the fact that she liked talking to him. She knew that she felt something else for him, something that she could not allow to dominate her mind. She liked him, wanted him as a friend, and knowing there could be no more than that, she pushed any other thoughts away.

Taking her tea, she settled into the small den off the living area, and she began to work.

Work was the one place that offered sanctuary.

CHAPTER NINETEEN

The following morning, at around eight thirty, Esme woke to find her phone ringing.

'I woke you?' Jacob said to her slightly dazed voice.

'Jacob! It was time I got up anyway – and I was going to phone you.'

'I'm in London,' he said. 'Would you like to meet?'

She explained then about Rose.

'There is a possibility that she might come home today, although tomorrow seems more likely.'

'I'll leave you in peace then,' he said.

'No, no. I would like to see you,' she said. 'I'll call you back when things are clearer. Give me an hour or so.'

She stretched, getting up from her desk chair, her neck stiff from having slept in such an uncomfortable place. Ringing the hospital, she was told that Rose had had a good night and could leave at midday. Lily appeared beside her, taking in her mother's pale face and the tiredness in it.

'Did you sleep in here?' she asked in surprise.

'One of those nights,' Esme said vaguely. 'I've to fetch Rose from the hospital. I'd better have a bath – I'm so stiff.'

'I'll run your bath,' Lily said kindly. 'You get your clothes sorted and then I'll call for a taxi.'

'Did you sleep?' Esme asked her.

'Yes, really well,' Lily said. 'I've decided to go with Jazz to Rose's work place, just to make sure – well, you know. Anyway, I'm just so pleased to be here. And Rose may be coming home today . . . it's great.' She smiled at Esme. 'Thank you, you're great.'

Esme had no idea why she might be considered great. She did not feel that it was a word that could come remotely near to describing her. She felt as if her serenity was shot. She felt more like crying.

She was lying in the bath thinking about Rose coming home from hospital, and then she remembered her own homecoming. It had been so awful. None of her clothes had fitted. She had lost so much weight, and she had grown. And it wasn't just that her clothes had not fitted, it was as if her whole life didn't fit. She remembered the coldness of the air the day she had come out of the hospital – it had hit her in the face and she wondered if that was what air always felt like. She simply could not remember. And then, sitting in the back of Harry's car with Susan beside her, she was afraid. She remembered that fear. Susan was holding her hand; she could see her mother's hand around hers, but she couldn't feel it. And yet there must have been warmth in the wrapping of their fingers around each other. But she had felt nothing. She told herself to stop. She must not think. She knew she must not think. She concentrated now on the suds in the bath. Lily must have put some foam into it. It smelled of fruit, or bubble-gum – something tangy anyway. After she had bathed and dressed she went and sat on the balcony and drank her morning coffee, and as she watched the Thames flowing past she remembered that was what she had watched when she came home from hospital all those years ago. And then with a start she realised that she had been in Dublin and had gone home there, and she wondered what made her think it was the Thames she had watched . . . so many things tangled together, things that she must not think about.

The day was fresh and clean with the sun shining brightly after the rain and the intensity of the heat had evaporated. It was a lovely day, the right day for Rose to be coming home. All my flowers will be with me, she thought. And for some reason that thought washed through her with a grief she could not explain. All my flowers, she thought again, my beautiful flowers . . .

Jacob came over in the late afternoon, in time to help with dinner and to eat with them. He looked just as she remembered him, his kind face searching hers, flowers in his arms, a bear hug once she had taken them and put them down, three kisses on the cheeks, French-style. The flowers amazed her. There were so many of them, and she knew they must be beautiful. She got out a large vase and filled it with water. Jacob helped her arrange them in the vase that they then put on the coffee table. The flowers seemed to dominate the room – a bit like how her daughters took over her life, she thought. And as they positioned the flowers they glanced at each other and she knew that something had changed.

Looking at Jacob, she realised that the strange talking relationship that had evolved between them in Paris had moved to a different level. There was real interest, real concern in both of them about the other. The only physical contact they had had before was when he had put his hand on hers in concern or empathy. Now they hugged like old friends. There was a deep warmth between them.

Rose appeared from her bedroom to find out what was happening. Esme introduced her to Jacob.

'I love the roses,' Rose said. 'I don't suppose I could take them into my bedroom?'

Jacob removed one rose from the vase into which Esme

had just placed them. The rose he took was red. With the clippers that Esme had used to trim the stalks, he carefully sliced away a few thorns and then handed it to Rose.

She smiled, delighted. Esme fetched a long glass for her, filling it with water, and then insisted Rose got back into bed.

'You've been told to take it easy for a while,' she said. 'And we're going to make sure you do. You've to sleep and sleep and then rest some more.'

'I need to get up and get better,' Rose said.

'You'll get better faster if you do what the doctors say,' Esme said. 'Well, at least, that is what they said.'

Rose laughed. 'Mum always quotes what other people say as though she doesn't quite believe it,' she explained to Jacob.

'In this instance she might just be right,' Jacob said.

'I hate being locked away in my room,' Rose said.

'You might be glad when Jasmine gets home,' Esme said gently.

'That's true,' Rose said. 'I hope she remembered to call into the hospital.'

'Don't worry, Lily went with her.'

Esme and Jacob sat out on the balcony in the late afternoon sun.

He watched her face carefully. 'Are you good, Esme?' he asked.

'Good?'

'*Bien?* Feeling reasonably all right? You look tired, if you don't mind me mentioning it.'

'I don't mind you mentioning it. I should look great after a week in the South of France but I feel exhausted. I think the stress of Rose in hospital – oh, just the last few days. I was worried about Lily. And now Jasmine is here too – and that is reason to be worried. Jasmine is . . . difficult, yes, difficult. I suppose that is the word. Irresponsible, actually, might be better.'

'And are you sleeping?'

'You sound like a doctor.'

'I am a doctor,' he reminded her wryly.

She was comfortable there with him sitting beside her. The sounds from the street below were far away, and the air was clear and bright.

Jasmine had woken early and, feeling very noble, got herself ready to go to Rose's place of work. Lily appeared before Jasmine left and said she would like to come too. Jasmine was going to object because she had plans for afterwards that included going back to Waterloo station and asking if any pets had been handed in. She wasn't very hopeful but Taliban was on her mind and she couldn't bear the thought of him lost in London. However, the fact that Lily wanted to accompany her to the hospital made the first part of her day more attractive, so she readily agreed.

They found the place easily enough and presented themselves in the hallway where some members of staff were leaving and some were coming on duty. Lily went to look at a notice board while Jasmine approached the reception desk. She decided the best thing to do was to pass the message about Roland first and then to explain about Rose.

'I've a message for Roland,' she said. She couldn't remember if her mother had given a surname.

'Roland Duval?' a nurse, coming off duty, asked.

Jasmine nodded.

'Are you a relative?'

Jasmine was not known for telling the truth, and now was not the time for her to start. She nodded. 'His sister,' she said.

Lily, coming up behind her and only hearing the word 'sister', said with a smile, 'I'm a sister too.' She was under the impression that Jasmine had been asked if she was related to Rose.

The nurse looked at them both and then at the receptionist. 'I'll look after this,' she said. 'Perhaps you girls would like to come with me.'

They were led to a small office down a corridor. 'I'm the staff nurse on Roland's ward,' she said to them. Her voice was sombre.

Lily was slightly puzzled at how this was progressing. Jasmine sat on a chair in the office and looked around with curiosity.

'What are your names?' the nurse asked them.

'I'm Lily Wassermann, and this is my sister, Jasmine Redmond. We have different surnames,' she explained. 'Different fathers . . .'

'I'm so sorry to tell you this,' the nurse said, 'but Roland died yesterday afternoon.'

Jasmine was thinking that that sounded very sad and she hoped that Rose wouldn't be upset. Lily was wondering why they were being told this.

'I'm sorry,' Lily said after a moment's hesitation.

'I wonder if you would like a doctor to come and talk to you about what happened,' the nurse said.

Lily was aware that there was something here that didn't make sense but she couldn't think what it was.

A doctor came in. He shook hands with them both and expressed his sympathy.

'When Roland came in, he said he had no next of kin,' he explained. 'This is why you weren't already contacted.'

'Do you think we are next of kin?' Lily asked somewhat tentatively.

Jasmine was looking a little uneasy.

'Aren't you?' The doctor looked from Lily to the nurse and back again.

'I think there may be some misunderstanding,' Lily said. 'We are Rose van der Vloed's sisters and we came in to say she is ill and can't come to work for, I don't know, at least a week, I suppose. And she asked us to leave a message for Roland. I think he was someone she read to . . .' Lily looked at Jasmine, still totally unsure how this mistake could have taken place.

'I thought you said you were Roland's sister,' the nurse said to Jasmine.

'I meant that we're Rose's sister,' Jasmine said.

'I think Rose was very fond of Roland,' Lily said, now trying to cover for her sister. It made no difference how the mistake had been made. It was done. 'If he has no next of kin,' she said cautiously, 'what happens? What happens now, I mean?'

There would be a post-mortem. And then Roland would be buried.

'Did he have friends?' Lily asked.

It didn't appear that he did. Neither friends nor family. No one had come to visit him, nor asked after him.

'My sister Rose is very ill but recovering. She's in hospital,' Lily said. 'I think she is going to be upset about his dying. Please can you tell me what happened? I don't know anything about him. But Rose is going to want to know.' She looked hopefully from one to the other.

'Rose?' the doctor said.

'She's one of the summer assistants on the ward,' the nurse explained.

'Yes. Yes, I see. Perhaps she would like to contact us when she's better,' he said.

Lily took Jasmine out for lunch after they had checked Lost Property at Waterloo station.

'What are you looking for, Jazz?' Lily asked her.

Jasmine had insisted on going into the place by herself, leaving Lily puzzled and waiting.

'Oh, I lost something here the other day,' Jasmine said vaguely, trying to make it sound as though it wasn't important.

'What did you lose?'

'Oh, a necklace Grandma gave me,' Jasmine said.

'You know, Jazz, you're a dreadful liar,' Lily said. 'No, I'm not cross, but I think if you stuck to the truth it would be better. Not just for you, but for everyone.'

'It's only a necklace,' Jasmine objected.

'I wasn't talking about that,' Lily said. 'I was thinking about what happened in the hospital. I don't know what you said that made them think we were this Roland's sisters, but you shouldn't mislead people like that.'

'I'm sorry,' Jasmine said, contrite. 'But think, if I had not misled them – and it was a sort of an accident anyway – then we wouldn't have found out what had happened to Roland, and Rose wouldn't know.'

'I'm not sure that we should tell Rose right now, anyway,' Lily said. 'Rose has been really ill. It might not be the right time to tell her that a patient of hers has died.'

'What do you think happened to him?' Jasmine asked.

'I've no idea,' Lily said thoughtfully. 'But whatever it was, they weren't going to tell us. And I think it could be a shock for Rose, and she might be better off without shocks until she's better. So, let's just keep it to ourselves, okay?'

Jasmine nodded as she looked at the menu.

'Can we go shopping afterwards, Lil?' she asked. 'I've some money from Dad and my grandparents.'

'What do you want to buy?' Lily asked.

'I don't know. Maybe something for Rose. She might like something to cheer her up.'

Lily smiled. 'That's really nice of you, Jazz,' she said.

*   *   *

When they got home in the early evening they found Esme in the kitchen organising dinner with a man called Jacob, who was cutting up peppers and onions, looking like he had been there for a long time. Rose was in bed asleep.

'Hi, Mom,' Jasmine said as she took in the kitchen activities. Lily appeared behind her.

'Jasmine and Lily,' Esme said. 'We wondered what had happened to you. This is Jacob Althaus, a friend of mine from France. Jacob, this is my youngest, Jasmine. And this is Lily.'

'I've sticky fingers,' Jacob said, 'otherwise I would shake hands with you.' Jasmine giggled. He waved the chopping knife instead.

'Where have you been all day?' Esme asked.

'We went shopping,' Jasmine said, eyeing the food hungrily. It seemed a long time since lunch. 'I had a brilliant, brilliant day. Lily and I had a great time.'

Rose now appeared in pyjamas. They were grey cotton with 'Biker's Bitch' embroidered in red across the chest.

'Jazz,' she said. 'Welcome home.'

'Hi, Rosie. I believe you've been pretending to be ill.'

Rose laughed. 'Yes. So ill that I'm being waited on hand and foot.'

'In fact, go and sit down now, Rose,' Esme said.

'Mum said you went to the hospital for me – did you tell them I was ill?' Rose said to Jasmine as she curled up on the sofa.

'I did,' Jasmine said.

'Did you ask them about Roland?'

'Yes,' Jasmine said. 'They said—'

'When you're better,' Lily interrupted, 'you're to call them and they'll talk about you restarting. I think you need a doctor's certificate to explain your absence.'

'I was going to buy you a present, Rose,' Jasmine said. 'But

I couldn't find anything that was right for you. I'm going to try again tomorrow.'

'Look what Jacob brought,' Esme interjected, gesturing towards the vase of lilies, roses and jasmine.

'That's beautiful,' Jasmine said.

'Each of my flowers is there,' Esme said, looking at the vase.

'Which flower is the most beautiful?' Lily teased.

'Stop that now,' Esme said, her voice sounding slightly frayed.

'Each is perfection,' Jacob said.

'That almost sounds like a quote,' Rose said.

'It is a quote,' Lily said. 'It's what Mum always said about us when we were little. Do you remember?'

Dinner was a noisy affair, with the girls outdoing each other and talking over and through each other.

'Do you think I'll be able to go back to work next week?' Rose asked. She was still lying on the sofa. 'I must admit I don't miss it. I hate the job – except for Roland.' She turned to Jacob to explain. 'He's one of the patients. He's been on suicide watch . . .'

'What?' Jasmine's mouth fell open.

'He's been very depressed,' Rose explained. 'But I like him. He is the only person in there I can relate to. He's very intelligent. Lovely eyes . . . grey. You know the way you sometimes feel empathy with someone? Well, that's how I feel with him. We're reading a play together.' She made it sound as if there had been more give and take than was in fact the reality. But it was difficult to explain what it was like.

'It sounds that, while you are not enjoying your work, you do actually like one individual patient,' Jacob said. 'I must say, I can sometimes identify with that.'

'I should never have done this degree,' Rose said. 'It seemed a good idea at the time . . .'

'You were young,' Esme said. 'You are young. You're allowed to change your mind. As we grow, different interests surface in us.'

'I don't know what to do,' Rose said. 'I'm twenty-one. I've invested all this time in doing something I don't like. No, it's not that I don't like it. It's more that it doesn't satisfy me.'

'Youth is on your side, you know,' Jacob said, cautious about intruding even though Esme's girls appeared to have accepted his presence with an equanimity that surprised him. 'As Esme said, you were young when you chose that particular career – you can still change, I would imagine, or equally you may find that it is a stepping stone to something in the same area.'

'Sometimes you have to dabble in different things until you find what you want to do,' Lily said.

'It's all right for you,' Rose said. 'You always knew you wanted to work with animals.'

'I know. But I meant, look at Mum.'

'What about Mom?' Jasmine asked.

'Well, my degree is in Philosophy and Linguistics,' Esme said. 'But now I work on a number of different issues.'

'And write novels,' Lily added.

'Isn't that all much the same thing, though?' Rose said.

'Not from the inside it isn't,' Esme replied thoughtfully. 'It might look like that to you, but it isn't really. What would you really like to do, Rose?'

'I don't know,' Rose replied.

'May I interrupt?' Jacob asked.

'Yes,' Rose said. 'I am open to any suggestions.'

'Well . . . what would you like to be doing, say, five or ten years from now, Rose?'

'I don't know. In an ideal world I'd like to be doing something that has some impact, something that has some meaning. But I don't know what that something is.'

'You know,' Esme inserted, 'we have impact in all kinds of ways without even knowing it.'

'I can't imagine not finishing this degree and yet I really don't want to,' Rose said.

'You could finish the degree and then start something new,' Lily said.

'Or you could seize the day,' Esme suggested, 'and work out what you really want and then do that.'

'How do you know what you want to do when you grow up?' Jasmine asked. 'I used to think I'd be like Dad and live on the plantation and play golf. But do you know something?' She helped herself to pasta and salad. 'I don't want to do that. I want to do something. I mean, really do something. Not just sit around. It's very boring. Sometimes I just sit and stare out at the trees.'

Esme shivered.

'What's so wrong with that?' Jasmine asked her. 'Did I say something?'

'Nothing,' Esme said. 'I just shivered because I was cold, nothing to do with what you said. The truth? I'm really glad you think like that.'

After dinner Jacob took her to a bar around the corner.

'Who is that man?' Jasmine asked Rose.

Rose was still on the sofa, and Jasmine and Lily were clearing up after the meal.

'Some friend of Mum's,' Rose said.

'Is he a boyfriend?' Jasmine asked.

'I've no idea,' Rose said.

'I rather liked him,' Lily interjected. 'He was interested in us in a way that wasn't nosy. And Esme seemed really cheered up. The last few days have been awful for her.'

'Don't you mind her having a boyfriend?' Jasmine said.

'Well, no. Not really. I mean, do you want a mother who does nothing except teach and write books and is probably very lonely? Or do you want her busy and happy?' Lily replied.

'I had wondered if there was a man in France – if that was why she was heading off there for her sabbatical,' Rose said. 'Looks like I was right.'

'Do you think he's okay, Rose?' Jasmine asked.

'Yes. He seems fine.'

'She's been by herself for a very long time,' Lily said. 'It's good for her to have company.'

'She doesn't have many friends, does she?' Jasmine commented.

'No. You're right. She's a loner,' Rose replied.

'A bit like me,' Lily said.

'Probably a bit like all of us.'

'I like your girls,' Jacob said to Esme as they walked down the street. 'You must be very proud of them. And rightly so. They are each unique and yet have similar strengths. They get that from you. Stalwart girls.'

'Stalwart! How nice. It's not a word I would have used, or indeed thought of. Stalwart. I like it,' she said. 'I . . . oh, I don't know. I'm proud of them but I worry about what I see as their frailties.'

'They are not frail,' he said. 'Not more than any human being. Look at Jasmine. With all your concerns about her lack of responsibility and her selfishness – your words, not mine – she in fact is growing into someone who wants to participate and achieve.'

'She has surprised me this evening,' Esme admitted. 'I've never seen or heard her talking about something other than what it meant to her or how she related to it. And yet, there she was talking about not wanting to do nothing. A complex negative, but you get my meaning.'

'And Rose sounds like she is going to reassess what she is doing. The only person left to sort out is you, Esme.'

'I'm not sure if you are joking or not,' Esme said.

'We can joke if you prefer,' he said. 'But somehow I don't think you feel like joking . . . this may not be the right time – you may prefer just to enjoy a brandy and coffee – or maybe it is the right time. Maybe you should talk to me. Shall we go in here?' he asked as they approached a small bar.

Esme nodded in agreement and, when inside, assented to the brandy and coffee he had suggested and waited while he ordered them.

They were sitting in a corner on comfortable round-backed chairs. He sat back and tore open a tiny packet of sugar, which he poured slowly into his coffee. She felt his eyes on her as she stared out the window into the night.

'You know about Molly Kilbride,' she said suddenly, breaking the silence.

'Yes.'

'I was Molly Kilbride,' she said.

He was about to say, 'I know,' when it occurred to him that she might not want him to have so quickly pieced that together. He also noted how she referred to Molly in the past tense.

'You are a woman who has invented herself many times over,' he observed, thinking about the different roles of wife and partner, student, lecturer and writer that she had occupied.

'Yes. I was Molly. I am no more. But I can't escape from what happened. In some ways it is always there.'

'What part of it is always there?'

'I think that that is who I was. I felt defined by the name

Molly Kilbride. People always wanted to know how I was feeling and how I was coping and handling things. And of course I wasn't. Neither coping nor handling, I mean . . .'

'We are all made up of our past,' he said. 'All the good and the bad bits. The secret, I think, is not to be defined by them. You are so much more than a child who was kidnapped and abused . . . but I think you know that.'

'Sometimes I think it is like there are ghosts that I was never able to lay. You lay a ghost, don't you?' She suddenly laughed. 'It just sounds a very unlikely combination of words. There is such a filthy irony in the words.'

'Tell me what happened when you stopped being Molly Kilbride,' he suggested.

'I was a mixture,' she said. 'A mix of anger and hope . . . no, maybe it was hopelessness. I was nearly nineteen when I finished school. I had this friend – I told you about her before, Jennifer Delmont. We went to university in Germany. She had this German boyfriend, although that didn't last once she got there. I thought that was why she wanted to go there, but later I thought it was because she was my friend. Now, looking back on it, I can't imagine why she wanted to go there.'

'Why did you want to go there?'

'I think because it was far away from home. My father had died . . .'

They were going into their last year at school. Her mother and father were constantly fighting. The arguments went on all night sometimes. Molly went to sleep hearing them downstairs, and when she woke in the morning, they were still going strong. She did not know if they had kept it up all night or if they had fallen asleep during the row and just recommenced it upon awakening. She tried not to listen. She knew they did not want her to hear, because they

clammed up when she came into the room. There was a
sense of accusation between them. Blame, perhaps. She
wasn't sure. Things had never been right between her parents
after the kidnapping. Molly knew that. But she could not
remember what they were really like before. Perhaps because
she had not noticed – there had been no reason to notice.
Now it was different. Her mother seemed more frustrated.
Yes, Susan tried to hide her frustration with her daughter,
but Molly knew it was there. Susan constantly tried to coerce
her into going with other girls to discos or to parties, but
Molly hated them. She went once to please Susan, but she
heard someone whispering, 'That's Molly Kilbride, you know
– the girl who was . . .' She moved away, horrified. There was
nowhere to hide. She preferred the silence of her own room.
Susan asked Jennifer to encourage Molly to go out.

But Molly was afraid. She was afraid of things no one else
could understand. She was afraid of crowded streets and of
empty streets; neither offered protection. Both could hide
the person she feared might stalk her. She was afraid of cars.
When Susan said she could take a taxi home if she wanted
to leave the disco early, Molly felt a clamp of terror around
her heart. Getting into a car, unless she knew the driver, was
almost beyond her. It evoked memories of being forced down
on to the floor where she could hardly breathe. Her days
were full of anxiety. She did not even feel safe when she was
out with her parents. She knew then that if she was going
to live, she was going to have to find some way to do it. The
arguments in the house escalated. Then out of the blue her
mother said she was leaving.

It was weeks later, when she and her father were having
dinner, silently picking at the food on their plates, that she
wanted to ask him if Susan had left because of her. She wanted
to apologise for the mess that she had made of her childhood.
She felt contaminated, unsure how to move forwards.

'Molly,' her father suddenly said, putting down his knife and fork, 'Molly, tell me that you know I would do anything for you. I need you to know that I love you.'

'I know that, Dad,' she said. She knew that. She didn't doubt it. But she also knew that he couldn't protect her. She knew that money bought comfort but not security. Parents gave love but not protection. She had learned many things the wrong way around.

'I would do anything to make you feel safe again,' he said.

She nodded her head politely. She knew that no one could do that.

But he did. At least he did his best. Two weeks later, the Eyes walked out of prison.

Harry Hastings thought of this man coming out of prison, looking at the world with new eyes, freed from the confines of cells and locked doors. He had been waiting for this day, hoping it would never happen, but knowing that if it did he must be ready. He knew enough people – colleagues, business people, bouncers in his clubs – many people who were not just shocked at what had happened to Molly, but who also liked Harry and knew that he had been destroyed by the crime – people who would help him once he worked out what to do.

At first he contemplated murder – it seemed the only fitting solution – but as time passed and it was clear that Molly was going to have to live carrying the memory of that nightmare week for the rest of her life, Harry's thoughts evolved into the notion of justice. The man they called the Eyes would live.

But he would live without his eyes.

Harry Hastings was charged with grievous bodily harm with intent. He had no regrets, nor was he afraid. He had confidence in the jury system.

Molly remembered that morning at the court only too clearly. She had visited her father the previous day and he had reassured her that it was going to be all right. She looked at him in disbelief. How could it be all right? How could anything be all right ever again? It was all back in the newspapers. In school they were talking about it. The anonymity she had craved and which had almost been hers was gone in two flashes of a very sharp knife. She did not know what to say to her parent. She loved him. He had done this for her. It would never end.

Then the morning of the court hearing, her father was brought in and he stood there while the charge was read out. She remembered him turning towards her and looking at her, and she remembered feeling an acute sense of despair, knowing that he was there only because of her.

And then he clutched his arm and seemed to wince, an expression of pain that was reflected in his face as his chest immobilised and he seemed to double over before falling to the floor.

It was four years to the day since she had been kidnapped. An irony not missed by the journalists. Her father was buried amidst the flashing of cameras, and she vowed then to leave, to get as far away as possible and never to return.

'There was nothing left, you see,' she said to Jacob.

'Your mother?'

'She could not protect me. No one could. That's how I saw it, anyway. My father had blinded one of the men, but now he was dead. I felt that his efforts to protect me had failed. I also – obviously – was devastated by his death. It was unbearable . . . you can imagine.'

'Tell me.'

'I had thought of killing myself numerous times over those four years. But I couldn't do it. Maybe I'm not the type. I don't know. Sometimes I took the blade from my father's razor, and I'd run the taps . . . but I couldn't do it. It wasn't in me. I don't know why. And after my father died, knowing that I couldn't kill myself, I decided then to leave. I had seen this psychiatrist years earlier, after the kidnapping. He had spoken to me about choice. He said that I could choose to be destroyed by what had happened or to fight it. Only now could I see that I really did have that choice. My father was not going to have died for nothing. I wanted . . . I wanted to do something so that he might be proud of me and know that he hadn't died for nothing.'

'I remember you said to me that you visited his grave and tried not to think. What were you trying not to think about?' Jacob asked her.

'I don't know,' she replied. 'I suppose how he died and why. You know the man – the Eyes – he killed himself shortly after my father blinded him.'

Jacob nodded. He did not pretend not to know what she was talking about.

'The Eyes only got six years – an accessory to armed robbery – and then, time off. Remission, I think they call it.'

'Have you any idea what happened to the other . . . the other . . . ?' He sought a word. 'Man' did not seem appropriate.

'Criminal? Rapist? Kidnapper? Armed robber? What a farce. Those were the things they were charged with, you know, armed robbery, kidnapping and rape. I used to think they should have been charged with murder.'

'Murder?'

'They murdered Molly Kilbride. At least that's how I saw it. She didn't survive what happened to her. And as a result her parents' marriage disintegrated. There are some ironies here, though, like the Wolf getting more for the armed robbery than he did for the rape. And no, I don't know what happened to him. I suppose he got back out. They were involved in the IRA. Did you know that? I know from living abroad that people are inclined to think of the IRA as freedom fighters. Freedom killers would be a more accurate description. The Wolf would probably have been released under the Good Friday Agreement if for some reason he was still in prison. I don't think about it. I don't want to know. I've never been back since that one visit to get the affidavit for my marriage.'

'You said you had no contact with your mother.'

'No. None. I said goodbye when I left. I told her I wouldn't be back.'

'What did she say?'

'Nothing. Absolutely nothing.'

'Esme, don't you think she grieved?'

'For my father? No.'

'I meant for you.'

'The awful thing,' Esme said slowly, 'is that I now know that she must have. She couldn't not have, if you see what I mean. So much of this I thought I laid to rest years ago, and yet as the years go by it is still there. It doesn't go away. Of late – perhaps in particular over the past few days – I have thought of her and how she must have felt. I mean, if one of my girls was kidnapped . . . it was bad enough Rose being so ill in hospital. I was terrified. Absolutely terrified and alone. Frightened. My child . . .'

Jacob said nothing. He watched the emotion in her usually impassive face. He did not know if she was referring to her own childhood experience or to the awfulness of Rose's illness.

'Did I do her an injustice?' Esme wondered aloud. 'Her marriage broke up because of me. I suppose they couldn't handle the whole thing. I was one long source of anxiety for them both.'

'You're going to blame yourself for being kidnapped?' he asked.

She smiled wryly. 'It does sound like that, doesn't it? No, that's not what I meant. I think I feel guilty because I didn't bounce back out of it and be like other girls. I couldn't fulfil my parents. They wanted their little Molly Kilbride back – but she was gone. And I couldn't remember what she was like.'

'I think they would be very proud of you,' he said gently. 'You grew into a wonderful woman – a mother, a scholar, a teacher . . . I think both your parents would be so proud and pleased with you. You survived. That in itself is an achievement.'

'I used to think the walls of my mind were too thin,' she said.

'You built them up again,' he said. 'You're strong – stronger than most. You've picked up the pieces time and again. You never caved in . . . what more could you want of yourself?'

What indeed? She did not know the answer. She only knew that she was, as she had once said to Jacob, only half a person. She did not feel emotions like other people did. She learned them by watching how other people reacted, and she tried to emulate them.

Jacob walked her back to the apartment and he kissed her lightly on both cheeks when saying goodbye. His face was caught in the streetlight and, looking into it, she saw the kindness and the concern in his eyes and she would have liked him to put his arms around her. They gazed at each other for a long moment before he turned to hail a cab.

Now she lay in bed, thinking about her girls. She wondered again how she had ever had the nerve to want children. Surely she, of all people, must have seen the risks in bringing a human being into the world. And yet she had wanted them.

Had loved them with all her heart, but had feared for them too. Feared as they grew up, and she supposed, became potential targets for whatever cruelty some potential criminal might choose to inflict on them. She had nurtured them through the years, and in a sense had heaved a sigh of relief as each hit the age of fifteen and had not been abducted or killed. She suspected that other people did not carry her fears – but then why should they? She knew from listening to colleagues in the department that other parents had trouble with their teenage kids, but she did not feel like that. As they made their small rebellions in life, she almost rejoiced at what she knew was normal. True, the noise they made when they were together was all-consuming, but in some way she loved it. They talked. They communicated. They supported each other. She loved their life and their energy.

She knew that the real reason she had decided to take a sabbatical was to try to get used to being alone. She needed those girls to give her life meaning, and of course they were growing up, carving their own way, forming their own existence in worlds they had created.

She knew she was now going to have to stay in London at least until Jasmine went back to school. She would put off learning to live alone for a while longer. She wondered how she would be able to work with that level of noise in the apartment. She would encourage Jasmine to get some kind of a job locally. Although that could be difficult. Rose would probably go on working in the hospital for the summer, once she was well enough. And Lily would be busy studying. It would be difficult in the evenings, though. Her mind was wandering; she knew that she was avoiding thinking about Jacob and their conversation . . . Jacob.

Before they had parted, he had mentioned, as though in passing, that he and his wife had separated. She had been shocked. She pulled back from him under the streetlight on the pavement. She knew what he was saying had to be momentous for him. They had been married since he was at university. And yet he had said it in a way that made it seem that it was inevitable, an event waiting to happen.

'Jacob, I'm so sorry. Here I am, talking about me . . . me, me, me . . . and you are in the middle of a crisis.'

'It's not a crisis,' he said. 'Yes, it is sad. But no, not something that I should not have seen coming. And, anyway, I happen to prefer to talk about "you, you, you", as you so succinctly put it.'

'Your marriage breaking up – please, tell me it is nothing to do with me.'

'It is nothing to do with "you and me",' he said. 'It is just one of those things.'

A taxi pulled up.

'I will see you tomorrow?' he asked.

'Yes,' she replied. 'Come again at the same time – if that suits?'

His pragmatism and his stoicism struck her. Her thoughts moved on, and she found herself thinking about her mother. From having believed the only way forwards was not to go back, not to look back and not to allow the past to impinge on the present, she knew that she was going to have to face certain things if she had any chance of finding peace of mind.

CHAPTER TWENTY

Two days later, airbound for Dublin, Esme looked down out of the window at the blueness of the Irish Sea on a sunny day, and she watched the long swirling beaches to the north of the city as the plane turned in over the coast and across the green fields of County Meath. Part of her was disbelieving that she had got this far, part of her apprehensive about what was ahead.

She had not notified her mother that she was coming. Indeed, she had not been sure that her mother was still living in the same place. It was Jacob who suggested to her that she might call Directory Enquiries, giving her mother's name and address, and if given the phone number she would ascertain that Susan was still there.

Directory Enquiries asked should they connect her. Esme had said no, that she just wanted the number to call later. She wrote the phone number down with a shaking hand. As she wrote it she remembered it from long ago, although there now seemed to be an extra digit. Dublin must have grown, she thought.

Of course she had heard from colleagues over the previous years about other people's trips to the city, about trendy bars and cafés, about a cosmopolitan city that had emerged from the shadows of the place where she had grown up.

The air coach took her through the heart of the city, down O'Connell Street, across the River Liffey, around the front of Trinity College where once it had been assumed she would study. It all seemed similar and yet different. Landmarks she recognised, but the amount of people on the streets was nothing like she remembered from the past. It was more like being in London. The traffic was slow and heavy.

She took the bus to a hotel in the suburbs, booked online the previous evening. Her bag was light, her return flight planned for the following night.

Walking down the road to the hotel, she was aware that every moment was evoking memory. Her parents had eaten there often in the past, long ago, and occasionally she was brought along as a treat. It was a place where birthday dinners sometimes took place, or drinks at Christmas. Her father had said she would have her eighteenth birthday there and would invite all her class. The idea of it had horrified her. She had not wanted a party or a dinner, could not bear to be the centre of attention. It was privacy she craved and she knew that she had hurt him when she said, 'No, no – I don't want that.' In the event it made no difference. Harry Hastings had been arrested on suspicion of murder before Esme turned eighteen, and he died the day after her birthday.

Inside the hotel, she was bemused by how it had changed over the years. Once it had been unique in Ireland in its modernity, but now she felt she could be anywhere, in any country. She wondered if that was the purpose of the hotel – to make the client feel secure because the surroundings were so similar to every other modern hotel. Once she would have craved the anonymity of it, now it left her somewhat cold.

Then she realised that she was cold. She felt chilled

through to her bones. She kept telling herself that she was not that person who had lived in this land so long ago. She was different. She had carved out a niche for herself in another world. And yet, and yet – she was a prisoner of the past.

A bit of her wanted to go straight outside and take a taxi back to the airport, but then she pulled herself up short. She had come so far. She was going to see this through. She thought of her girls in London. Lily at home in the apartment, caring for Rose and writing up her notes. Jasmine, Esme hoped, not up to mischief. Rose in bed, resting and recovering.

Recovering – that was what she was here for. She was trying to recover the past and to put the pieces together.

In her room she braced herself and rang the number she had jotted down. The phone rang and she waited, almost unable to breathe.

'Hello.'

She inhaled before saying, 'Is that Susan?'

There was silence for a moment at the other end.

'Molly?' The voice sounded older but still the same.

Esme wondered for a moment if her mother could have known that she was going to call. And then she knew that she had not known. And it dawned on her that maybe every time the phone rang, her mother wondered if it was going to be this call.

'Susan,' she repeated. She remembered once wishing that she had been like other girls and called her mother 'Mummy' or 'Mum' or some other normal name for a parent.

And then her mother's voice, different now, uncertain, perhaps shaken: 'Molly, it is you, isn't it?'

Was it pleading? Was it frightened? Molly could not identify what she was hearing.

'I'm in Dublin,' she said. 'I wondered if we could meet.'

'Of course,' her mother said. There was more control back in the voice. The crisp organised voice that Esme remembered had returned. 'Where are you staying? Or would you like to come here?'

Now Esme wanted to step back. She wanted time to think. She wanted to work out where was the best place for them to meet. In the hotel might be awkward. There would be less privacy. In her room would be worse – she would not be able to walk away.

'Yes, I would like to come and visit, if that suits,' she heard herself saying. This way she would be in control. She could get up and leave at any point.

'Can you come now?' Susan asked. 'I'm free now . . .' Her voice sounded hopeful, suggestive, and yet there was the implication that later she might not be free.

'I'll come now,' Esme said.

Before leaving she checked in the mirror, redid her hair, removed her green contact lenses, sprayed a little perfume, and she was ready.

It was a short walk. There were high gates at the front of the mews house, with an intercom and a camera. These functional accessories were new. Esme pressed the bell. She knew that her mother would see her on the camera and would have time to look at her, time to see how she had changed. Esme felt that she was no longer recognisable as that teenager who had left and walked away some twenty-three years earlier.

A buzzer released the gate and it opened. Esme walked through to the courtyard, more modern now than she remembered it: whitewashed walls, trellises of ivy, and a tiny fountain in the middle of the tiled square; a small car parked at one side. And then her mother was standing at the door.

'Molly,' her mother said.

They stood there looking at each other. Her mother had

aged. Her hair, now grey, was tied back into a chignon just as Esme's blonde-streaked hair was. Her mother's face was carefully made up, her eyes the same as she took in her daughter. They approached each other, searching each other's face.

There was a moment's awkwardness. Neither knew if they could or should embrace the other.

'I quite like a drink at this time of the day,' her mother said suddenly. 'Or would you prefer coffee or tea?'

They went inside. The house was clean, tidy to a fault. Just as Esme remembered her mother's life always to be.

'A drink sounds perfect,' Esme said. She tried bringing a smile to her face, but the muscles did not seem to remember how.

'Come and sit – no, we'll take these outside,' her mother said. She was fishing olives out of a jar and putting them in a cut-glass bowl. She got out two glasses and poured gin into both. She was about to pour in the tonic when she turned to Esme. Esme could see her hand was shaking slightly.

'I don't know what you drink,' she said.

'One of those would be lovely,' Esme replied.

They sat on the whitewashed patio, with the early evening sun shining down on them.

'How are you?' Susan said. She seemed so poised, sitting with one leg crossed over the other, her summer dress falling neatly across her calves, a thin cardigan over her shoulders. Esme remembered how neat, to the point of perfection, her mother had always been.

'I am fine, thank you,' Esme replied. 'And you? Are you well?'

It was so formal. They were so formal. They looked at each other as strangers. They sipped their drinks.

'Are you keeping well?' Esme tried again.

'Yes, Molly. I am keeping well, thank you.' There might have been irony in her mother's voice.

There was silence. Both sat as though caught in time. No give. No take. The barrier between them was as high as it had ever been.

And then they spoke together. Simultaneously one said, 'Why did you come?' and the other, 'I needed to touch on the past with you.'

Her mother's eyes seemed frightened now.

'I had hoped you had come just because you wanted to see me again.'

Now Esme saw sadness in her mother's eyes. She tried to fight against the compassion she was feeling, but it was stronger than she.

'Mother, I had to leave. I had no choice.'

'I know. That's why I let you go,' Susan said.

Esme looked at her, startled. 'I left – you didn't *let* me go. It was my choice. I left.'

'I don't think it was quite that simple,' Susan said. 'Letting you go was not easy. You needed to go. That is why I did nothing to stop you.'

'You couldn't have stopped me.'

'I know. But I could have made it more difficult for you. I could have pleaded, I could have made you feel guilty, I suppose . . . but I didn't do that. I let you.'

'You're making it sound like it was hard.'

'Hard? Hard, Molly? You have no idea. It was the most difficult thing imaginable. After we got you back, after the kidnapping, I mean, I knew I would never ever be able to let you go again. And yet I did. And do you know why? Because it was the only thing I could do for you.'

Esme swallowed hard. She had not seen it this way. She had thought somehow that her mother had been glad to see the back of her. When there was no contact from her, this confirmed her feelings.

'You look very beautiful,' her mother said suddenly. 'I so

often wondered what you were like . . . Jennifer gave me news of you from time to time. You married an American?'

'I'll tell you about that in a minute,' Esme said. 'I don't want to let this go . . . please. I need to know, did you blame me?'

'Blame you? For leaving? No.'

'I didn't mean for leaving. I meant for the past. For what happened to me, and then Harry.'

Susan looked puzzled. 'Blame you? Of course not. Why would I blame you? Blame? The blame is mine. No one else's.'

'I always thought you blamed me,' Esme said.

'Molly – you are blameless. I don't know how strongly I can put this. What on earth do you think you could be blamed for?'

'I don't know. I let you down?'

'How? How did you let me down?'

'I . . .' Esme sought for the words. 'I let you down by being kidnapped, by being raped, by being not able to pull myself together. You liked perfection. I was flawed . . .'

Flawed. Strange word I chose, Esme thought.

'Flawed? Strange word,' her mother said, echoing Esme's thoughts. 'Molly, you were my child. You were this perfect child – no one could have asked for better. You were everything parents could have wanted.'

'Until that happened,' Esme said. 'Then I wasn't anything that anyone could have wanted.'

'No, no, no,' her mother said. 'Oh God, no. No, nothing was your fault. Not then. Not afterwards. We did our best, your father and I, but it wasn't good enough. Nothing could have been. Nothing could repair you. Repair? Yes, repair. That is the word I meant. When you left I knew that that was your only chance. Molly, I grieve for you. I grieved and I grieve and I will grieve for ever. And I grieve for me. I grieve for what happened in the past and I, as your mother

– your *mother* . . .' Words failed her momentarily. 'Mothers are supposed to protect their children. I couldn't protect you. I can't forgive myself for that.'

'I had no idea,' Esme eventually said. 'I had no idea . . .'

'Somehow, we lost the ability to communicate. I don't think it was anyone's fault – the lack of communication, I mean. You had closed up, and I couldn't reach you. No one could reach you. And yet even though we couldn't reach you, you still stunned us with your resilience. You worked so hard, did so well . . .'

'But it wasn't enough, was it?'

'How do you mean?'

'It didn't keep you and Harry together . . .'

'No. You're right about that. But that wasn't to do with you – it was to do with us. There was blame between us, blame because of decisions we took that the other thought was wrong – the strain of it all was too much for our marriage. But that was not your doing. That was your father and me trying to work out our own lives. What are you supposed to do as a parent? Hang in there where there are constant arguments and where both of you are miserable, or do you cut your losses? I remember one day, one awful day after one of those endless rows, thinking to myself, what would I want for you in such circumstances? And I knew that I would not want you to waste your life in a marriage where you were unhappy. I would want you to get out and restart – and because of that I decided to leave. I wanted you to have the right example. Maybe I was wrong. But I did what I thought was best for you. You don't know how hard it is to be a parent . . . I'm so sorry. I should never have said that. I apologise.'

Esme was puzzled. 'Why are you apologising? I am a parent. I do know how hard it is to be one. I don't fault you for leaving Harry. I just didn't know why you had. I don't remember ever being told.'

Susan was looking at her carefully now. 'You *are* a parent?'

'I have three daughters,' Esme said, suddenly realising that Jennifer must not have told Susan this.

'You have three daughters? I never thought you would have another child,' Susan said. 'I can't believe this. I had no idea.'

Esme said nothing. She watched her mother's face. She did not know how to proceed. There were questions she wanted to ask, things she had to know, decisions that had been made; she now wanted to understand. She was afraid. She knew that the doors to the past were going to be thrown wide open.

I must take control of this, she thought. I can handle this.

'Right,' Esme said. 'Let's start again. First of all, people call me Esme now. And that is how I like it. I have three daughters. Lily, Rose and Jasmine. They have three different fathers, Günter, Arjen and Grayson. Günter is now married to Jennifer. Arjen died, and Grayson lives in the States.'

'How old are they? These daughters . . . my granddaughters . . . '

'Twenty-two, twenty-one, and fifteen. Now, Susan – Mother – Susan . . .' Esme stood up, and then she sat down again. She was struggling to find the words. There seemed no easy way to face into why she had come and what she wanted to ask. 'Mother, please, I need to know why you let me carry that child, why you let me give birth. I need to know what happened and why.'

Susan was now looking very uneasy. 'Molly, I don't know how to talk about this, I really don't. We didn't know what to do.'

'Please tell me.'

Molly was pregnant. Fourteen years old. Susan knew it the moment it dawned on her that Molly was throwing up in the mornings, three days running. She got her daughter back into bed. Time had passed. Molly had gone back to school some six or seven weeks after the kidnapping. Harry or Susan drove her there in the mornings. One or other collected her. If Molly was uneasy about returning to school, she didn't say. She didn't say anything. She just did what she was told. She didn't look well. There was a sort of greyness about her. She seemed wispy and non-consequential, a wraith in a school uniform, a shadow that did not react like she ought.

Weekends had passed, weekends in which Molly stayed in her room and studied, or read the books Susan helped her choose from the library. There was an air of people trying to make everything seem normal, and of course it was not. Christmas came and went. Visits to and from relatives. So much concern shown for Molly, with kind aunts and uncles kissing her gently, telling her she was a brave girl. Susan and Harry hovered, hoping that Molly's polite veneer wouldn't crack. School reopened.

Another week passed.

It was a Monday morning. Molly came downstairs looking worse than usual. She was still in her pyjamas. She said she didn't feel well. But she had been saying that all the previous week. Susan kept telling herself it was just the difficulty of getting back into a routine, and getting Molly to see that this was all normal. And then as Molly sat looking at her cereal, she suddenly threw up.

Susan took her back upstairs. There were alarm bells ringing in her mind. She tried to quash the notion that had suddenly occurred to her. Molly's school uniform was hanging on her wardrobe door, her blouse crisply ironed. Harry had polished her school shoes as he did every Sunday night. They were on the floor by her chair. Susan got Molly to lie down on the bed and she stroked her head. Molly had been sick on the Saturday and on the Sunday morning. Susan got a wet face cloth and wiped her daughter's forehead. The alarm bells were ringing louder. A cold and horrifying sensation was wrapping itself around her heart, penetrating her brain, numbing her in disbelief.

'I'm going to get you a cup of tea,' she said to Molly. 'And some toast.'

'I can't eat,' Molly said, her eyes closed, her hair matted on her head.

'It will be all right,' Susan said. 'It's going to be all right.'

She went downstairs to the kitchen. She made the tea as if in a daze. She put a slice of bread in the toaster. Her mind was in a whirl. She didn't know what to do other than to go through these motions, doing something to make Molly all right. All right for this moment. But not for the next. How could she fix this? She felt as powerless as she had when Molly was kidnapped. She kept saying to herself: 'This is not as bad.' Nothing could ever be as bad as Molly gone and the endless days and nights of waiting to see if her daughter would ever return. Nothing. She kept repeating it, over and over. 'This is not as bad as what has already happened. Nothing can be that bad. This I can handle. The other I couldn't.'

'I'm not sure I can go to school,' Molly said. 'I feel awful.'

Susan had put the cup of tea beside her bed. The toast was cut into four little triangles.

'I want you to try to eat one of these,' Susan said to her. 'Forget school. You won't be going in.'

Harry had left early that morning. Susan wanted to get back downstairs and to phone him at work, but she couldn't leave Molly alone like this. She wanted to hold her daughter in her arms. She wanted to put back the clock, not just back a couple of weeks, but back every single year of Molly's life until Molly was safely back in her womb. She wanted to rewind time and not to give birth to this child who had had to endure so much.

This was not fair. This was too much. No child should have to go through this on top of everything else.

She stayed with Molly until she slept. She sat by her bed and watched the long dark lashes on Molly's pale face and she wanted to scream at God for doing this to her child.

'You cannot be serious,' Harry said. He had by now digested the fact that Molly was pregnant. His anger was acute. 'You cannot be fucking serious.' He never used bad language in their home. He was now. He was irate.

'Didn't they check in the hospital if she was pregnant?'

'It was too early to check.'

'But isn't there a morning-after pill or something like that? Shouldn't they have given her something to prevent this from having happened?'

'They did give her something. It's not legal in Ireland, but none the less they did because of what had happened. And it clearly hasn't worked.'

'I'll get something – there's got to be something we can give her that'll get rid of this.'

'But what, Harry? What can we get and how can we get it?'

'Leave it with me,' he said. There was a man at the club – one of those men from the North of Ireland. Harry had wanted to fire them all after the kidnapping because he no longer knew whom to trust. But now he remembered hearing something about a girl getting pregnant and one of the men got some drug for her to take and it got rid of it.

'There's no time,' Susan said.

'Don't worry. We'll fix this,' Harry said with a determination that had been lacking in the days since the kidnapping when fear had followed on fear, and the return of his daughter had been like looking into a lifeless pool where only horror and panic were reflected.

'Drink this, Molly,' Susan said, giving her daughter the concoction Harry had brought home.

'No, you must drink it all down,' Susan said, as Molly pulled a face at the first sip. 'Just drink it. It's going to make you all right.'

Molly drank.

Some six hours later Susan tried to hold her sweating moaning child. She helped her into the bath as Molly made a noise like an animal howling. The night was long. And in the morning the pains eased and Molly lay limp in her bed, staring at the ceiling.

'Oh God, Harry, what are we going to do?'

'I'll try and get something stronger.'

'Harry, we can't put her through that again. You know we can't. Last night was unbearable.'

'Maybe it will still work. It could take time. We can give it a day or so.'

'And then?'

Then it was too late. Harry tried to get an appointment at a series of private clinics in England. He was having a problem finding a clinic that would perform a late abortion. He could get nothing. Susan sat in Molly's room, the turmoil in her mind driving her to distraction.

'Susan.' It was Harry calling.

She went downstairs to him. She could see the relief in his face immediately.

'I've got an appointment in three days' time. In London. I've booked the flight. We'll all go over. We'll handle this.

We have to.' They were both exhausted. 'One more week and we'll have this sorted.'

But Susan knew it was only one aspect of things that would be sorted. Molly would still be there – maybe in a worse condition psychologically.

And then, the day before they were to fly to London, it snowed. It snowed and it snowed. They woke to find their world a glittering freezing white, and the airport was closed. It stayed closed for three days. Molly caught a chill that developed into flu and she lay shivering in her bed with a raging temperature. She was ill for over three weeks, and then she was so weak there was no question of her flying. Susan and Harry nursed her, trying to speed her recovery, but weeks passed and then Harry couldn't find a clinic that would do the required operation. 'She's too far gone.' 'It's against our policy.' 'I'm so sorry – we can't help you.'

Spring came, unnoticed by them all. Harry shook his head in despair and Susan knew that she must get Molly away. She would take her abroad, find somewhere for Molly to give birth to the offspring of her rapist and leave the child there for someone else to take and rear as their own.

The row got heavier and heavier.

Harry could not believe that Susan would want Molly to carry this child inside her for another two and a half months.

'For Christ's sake, Susan. She was raped. How can you want to let her carry it inside her – a perpetual reminder for the rest of her life about what happened?'

'Do you think she is likely to forget what has happened?' Susan shrieked at him. 'That is never going to go away . . .'

'So why prolong it all by making her give birth to that bastard's baby?'

'But what can we do?' Susan asked. 'You've tried every place you can think of.'

'We should try that concoction again – the stuff I got before.'

'Harry, we can't. I can't do that to her. I cannot put her through another night like that one. And she's weak and ill anyway from the flu now. She mightn't survive. Go upstairs and look at her.'

In her room, occasionally visited by one or the other of them, Molly lay looking out at the trees.

'We'll ask Dr Gumm what he thinks,' Harry said, confident that Harper Gumm would see Susan's insane idea for what it was.

'It's nothing to do with Dr Gumm,' Susan said. 'This is nothing to do with anyone. The newspapers will find out about it. She will be all over them again. All the intimate details of our lives, of the awful things that were done to her . . . no. No. I won't have it. I'm taking her away as soon as I can. We can tell the school that she needs rest and that we've been advised to give her a holiday. She can go back to school next September. A fresh start. A new school year.'

'And in the meantime our child has a baby?'

'What choice do we have? What can we possibly do?'

And in despair, Harry agreed. They had no choice. He found them a place to live in London, near the river, on the Piccadilly line so that he could fly in to Heathrow and visit them often.

'I'm trying to take this in,' Esme said to Susan. The sun had gone down now. The evening seemed exceptionally chilly. The lighting had come on automatically and the small patio was lit up. They sat there and both were now shivering. 'That night I was ill – I do remember it, you know. It was a night of agony. You and he had given me something to get rid of the baby?'

'Let's go inside,' Susan said to her. 'I need to . . . I can't talk about this – I need a break. I can cook for us.'

'I don't really feel hungry,' Esme said.

'I'm going to put something on for us,' Susan said. 'I think we should both eat.'

Esme laid the table as Susan placed two meals in the oven and put together a salad.

'You were always so good at this,' Esme said. She was trying to behave normally.

'At what?'

Esme gestured to the table, where Susan had lit a candle and placed two white napkins. She was opening a bottle of white wine that she had taken from the fridge. Two crystal glasses appeared from a sideboard.

'At this – at making things nice.'

'The perfectionist in me,' Susan said. 'It's not always a blessing. It makes it more difficult to deal with things that go wrong.'

'I'm like you,' Esme said. 'Much more than I knew, in fact.'

They were talking now, passing time until the meal was ready as there was still so much more to say but it was as if they needed a small break from it.

Esme, who was still trying to take in what her mother had told her, was struggling in her mind to hold on to the present moments and not to think. She had not known that they had tried to kill the baby – to abort it themselves and, when that failed, to get her an abortion. She had no recollection of anyone ever explaining any of that to her. But there was something else. She felt there was something there, something tapping on her memory. Her mother was now preparing a dressing with oil and vinegar, mustard and garlic. She tossed the salad leaves in it, as Esme sat on the arm of a chair the other side of the kitchen partition.

'You even look like me,' Susan said. 'No, no – I don't mean now. I am old now. And I feel old. I mean when I was your age. Even I can see it. And one doesn't usually see similarities to oneself. Who do your girls look like ... your girls ... my grandchildren?' She smiled suddenly. 'I never thought I would be able to say I had grandchildren.'

'Mother, Susan ...' Esme hesitated. 'We still have things to talk about. I don't know what happened after I gave birth. I really can't remember. I don't know if I gave birth to a boy or a girl. I just can't remember. I don't know if I was ever told. I don't know if I even asked.'

'Give me a few more minutes with this,' Susan said, pointing towards the salad. 'We'll talk more while we're having dinner. I just want to savour the idea of grand-daughters.'

Esme nodded.

She went to find the bathroom and she washed her hands and face, brushed out her hair before pinning it back up again. It made no difference how fast or how slow her mother told her the story of the past. Either way it would be the same. Either way she would know what had happened, and maybe then everything would make sense. She took her time in the bathroom, looking in the mirrored glass-cabinet at her mother's neatly arranged cosmetics. Everything so orderly, so clean and tidy. Even the bathmat was neatly folded over the side of the bath. A little yellow duck, which she had picked up in a hotel as a child, was sitting in a corner of the bath. She leaned across the bath and reached for it. She remembered how it felt in her hands, could remember it bobbing in her bathwater, sometimes submerged in foam until the bubbles disappeared and left its round yellow head and orange beak popping up again and again, no matter how often she pressed it down. She wondered if her mother put it in the bath or if it was just there for show. Or maybe, just maybe her mother had kept it as a reminder of Esme's childhood – a reminder of the childish innocent days before the Wolf and the Eyes.

The food was on the table when she got back downstairs.

'It smells great,' she said.

'Not gourmet cuisine,' her mother said. 'But not bad for something straight out of the freezer.'

They raised their wine goblets to each other and touched them lightly. The clink of glass echoed slightly in the silence of the room.

'A boy or a girl?' Esme asked.

'A boy,' Susan said briefly. Esme had the feeling she had been preparing words in her absence.

'He died,' Esme said. 'I know he died. I remember so clearly you telling me. But, why did he die?'

'Deformed. Badly. He died seconds after he was born,' Susan said firmly.

'I saw him,' Esme said. 'I saw him, didn't I?' She was remembering something now. 'I remember seeing him for one moment. No one said whether he was a boy or a girl. I've never known.'

'Do you really want to go into these details?' Susan asked her.

'I remember you saying the baby was dead and then they took it away. All these years I've wondered if I had a boy or a girl. All these years. I never touched him. Oh, God, he was mine.'

She put her fork down on the plate. Waves and waves of grief washed through her as she allowed herself for the first time to look back. And suddenly she was crying. There were tears streaming down her face.

Susan sat for a moment as though not knowing what to

do, and then she got up and came around the table. She took her daughter to the sofa and she held her while Esme cried. She cried and cried as though she would never stop. She cried for the years of forgetfulness, for her father dead in his grave, for the anguish unleashed on her family by the kidnapping. She cried for a baby she had never held. A baby no one had wanted. She cried too because Susan was holding her.

Susan held her as she would have liked to have held her all those years ago, as she should have held her, but there had been no way to get through to Molly back then. And when she finally finished crying she lay in Susan's arms.

'It's all right,' Susan whispered to her. 'It's all right now. It's over. It's long over. It was long ago. And it's over.'

In her hotel, late that night, Esme phoned Jacob. She was calmer now – at least on the surface.

'I couldn't phone the girls. It's too late. I was afraid of waking them. I hope I didn't wake you.'

'No, it's fine,' he said. 'I hoped you would call. I hope it is all right with you, but I took your girls out to dinner tonight. I phoned to make sure Rose was still recovering, and it seemed a good idea that I would drop over. We got a taxi. We just stayed out for an hour so that Rose wouldn't tire.'

'Are they all right?'

'They are each fine,' he said. 'In their own inimitable ways. Rose is much better. Lily has been working on her notes and is confident that she has enough for her paper. And Jasmine is looking in the newspapers for some kind of work. Lily said that she saw a notice in that hospital where she and Jasmine went the other day – you know, where Rose was working. Well, the advertisement was for someone to read to children in the children's ward. Jasmine is going to check it out tomorrow. It's voluntary work. You would be very pleased and proud of them.'

'Thank you,' Esme said. She knew it was odd that Jacob was telling her these things and equally strange that she was not disturbed by what some might see as interference. But she knew that it was not that. Their friendship was such that she instinctively felt that he had her best interests at heart. He knew that she needed reassurance about her girls. And that was what he was giving her.

'An interesting anecdote in today's papers,' he continued. 'A tarantula was spotted on the Jubilee line.'

'What?' Esme gasped.

'Don't worry. Jasmine denies all knowledge. She says she took her Taliban to the zoo.'

'Thank heavens.'

'Although she did say, it was the Bakerloo line, anyway. That's a quote, by the way.'

'Hmm,' Esme murmured thoughtfully.

'And how are you getting on?' he asked.

She wanted to tell him, but did not know where to begin.

'I'm going to spend tomorrow with my mother,' she said. 'I'll be home on the seven o'clock flight as planned.'

'I'll meet you at the airport. Will you tell me then?'

'Yes. And Rose is feeling better?' Esme asked.

'Yes. Despite today's events, she is still on the mend.'

'What happened today?'

'Rose phoned the hospital to say she would be back in next week, and she asked after a patient of hers. They told her he had died.'

'Oh, no. Oh, poor Rose. Is she coping?'

'Yes. She was upset. Very upset. It appears he killed himself. He got hold of something and slashed his wrists with it.'

'My poor Rose.'

'When I phoned, Lily told me what had happened and I

suggested coming over. I wasn't sure if they would see it as an intrusion but Lily thought it might help. When I arrived at the apartment Rose was crying and Jasmine was comforting her. It appears that Lily and Jasmine knew this man was dead, but thought it better not to tell her until she was better. I don't think it occurred to them that she would phone the hospital quite so quickly. Lily seemed less able to cope with Rose's distress, but Jasmine was curled up with her on the sofa.'

Esme thought of Lily and her own problems and crisis of confidence, and Jasmine with her usual histrionics over everything. She thought of her screaming about the alligator's eggs all those years ago, and how she always tried to take the limelight in front of her sisters, and it suddenly occurred to her that Jasmine was growing up. And what Jacob was describing was like a baptism by fire, and yet her youngest flower was coping and caring for her sister.

'I wish I were there with her,' Esme said. 'With Rose, I mean. She is only twenty-one, you know. Nearly twenty-two, but such a child in so many ways.'

'I know. But strong. Like her mother. Don't forget that.'

'Oh,' Esme sighed. 'We would do anything to protect our children, but we can't.'

'No. You can't. That is life. It throws things in our faces and we do the best we can. All of us, each in our own way.'

'My poor Rose.'

'Do you want to talk?'

'No, not now. I think that I need to think,' Esme said. 'We'll talk tomorrow evening. There is one more thing to tell you, but it will wait until tomorrow.'

Esme lay in bed with the phone now turned off. She thought of Rose and how she had spoken of that poor man with such kindness and such a strong sense of protection. She hoped her daughter was asleep, and that if she wasn't, hopefully Lily or Jasmine, or maybe both, was sitting with her, maybe talking to her. She wished that every child in the world had someone to lean on when they were tired, distressed or broken by life. She hoped that somehow human nature would ultimately evolve into something kinder than it was. She thought of her own child born long ago when she was only a child herself and she wondered if he had ever been named, or if he was just taken away and buried.

Other thoughts came in now. She remembered, before giving birth to Lily in the German hospital, the midwife saying to her, 'This is not your first child,' and she had said that it was. Of course it was. She was not going to admit to anyone she had been in that position before. Lily was her firstborn. The other had not counted. Her mother had said to her way back then that it was over and need never be thought about again.

But of course that baby had counted. Everything counted. One way or another every human action counted. Everything had a knock-on effect somewhere, somehow. She wondered now if she should have faced all of this before rather than just pushing it with all the other awful things into the depths of her mind, there to eat away at her. She knew that that whole time had been spent in learning to forget and not to remember. Sometimes that was the only way of coping with life. You had to let things go. Now she wondered what she had felt when that baby was born. She could remember nothing but the tiny blood-covered body being carried across a room, and a vague memory of looking out the window and seeing trees blowing in the wind and knowing that nothing in life could ever be the same again.

If you can look into the seeds of time,
And say which grain will grow and which will not . . .

Her mother had blocked her view of the baby then, and she thought she heard it cry. She wondered again if the baby had been baptised or christened. Had they named him? Where was he laid to rest? She also wondered, did she need to know the answers to these questions, or was it not sufficient that she now knew that he was a boy?

She had wondered – so often wondered. She did not know what she was supposed to feel. Little by little other fragments of memory wisped like ghosts into her mind. Someone saying to her, 'It's over now. It's all over.' And her mother, Susan . . . Susan said to her, 'It's done. Now you must forget this. This has no place in your life.' 'What's done is done, and cannot be undone,' Esme thought. The quote reminded her of her work, and she had to force herself back to contemplating what she and her mother had spoken of. Hiding in her work was by far the easier option. She thought now about moving on in life again and disclaiming the past.

But could one do that – eradicate things so completely that they were no longer part of you, and yet still live a full and satisfied life?

What should they have done, these parents of hers, Susan and Harry? What did they go through during those long months? What alternatives did they have? Of course, Susan had not known that the child was going to die. What a relief that must have been for her. Esme did not know what she had felt during those awful nine months. She remembered very little other than the hours with Dr Gumm and, later, time in London where she read and read. Of the actual pregnancy there were no memories at all.

She lay in the dark in the hotel as she pursued her thoughts. She knew that she would not have wanted, would not want, one of her daughters to give birth to the child of a man who had raped her. Just as her mother had not wanted it. What more could her mother have done to protect her? She knew now that her mother had done her best.

In her mews house, Susan sat up in bed with a book. She wasn't reading. She was thinking about Molly. The initial composure of her daughter had surprised her, and then she had seen that it was a cover. Molly was covering up as she had always done since the kidnapping. All her emotions obliterated until that moment when she had begun to cry. Susan knew that Molly should have cried a long time ago. They all should have. But it was as if they didn't know how any more. She recalled too clearly the day Molly was kidnapped and she remembered crying in the police station, and she remembered days and nights after that, huddling in Harry's arms as they both cried, and then suddenly there were no more tears. It was as if they didn't dare to cry any more. Molly had come home and they wanted to howl at the injustice of life, at the terrible things that had been done to their little girl, but they couldn't. They couldn't begin to formulate their anger. Susan remembered those days and nights then, sitting in the hospital holding her child's hand and trying to communicate with her, telling her over and over that it was all right. And of course it was not all right. It could never be all right again.

She hoped she had made the right decisions. She had described the child as being deformed. Well, having only three fingers and a thumb on each hand was a deformity. She had not lied there. It was unclear if the stuff she and Harry had given Molly had caused this. She never asked. It made no difference.

And what would it avail Molly to know that the child had lived? There were things best left untouched. She and Harry – they had done their best. The centre of their relationship was not strong enough to hold intact when their world had fallen apart. They had argued and fought with each other but only because they both wanted the best for their child. They never seemed to be able to agree on how to handle things. She remembered when Molly was gone – that awful week of the kidnapping, Harry was the only person who understood. She knew that when they sat together in the kitchen with people dropping in – police, family and friends – it was only Harry who knew the depth of her despair, and that was because his was the same.

That was the last time they were in a kind of unison. After that it was as if they were looking at things from different angles. There had been that awful row when she had said to him, 'If only you did your own bloody banking,' and he had turned on her and said, 'You should never have let them take her that day. I wouldn't have.' And she said, 'You employed that awful man. You brought him to our home for dinner.' And then they had looked at each other in a kind of horror as they saw the blame and the possibilities for the fault to be laid at one or other of their doors.

After they had tried to get rid of the baby, she did not know what more they could have done. They would have done anything but they had no idea how to go about it. Had they only realised earlier that she was pregnant . . .

No matter what had gone wrong, they were true to Molly all the way. Both of them in their own ways. Molly must never find out that the baby had survived. Susan had already made plans to ensure that. If Molly asked her where the baby was born, Susan was going to give her the name of a hospital that had been destroyed in a fire. It was now rebuilt but there were no records from the past. Molly must never find out the truth. She remembered so clearly the day after the birth, her daughter lying in bed, staring vacantly out the window at trees blowing in the wind. And

Susan knew she must get her out of there immediately, before someone started looking for more papers to be signed. She had given a false address and they left the country within the week, ensuring they could not be traced. Harry took them to Switzerland for Molly to recover in the clear mountain air.

Who knew how long Harry would have got for the attack and blinding of the man Molly called the Eyes. Maybe the judge would have been lenient. Surely he would have been. Would any father have done differently? Who knew? Harry's mistake was in being caught. He might never have had that fatal heart attack if he had not been arrested.

Molly had not asked what had happened to the other man – the one she called the Wolf. Susan was unsure what she would have said. It might yet come up. She should stick as closely to the truth as possible. He had been released. Time off for good behaviour. That was what had happened to the Eyes. It had driven Harry insane that one of those men could get time off when there was no time off for Molly, Harry or Susan. She knew that Harry would have wanted the Wolf killed, but she had no idea how to go about it.

But Susan had kept track of him. It was all she could do. To know where he was and what he was doing. She was sure – even if the courts had decided otherwise – that he would commit further crimes. Now he was in Australia. She was sure that sooner or later he would end up in prison there. She thought that prisons in Australia might be harsher than in Ireland. She hoped so.

When he had been released from prison in Ireland, he had emigrated. She hoped it was because he was afraid that Molly's family might come after him. She liked to think of him living in fear. Why should he have been allowed to rebuild a life? He had destroyed Molly's. He had destroyed their family unit. He had taken away years and years of potential happiness.

But she had grandchildren now. Molly had said she would meet them soon. She would come to London and stay with them in their apartment. Molly said that would be easier than them all landing on her in her small house. There suddenly seemed so much to look forward to.

She wondered that Jennifer Delmont, on her visits to Ireland, had never mentioned that Molly had married and had had children. But then, Jennifer never liked Molly having anything she did not have herself. Even the awful attention that Molly had been given years ago, even that Jennifer seemed to have envied.

Tomorrow she would phone Bluebell – Bluebell Mortimer, her friend, who had stuck by her after Harry had died and Molly left. Bluebell would be so pleased to hear about Molly. She never asked, or at least she had not in a long time because she knew there was only pain there for Susan. Sometimes she told Susan about Andrew, her son. Dear Andrew, who had found Molly. Bluebell worried for him. He had never been the same since the kidnapping. He had finished his Ph.D., and although he got the results he wanted, nothing in life appeared quite the same. The solidity that numbers and figures had offered him had been eroded by the awareness of the accidental nature of all things – of a man noticing a light in an empty house at odd hours of the night . . . of a friend in Brussels deciding to come home to investigate . . . of waking with a hangover and thinking they should go to the house . . . of the horror of what they had discovered . . . of what *he* discovered. That was when he found there was no mathematical formula or equation to explain or predict anything. Bluebell said he lived in Las Vegas now, in the gambling or the poker rooms, where he made a good living but did not appear very happy. Bluebell said his world too had been undermined.

Esme had a bad night. Four in the morning saw her pacing her hotel room, then making coffee. She wondered over and over at her mother's actions. She could see that her mother and father had done what they could so that she wouldn't have to carry that baby. But their efforts had failed. She wondered what she would have done had she been in their position. They had explained nothing to her back then. And she had believed that her mother had insisted on her having the baby. She thought it had been part of her mother's religious beliefs. She had had no idea of the efforts they had gone to in their endeavours to help her. She thought briefly of that moment when her baby had been born, and her mother telling her it was all over. Did her mother really believe that everything could be compartmentalised and that life would go on? And yet there were clearly other instincts that were equally strong. Letting Esme go and live abroad and letting her cut all ties obviously had hurt and yet, as a mother, she had done it because she saw that as being the best way forward for her child.

Esme found herself thinking about what would have happened had her baby survived. Her mother had said they would have given it up for adoption – they would have left it behind and moved on. She wondered where the justification lay in that decision. She had no answers. She only knew that everyone's problems were resolved in that baby dying.

Shortly after dawn she fell asleep.

Lily phoned her in the morning.
'Hello, Mum.'
'Lily, talk to me – how are you all?'

'Jasmine and I are fine. Rose is very upset.'

'Jacob and I spoke last night. I heard her patient had died.'

'Yes. But he left her a letter and a book. I think the book was hers – a play, *Macbeth* perhaps. They were reading it. But in the letter, Mum, he thanks her for being so good to him. And he tells her a story – about his life, I think. She can tell you about that when you get back. But, Mum, there is no money, no relatives, nothing, and after the post-mortem he needs to be buried. And Rose doesn't want him just . . . well, I don't know . . . she said something about a pauper's grave. I don't know if she was exaggerating or not. I don't know what happens to someone when no one wants them or claims them. She's terribly upset.'

'I'll be back tomorrow,' Esme said. 'But just tell her, I'll pay for the funeral.'

'Thank you,' Rose said. 'Thank you. I don't know why you would pay for his funeral, but I'm so grateful.' She was crying again.

'Rose, tell me why you are crying?'

'I'm crying because . . . I don't know. The complete and utter sadness of it all. Mum, he had no one. No one. He was fostered over and over during his life. He never got a break. He was abandoned at birth. No one ever seemed to want to keep him. Mum, it's so unfair. He was brilliantly clever and all he wanted was his mother to find him and to love him. I can't thank you enough for paying for his funeral. I don't know why you are. But it's not right that his life should not be acknowledged in some way.'

'I know, Rose. Let me tell you a story. A long time ago, when you were very little, maybe you remember a German woman called Christa?'

Lily said she remembered her. Rose wasn't sure.

'Christa told me a story about passing on an act of kind-

ness. I'm paying for this man's funeral because it is the first
time in my life I've had the chance to actually pass on that
act of kindness.'

'That's nice,' Jasmine said.

'It's nice that I've been given the chance to pass it on,' Esme
said. 'I remember saying to Christa, what would I do if I never
got the chance?' Her voice was thoughtful now as she remembered the lined but kind face of that woman – the only person
who visited her in hospital after Rose was born.

'What did she say?' Jasmine asked.

'She said that even if one never got the chance to pass the
act on, I could make sure that if any cruelty or unkindness
happened to me, that I would not pass that on. You know
. . . days where nothing goes right, and someone says something cruel or unkind or whatever to you. Well, that's an
example. That's when you choose not to take that out on
someone else. Instead, you bite it back. You turn the other
cheek. It's the only way to make the world a better place.'

'Do you think you can make the world a better place?'
Rose asked, drying her eyes yet again.

Esme shook her head. 'No. I don't. I can only hope that
my actions leave no one worse off. If we all lived like that,
then maybe, just maybe . . .'

She glanced at Jacob. He was sitting quietly in a chair,
listening to them.

'Rose,' she said. 'I want you to come to bed. You're still
not well. And you're very upset. I want to tuck you in. I'll
sit with you a bit.'

Rose slowly and very tiredly got up.

Esme made a sign to Jacob that he should get a drink,
and she went with Rose into her bedroom.

'I was going to paint my walls this coming weekend,' Rose
said.

'I think it'll take more than a few coats,' Esme said. 'The

black will show through. Maybe we could get someone in to do it, and you could choose the colours.'

'Why are you being so nice to me?' Rose asked.

'Am I not usually?'

'No, I didn't mean that. You *are* nice to me. I mean . . . I don't know what I meant. I just feel so terribly sad. Mum, he wrote this letter – I know it was given to me, but I don't think it was meant for me. There is nothing I can do. It's over. But it's not fair what happened to him in life. It's just not fair.'

'Tell me about it,' Esme said gently, sitting on the bed beside her second daughter.

'Mum, he was really clever. Like really, really clever. Sometimes when he was talking it was like talking to you. He was so reasonable, so clear-thinking in some ways, but so terribly sad. A life of not being loved and never fitting in, no money for university, so he borrowed and he got himself there. He got himself into debt and couldn't see a way out of it. He was brilliant, but could never have fitted in anywhere. He wrote hundreds of letters to his real mother, which he sent to this adoption or fostering place where you can register and hopefully your real mother will make contact. But she never did. He even dreamed of her. All he wanted was for her to want to find him and to tell him that she had loved him.'

Esme shivered. 'The poor boy,' she said. 'That is so sad.'

'He said in the letter that he felt like half a person. I never realised how lucky I am – how lucky *we* are – Lily, Jasmine and me. We take so much for granted and complain about things because they aren't exactly the way we want them. And yet we have everything. Everything that counts. People who love us and watch out for us . . . I mean, even if it wasn't or isn't ideal – like my father dying and my never knowing him – I still got the love from his family and I still had you. I never thought about the importance of these things. I never realised that I had so little to complain about.'

'That's all right,' Esme said. 'We mostly don't realise our fortune until we lose something or someone. To see life through someone else's eyes and to learn from it, that surely is something. Rose . . .' She felt cold now, very cold, as though a hand was clasping her heart and stopping the blood flowing through her veins. 'Rose, Jacob said he thought you were reading *Macbeth* with this man.'

'Yes. His choice,' Rose said. 'Not mine. I'd have preferred something less . . . well, less heavy, I suppose. He liked Shakespeare. He said that all of human life was in it. He said that every story was repeated over and over again in history. Look, let me show you his letter. The end of it. We had nearly finished Macbeth the other day. He quotes from it.'

She reached under the bedclothes and pulled out some pages. Choosing one, she passed it to Esme.

Esme took it from her.

It said:

> Tomorrow, and tomorrow, and tomorrow,
> Creeps in this petty pace from day to day,
> To the last syllable of recorded time;
> And all our yesterdays have lighted fools
> The way to dusty death. Out, out, brief candle!
> Life's but a walking shadow, a poor player,
> That struts and frets his hour upon the stage,
> And then is heard no more; it is a tale
> Told by an idiot, full of sound and fury,
> Signifying nothing.

Esme read it twice.

'I think he felt he signified nothing,' Rose said. There were tears on her cheeks again. 'And I think he was special. Very special.'

*   *   *

'I have the strangest feeling,' Esme said to Jacob. They were sitting on the balcony with the girls inside in their beds. She had finally told him about the baby who had died so long ago.

He held her hand at first, and then he stroked it as she spoke.

'I have always refused to think about it. My mother had said to forget it. She said the only way forward was to put it so far behind that it couldn't touch me. And I did. My sleep is haunted by what happened, but also by the sound of a baby crying. I now – only now – can acknowledge that. Facing this, talking about it with my mother – well, it's like my child has only just died. All my life I forced myself not to think about what happened, never to ask any questions, just to let it all go so that I could live. And now I've faced it.'

'What are you facing?'

'I am only now acknowledging that I gave birth to a baby that no one wanted, and that it mercifully died. But someone should have grieved for it. It was not that baby's fault. Someone should have held it with some love as it died. And that someone should have been me. And I don't know what to do.'

Jacob took both her hands in his. 'I know what you will do, Esme,' he said. 'You will pick up the pieces, just as you always do. Only this time, you are going to allow yourself to grieve. And I will be here for you. And with you. No one, but no one should ask a fourteen-year-old child to hold her unwanted dead baby, and the woman that fourteen-year-old child grew into knows better than to berate herself for that.'

'I don't know what I'd do without you, Jacob.'

'You would survive,' he replied.

*   *   *

Jacob, back in the Delmonts' house, sat with Henry before going to bed.

'I find myself torn in a strange way,' he told his friend. 'I feel . . .' he searched for the words, 'strong feelings, that's the best way I can describe it. Yes, strong feelings for Molly, as you know of her. She has got under my skin. I should be in shock over Naomi's departure and yet I am not. That in itself evokes feelings of guilt.'

'Do you think you should try to get Naomi back?'

'We don't love each other any more.'

'When love is finished – it is just that, finished,' Henry said. 'It's easy for me to say, I know, because Sally and I are very close. And I am aware of the comfort of habit. But I don't see the point of stagnation when there is the chance of growth. Most of my patients are coming to me because of the misery of their own situations – or the lack of fulfilment within those relationships. Are yours any different?'

'No. Like you there are patients with other problems, but there are many who are trapped in a watershed and either have not the energy to do something about it, and so have developed psychological problems, or they lack the imagination to see that they can, if they want, start over.'

'You want a relationship with this Molly?'

'I feel I am too old for her. In years, I mean. We communicate very well, but the age difference . . .'

'What about the age difference? What does age matter? If you communicate, if you have strong feelings – well, where is the harm?'

Then in bed, Jacob thought of her again. On the one hand he knew that what he wanted from her was everything. He wanted to waken beside her in the morning – every morning. He wanted to love her and to protect her. To listen to her and to talk to her. To live her story. To be part of her life and her history. And yet to do that, to give her those things,

would ultimately mean to take them from her, because he
was so much older. He worked through these thoughts,
knowing that what he feared was his dying and leaving her
– not for himself, but for her. And then he thought of her
resilience, and how she had pulled herself up time and again.
She would always do that. What a fool he would be not to
try to share some time with her. Who knew anyway what
life would throw at them?

Jasmine bought a pink-eyed white rat in a shop in London
and she brought it home to cheer up Rose. Rose, curled in
her bed, looked at it in dismay. Lily, however, went into
ecstasies about its perfect colouring.

'Pure white,' she said. 'Perfect for breeding. But make sure
you only breed with another pure white rat, or you'll have
spotted babies.'

'I wasn't really thinking of breeding,' Jasmine said. 'I just
thought that Rose would like the company.'

Lily and Rose exchanged a look. Lily knew that Rose was
not as keen on animals as Jasmine seemed to think.

'I'm not sure that it would be my first choice of pet,' Rose
said as kindly as she could bring herself.

'But we can't have a dog or a cat in the apartment,' Jasmine
said. 'It wouldn't be fair on them.'

'Not to mention that dogs and cats aren't allowed in the
apartment,' Rose said.

'You like him, though, Lily, don't you?' Jasmine said hopefully.

'Of course I do,' Lily said to her, stroking the rat's head.
'Have you thought of a name for him?'

'Not really,' Jasmine said. 'I thought Rose might like to
christen him.'

Rose sat up in bed to take a closer look at the little fur
ball in Jasmine's hands.

'How about Macduff?' she suggested.

'That's an odd name for a rat,' Lily said.

'I think it's perfect,' Jasmine said. 'Macduff.'

'"Lay on, Macduff",' Rose quoted. 'They were Macbeth's last words.' She reached out a tentative hand and touched the little rat. 'I might get used to him,' she said after a moment.

Jasmine smiled. She felt she had got this one right. It wasn't like Taliban – no one had really understood Taliban.

Four days later, Jacob went with Esme and her daughters to Roland's funeral. He went to be with Esme, who had gone to support Rose. Roland's body was lowered into the ground on a warm summer's morning and Rose cried for him. Jasmine stood on one side of her, holding her hand. Lily, on the other side, slipped her arm around her sister's shoulder.

'Don't cry,' Jasmine said to her after Rose had thrown a red rose into the open grave.

'I'm crying because he was special,' Rose said. 'Please believe me. You'll never know, but he was special . . . and someone should cry for him.'

'I've decided to trace my baby,' Esme said to Jacob as they walked back to the car. 'My mother will give me the name of the hospital where he was born and they will tell me where he is buried. Here I am, standing by the grave of a man I don't know. Don't misunderstand me – I have no problem with that. I came, like we all did, for Rose. But I want to stand by my son's grave and I want to think of him. It wasn't his fault. Do you see? Tell me you see.'

'I do see,' Jacob said. 'And I would like to make that journey with you.' He had his arm around her and she leaned against him. 'Would that be all right with you?' he asked.

'Yes,' she said, very slowly. 'It would.'

CHAPTER TWENTY-ONE

'When shall we three meet again?' It was the last day of the summer holidays. Rose asked the question.

Lily, Jasmine and she were all lying in Esme's bed eating a breakfast of toasted bagels that Jasmine had prepared.

'Mum is coming home from Paris tomorrow to see me back to school,' Jasmine said.

'We need to change the sheets on her bed,' Lily said. 'I don't think she'd like to sleep on bagel crumbs.'

'No, really – when?' Rose reverted to her question.

'Well, Mum said she'd be back for my first weekend off,' Jasmine said hopefully.

'Right,' said Rose. 'We'll all come here then.'

'Do you think she's going to marry Jacob?' Jasmine asked.

'Would you mind if she did?' Lily asked.

'I don't know,' Jasmine replied.

'I don't think it really matters,' Rose said. 'She seems so happy just the way things are now.'

'That's good, isn't it?' Jasmine said carefully. She was looking for guidance from the other two.

'She's happier than I can ever remember her,' Lily said.

'That's all right then, isn't it?' Rose said.

Jasmine smiled. It was all right.

Macduff appeared at the end of the bed and Rose gave him a bit of bagel.

'We could just take the quilt off,' Jasmine said, 'and let Macduff clean the bed.'

Lily laughed. 'He might leave some other traces, though,' she said. 'I'm not sure that's the best idea, Jazz.'

In South Carolina, Grayson Redmond sat back on the sofa and stared at the curtain rail. The owl was back, and was sitting there looking at him with one beady eye. Grayson was feeling slightly disorientated. He had been for a ride out towards the hills.

Reining in his horse when he reached the shagbark hickory trees, he had looked up to see hundreds of geese flying in over the hills in perfect V-formations. His horse rose slightly on its rear legs, before moving around so Grayson could follow the flight of these startlingly large birds. Out of curiosity he started to gallop after them, and his horse raced with equal excitement back across the fields in the direction of the mansion. The geese arrived first, and Grayson had the singular privilege of watching some four hundred of them land on his back lawn. Even his horse pulled up in amazement. Dismounting, he led the beast around to the stable, handing him over to the stable boy before emerging to take another look at the interlopers on his land.

Esme went to Paris for a long weekend with Jacob, who was now back at work. She checked her email after he had left in the morning. There was only one and she looked in surprise bordering on dismay as she saw it was from Peter Carew. She had a momentary memory of him standing beside the taxi as she left the resort outside Nice.

Dear Esme,

I am back in Australia, sport, corks swinging from my hat and a tinnie in my hand. I may be wrong, but it occurred to me that the enclosed cutting might be of interest to you. Forgive me if I am wrong. And indeed if I am wrong, it will be meaningless to you, so just forget it.

Anyway, the holiday is over, and I'm back at work with all that that entails. Drop me a line when you have time.

Yours,
Peter

Esme opened the attachment. It was a scan of a newspaper article entitled 'Sentenced to Life' by Peter Carew, lawyer and legal journalist.

The safety of the public can only be secured by long sentences for the most dangerous criminals in our society. The popular perception is undoubtedly that, generally speaking, sentences are not harsh enough. Too often we learn of a violent criminal being released after serving only a relatively short sentence, whilst the victim of the crime is, all too often, 'sentenced to life'.

Perhaps then the recent sentencing of Jeremy Coyle to life imprisonment will go some way to allaying public fears. Coyle, an armed robber, kidnapper and rapist, who was released from prison in Ireland under the terms of the Good Friday Agreement, was today sentenced to life imprisonment in Australia.

Jeremy Coyle, whose perverted 'trademark' was the carving of a star into his victim's flesh, appealed to the Court for leniency on the grounds that he had given evidence against his co-accused. His claim that the crime was a burglary that had gone wrong had little to support it.

His Honour, Judge Alex Pickering, before sentencing Coyle, told him that he was as cruel and twisted a man as he had encountered in all his time on the bench, and reminded him that many of his victims had pleaded for mercy, but were shown none.

Coyle's co-accused received a fifteen-year sentence.

Perhaps we might all sleep a little easier tonight knowing Coyle will be well into his nineties before he has any realistic prospect of release.

Jacob Althaus closed his office door having said good night to his secretary. On his way down in the elevator he thought of Esme, crying out in her sleep the previous night. 'Jericho, Jericho,' she had said, as her head moved from side to side on the pillow. In the moonlight coming through the open window he could see the beads of perspiration on her face like a thin film.

He had held her in his arms and she had half woken.

'Yavay?' she whispered.

He murmured reassuring things with his face close to her ear, smelling her perfume, feeling her hair on his skin.

'I am here,' he said. 'And I'm not leaving you.' And she slipped back into a sleep that seemed more peaceful.

'What are you going to do with them?' Grayson's father asked, looking in surprise out of the back windows at the geese.

'I'm going to let them stay,' Grayson said.

'But why, son?' the old man asked, raising his voice above the honking. The windows were open because of the owl.

'I was thinking they might help Lily with her research,' Grayson replied. 'I got one of the men to count them – and if some of them stay on, Lily will have very precise figures about this.'

'There's a helluva lot of them.'

'Are you breeding chickens?' Grandma asked, looking at the now dozing owl and reclining on the sofa with her martini.

'No, Mother. Anyway,' he continued, addressing his father, 'how can I get rid of them, bar shooting the whole flock? And Jasmine would never forgive me, anyway. I like them. I think they add to the place.'

'More money in oil,' the old man said.

'I'm off to the Netherlands the day after tomorrow for a week,' Rose said. 'And then Billy is picking me up on his bike and we'll come back together.'

'Give our love to the Grootouders, won't you?' Lily said, coming back into the room and catching Rose's observation. Lily was looking particularly happy. Grayson had just phoned and said he would pay her flight and that she simply had to come over.

'He's gone and acquired four hundred and thirty-two geese,' she grinned.

'What?' Rose was surprised.

'Good old Dad,' Jasmine said.

'We're so lucky, aren't we?' Lily said. 'Who else has as many strands to their family as we have?'

'And we all look out for each other,' Jasmine said. She felt pleased that it was her father that had made Lily light up with joy.

'AND,' Lily said, 'the owl is back again. I can't wait to see him. I loved that owl so much and I was so sad when he flew away.'

'You loved the alligators too,' Rose said. The three of them laughed.

*   *   *

Home from their holiday in Hungary, Günter and Jennifer Wassermann were back in their apartment. Günter was already at his desk, sorting through the post, opening several packages of books he had been asked to review, and leafing through his schedule for the next term. He was feeling quite content.

Jennifer was unpacking their cases in the bedroom. The washing machine was already running. She laid out the contents of his washbag in the bathroom just as he liked it, carefully storing her cosmetics and all the bits and pieces that she used to keep herself looking the way he liked her, away in the cupboard under the basin – out of sight, to keep him happy.

As she did it, she remembered long ago Esme telling her how Günter liked the place kept so tidy, how he liked his life undisturbed, and of what he saw as perfection. She went back to the bedroom and took the sheets off the bed to wash, in case there was any dust on them after their weeks away.

The window was open and far below she could hear the splash of oars in the river and she knew if she looked out she would see that timeless scene that she and Esme had observed so long ago. And not for the first time, she thought how she missed Esme.

She thought she might write to her. It would be nice if they could be friends again. She wondered what Esme was doing. They hadn't heard from Lily all summer and she missed the tiny trickle of information that Lily had occasionally released. Before putting fresh linen on the bed, she carefully dusted the surfaces in the room and then vacuumed. She would iron Günter's handkerchiefs and then go down to the market to buy some flowers. A splash of colour would be pleasing.

*   *   *

Esme Waters sat at a table outside the café near Jacob's place of work. She was toying with a coffee, waiting for him to join her when his work was done. She had her laptop with her, and she was busy typing. The first draft of her novel was coming to an end. Those who had abused their power, controlled others and destroyed them were dead or soon would be. A semblance of normality would return to the survivors as they continued the struggle to rebuild their lives.

Jacob approached and kissed her. Her face lit up in greeting.

'You were talking in your sleep last night,' he said after he had settled himself at the table.

'Oh?' She looked surprised. She had no memory of a disturbed night.

'Don't worry,' he said.

'I'm sleeping so much better.' She said it almost hopefully, fearing it would not last.

'I know. And that's how it's going to stay. By the way, I've taken next week off work so that I can come over to you in London – if you would like, I mean.'

'Of course I would like. I'm taking Jasmine back to school, and then my time is my own again.'

'And then you will come back here for the next few months.' He caught the reluctant waiter's attention and ordered a pastis.

'I had promised my mother she could come and visit and meet the girls,' Esme said thoughtfully.

'It wasn't the right time,' Jacob said to her. 'I was thinking that maybe for that long weekend you mentioned that Jasmine has free from school – what if she came to London then?'

'That could be good,' Esme replied. 'I'm nervous about a lot of things to do with that. I've told her that my name is now Esme. She's seen me with my green contacts . . . but I suppose I'm afraid she will let something slip. I don't want my girls – or indeed anyone – to know about Molly Kilbride.'

'It will be all right,' Jacob said. 'I'll be there – there will be no slip-ups. Don't worry. Nothing bad is ever going to happen to you again.'

'It's so sad that the hospital records are gone,' Esme said. Her mother had told her about the fire that had destroyed the administrative floor of the hospital.

'Did you phone them?' Jacob asked.

'Yes, I phoned them this morning. My mother was right. All the files were gone. There is no trace of my baby ever having been born there – like he never existed.'

Jacob covered her hand. 'I think,' he said slowly and very gently, 'I think it is time that you let the past go.'

'Oh, Jacob,' she said, 'I got an email this morning – look, let me show you.' She brought it up on her screen, and Jacob read Peter's words.

'He was a legal journalist after all,' she said.

Jacob nodded.

'I feel a bit guilty about my suspicions about him,' she said ruefully.

'But what do you feel about the content of his article?' Jacob asked thoughtfully.

'I feel – I don't know what I feel. Is it relief? Complete and utter relief. I will never again be looking over my shoulder, wondering if he is there.'

'Did you ever think he might be?'

'Not in a realistic way,' she replied. 'More in a vague way – the knowledge that he was out there somewhere . . . I suppose that is haunting in some ways. The idea that he might ever do that to someone else . . .'

'He won't be doing it to anyone else now, you know,' Jacob said, thinking about the brutality in prison and the reaction of other prisoners to certain crimes. And there was no doubt that his co-accused had not taken the turn of events very well. He wondered how long Jeremy Coyle would survive.

In the steamy heat of the Central line at the evening rush hour, a very tall man with a briefcase in his hand and a hat on his head entered a carriage at Chancery Lane. He had just finished his last day's work and the joys of retirement stretched ahead of him. He was interested in exotic horticulture and, recently, had had constructed a tropical greenhouse in the gardens of his suburban home. If he was going to miss anything about his legal career it was that sense of excitement when involved in a case, the obfuscation of truth, the twisting of facts, the adversarial cut and thrust of a day's work, the moment of realisation that a witness had contradicted himself, and the winning of a challenging case. It had occurred to him that he needed to find something with which to replace that particular thrill.

At six foot two, with a hat, he was not far short of the large vent in the roof. There was no room to move; the air was thick and heavy. He stood holding the rail with his free hand, thinking about his conservatory, looking forward to pottering in it of an evening. He wondered if he should buy some exotic animal to house in it – a snake or an iguana, something unusual that would add to his sense of adventure among the orchids and the foliage he was planning on propagating.

A large mouse-brown tarantula took that moment to silently drop out of the vent into the fold on the top of his hat. The man thought he felt something on his head but declined putting his hand up to check it out. It was a wise decision and a fitting conclusion to his distinguished legal career.

He and Taliban journeyed home to suburbia together.

*   *   *

Jacob held Esme's hand as they walked along the pavement
to the restaurant for dinner. She looked up at him with her
glass-green eyes and her composed smile. But he saw a soft-
ness in her face that he was sure had not been there in the
past. He believed that she was approaching some form of
reconciliation in her mind.

He thought then, as he often did, in what sense did the
past exist – for her, for him, for anyone? He knew it only
existed in so far as it could be remembered, or in the way
it influenced someone. He knew that she had run and run
from it, but that she could not hide from it, and that accept-
ance, with as much understanding as possible, was the only
way forward.

She might run again – he knew that.

But he also knew something else, something that had
puzzled him earlier. She had covered so much of her life,
both by hiding from it and by disguising herself with her
contact lenses and her dyed blonde hair, changing her
name, avoiding the country of her birth. But she had not
had the scar removed from her chest – that cruel star
carved into her skin. And he knew why. It was the same
reason he had never had the tattooed numbers on his
forearm removed by surgery – it was because they were
part of him. They were the reminder of who he was and
where he had come from. The very fact that she had
retained that scar was her reminder. It was the link between
before and after.

She slipped her hand through the crook of his elbow and
he knew with clarity that he would stay with her for as long
as he lived or as long as she wanted.

They went to London and Esme took Jasmine back to school.
On her return to the apartment, Jacob said that friends of
his, Henry and Sally, had invited them to dinner.

'I think you may have known them some time in the past,' he said.

'Oh?' Their names meant nothing to her.

'Their surname is Delmont,' he continued. 'Jennifer's uncle and aunt, in fact. Will you be comfortable with that?'

'I'm delighted to meet friends of yours,' she said. She was surprised but not displeased. It was a coincidence that he knew Jennifer's relatives, but then she knew that life itself was a series of coincidences. In Esme's view, everything was random and some events collided.

And so she went with him to the Delmonts', and she was charmed by them and they by her, and they were so blatantly pleased to meet her.

Sally put her arms around her and hugged her.

'It is lovely to meet you again after all these years,' Henry said. He patted her shoulder. 'Lovely,' he repeated.

'Come, let's go into the garden,' Sally said. 'We're going to have a drink out there before coming in for dinner. Now, watch the step, Esme,' she added. 'We had it rebuilt a week ago, and last night, for some unknown reason, a fissure appeared in it.' Esme looked down. There was a crack on the step – long and narrow. It reminded her of something – she closed her eyes briefly, then looked again. The crack looked like the mountain range, or maybe the coast of South America – Americay, her dad used to say, long ago. It seemed to point towards the garden. She followed its line, onto the patio, into the garden. She looked around in disbelief. Flowers of every hue filled the earth – dahlias, hollyhocks, roses, lilies, jasmine, peonies, marigolds, giant daisies, trellises of sweet pea. All she could see was colour, and then the fragrance reached her.

She moved as in a dream down into the garden on the tiny stone pathways between the beds, seeing with clarity the different colours, inhaling the perfume, her mind filling with each intoxicating colour and scent.

Jacob, Henry and Sally stood on the patio watching her. Sally touched Jacob's hand and smiled at him. Henry nodded in approval.

Among the flowers a spider was weaving a web, strand upon extending strand as he wove forwards and back, the sunlit threads interconnecting with perfection.

On the patio they could not see him.

But Esme did.

A noiseless patient spider,
I mark'd where on a little promontory it stood isolated,
Mark'd how to explore the vacant vast surrounding,
It launch'd forth filament, filament, filament, out of itself.
Ever unreeling them, ever tirelessly speeding them

And you, O my soul where you stand,
Surrounded, detached, in measureless oceans of space,
Ceaselessly musing, venturing, throwing, seeking the
    spheres to connect them,
Till the bridge you will need be form'd till the ductile
    anchor hold;
Till the gossamer thread you fling catch somewhere, O
    my soul.

Walt Whitman

MARY STANLEY

Searching For Home

Ireland, 1944. In a violent storm, a German plane heading for Britain is blown west, far off course. When it plunges down on a family in the Wicklow mountains, a father and his young daughter are lost.

The children who survive that terrible night try to leave the past behind, but it will not let them go. And as Mattie and Amelia search for a place to call home, they accidentally uncover the cruellest secret of all . . .

Mary Stanley's enthralling new novel moves from 1940s Ireland through post-war England to golden Malta. Her vibrant characters and beautifully perceptive writing bring to life a compelling tale of survival and self-discovery.

Praise for Mary Stanley's writing:

'A compulsively different read . . . imaginatively and stunningly written . . . warm and poignant. Thought-provoking and compassionate, the tale is as strong as its characters. Spellbinding' *Irish World*

'The pages turn with ease' *Observer*

'A perceptive and poignant novel exploring the rami-fications of loss and abandonment with compassion and a wry, perfectly pitched wit' *The Big Issue in the North*

0 7553 2506 0

review

MARY STANLEY

Missing

Missing (adj.) 1. not present, absent or lost. 2. not able to be traced and not known to be dead. 3. **go missing** to become lost or disappear.

To the outside world we were this perfectly contented happy family – a mother, a father and three little girls. And the truth? Really it was a conspiracy of silence – everyone living a life on the surface while underneath reality bubbles away – until the day that it blows up . . .

John and Elizabeth Dunville believe they have the ideal family. Their three daughters – beautiful, vivacious Baby; clever, industrious Becky; and lively, if mischievous, Brona – attend Dublin's most prestigious covent school, and all have bright futures. But denial and deception go hand in hand, and one night, one of the girls slips out into the winter fog, and doesn't come home . . .

Praise for Mary Stanley's writing:

'*Missing* is a perceptive and poignant novel exploring the ramifications of loss and abandonment with compassion and a wry, perfectly pitched wit' *The Big Issue*

'A gripping and mesmerising novel . . . Skilfully written with bursts of humour, Stanley weaves a compelling web of deception and intrigue' *Glasgow Evening Times*

'The pages turn with ease' *Observer*

'Warm, and even at its darkest, never entirely black. An engrossing read' *Irish Sunday Independent*

0 7472 6737 5

review

Now you can buy any of these other bestselling
books from your bookshop
or *direct from the publisher*.

FREE P&P AND UK DELIVERY
(Overseas and Ireland £3.50 per book)

Searching For Home	Mary Stanley	£7.99
The Mermaid Chair	Sue Monk Kidd	£6.99
The Island	Victoria Hislop	£6.99
The Wedding Day	Catherine Alliott	£6.99
Secrets of a Family Album	Isla Dewar	£6.99
Atlantic Shift	Emily Barr	£6.99
Anyone But Him	Sheila O'Flanagan	£6.99
On Dancing Hill	Sarah Challis	£6.99
The Distance Between Us	Maggie O'Farrell	£7.99
Amazing Grace	Clare Dowling	£6.99
The Woman on the Bus	Pauline McLynn	£6.99
Play it Again	Julie Highmore	£6.99

TO ORDER SIMPLY CALL THIS NUMBER

01235 400 414

or visit our website: www.madaboutbooks.com

Prices and availability subject to change without notice.